Rethinking Mission to the Educated Middle Class

Rethinking Mission to the Educated Middle Class

Sunil Kolhar

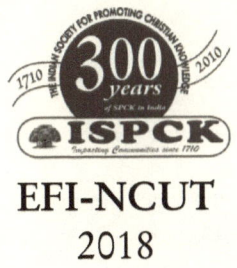

EFI-NCUT

2018

Rethinking Mission to the Educated Middle Class— published by the Rev. Dr. Ashish Amos of the Indian Society for Promoting Christian Knowledge (ISPCK), Post Box 1585, 1654, Madarsa Road, Kashmere Gate, Delhi-110006 and the EFI's National Centre for Urban Transformation (NCUT), No. 6, City Serve Mansion, Chikkenappa Layout 2nd Cross, Byrathi Extension, Kothanur, Bangalore-560077 under the Urban Transformation Series (UTS-1).

© EFI-NCUT, 2018

Online Order: http://ispck.org.in/book.php

Also available on amazon.in

ISBN: 978-81-8465-674-9

Cover credit: Internet sources

Laser typeset by

ISPCK, Post Box 1585, 1654, Madarsa Road, Kashmere Gate, Delhi-110006
• *Tel:* 23866323/22

e-mail: ashish@ispck.org.in • ella@ispck.org.in
website: www.ispck.org.in

Contents

Foreword

We live in a globalized world which is rapidly turning urban, consequently creating a huge middle class, that poses a big challenge to the global church. In 2014, about 54% of the world's population lived in urban areas, and it is projected that, by 2050, nearly 70% of the world population will be urban. Given the surge in urbanization in India today, it is projected that about half of India's population will be living in urban areas by 2030. A significant portion of urban population consists of the educated Hindu middle class and this scenario presents the urban church with greater opportunities of engaging them with the claims of Christ.

National Centre for Urban Transformation (NCUT), a timely initiative of Evangelical Fellowship of India (EFI), exists to ensure that the urban Christian leadership is adequately informed, effectively equipped and strategically mobilized to bring about holistic transformation of the cities of India. NCUT is committed to fulfill this vision by providing focused urban seminars, workshops, think tanks, regional and national conferences. Simply put, NCUT's primary desire is to cast the urban vision in the psyche of the churches and mission organizations and provide them with necessary information, skills and tools to meaningfully engage with various segments of urban population.

One of NCUT's primary endeavors is to carry out research and writing projects on various contemporary urban issues that have a bearing on the ministry and mission of the church with a view to provide relevant resources for the urban church in India. Our efforts to fulfill this goal has resulted in the publication of this manuscript, the first of what we would like to call as the Urban Transformation Series. This series was initiated to provide the urban church, academicians and mission practitioners with relevant and useful tools that will enhance their understanding of urban challenges and contexts of India and provide innovative insights to engage strategically with the urban population.

This first publication, entitled *Rethinking Mission to the Educated Middle Class*, turns the attention of our readers to the educated Hindu middle class, an important segment of our population that has not been receiving adequate attention for long. For over two centuries the Christian missions have been exclusively focusing on the tribal and Dalit population, with some degree of response from them. Interestingly, most missionary efforts in the previous century had initially focused on the upper castes of the dominant religion and attempted to make the gospel message relevant to them. With the publication of this work, we are glad that we are beginning to refocus our attention on such neglected groups. Dr. Sunil Kolhar, the author of this book, had undertaken strenuous efforts to study the changing trends among the urban middle class, especially the Hindu middle class in Ahmedabad, Gujarat, with a view to develop contextually relevant means of reaching out to them. This research was undertaken as part of his D Min Studies under my supervision at South Asia Institute of Advanced Christian Studies (SAIACS) in Bangalore. I found in him a keen and meticulous scholar who had diligently pursued the topic with a professional commitment. Dr. Kolhar's entrepreneurial, pastoral and missional experiences, as he recounts in the Preface of this book, have enabled him to unearth the ground realities of the contexts of his research. As Founder of Citylight Foundation and Pastor of Citylight Fellowship in Ahmedabad, as well as an initiator of five urban church planting initiatives in the city of Ahmedabad, Dr. Kolhar continues to contribute to the understanding of urban mission and practice. He serves as a regular resource person of NCUT in its various training programs.

With a few more manuscripts dealing with urban realities getting ready for publication, we are also committed to developing appropriate urban theological/missional curriculum for the Indian Bible colleges and seminaries through consultations and workshops, with assistance from a select group of missiologists, theologians and mission practitioners. We do hope that like-minded stalwarts in this field will extend their hands of fellowship and partnership so that NCUT's efforts will increasingly benefit the urban Indian church in the years to come.

We are delighted to present to you this first book in the Urban Transformation Series, jointly published by EFI-NCUT and ISPCK. We express our sincere thanks to Rev. Dr. Ashish Amos, Executive Director of ISPCK, and Mrs. Ella Sonawane for their assistance in getting this manuscript published. It is hoped that this book will provide its readers insights and skills to engage with the educated middle class in a contextually relevant manner.

Rev. Dr. Atul Y. Aghamkar
National Director, NCUT, Bengaluru
March 2018

Preface

The educated Hindu middle class in India is almost always a neglected group as far as Christian witness is concerned. The Christian professionals connected with this group of people are not adequately equipped to witness to their colleagues nor do we find enough trained missionaries working among this group. God enabled me to see the tremendous need to empower our professionals and missionaries to be effective witnesses to this group.

I had a tryst with the corporate world at two different times, one as an unbeliever and the next as a believer. With an Engineering degree and a Post Graduate Diploma in Management, I was well placed in a MNC to make a good career. But I knew there was something missing in my life. I know now that this was because the place that God should occupy in my life was empty.

God, who is always good, brought about circumstances in my life that led me closer to him. Accepting Jesus as my Savior, and realizing his call on my life, I enrolled myself for theological training at Union Biblical Seminary, Pune, and completed it successfully. I began my ministry with the Methodist church. However, soon I realized that I was totally cut off from the secular world. As per God's leading, I went back to my secular work and, by the grace and plan of God, I got back into the same company that I worked for earlier. But this time I was there as a believer and also a trained theologian. I spent about eight years in my second phase in this company and this time I was able to see the tremendous need of the corporate executives. They had all the money they needed, and all the luxuries required for one to live a happy life and yet they were without an anchor. Their education did not help them to live a life of integrity. This is where the Lord gave me tremendous opportunities to witness for him. I saw that these high flying corporate executives were open to the gospel.

Experiences such as these instilled in me a desire to research and study this segment of people to know better about them. My Doctor of Ministry (D. Min.) study program at South Asia Institute for Advanced Christian Studies (SAIACS), Bangalore, focused squarely on the changes that the educated middle-class Hindus have undergone due to urbanization and to deliberate on a contextually appropriate model for Christian witness among them. It has been an educative experience for me, personally, to study the patterns of change among the Hindu middle-class in Gujarat, particularly Ahmedabad, where I'm currently serving the Lord as Pastor of Citylight Fellowship. This book, in fact, is a result of my doctoral research. My desire is that this book may empower many to witness to the educated middle-class Hindu.

I'm indebted to many people who have contributed to the successful completion of my research and helped me in re-working on the manuscript for publication. First and foremost, I would like to thank Dr. Atul Aghamkar, Director of National Center for Urban Transformation (NCUT), the Urban Commission of Evangelical Fellowship of India (EFI), for arranging to publish this book. I carried out my research program under his guidance and he has been a special motivating force for completing this work. My special thanks to Mr. Vadivel Victor, Research Editor and Publication Coordinator, NCUT, who has taken great pains to edit my thesis and bring it to its present shape.

I would especially like to acknowledge the role of late Dr Edwin Masihi, former faculty of the Dept. of Sociology in Gujarat University and who was heading his own Research agency. He was extremely helpful in suggesting the different sources for books, articles and reference material. He also suggested various reading material for the subject and interacted frequently which helped me to gain insight in the subject. He, through his staff Ms. Aruna Parmar, helped to collate the information collected through the questionnaire.

I am thankful to many of my church members who took active interest in giving the questionnaire to their colleagues and acquaintances. My special thanks to Mr. Harold Frank who translated the questionnaire into Gujarati. This helped immensely for many of the respondents filled up the questionnaire in Gujarati.

My heartfelt thanks to my family for bearing with me and encouraging me to complete this book, particularly my son Sudeep who helped me in all computer related works.

Rev. Dr. Sunil Kolhar

Pastor, Citylight Fellowship, Ahmedabad

March 2018

Abbreviations

AWAG	Ahmedabad Women's Action Group
ECI	Evangelical Church of India
NGO	Non-Governmental Organization
NRI	Non-Resident Indian
OM	Operation Mobilization
RZIM	Ravi Zacharias International Ministries
SEWA	Self Employed Women's Association
UA	Urban Agglomeration
UESI	Union of Evangelical Students of India
UN	United Nations

Glossary

Panchayat	Local Governing Body
Patidars	Land Owning Community
Zamindars	Land Owners
Gnati Samaj	Caste Society
Mukti	Salvation
Moksha	Salvation
Maya	Illusion
Marga	A way of achieving salvation
Jnana Marga	A way of salvation through achieving knowledge
Karma Marga	A way of salvation by works
Bhakti Marga	A way of salvation through devotion
Shastras	Hindu Scriptures
Katha	A style of telling a mythological story
Pooja	Hindu Worship
Vedas	Hindu Scriptures
Puranas	A collection of ancient stories of moral content used by Hindus

Mahajan	Merchants guild
Panch	Artisan's association
Pol Panch	Community Council
Nagarsheth	Title given to leader of the city
Mukadam	Supervisor
Bhagwat Vidyapeeth	A Hindu Seminary to train Hindu Pandits
Swaminarayan Gurukul	A school based on Hindu Traditions
Yatra	A Spiritual Journey

Introduction

The world is urbanizing at a very fast rate. Today more than fifty percent of the world population resides in urban areas. This is the first time in history that there are more people living in urban than rural areas. India is not far behind with 31.16% of the total population being urban. We may seem to be lagging compared to population trends in other parts of the world. However, we need to appreciate that we have come a long way from where we were a century ago. Looking at the population of India which is put at 1210 million, the fact that 377 million people live in urban areas is huge in terms of absolute numbers. India can boast of 53 million plus cities with eminent sociologists and demographers predicting that this could rise to 68 in the next 15 years. Very few countries can come even close to this. The urban population itself is predicted to rise from the present level to around 590 million in this period. This would mean that around a tenth of the urban world population would be living in Indian cities. I am sure you would agree that the implications of this projection for the church is staggering.

The question that obviously would rises at this point is: why is there an urban explosion in our country? India has always been known as a rural agricultural economy. Even Nehru's initiation of the industrial revolution did not cause the urban explosion that was expected. It was only in 1991 that Mr. Narshima Rao, the then Prime Minister, initiated under the guidance of Dr. Manmohan Singh, several economic reforms wherein he opened the country for foreign investments. This gave a tremendous boost to the sagging economy and, within a short span of time, jobs in the service sector—mostly in IT sector and to some extent hospitality sector—multiplied in leaps and bounds. Cities like Mumbai, Bangalore, Pune and Hyderabad and, to some extent, Ahmedabad became the new destination of the IT professionals. With IT parks developed in many of these cities and new infrastructure in place, the cities themselves began to gain a new look. In the process, these professionals are the ones who redefined urbanization, and were added in great number to the Indian middle-class. In fact, as Gurcharan Das says, during the eighties and nineties the middle-class increased more than tripled.[1] It cannot be denied that the middle-class came into focus sharply after the economic reforms. It is true that these economic reforms gave rise to many new entrepreneurs who through their ingenuity and hard work have made a fortune. A survey of the Confederation of Indian Industry (CII) concluded that there were 180 million people in India with an annual income exceeding Rs.1,20,000.

Urbanization, obviously brings about many changes. The external changes are obvious. People start dressing up differently. Their food habits change. Social interactions which were probably forbidden in a rural society now become a normal way of life. Even the way people choose their residential areas change. These are changes for everyone to see. But does urbanization change people at a deeper level? And if it does, to what degree are they affected? The building blocks of the Indian society are caste, family and religion. All the three are very sensitive subjects and we need to tread the path very carefully, as we cannot brush them under the carpet. India is distinctly a caste-based society. Caste defines every aspect of life for an Indian. The joint family system, though not distinctly Indian, was predominantly Indian. As in the case of caste, the joint family system also defined unambiguously the role of each in the family. Religion was by and large a community affair, though it did have its individual ramifications. In short, these three institutions governed the life of a Hindu. This was true not only in the rural but in the urban also. So then, has the urbanization explosion really impacted these three great pillars of the Indian society? It is worth a study to know the mindset of a large cross-section of the urban society.

With a view to understand the process of change due to urbanization and assess its impact on the educated Middle-class Hindus, the research specifically focused on Gujarat and its capital Ahmedabad.

Gujarat is the third most urbanized State in India. The Encyclopaedic District Gazettes of India shows that the urban population of Gujarat has maintained a steady growth of 33% per decade since 1930. This increase in the urban population is due to both interstate and intrastate migration. It has at least four 'million-plus' cities and several smaller ones distributed throughout the State.

This demographic growth has happened mainly due to the all-round industrial growth of the State coupled with good infrastructure and some excellent educational institutions. If Ahmedabad was once called the Manchester of the East for its several cotton mills, it now houses several huge pharmaceutical, chemical and automobile industries. Apart from that, there are several premier educational and research institutions such as Indian Institute of Management, Physical Research Laboratory, Indian Space Research Organisation, etc. Surat is known for its textile, silk and diamond industry while Rajkot is the centre for cast iron products and groundnut oil. Baroda remains the cultural centre of the State. Apart from these million-plus cities, Jamnagar has a huge refinery, Bhavnagar has the Alang ship breaking industry, Anand has the famous Amul dairy and places such as Ankleshwar, Bharuch and Vapi are part of the prosperous industrial belt. The State's long coastal belt has made its fishing industry quite prominent. Gandhinagar has developed into an important IT hub. Apart from this, Narendra Modi's Vibrant Gujarat program has brought in several international business houses to invest here.

Urbanization of Ahmedabad is not a recent phenomenon. The population of Ahmedabad district is around 6.58 million of which 84% live in the city of Ahmedabad. It is also the seventh largest city of our vast country. It was a thriving business centre from the time of its inception. Though it went through a rough patch during the Maratha rule, the British set the pace for its urbanization through industrialization and various reforms. The business guilds or Nagarseths played an important role in developing and maintaining the business of the city. The city began to get so prosperous that Achyut Yagnik and Suchitra Sheth note that it prompted famous historian Maganlal Vakhatchand to call this phase as "ramrajya or the reign of Lord Ram, a metaphor for a paradise of wealth, opportunity and justice in his account of the city in 1851."[2] From then on, the city has progressed not only in industrialization but also in education. Today, it boasts of having a highest number of Malls in any city. The recently built Alfa Mall is said to be the largest in Asia. The Gujarati theatre and to some extent the English and Hindi theatre are quite active. The national level classical music program known as *Saptak* is very well attended. Several NGO's such as SEWA and AWAG, which work towards the empowerment of the downtrodden women, are housed here. Despite all the advances that this city has made, it has been a traditional and conservative society. This was more obvious a few decades ago when they preferred to reside in ghettos and stuck to the age-old culture. The last few decades, however, has seen a vast change even in this society. Therefore, Ahmedabad has been taken as the base of this study. Yet, obviously, changes in many of our cities would be comparable to what we have seen in Ahmedabad and hence the results of the study can be conveniently used in most million-plus cities.

Finally, and importantly, we as Christians, as part of the church in India, need to assess the implications of these societal changes for Christian witness. If the pillars of any society are shaken, can we as Christians provide a foundation that is more solid and would endure the passage of time? A prior question that we need to ask ourselves in this regard is whether Christianity is for this class of people. Christianity in India has by and large touched the lower segments of the society and is known as the religion of the have-nots, the proletariat. This is very much true of Gujarat. Robin Boyd[3] traces the history of Christianity in Gujarat back to the 13th century, but the real impetus came only after the 1830's. Though the initial concentration was on cities and the educated, it later became a movement for the oppressed, downtrodden and the outcaste. In these initial years, there was a slow and steady flow of the educated middle-class into the Christian fold, but with the mass movement of the outcaste, the flow not only stopped, but there was a general antagonism towards Christians and Christianity in Gujarat.

Efforts in the past to evangelize the educated middle-class Hindus met with some success. RZIM has had several programs in the past two decades to present Christianity as a viable logical worldview which have been well attended. Jesus Calls has been a late entrant in Gujarat, but their Prayer Tower in Ahmedabad receives several prayer requests from this class of people from all over the State. Several of them visit the prayer tower for counseling. Quite a few of them also attend their weekly healing and family blessing meetings. OM India, ECI and several Pentecostal churches have tried to evangelize this group of people with some success. The work of a few individuals is also laudable. Sanjay Masih, a young Creative Engineer has done this through his paintings. He has had several exhibitions on various Biblical themes which have been well attended by the educated middle-class. EUSI has several Bible study groups where quite a few non-Christian educated people attend. While some who attended these Bible studies have taken baptism, many of them have not, although they claim to believe in the atoning work of our Lord. These are evidences of some concrete work happening among this segment of the people, and there is scope for a more to be done.

On the other hand, we need to probe the biblical teaching in this regard. Was the church of the first century predominantly the church of the poor? Were people of the 'middle-class' part of the church too? In other words, what was the social composition and status of the first century Christians? These are some of the questions that I have tried to engage in so that we have a base to build on.

I should also mention that the findings of my study in the city of Ahmedabad are based on an extensive field research. Questionnaires were prepared in English and Gujarati (the local language). Snowballing method was then used to give these questionnaires to a good cross section of the society. Care was taken to see that different age groups were represented and that there was a balanced representation of male and female ratio. There was a good mix of locals which included people who had migrated from within the state and people from outside the church. Though the sample size was substantial, the results can only be taken to be indicators or signs. It certainly can show us the way forward.

I sincerely hope that this book may prove to be a useful tool in the hands of readers grappling with urban challenges and issues, particularly in relation to Gujarat, and inspire them to develop contextually appropriate paradigms for Christian witness among them.

Endnotes

[1] Gurcharan Das, 'Middle-class Values and the Changing Indian Entrepreneur', in Ahmad and Riefeld (eds), *Middle-class Values*, 196.

[2] Achyut Yagnik & Suchitra Sheth, *Ahmedabad-From Royal City to Mega City* (Delhi: Penguin Books, 2011).

[3] R.H.S. Boyd, *A Church History of Gujarat* (Madras: The Christian Literature Society, 1981).

Chapter 1

Urbanization, Change and First Century Christianity

It is often thought that urbanization is a recent phenomenon and thus the setting of the Bible is perceived to be rural. A cursory reading of the Bible narratives will show that many of the events occurred in urban settings. So, it is important that we see and understand those narratives against an urban background. My primary intention in this opening chapter is to show that urbanization and urban settings during Bible times provide an immense help in our effort to grasp the biblical truth. I will first examine briefly the biblical perspective of cities and then go on to show how urbanization helped the advance of Christian mission.

1. BIBLE AND CITIES

Surveying the mentioning of cities in the Bible yields interesting results. According to David S. Lim, "In the Scriptures, the term 'city' appears about 1600 times in the Old Testament and 160 times in the New, without counting the instances in which the cities' proper names are used."[1] Life in the world of the Bible was influenced by its urban centers. Robert Linthicum, who with his intentional research over a decade developed an urban theology that would bring theological sense to his city ministries, says this:

> It comes as a surprise to all of us: The Bible actually is an urban book!
> It is hard for us to appreciate that the world of Moses and David, Daniel

and Jesus was an urban world. But it was—their world was probably more urban than any civilization before it or any after it for the next fifteen hundred years.[2]

Such realization does not come as a surprise for some of us in the urban theological academia. However, it is certainly an eye-opener for many who are accustomed to think otherwise. So, with a survey of the Bible and a description of how the story of the Bible is played out in the cities, we will try to decipher the theological significance of the cities.

Cities in the Old Testament Times

The story of the Bible begins in a garden. When Cain had to leave the Garden of Eden, he virtually became a wanderer—till probably he thought that he needed to settle somewhere. And what did Cain was to build a city which he named after his son Enoch (Gen 4:17).

The next person mentioned building cities is Nimrod. He certainly was a man of great achievement for he built cities like Nineveh, Rehoboth, Ir, Calah and Resen (Gen 10:12). In Gen 11, we see people building a city in the plain of Shinar with a tower reaching the skies.

Sir Leonard Woolley from his study of the excavations of Ur concludes that it had a population of about 2.5million.[3] Keller says that "Ur of the Chaldeans was powerful, prosperous, colorful and busy Capital city of the second millennium BC."[4]

We read about a series of cities in the Exodus narrative. Pithom and Ramases were cities built by the Israelites for the Pharaoh (Ex 1:11). During their conquest of Canaan, what the Israelites captured were predominantly cities, of which Jericho was the first one to be destroyed (Josh 5:13ff). Judges chapter 1 gives us a good picture of the number of cities that the Israelites captured: Jerusalem (v8), Kiriath Sepher (v12), city of Palms (v16), Zephath (v17), Gaza, Ashkelon and Ekron (v18), Bethel (v22), Beth Shan, Taanach, Dor, Ibleam Megiddo (v27), Gezer, Kitron and Nahahol (v30), Acco, Sidon, Ahlab, Aczib, Helbah, Aphek, Rehob (v31). The cities of the Philistines, Ashdod, Gaza, Ashkelon, Gath and Ekron were actually city-states. These were fortified towns with their country villages (1Sam 6:17-18).

Assyria and Babylonia—the great empires that ruled the Ancient West Asia during the 7th and 6th centuries BC—also built up great cities. Nineveh, the ancient capital of Assyria, was an important city, three days' journey in breadth. Lewis Mumford, in his study of Babylon, says that at the time of Nebuchadnezzar it was an amazing city, with eleven miles of walls and a water and irrigation system (perhaps even including flush toilets) not equaled again until the end of the 19th century.[5] Susa, the capital of the later Persian empire was also known to be a great city (Est 1:2). These cities or city states were usually walled, thus offering security to its inhabitants from their enemies. They were self-sufficient where the central area was reserved for commerce and law while farming was done in the suburbs (cf. Nu 35:2, Josh 14:14, 1Chron 5:16). In many of the cities now excavated, there were several gates where the judges would sit and give their decisions on issues and problems of people therein (cf. Gen 19:1, Am 5:10).

Certain cities were built for specific purposes. There were these cities of refuge that God told Moses to keep aside for people having committed unintentional crime and wanting to escape the wrath of the victim or his relatives for a time. There were cities like Pithom and Ramases which were built as storehouses or treasure cities. Solomon had cities for chariots and horsemen (1Kgs 4:26, 9:19) which were meant for defense.

God and the Old Testament City

How did God look upon the cities in the Old Testament? Scholars differ in their views on the biblical meaning of a 'city.' Ellul thinks that the city is evil and stands opposed to the purposes of God from the time Cain built the first city.[6]

Scholars like Conn and Ortiz who look at cities more positively say that the cultural mandate of Gen 1:28 could be called an urban mandate because it would be accomplished through more than farming or husbandry. "The future of humankind outside the garden was destined to play out in cities."[7] So, the city would signify security, prosperity and progress.

Linthicum sees the city as the battlefield between God and Satan. He says: "Whether it is put in terms of Yahweh and Baal, God and Satan, or Christ and Caesar, every city is the city of conflict. It is a city of conflict between the Yahwehs and "Baals" of life—between the forces of freedom and the forces of license, between the forces of justice and the forces of exploitation, between the forces of love and the forces of lust, between the forces of God and the forces of Satan."[8] Linthicum's description of the city as one of conflict is more realistic than the pessimistic picture of Ellul or the more optimistic picture of Conn and Ortiz. Though the city does signify security, prosperity and progress, it always has a downside to it and this is because the city represents the conflict either between the flesh and the spirit or at another level between God and Satan.

Inevitably, the Bible makes it clear that God has a special place in his heart for the city. The negotiation between God and Abraham for the cities of Sodom and Gomorrah is the first instance where God shows his love for the city in spite of all the evil that was there. Much later in history, we see God's concern for Nineveh in his deputation of Jonah as the first cross-cultural missionary to warn them of the impending destruction.

The New Testament and Cities

The Ministry of Jesus

It is often wrongly assumed that the ministry of Jesus was limited to the country side. We know this is not so. Jesus was born in Bethlehem, brought up in Nazareth and had a major ministry in Capernaum. It is estimated that these places then had a population of about fifteen thousand. By today's standards, these certainly would be called villages, but is it right for us to judge them according to today's standards? There is a huge gap between the industrial and preindustrial world. The definition of urbanization also changed with industrialization. The demographics of the city changed drastically. Hence it would be unfair on our part to judge the preindustrial world according to today's standards or definition of urbanization. The New Testament tells us that both Nazareth (Mt 2:23, Lk.1:26, 2:4) and Capernaum (Lk.4:31) are designated cities in the gospels. In fact, Luke designates Bethlehem as a town in Luke 2:4. Conn and Ortiz also say that the vocabulary used of the ministry of Jesus in Galilee certainly shows that it was an urban area. References to institutions like courts (Mt 5:25) and city market squares (Mt 23:7, Mk 5:56), financial analogies built on interest-bearing accounts (Mt.25:27, Lk.19:23), the metaphors of God as an absentee landlord (Mk 12:1-12), centurion leaders of one hundred soldiers (Mt.8:5), and bureaucratic tax collectors controlling even fishing rights (Mt 9:10, Lk 5:27) etc. all show Galilee to be an urban centre.[9]

The gospel accounts show Jesus constantly surrounded by crowds. He was either followed by crowds or was teaching or feeding crowds. And obviously, the crowds were in the towns and cities.

Jesus' Urban Mission

As observed earlier, Jesus came into an urban world and worked in an urban world. Conn and Ortiz say that with his coming began the inauguration of God's urban renewal plan. Jesus is the stairway, the one in whom heaven comes down to the cities of the world and through whom we ascend to the heavenly city. They go on to substantiate this by saying that in Jesus' preaching "something greater than Jonah" calls the cities to repentance and the sign of his power will be his Jonah like resurrection from the dead after three days (Mt 12:39-40).[10] Conn in another article says, " As Jesus wanders like the Patriarchs, his presence signals both grace and judgment for the cities and their people."[11] He substantiates that by showing the work of Jesus in the cities and yet how many of them rejected him and what that would spell for them.

> Jesus raises the widow's only son from the dead in the city of Nain (Lk.7:11-17). A prostitute "from the city" (Lk. 7:37) receives her forgiveness of sins. To the cities he sends his disciples, empowered to heal the sick and announce the approach of the Kingdom in the approach of Jesus (Lk. 10:1, 9, 17). And at Calvary, "outside the gate" of the city, he suffers "to make the people holy through his own blood" (Heb. 13:12). But the response to grace is not always repentance and obedience. In the region of the Gadarenes, he drives out demons. But "the whole city" responds by pleading "with him to leave the region" (Mt. 8:34). "The cities in which most of the miracles had been performed" reject him (Mt. 11:20). He warns his disciples about the cities where the gospel's good news will not be received (Lk. 10:14-15). Chorazin, Bethsaida and Capernaum will fare worse in the judgment day than Sodom and Gomorrah (Lk. 10:10-12, cf. Mt.10:15; 11:24). They have tasted, in the miracles and words of Christ, the redemptive power of the kingdom of God. They have seen the signs pointing to the coming of God in Christ. But they have rejected God in rejecting Christ.[12]

Jesus obviously concentrated on the cities and towns because that is where the action was and that is where the need was. He was accepted by a few while many rejected his claims in the cities where he ministered. And things haven't changed in the past twenty centuries because the testing ground for the authenticity of the gospel remains the city. It is here that the gospel faces its challenges—be it in terms of its intellectual veracity or spiritual content or sociological implications.

Greenway and Monsma further offer a succinct description of the eschatological city by saying that "the world to come, Scripture teaches, will be an urban world. The redemption drama that began in a garden will end in the city, the New Jerusalem. Heaven's citizens will be urbanites. Drawn by bonds of grace, from all races, nations and language groups, new-city citizens will live together in perfect harmony as God's redeemed people, his new covenant community."[13]

Paul's Urban Emphasis

Paul's emphasis on mission is urban in nature. But what was his strategy? Bosch says "Paul thinks regionally and not ethnically; he chooses cities that have representative character. In each of these centers, the gospel will be carried into the surrounding countryside and towns."[14] This observation of Bosch is quite revealing. Paul was aware that the city breaks down many of the ethnic barriers and hence it was unwise or short sighted to think and work ethnically. It is sad that we often think of urban mission in terms of reaching ethnic groups rather than realizing that one's social circle is usually people of varied cultures.

Explaining Paul's missionary strategy, Bosch says in agreement with Ollrog that Paul was engaged in Zentrums mission, i.e. mission in certain strategic centers. He points out that Paul concentrates on the district or provincial capitals, each of which stands for the whole region: Philippi for Macedonia (Phil 4:15), Thessalonica for Macedonia and Achaia (1Thess 1:7f), Corinth for Achaia (1Cor 16:15, 2Cor 1:1), and Ephesus for Asia (Rom 16:5, 1Cor 16:19, 2Cor 1:8).[15] Quoting Haas, he says that these 'metropolises' were the main centers as far as communication, culture, commerce, politics and religion are concerned.[16] Commenting on Paul's strategy, Roland Allen says, "He seized strategic points because he had a Strategy. The foundation of churches in them was part of a campaign. In his hands they became the source of rivers, mints from which the new coin of the Gospel was spread in every direction."[17] If the proverb 'all roads lead to Rome' is true, so is the opposite that all roads form Rome led to all parts of the Roman Empire. Whatever happened in the cities found its way to the surrounding towns and villages as people travelled on business or to their native to meet their families. Thus, urban mission was a sensible thing for Paul and for us also for the gospel would ultimately find its way to remote places. Randy White on the other hand speaks of his strategy within a city. Taking Paul's brief evangelizing effort at Athens, he says "Paul's urban tour formed his strategy for unveiling the forces that shaped the perspectives, behavior and beliefs of Athens. Once revealed, he would plant seeds that would take root in uniquely Athenian soil, an urban garden like no other."[18] He further informs us that "By the sixth century, many of the pagan temples, including the Parthenon on the Aeropagus, had been converted into Christian churches."[19] Paul was certainly a master strategist. As the city doors opened for ministry, he worked so strategically that the gospel would spread not only in the chosen cities but throughout the then known Roman Empire.

2. URBANIZATION AND EARLY CHRISTIANITY

We have already mentioned that Paul established his mission stations in the four provinces of the Roman Empire. He knew that the arteries of the city lead to the countryside also. However, the question that needs to be answered is whether urbanization created the right environment for the growth of Christianity. We explore this question in the following sections.

Urbanization in Antiquity

As the Roman Empire moved to the East, they adopted the policy of founding and reestablishing the ruined cities for they recognized that this would be to their advantage. They knew that if they had to rule these newly conquered areas efficiently, it needed a thriving economy and a good administration. They did this by not only developing the cities but also developing a good infrastructure to connect these cities through roads and developing ports. Along with this, they also brought stability to the cities by giving them military protection and the law courts where the common man had a chance to get justice. For the administration they involved the local monarch or the local aristocrats who already had a large clientele and gave them adequate powers to rule these cities and yet not so much power that they could think of independence. "The Roman empire," says Rostovtzeff, "was to become a commonwealth of self-governing cities."[20]

Cities and Christian Mission

Christian mission advanced in the first century due to several factors. We need to recognize that the cities then were smaller in size and population compared to the cities of modern times. Most of the cities would have a population ranging from 40,000 to 100,000 with only Rome reaching figures of about 400,000. Further, we need to understand that, although the cities were small, they were highly dense. With the density figures reaching as high as 130 per acre in Antioch and 300 in Rome, which is more than double that of modern Calcutta, one can only imagine the kind of congestion in the city. This congestion was coupled with open sewers, lack of proper water supply, extremely small and smoky rooms without any chimneys or proper ventilation, as people lived in houses built with wood covered with stucco. There was a constant danger of not only fires but also plagues and other deadly diseases in the cities. "It follows that privacy was rare. Much of life was lived on the streets and sidewalks, squares and porticoes—even more than in Mediterranean cites today."[21]

This lifestyle in the ancient cities had a two-fold effect on Christian mission. First, there was nothing which was hid from anyone's eyes in the city. Word about any event or new teaching or a new cult spread like wild fire in these cities. We know of one example, that is, of Paul in Athens (Acts 17). While Paul was discussing the gospel in the market place, some people noticed it and brought him to the Aeropagus to discuss the same with the intellectuals of the city. Thus, the speed with which news spread by word of mouth helped Christianity spread faster in the city.

Second, it is said that people in antiquity lived in extreme misery and such situations helped Christianity make inroads into the city. This, however, is debatable since scholars differ in their opinion. E.R. Dodds, for instance, says that people turned to Christ out of revulsion "from a world so impoverished intellectually, so insecure materially, so filled with fear and hatred as the world of the third century, any paths that promised escape must have attracted serious minds."[22] But we know even from today's experience that this is not so. In a place like India where misery abounds, such teachings of eschatological bliss also abound, and yet the people do not lap it up to escape the present misery. Rather, it was the teaching in Christianity which was different from any other cult that gave it impetus. The Christian teaching about love and charity and helping your neighbor who was in need was found attractive. And this was coupled with the life and work of its founder, Jesus Christ, who showed what real love was all about by his example on the cross. All this had a great effect on the followers of Christ which resulted in them taking care of the sick and needy, the poor and powerless. "In short," remarks Rodney Stark, "Christians created a miniature welfare state in an empire which for the most part lacked social services."[23] Such urbanization factors certainly provided a great impetus to the growth of Christianity in the first century.

Theissen investigates early Christianity in the light of the conflict theory of sociology which corroborates with the above observation. Every society has struggles between the haves and the have-nots. Christianity became a reason for conflict in the society because it presented a 'revolution of values' which were supposedly meant only for the aristocratic and which was resented by the poor or have-nots. Everything in Christianity, from the origins of the founder to the values presented to its ordinary adherents was too revolutionary. Jesus, the founder, was not from an aristocratic family but a carpenter's family. He spoke not just of earthly powers but rather of all powers in heaven and earth (Mt. 28:20) as belonging to him. The disciples were his household who participate in his power and therefore "form a community which is as universally organized as the worldwide power of their ruler"[24] The values they held of philanthropy, which were supposedly for the rich and powerful, are now something that gave dignity and value to even the ordinary people. Their refusal to participate in official cults, including emperor worship, enhanced their struggle against the rich and powerful. They were ready to give up high offices which would require them to come in contact with idolatry, and yet were not dissidents of the state. In fact, what would have confounded their opponents was their adherence to the rules of the state like no one else. They excelled in family values, civic values and in treating women and slaves with equality. Theissen, along the lines of Rodney Stark, thus concludes: "Here the surrounding world was confronted with an "aristocratic attitude from below" which, as an expression of a personal decision had a provocative effect."[25] Such exemplary attitude and value system had a profound effect on all the aspects of the society.

Theissen further makes this wonderful assertion: "The history of primitive Christianity was thus shaped even in the first generation by a radical social shift which altered socio-cultural, socio-ecological and socio-economic factors through the processes of Hellenisation, urbanization and the penetration of society's higher strata"[26] He goes on to explain that it was in these urban churches that a new kind of society developed due to what he calls 'Christian love-patriarchalism,' the equality of status that was given to all irrespective of status or background.[27] So, it would seem that a good number of people embraced Christianity for sociological reasons. There have been those who have advocated the social gospel based on such arguments, but it remains true, as Roger Greenway says, that "that power according to the gospel comes from the Holy Spirit's indwelling the believer (Rom 8:2-4). That is why conversion has beneficial social consequences."[28] When those advocating the social gospel see the evidence of the gospel in the changed social behavior and call that the gospel itself, it is like placing the horse before the cart. There is enough evidence in the gospel narratives that it is the lordship of Jesus and the power of the holy spirit that bring about any change whatsoever. So, though there cannot be any compromise on the gospel of our lord, one can still think in terms of a paradigm shift in making the sociology of religion as the spearhead of evangelism and mission among the middle-class.

Religious Context

The Roman cities thrived with multiple religious traditions and cults. These were basically Hellenistic cities and they already had a plethora of gods and goddesses. Urbanization brought in people from various parts of the empire to the cities. People moved either to establish a trade or earn a livelihood. When armies conquered territories, they settled their people there. The Romans, in particular, formed numerous colonies by bringing their own people and army veterans into areas under their administration. Good roads and excellent maritime facilities facilitated migration. The migrants brought in not only their culture but also their gods and goddesses. These were far away from their homeland; hence, the only connection that made them feel at home was the religious associations or clubs that they formed.

It is to be noted, however, that excessive pluralism had its downside also. As Dodd rightly points out, the empire suffered from "a bewildering mass of alternatives. There were too many cults, too many mysteries, too many philosophies of life to choose from; you could pile one religious insurance on another and yet not feel safe."[29] While such a scenario proved to be a bane for the cults, it certainly proved to be a boon for Christian mission. Due to the multiplicity of gods, the patrons were divided, and this provided the impetus for their downfall, though in no way was this sudden and complete. But as Stark points out, "the rapid procession of the new gods created a cultural fluidity that made it progressively easier for new faiths to gain a foothold."[30] This is where the Christian mission benefited in the cities. Where people are steeped in traditions, it becomes much more difficult to push in new ideas, but where there is cultural fluidity; people are open enough to at least test the new ideas.

This religious pluralism helped many of the Diaspora Jews to accept Christianity which I propose to see at a later stage.

Physical and Social Mobility

Good roads in the Roman world aided easy travel. Presence of many religious cults proved to be a fertile soil for Christianity to grow. As one author has estimated, Paul in his lifetime would have travelled at least ten thousand miles. The letters of Paul record details of not only Paul's travel but also of his companions and others who travelled to report to him what was happening in their cities and thus in their churches (1Thess 3:2-6, 1 Cor 4:17, 2 Cor 2:13, ...) his certainly would have helped in the growth of Christianity. Interestingly, Rodney Stark says that it was not the road travel but maritime travel that helped Christian mission. He explains that the roads were so hard that it would be impossible to travel long distance on foot. It would simply tire out a person. On the contrary, many of the towns had excellent ports and travel by boats was quite safe, and people perhaps preferred to travel by sea. This, according to Stark, is the reason for the fact that port cities like Corinth, Antioch, Pergamum, Sardis and Ephesus were Christianized earlier than the cities inland.

Apart from the physical mobility, the social mobility in the cities too played a major role in Christian mission. There was often a reasonable movement from one *ordo* to another among the aristocrats who formed the ruling class. Such a movement was hardly detectable among the common man below the *decurions*, and yet it was not uncommon. The fundamental change of status of a person of the lower classes was from slavery to freedom. In the social order, the freeborn was of a higher status than the freedmen. This status order overruled even the difference between male and female and was the order of a Roman household. Thus, a freeborn son was of a higher status than a freedman father; a freeborn woman was again of a higher status than a freedman husband. Apart from such stratifications, there were also the slaves and freedmen of the house of Caesar who had great opportunity to rise in the social order. This change of status gave rise to opportunities for economic advancement also.

The rise of the freedmen aroused deep resentment among many people who thought themselves their betters. Meeks points out that it was during the reign of Nero that Petronius wrote his satire of the freedman Trimalchio's dinner party. "What the critics find so outrageous in the parvenus is their crossing of social boundaries. They had dared to claim the status to which their education, intelligence, skill power and wealth accord but which is forbidden by their birth, origin and legal rank."[31] This is similar to the situation of Dalits in India where they never get their due even when they cross the boundaries. Such resentment of the upper class resulted in what sociologists call as 'status inconsistency,' thus causing dissonance of status. This is important to our discussion because as Meeks points out that "such feelings would find some form of religious expression or-contrariwise-that some kind of religious symbols, beliefs and attitudes would enhance, or channel social mobility differently from others."[32] In other words, according to Meeks, this status inconsistency which resulted in discrimination found its antidote in the new society formed by Christianity. He is right in saying that though the social mobility in this new society would be different from the one outside, it nevertheless satisfied the need that their new status demanded.

We also know from biblical accounts that women were involved in business, played leadership roles in the church, travelled for various reasons, and so on. History shows that many women stood equal to men in various fields. MacMullen, drawing evidences from Italy and the Latin speaking provinces, has estimated that "perhaps a tenth of the protectors and donors that *collegia* sought out were women."[33] As women had no legal rights, this status inconsistency and status dissonance would certainly have been felt by them also and they were also the ones who got within the church the status they deserved.

Theissen explains this from a sociological point of view. He explains how Christianity as a sociological phenomenon acted to build society on lines which was at times disruptive to the existing society, and yet which brought integration in a way never experienced before. The new worldview advocated by Christianity and experienced through conversion was totally opposite to the existing worldview of the time, and yet this new Christian worldview could breach the gaps in the old, satisfying the deepest needs of people. So, early Christianity, with its reversal of social and spiritual values, virtually turned the world upside down, and this explains why many who experienced status inconsistency turned to Christianity. We will discuss it briefly here, since this aspect of the growth of Christianity and its connection with urbanization is discussed in the next chapter that deals with the stratification of the Roman society.

First, the social characteristics of the city also play an important part in the unity of the city. Theissen says: "The three most important integrating factors were loyalty to the central authority; a unifying supraregional upper-class culture in towns and cities; and the local community of the *polis*."[34] But there were groups in this society who did not fit into this structure and they looked for new forms of integration and the Christians congregation was one of them.

The emperor, of course, was the central figure in the Roman empire. In spite of the heterogeneity of the empire, the aristocrats and the bureaucrats were related to the emperor through a strong judicial system. However, there was a larger group of people who probably were not bound to the emperor with a strong loyalty, and it could be ascribed to the hierarchical distance between them and the emperor. There were some who found this loyalty in their relationship with Jesus Christ which supposedly overrode all other loyalties because of its universal nature and "which gave to all men and women a value independent of social status—irrespective, that is, of local origin, ethnic affiliation, and social status."[35] So, socially, Christianity could offer what the State could not, and this gave Christianity a great impetus for growth. Perhaps the same could be said as the reason for the growth of Christianity in India among the depressed and oppressed classes, and for the upward mobility and expansion of the middle-class.

The second reason for integration of the society was, as pointed out, a unifying supra-regional upper-class culture in towns and cities. Though the Roman-Hellenistic culture did act as a binding force in this heterogeneous society, it was not able to include the Jews. The Jews were at constant loggerheads with the Roman administration. It is here that Christianity stepped in to act as a bridge. As Paul often explains, and particularly so in Eph. 2:15, the dividing wall between the Jews and the gentiles had been broken down through the work of Jesus on the Cross, thus bringing the Jews and gentiles together. Thus, by bringing together Jews and gentiles, Christianity did at the social level what the Romans could not in terms of integrating the society. We need to remember that, though the integration took place at the social level, the reasons were theological.

Thirdly, the city was supposed to act as an integrating factor because it is here that all had equal rights. However, it was only a myth for we are aware that a large part of the population consisting of women, the *liberati* or slaves did not have rights at all. It is quite clear that the differing status of citizens in society overrode the equal rights of citizens in a city. Christianity brought in all the excluded members of the society under one-fold and thus acted as a greater unifying factor than the powerful Roman Empire. In Gal. 3:28, Paul says "there is neither Jew nor Greek, slave nor free, male or female, for you are all one in Jesus Christ." He is specially focusing on the Jew, the slave and the woman for they were that section which had no rights and he is affirming that they are equal irrespective of their religious background, gender or occupation.

Hellenism and Christian Mission

It has been already noted that Hellenism was one of the factors contributing to the spread of Christianity in the city. The importance of Hellenism for Christian mission requires an explanation here. The Greco-Roman cities all had a common Hellenistic culture. Even where the Roman colonies existed, Hellenism was the dominant culture.

The first and prominent thing to note is that Greek was the spoken language. The Old Testament has already been translated into Greek (Septuagint) in 3rd and 2nd centuries BC, and all the New Testament writings were also in Greek. Apart from the language, there was a commonality observed across the cities, be it the decrees announced by the city councils, or the way the clubs honored the patrons, or even the handbooks used by students for studies. There was also a similarity in styles of pottery, glassware, furniture, and so on. It is important to note that such commonality could be observed only in the cities, while in the countryside people differed greatly in their lifestyle and culture.

Does this mean that there was a uniformity of culture in the city? Meeks concludes by saying that "the city then, was where novelties first could be encountered. It was the place where, if anywhere change could be met and even sought out."[36]

Therefore, though Hellenism was a dominant culture, there were many others competing with it. Explaining the culture of Corinth, Theissen says that "they did not live in the culture. If in many aspects of life, they stood in continuity with Greek tradition, the use of Latin in their inscriptions and the construction of the amphitheater show how un-Greek they were in other ways. Such circumstances are particularly unsettling to those strata of society for which culture (real or imagined) is a part of social status."[37] He further explains that "in a newly founded culturally heterogeneous city the desire for new cultural and social identity is much more likely to arise than in the established cultural centre of Athens."[38] Philippi on the other hand was colonized by the Romans and the conquering Kings settled their veterans here. According to Meeks, "the double colonization and the constant passage of troops through Philippi thereafter, because of its strategic location assured to this city a much more Latin character than any others..."[39] Philippi had basically agricultural economy though trade also flourished there due to the high concentration of migrants. Thessalonica, apart from being the capital city of the province of Macedonia also had a thriving business of purple dyeing. Commerce brought in a constant flow of immigrants like the Egyptians and the Jews. So, what do we find in these cities? Hellenisation had brought in a commonality of culture and yet there were other cultures thriving alongside it. The constant flow of new people to the city brought in new cultures which may not have been dominant and yet they were very much part of the city culture. Thus, on one hand, the Christian missionaries would have found it easier to connect with the city folk because of a common culture, yet on the other hand, the unsettled culture of the city would make it difficult for them to share the gospel in such manner that the city folk can assimilate it.

Jewish Diaspora and Christian Mission

The Jews had, for a long time, started settling in cities outside Palestine, especially in the cities of Greece. They came mainly as traders though some of them would have been artisans. In every city they formed a community, centered around the synagogue. It is possible that they assimilated the Greek culture. However, did they keep their distinctions as Jews or did they lose their identity completely? There are differing views on this subject. Rodney Stark cites various examples to show that the Jews had virtually given up their distinctions. "For example, the prohibition against eating with non-Jews probably was widely ignored."[40] He gives many examples to show that they compromised even their religious convictions, which was their trademark. But he goes on to say that "if they were no longer Jewish, neither was they Greek. Instead they were trapped in marginality, their Hellenism compromising their Judaism, and the latter preventing their full embrace of the former."[41] It is here that Christianity would have been attractive to them as they would have their Jewish root without the law to hinder their relationship with the Hellenized neighbors.

Meeks, on the other hand, gives a lot of evidence that the Jews at various times and in various cities made rigorous petitions to the then governors or the emperor to keep their distinctions which were graciously granted. Their desire for full citizenship, however, was turned down. He also says that "the ambivalences which affected their lives as simultaneously members of the Jewish community and residents of the Greek city would have varied somewhat from place to place and considerably with their means and rank."[42] Though Meeks has not elaborated on this, what he means probably is what Stark is showing very clearly. There may have been a certain segment of the Jewish community who had virtually left their Jewish distinctions and in all probability, these were the people who were more receptive to the Christian gospel.

Stark brings in another concept which helped the growth of Christianity among the Jewish Diaspora. He says that every religion has a culture attached to it which he calls 'religious capital.' He says that "people are more likely to change faiths to the extent that they are presented with an option that allows them to conserve much of their religious capital."[43] Christianity presented this to them as it preserved the heritage of the Old Testament and only added to it. There were no new laws added, the worship pattern was like that of the synagogue, it was conducted in Greek etc. So, there was much continuity between Judaism and Christianity due to which many of the Hellenized Jews readily accepted Christianity.

Thus, urbanization in the first century played a major role in the spread of the Christian faith. The compactness of the cities helped the Christian message to spread rapidly. The multi-religious context characterized by religious fluidity also helped Christian faith to make inroads into the city. The excellent roads and marine facilities that the Romans developed were of great help to Paul his companions in their long travels to spread the Christian faith. Further, Christianity paved the way for a respectful and dignified social order that could satisfy people from every stratum of the society, something the existing social order could not achieve. Hellenisation of the city brought about a common culture, which again helped the Christian missionaries to connect with the people of the city. Lastly, it integrated the city in a way that no previous society could. Urbanization, therefore, played a major role in the spread of the Christian faith.

3. THE SOCIAL STATUS OF THE FIRST CENTURY CHRISTIANS

Having examined the evidence of Christianity growing in an urban environment, we are now ready to look at the social status of those who accepted Christianity. It is generally believed that Christianity was a religion of the proletariat, but we need to again examine evidence to see how true this is. It is my endeavor to show that there were a good number of people of moderate means who accepted Christianity. More so, these were the people whom God used for the furtherance of the gospel.

Social Stratification of Early Roman Society

Social stratification is important in any society not only to describe it but also to analyze any changes that are taking place within them. The social stratification in India is rather very complex, with caste and class crisscrossing each other at various points. A general reconstruction of the Hellenistic-Roman society is far from complete owing to vast disagreement among the scholars on the subject. Yet, we may be able to draw some conclusions based on the clues that various authors have given in their writings, however fragmentary the evidence may be.

There have been quite a few who have considered the economic criteria as the basis of stratification of the early Roman society. Others have tried to combine it with the status a person acquired based on various parameters. Stambaugh and Balch say: "In terms of power, influence, money and the perceptions of the time, we can divide the population into two main categories, those with influence and those without it, the 'honorable' and the 'humble', those who governed and the those who were governed, those who had property and those who did not. The upper category was very small, the lower one very large."

Meeks says that "we would do well to follow the lead of M. I. Finley (who in turn was adapting the views of Max Weber) in distinguishing in ancient society three different kinds of ranking: class, *ordo* and status."[45] By this he is speaking of not just the economic criteria, but the status attached to the top order of the society.

The *ordo* or *ordines* were probably the only well-defined category in that society which majority of authors agree with and elaborate upon. At the top was the Senate consisting of some 600 members drawn from several aristocratic families followed by the *equites* or knights. This was followed by a hundred senior men called *decuriones* followed by the freeborn, the freedman and then the slaves. Jeffers puts this as a pyramid in Fig. 1 which gives us an idea of how very tiny or miniscule the upper class was in terms of numbers. But in terms of wealth, status and power, there was an immense gap between these ruling elite and the masses. Esler's comment on this is revealing when he says, "Attached to all three *ordines* were property qualifications. A Roman senator had to possess 250,000 *denarii* and an *eques* somewhat less than half that amount, while a typical figure for a *decurion* was 25,000 *denarii*. The immensity of these amounts can be seen by comparison with the daily wage earned by laborer—one *denarius*."[46] It was thus natural that the upper class regarded themselves as morally superior to the masses. Esler further thus rightly comments that the upper classes came to refer to themselves as *honestiores*, possessors of *honos*, or esteem, while the rest were simply *humiliores*, those of lowly birth and status.[47] Was this stratification of society good enough to describe the first century society adequately? The *ordo or ordines* were good enough to describe only the top aristocratic society. It only bunched the rest of them into one homogeneous group which was totally incorrect. Even this mass was highly heterogeneous and very complex. Hence, we could never get an idea of the Greco-Roman society by using just the class of *ordines*.

There have been attempts to combine this with the concept of class to describe the stratification in the Roman world. We have already referred to the Pyramid structure of Jeffers to describe the *ordines*, but he puts another group just below the *decurions* and above the poor and destitute.

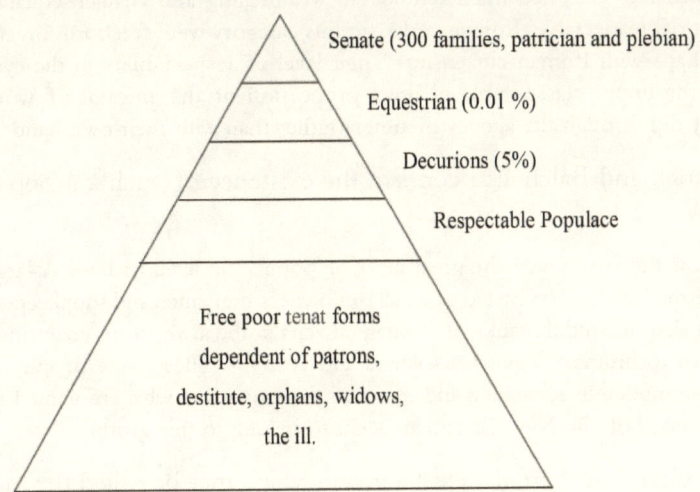

Senate (300 families, patrician and plebian)

Equestrian (0.01 %)

Decurions (5%)

Respectable Populace

Free poor tenat forms
dependent of patrons,
destitute, orphans, widows,
the ill.

Figure 1: Stratification of Roman Society (Source: J.S. Jeffers)

J.S. Jeffers calls this fourth category as 'respectable populace' below which was a huge number of poor, destitute etc. as seen in the above figure. He says,

> Below the ruling classes, there existed a large group of persons of middling wealth and status, whom the Roman historian Tacitus called the populace integer, the "respectable populace". This group was composed of small land owners, craftsmen and shopkeepers, including those who worked alongside their slave and wage owners...[48]

Esler goes a step further when he gives us an idea of the status of this group. He says that

> The most fortunate were probably the wealthier merchants and traders who could normally earn a reasonable living, even though they were barred from sitting on the provincial city councils because they were thought to engage in a degrading livelihood. Then there were the artisans and those engaged in the service industry...[49]

Jeffers further elaborates that

> These were the people of some moderate substance, though with various social backgrounds. Included were former slaves, who had gained Roman

citizenship. They had attained moderate wealth and status virtually equal to
that of 'respectable' Romans. Also, in this category were freeborn Greeks
perhaps with Roman citizenship. Their level of respectability in the eyes
of the upper classes was in direct proportion of the amount of work
they did through the agency of others rather than with their own hands.[50]

Stambaugh and Balch also confirm the existence of such a group when
they say:

> Below the aristocracy, the great mass of population lived its lives. A large
> intermediate level consisted of small landowners, craftsmen and shopkeepers
> and also the middle ranks of Roman citizens in the army, from centurions
> down to ordinary legionary soldiers and veterans. These were people of
> some moderate substance and most of the Christians who are named in
> the pages of the New Testament seem to belong to this group...[51]

So, it is clear that there did exist a group which may be called the middle-
class between the aristocrats, on one hand, and the poor masses, on the
other. But we need to take notice that their status in the society was not
based on their economic levels. Some of them may have possessed as
much or more wealth than the *Decurions*, but their status was not the
same as the *Decurions*.

It appears that most authors use the economic criterion as a basis for
describing the social status of the early Christians. A general impression is
that Christianity in the early years was a religion of the oppressed and it
was only the people of lower status that came to believe in Jesus. Several
authors hold this view. Kautsky, for instance, said that it is generally
recognized that the Christian congregation originally embraced proletariat
elements almost exclusively and was a proletarian organization. And this
was true for a long time after the earliest beginnings.[52]

Adolf Deissmann was one of the first who strongly advocated that
the early Christians were of a low social status, the proletariat. He justified
his position by pointing out that the literary culture of the New Testament
was low compared to it contemporary Greek culture.[53]

E.A. Judge, however, held the opposite view: "Far from being a socially
depressed group, then, if the Corinthian are at all typical, the Christians
were dominated by a socially pretentious section of the population of
the big cities."[54] Authors like Meeks and Theissen also seem to agree
with Judge. They both have written extensively to show that there were a
good number of people of moderate means within the Christian Church.

These opposing views have been called the old and the new consensus. But there have been various arguments against this so-called consensus. Richard L. Rohrbaugh has questioned the very methodology of calling this group either as 'middle-class' or even as people of 'middle social status'. Arguing against such stratifications, he says:

> In summarizing this review of current use of class terminology among New Testament scholars, several points can be made. To begin, we note that popular and nontechnical use of the terms abounds. It would be obvious to assert that confusion is the result, yet more to the point is the fact that assumptions about class are made by default more often than by design. The most common assumption is that vaguely defined income levels are an adequate criterion for designating social class. The possession of a lot of money is suggested as evidence of upper class position, while having little puts one in what is assumed to be a middle-class. So also, it is widely asserted that items like the ability to travel, evidence in the modern world of having money and status, must imply the same thing in antiquity. Such unexamined assumptions make social anachronism a constant problem.[55]

Is Rohrbaugh's critique a valid one? It appears that his conclusion is premature and forced. While many of the authors have taken income levels as a consideration to determine the 'class' levels in antiquity, it is not appropriate to include Meeks and Thiessen in this group. Meeks in fact rejects the concept of class and tries to stratify the society based on status as discussed below. Although Thiessen seems to have used the terms social class and social status interchangeably, or rather in a loose manner, he also talks of people of 'dissonant status', in line with what Meeks calls 'status inconsistency,' which uses the status criteria as a stratification tool. So, it is important to note that both these authors have not considered the income levels as their criteria to understand the society in antiquity.

In addition, Richard Rorhbaugh has based his analysis of class in antiquity on the Marxist and Weberain theory of class. He concludes that class differentiation is based purely on the power that one possessed. Speaking of the people below the *decurions*, he says that "the precarious position in antiquity was one of having money without power. It left one extremely vulnerable to the confiscatory powers of those who controlled the political system"[56] Meeks, however, points out that we cannot use the definition of Marx or Weber to describe or analyze society in antiquity for "they lump together groups who clearly were regarded in antiquity as different."[57] Further, there is enough biblical evidence that Rorhbaugh was not totally correct in stating that the common man did not have any rights or was totally powerless. Consider the case of Paul who, when arrested, evokes his Roman citizenship to avoid being flogged unjustly (Acts 22:22ff). It is obvious that even common people had their rights, provided they had the right status qualifications. Political power certainly lay in the hands of the elite, but it did not imply that the masses were without any rights at all.

So then, what was the best way to describe the Greco-Roman society in antiquity? The only alternative left now is the use of social status to describe this society. Though the concept of status is complex, it is probably the best way to describe the Roman society. Jeffers says: "Status is a more fluid term in that the various markers of status could change over time and might conflict with one another."[58] He further says that

> the Romans evaluated a person's status based on whether the person was a citizen or a foreigner, patron or client, free or slave, ethnic Roman/Latin or not, voluntary ally or conquered enemy, male or female and married or unmarried. These categories each had a specific value for Romans. For example, a well-educated wealthy non-citizen former slave would have been thought lower in status than a poor, uneducated freeborn citizen.[59]

Meeks confirms this view by saying that "Most sociologist have come to see social stratification as a multidimensional phenomenon; to describe the social level of each individual or group, one must be able to measure their rank along each of their relevant dimensions."[60] He goes on to list a number of variables like power, occupational prestige, income or wealth, education and knowledge, religious and ritual purity, family and ethnic-group position, and so on, as the basis of placing a person on a social scale. We need to understand that a person's ranking on the social scale was not just the average of these variables, but rather the weighted average where each parameter would have its own weightage. This in turn would depend on the person doing the analysis. There is an element of subjectivity in this ranking. Meeks brings in one more aspect which is important. He says that "the degree of correlation among one's various rankings constitute another kind of variable that affects how one is evaluated by others and how one evaluates oneself. This is the dimension of status consistency, status congruence or status crystallization...."[61] In fact sociologists call this phenomenon as 'status inconsistency' or 'status dissonance,' as already mentioned above. A person's behavior is often a result of the gap between attributed status and one's own understanding of it. This is the factor that leads to social mobility where one tries to reduce that gap. This could be compared to the stratification in India based on caste. A Brahmin enjoys a high status irrespective of his education or his wealth. So, it is important to recognize that social stratification was as complex in the Roman society as it is now in our country.

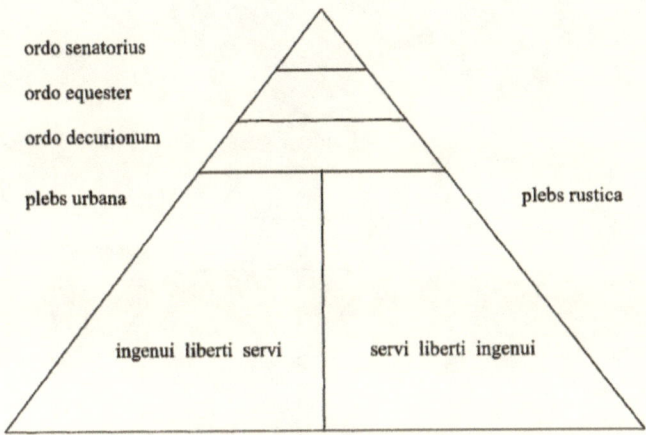

Figure 2: Stratification and Rank in
Roman Hellenistic Society (Geza Alfoldy)

The depiction of the Greco-Roman society by Geza Alfoldy, shown above, is an improvisation of the social classification by Jeffers. While Jeffers based his classification only on economic levels, Alfoldy bases his stratification on status. The society below the aristocrats was divided into the *plebs rustica*, signifying those from the villages, and *plebs urbana*, depicting those from the urban areas. Each was further stratified according to status, the *ingénui*, signifying the Romans consisting mainly of those brought in by the Roman empire from Italy, most of them being army veterans and probably the freeborn. Next were the *liberati*, also called freedmen. These were those freed from slavery and yet had obligations to their previous masters. They were followed by the slaves.

The Christians were mainly from the *plebs urbana* with differing status. There would have been from each of the status groups, the *ingénue*, the freeborn, the freedmen and the slaves. However, as seen from the figure below, two things are to be noted. First, the church consisted of people of differing social status where wealth also plays an important part. Second, there are people who in wealth are comparable to the aristocratic *decurions*, and yet are outside the status criteria. These would have been the foreign immigrants or even the women in that society. Such people are called those of 'status dissonance' or 'status inconsistency.' Many of these people chose to convert to Christianity, the reasons for which have been discussed earlier.

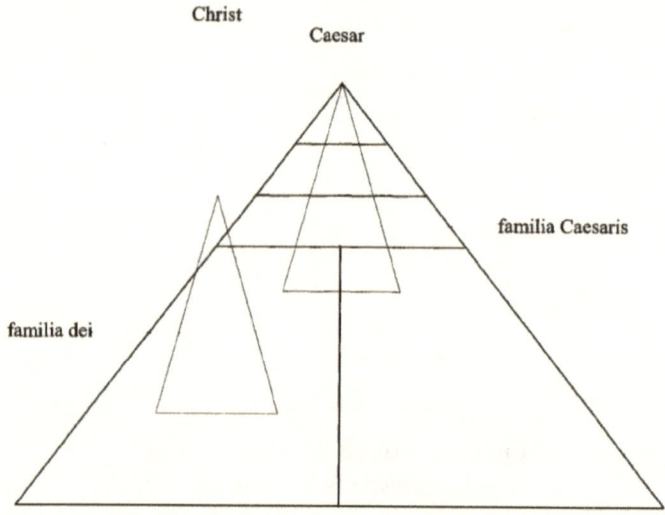

Figure 3: The Christians as *familia die* in
Hellenistic-Roman Society (Source: Theissen)

Steven J. Friesen feels that Meek's idea of evaluating a person on status ranking is not without its problems. It has already been pointed out earlier that the status evaluation is highly subjective as one does not know the exact value of each variable in antiquity. Moreover, he questions whether we really know the status variables of those in the Pauline congregations. So, in line with Justin Meggit, he concludes:

> So, social status is indeed a complex concept, and laying out the variables within it gives the appearance of sophistication. When it actually applied to Paul's assemblies, however, what we end up with is actually an 'impressionist sketch' as Meeks rightly noted. That sketch is based on very little information and is fraught with arbitrary conjectures that are gradually elevated to the status of conclusions.[62]

Friesen also thinks that the economic level assigned to various people in Paul's congregation has been done arbitrarily and does not have any base. Though he concedes that economic criterion is the only one you can apply to antiquity, he thinks that it has to be done scientifically. He thus has developed seven economic levels (PS1-PS7), where he has measured wealth in terms of subsistence. The first three levels comprise the super-rich, and the last two comprises of those living at or below the level of subsistence. He goes on to show that the early Christians in the Pauline assemblies were from the last two levels. He nevertheless acknowledges that there were some from the middle level of PS4 and PS5 which were supposed to be people of moderate and surplus means. In sum, according to Friesen, the early Christians were from an extremely poor background.

Although Friesen's thesis is attractive, he has been selective in choosing material to prove his point. The same argument would go against Meggit whom Friesen follows. First, neither of these authors has taken the evidence in Acts seriously, which may go against their line of argument. As will be shown later, there is ample evidence in Acts to show that many of the early Christians were of a high as well as good economic status. We are aware that quite a few authors question the authenticity of Luke-Acts. Tidball says that

> it could be that the picture has been deliberately painted in this way, since it is commonly thought that part of Luke's purpose in writing Acts is to demonstrate to the Roman authorities how acceptable and politically unsubversive the preaching of Christ was. If that was the purpose, it would be natural for him to emphasize the status and wealth of the converts at the expense of the common followers.[63]

Meeks agrees with this view when he says that "the author of Luke-Acts was evidently interested in portraying the Christian sect as one that obtained favor from well-placed substantial citizens."[64] Thiessen, however, argues: "No matter how one assesses the historical value of Luke-Acts, Luke is undoubtedly an irreplaceable witness for the social history of the end of the first century."[65] He is probably right in making his point because every author who does an analysis of the level of early Christians takes support of Acts in some way or the other. One glaring example would be that of trying to study the social level of Paul. That he was from Tarsus and he was a Roman citizen, and so on, is obtained from Acts. Thiessen also rightly points out:

Above all he dedicates his double volume to a 'most excellent Theophilus', whom he addresses in the same way as some high Roman officials are addressed in his work. ... He may have tried to impress Theophilus. But he must have ensured, nevertheless, that his image of the early Christian congregation would be plausible to his readers at the end of the first century.[66]

Second, he is not right in totally ignoring 'status' as a means of stratification. There is enough evidence in extra biblical literature of the different parameters used as status indicators—as stressed and elaborated upon by Meeks, Jeffers and others. Theissen points out that Meggit (And also Friesen for Friesen bases his thesis on Meggit) has also ignored the discussion on 'dissonance of status' and 'social deviance' which enriched social history in the 60s and 70s.[67] As said earlier, this refers to people who were wealthy, whose manner of life resembled even that of the *decurions*, and yet were not considered to be enjoying a high social status for various reasons: They may not have been born free or their origin was from a foreign land or some social variable was attached to them that was not rated very high. In many ways, these people were a disadvantaged lot, although their economic status was comparable with those in higher social status. So, it is very clear that the status of a person played an important role in the understanding of the social stratification in antiquity.

Thirdly, the list of Friesen of people of moderate surplus wealth (PS4-PS5) is comparable to what Theissen and Meeks call people of middling status. Stephanas is the only exception in Friesen's list. In addition, in the economic levels that he has developed, there is very little discussion on the middle level and much of what he says of these levels is speculative. He also seems to follow Meggit who has divided the society into just two levels—a small minority of the super-rich and the rest are the poor and the destitute. This kind of bunching a mass of people (more than 97% of the population) into just one group as "poor" is sociologically not plausible and hence incorrect. As in any other society at any time in history, there would have been people doing different kinds of jobs and each would have its own prestige with which would be attached an economic value. This certainly would bring about distinction among these people. Theissen rightly points out that

the Shepherd of Hermas speaks of the rich and the poor among Christians and attaches great significance to their relationship (Hermas, *Sim.* 2.51; cf. Jas 1.9-10; 2.1-11). Both in reality and in its interpretation, there existed

distinctive social differences among the population below the local power
elite, even if all groups were far removed from the huge possessions and
the power of the imperial upper class.[68]

However, the question that still remains is this: Was there a middle-
class in antiquity comparable to that we have had in the industrial and
postindustrial period? Theissen says that though we do not have a complete
picture of the Greco-Roman society, research has brought about some
accepted results and "it does not speak of a middle-class which indeed
is misleading in antiquity."[69] We may categorize this group as comprising
of (a) people of high status with a good economic status and (b) those
whose status was low but were as wealthy as the former group. There
may have been tensions between these groups, although this is not very
evident from biblical accounts. Hence, in trying to analyze levels of
social status enjoyed by early Christians, we will have to keep both these
in view and differentiate them from those who were economically poor
and probably of a low status.

Paul's Background
Church growth in the first century AD is associated with the missionary
journeys of Paul and hence it is pertinent to analyze the class that Paul
belonged to. It is important to locate his class because it is with his own
class that he would be able to come in close contact more easily and also
communicate the gospel more comprehensively.

Troeltsch does not give Paul a high literary status. Tidball, however,
rejects his estimate and says that though it is not possible to come to a
firm conclusion, there are a number of factors which tend to make us
place him solidly in the middle-class and possibly in the upper middle-
class.[70] Feirsen on the other hand puts Paul at the bottom of his economic
levels. He says that "while Paul's economic situation certainly vacillated
throughout his adult life (Phil. 4:12), his experiences would have been
primarily in categories of 5-7 on the poverty scale."[71] We have already
discussed what the different categories of Friesen indicate and, accordingly,
it suffices to know that he puts Paul at the below subsistence or destitute
level. Both these arguments against his high literary status or his low
economic level are unfounded.

Paul was a citizen of Tarsus which was a centre of learning. He claims
to have studied under Gamaliel (Acts 22:3) and it is possible that he had

secular learning also. Moreover, to become a citizen of Tarsus, one had to have property worth at least 500 *drachmae* (equivalent to 2000 *sesterces*, which was equal to two years' salary of legionary). Paul and his family must have fulfilled this condition. This is adequate evidence that Paul was from a middle-class family. He is being a citizen of this city would have come as a special privilege for some special reason and this certainly put him among the social elites of the empire. His attitudes towards work and ethics also show that he hailed from a middle-class background. If he chose to work for a living along with Barnabas, it was a deliberate choice and it tells us nothing about his economic status. His attitude towards work and ethics show that he hailed from a middle-class background. Thus, Tidball concludes: "It would seem that Troeltsch's judgment of Paul is ill-founded and that, instead of being an 'unliterary man', Paul was educationally and socially of more than average standard."[72] From the available evidence, we would not go wrong if we conclude that Paul had a good literary background and was from a reasonably wealthy family.

Paul's Converts in Acts

A careful study of Acts reveals that Paul's converts, associates or sponsors were socially mixed . In his first missionary journey, Paul's first convert is the Proconsul of Cyprus (Acts 13:12). In Philippi, one of Paul's converts is Lydia, a dealer in purple cloth from the city of Thyatira. As a dealer of imported expensive cloth, she obviously was wealthy. This is again confirmed when she invites Paul and his associates to come and stay in her house which meant that it was big enough to accommodate quite a few guests. Acts 16:34 tells us that the jailer and his household believed in the Lord. This jailer would certainly be from a considerably high social standing. In Thessalonica there are quite a few prominent women who are convinced and converted by Paul's preaching (Acts 17:4). Also, the fact that Jason was forced to sign a bond on behalf of Paul, which would involve depositing a considerable amount of money, shows that he was also among the wealthy (Acts 19:9). Again, in Berea, there were quite a few prominent Greek women among those who believed. At Athens, Paul is taken to the Areopagus where the elite of the city met. He has no difficulty in presenting Jesus taking into consideration the philosophical bent of mind of his listeners. Dionysius, one of the intellectual elite listening to Paul got converted, along with Damaris who perhaps was also a woman of some social standing. In Ephesus, he hired the lecture hall of Tyrannus where he held discussions for two full years. It is certain that the people who came to discuss with him would have been from the intellectual elite with a high social standing. Some of the officials of the Province of Asia were friends of Paul (Acts 19:31). Esler in fact points out that "with the exception of Sergius Paulus, who was of Senatorial rank, all these individuals must have had a status equal to that of *decurions*."[73] He further states that "the care which Luke takes to mention them is best explained as indicating that they were members of his community who could identify with these early heroes of faith by virtue of having a similar, or slightly inferior, position in society."[74] Thus it is beyond doubt that there were a number of people from the higher echelons of the Roman society who had come into the Christian fold. Though the number may not have been substantially large, one cannot say either that they were so negligible.

Paul's co-workers too are cases in point. One is Barnabas. We are aware from Acts 4:36f that Barnabas came from a reasonably well to do family. He was a Levite from Cyprus who voluntarily sold a piece of land he owned, donated the money to the early apostles, and took to being an itinerant preacher and missionary. Though Paul and Barnabas decided to work for their living rather than burden the Corinthians, it was very much a voluntary act. Another is Apollos. He is a Jew, a native of Alexandria who came into the circle of Paul, courtesy Aquilla and Prisca. Bruce comments: "Luke applies to him the adjective *logios*, which meant "learned" or "cultured" in classical Greek, but acquired the sense of "eloquent" in Hellenistic and later Greek; the latter sense is what Luke intends though the former need not be excluded."[75] He further says that "Apollos seems to be one of the travelling Jewish merchants of whom some others receive mention in the Near Eastern history of this period for combining a readiness to give religious instruction with whatever other business that took them from place to place."[76] If he was a merchant and was capable of travelling from place to place for preaching and probably for his business, this certainly shows him to be a person of wealth.

Paul's converts in Acts who come from the middle level of the society would compare well with the educated middle-class of India with some differences. If we set aside the interplay of regional languages, religion and caste, then, the middle-class status in India is based primarily on education, income and occupation, although there are other factors at play in deciding the status of a person.

It is quite clear from this brief survey of Paul's converts and his co-workers in Acts that they were a socially mixed lot. If there were people from the lower strata, there were people from the higher strata also.

Prosopographic Evidence from the Epistles

Paul in his epistles has mentioned various names. These, along with those mentioned in Acts, add to about eighty. Studying these names and analyzing their backgrounds may provide us clues that will help us draw some conclusions on the stratification of the society in New Testament times. Meeks says there are at least thirty of these names that we could consider since we may get a clue of their status from their name, or from their origin or the cities they came from, and so on. Such information, coupled with their wealth as indicated by their ability to travel, or the service they rendered, would give us a fairly good idea of their overall status in the society as well as in the church. We will consider each separately to determine what each may indicate to us.

By Name

One may get a clue of one's status from his/her name. This method of determining one's status would largely apply to the Indian situation also where the surnames mostly depict the caste of the person. Thus, a Purohit or Dave would immediately be put in the Brahmin high caste while a Prajapati or Darji or Mistry would be the artisan or low caste. Meeks points out that Achaicus and Fortunatus (1 Cor 16:17), Quartus (Rom 16:23), and Lucius (Rom 16:21) in Corinth, and Clement in Philippi (Phil 4:3) all have Latin names coming from the two Roman colonies where Latin was the dominant official language. This *may* indicate that their families belonged to the original stock of colonists, who tended to get ahead. Euodia and Syntyche (Phil 4:2f) are Greek names and they may be from the merchant groups in Philippi. Tertius is another Latin name among the Corinthian Christians. We are told that he was a trained scribe who wrote letters for Paul (Rom 16:22). Though it is difficult to gauge his status, Theissen says that nothing is said about him which would place him among the proletariats. Perhaps he was a scribe employed in the imperial provincial administration.[77] This certainly shows that he was a man of letters and would be counted at a reasonable level in the social ladder.

Luke is another professional with a Latin name who is a Physician (Col 4:14) and a travelling companion to Paul. Doctors were often slaves. So Meeks says: "We might speculates that Luke had been a *medicus* in some Roman *familia*, receiving the name of his master (Lucius, of which Lukas is a hypocorism) on his manumission."[78] Esler, on the other hand, places Luke in the upper echelons of the Roman society, by reasoning that, "the high literary style of Luke and Acts, especially of the Prologue (Lk.1:1-4) and the sea voyage and the shipwreck description in Acts 27, implies that the author came from the upper segment of the Greco-Roman Society."[79] So a study of a sample of the names given in Paul's letters show that there was a fair sprinkling of those from the fringes of nobility, those involved in business and a few from the literary stalwarts.

Travel

As travel necessarily involved finances, the ability to travel shows the financial status of a person. However, we need to be cautious of drawing conclusions about the status of the people involved in travel as trips could be made on behalf of someone else or as companions of some wealthy persons. Nevertheless, we may be able to get a clue of the status of at least some people involved in travel. In today's world, it is not the ability to travel that would show the status of a person as much as the mode and class of travel would. Though many who travel by air or by the upper class in trains do so on behalf of the company they represent, these are mostly the educated ones hailing from the middle-class in our country.

In 1 Cor. 1:11 we read about the members of Chloe's household who travelled from Corinth, from whom Paul learnt of the problems in the Corinthian church. These probably were servants or slaves in Chloe's household and were probably of an inferior social status. Ampliatus (Rom 16:8) is a slave name and would fall in the same category. Andronicus and Junias who Paul says were his relations and were with him in prison somewhere are now in Rome (Rom 16:7). Eck assumes that the name Andronicus marks him as a freedman and, therefore, Junias was also a freedwoman. Meeks, however, refutes this assumption by making it clear that not every Jew with a Greek name in Rome was a former slave. He goes on to state that probably they were husband and wife.[80] Epaenetus (Rom 16:5), identified as the first convert of Asia, travelled to Rome and his name suggests that he was a slave. Silas (1Thess 1:1, 2Cor:1:19 etc.) is seen travelling widely with Paul and having a high status in the church. This, however, does not necessarily imply anything about status in the larger society. So, these few people we have considered here do not seem to qualify as people of a high social standing. Of course, there were others like Aquila and Priscilla, or Phoebe, who travelled for various purposes but who also qualify in other categories and hence they will be considered there.

Services Rendered

There were people in many local churches who rendered services to the church. We need to investigate if the kind of services they rendered would provide us any clue regarding the social status of the person.

Gaius (Rom 16:23, 1Cor. 1:14) is also a Latin name and is one of those whose ancestors migrated to Corinth. He seems to be a man of considerable wealth looking at the fact that he had ample space to accommodate not only Paul but the church also in Corinth. Theissen makes an interesting observation about the church that met at Gaius' house. He says that "Paul does not speak of a 'house congregation' (as in Phlm. 2) but of the 'whole congregation'. From this it could be concluded that the church also met at other places in smaller groups."[81] Quoting other well-known sources, he concludes thus: "In any event, the whole church met at Gaius' house which presupposes that he had sufficient space at his disposal, since the congregation at Corinth was a large one. This certainly shows that Gaius was a man of considerable wealth."[82] It is quite evident that Tertius also wrote the letter to the Romans from here and hence this would have been the place from where a number of activities of the church were carried out (Rom.16:21-23).

Aquila and Priscilla also fall into this category of those who rendered service to the church. Twice it is mentioned that the church met at their house (Rom. 16:3 and 1Cor 16:19). Paul calls them his fellow-workers and commends them for they had risked their lives for him. They had migrated from Italy due to political compulsions and they were tentmakers by profession (Acts 18:1-4). As artisans they would be placed in the middle to lower social status, but they seem to be wealthy for they could travel with Paul to Ephesus (Acts 18:18-19) and establish a home and ministry there. Underlining this fact, Bruce makes this statement: "They appear to have been a well to do couple, and their tent making business may have had branches in several centres, with a manager in charge of the branches in those places where they themselves were not resident. They were thus able to move back and forth easily between Rome Corinth and Ephesus."[83] According to E.A. Judge, "the fact that Prisca's name is mentioned before her husband's once by Paul and two out of three times in Acts suggests that she has higher status than her husband."[84] Tidball says that "whilst this suggestion is not impossible, is based on very slender evidence."[85] Bruce on the other hand says that "it may suggest that she was the impressive personality of the two."[86] If Luke or Paul has done it with some purpose, then, Judge is the one who seems to be correct in linking it with status.

Philemon also falls in this category. He seemed to have had a house big enough for the church to meet (Phlm. 2) and Paul requests him to reserve a room for him when he comes to meet him (Phlm. 22). The fact that he has at least one slave, Onesimus, further suggests that he is a man of reasonable wealth. Friesen says that "New Testament scholars have tended to assume that reference to a house and a slave are strong indicators of wealth and/or high social status." Although Meggitt has argued that "many poor people owned slaves in the ancient world and that a mere reference to a home is not a good indicator of wealth,"[87] Theissen has clearly pointed out that "in all events the proprietor of a slave was richer than his neighbor without a slave. ...Therefore, we should exclude the houses from our list of status indicators especially if their significance is confirmed by other indicators or individual observation."[88] Moreover, Friesen has tried to show that poverty was rampant, and housing was scarce. If that was so, then, a house and a slave are sure indicators of one's social standing.

Paul recommends Phoebe to the Roman church for the help she has rendered to many including him. She is called the *diakonos* of the church in Cenchreae (Rom 16:1), a title which has evoked endless discussions. Robert Banks points that the term *prostatis* (in v.2, generally translated 'helper') may explain what this means. He says:

> While it could refer to her involvement in Paul's mission as a patroness, cognate terms from the same root are used elsewhere to describe the activities of those who exercise important functions in the churches, this could suggest that Phoebe was engaged in "teaching" and "leading" in her local church as Cenchreae.[89]

She is probably travelling to Rome on business and hence it can be inferred that she is a woman of some wealth.

The household of Stephanas is mentioned twice (1Cor.1:16 and 16:15-17) which probably shows that it was an important family. A household could include slaves as well, which Theissen takes as an indication of high status. Authors like Meggitt contend that the mention of 'houses' is not a good enough indication of one's status. However, Theissen says: "What is striking is that he insists on subjection not only to Stephanas but also to the members of his house. The whole house community participates in the prestige of the master. Stephanas and correspondingly his household community must have a high social status."[90] They held the distinction of being the first converts in Achaia and are said to have devoted themselves to the service of saints (1Cor. 16:15). Meeks says that his name suggests that he was a Greek, either indigenous or immigrant and that would not give him a very high status. But he continues that "the service he has rendered to the Corinthian Christians seems from the context to be of the sort rendered by patrons rather than by charismatic gifts (*Charismata*)." Further he clarifies that "it is precisely in contrast to the sometimes-disruptive roles of the *pneumatikoi* that Paul urges recognition due to people like those (*toioutoi*), namely Stephanas, Achaichus and Fortunatus."[91] Paul thus urges the congregation to submit to them and to others who similarly join in the work of God. Moreso, Stephanes along with others are involved in travel (1Cor.16:17), to meet Paul. Both Meeks and Theissen place him at a reasonably high level in terms of wealth (despite the fact that their social indicators differ), although not as high as Gaius or Erastus.

Another person to host Paul is Titius Justus (Acts 18:7). What could be the reason(s) for Paul to move from Aquila and Priscilla's house to Justus' house? Several reasons may be possible. It is possible that Aquilla and Priscilla being immigrants could not find a suitable spot to locate their business establishment. On the other hand, Justus' house was located very near the synagogue which may have been at the centre of the city. His house probably would have been more advantageous for Paul's mission. It would probably have offered him a place where he would have been able to carry out his work without interruption. Concerning his status, Thessien rightly says that "it can be assumed that it was not inferior to that of Aquila and Priscilla, as Paul would hardly have made claims on anyone who would have found it a greater burden that they had. The opposite is more probable."[92] Meeks is more specific about his status. He says that "his name indicates that he may be a Roman citizen; he belongs to the dominant Latin group of the colony."[93] This would place him at a high level as far as status is concerned. Further, his ability to host Paul would also mean that he was reasonably wealthy.

Paul specially mentions Rufus' mother who he says is his mother also (Rom. 16:13). Is it possible that Paul is hinting that she had taken care of him as a mother? Meeks says "If what Paul means by calling him 'my mother too' is that she was his benefactress, then she too had travelled or resided for a time in the East and had some wealth."[94] Acts 12:12 tells us that when Peter was miraculously released he went to the house of Mary, the mother of John Mark where many people had gathered and were praying. If Mark's mother was able to host a prayer meeting for many people, it shows that they had no space constraint. This in turn shows that they were people of some means of sustenance. We are also told in the same incident that Rhoda a servant girl came to open the door. If Rhoda is a servant of that house, then it certainly shows that Mark's family could afford one, which again is an indication of their social standing.

We have seen in this section that one of the main services rendered was hosting the church in their homes which we linked with their wealth. Who would better understand this than we in India where housing in the cities is scarce and is always bought at a premium? A few decades ago, it was only the upper class who could claim their own palatial houses. But buying or building a house is no longer the prerogative of the upper class but the dream of the middle-class. If it was the middle-class who organized housing societies, it is the New Middle-class who occupy the posh multi-storied apartments. Owning a house in our overcrowded cities is certainly a status symbol and a sign of being part of the middle-class.

References to Offices

The references to particular offices may show their status in the social realm. There aren't many names to be considered under this heading, but the few that are there do give a certain clue of their position in the society.

Acts 18:8 tells us that Crispus, the synagogue ruler, and his entire family believed in the Lord and this led to a wave of conversions in Corinth. Crispus is also mentioned among the few people that Paul baptized (1 Cor. 1:14). A synagogue ruler was usually in charge of the worship service controlling the reading of Scriptures and the homilies. Theissen points outs that

> for our purposes, it is particularly important to note that he had to assume responsibility of the maintenance of the synagogue building. Since upkeep of the synagogue required money, there was a reason to entrust this office to a wealthy man who would be in a position, should the occasion arise to supplement the community's funds with his own contribution.[95]

He further quotes E. Haenchen who on studying the different inscriptions comment that

> a majority of the inscriptions preserved from synagogue rulers emphasize that those who held these offices rendered a service to the Jewish congregation through their initiative and generosity. They certainly were not the poorest members of the community. So, we may assume he says in the case of Crispus that he possessed a high social standing which would explain why his conversion had such a great influence on others.[96]

Another person who held a high secular office, according to Rom 16:23, is Erastus. Paul calls him the city's director of public works (*oikonomos tēs poleōs*). There is a confusion and controversy over this title given to Erastus. H.J. Cadbury argues that though this title was given to high officials, it was also given in some cases to public slaves, and Erastus falls in this category.[97]

Is Cadbury correct in ascertaining that Erasmus could be a public slave? Or was Erasmus the "city treasurer" as understood by others? The King James Version, for instance, renders the term *oikonomos* as Chamberlain which means 'city treasurer.'

In this Roman colony of Corinth, next to the *duumviri,* who was the head of the constitution, the two most esteemed officials are the two *aediles* whose duty was to oversee the maintenance of the public buildings. There is some evidence that a certain Erastus did serve as a Corinthian *aedile.* Some Latin inscriptions were found naming Erastus as the donor of laying a pavement. The reconstruction of the inscriptions found in 1929, supplemented by those found in 1928 and 1947 read thus: "Erastus laid [the pavement] at his own expense in return of his *aedileship.*" Thus, it is tempting to identify the Erastus of the Bible with this *aedile.* But against this stood the fact that the Greek translation of *aedile* was *agoranomos* and not *oikonomos* mentioned in Rom 16. Kent thinks that *aedile* could be translated as *oikonomos* because an *aedile* was supposed to oversee the famous Isthmian games, but now a separate officer was chosen. So, the role of the Corinthian *aedile* was confined to local economic matters. He further comments that, for this reason, Paul does not use the customary word *agoranomos* to describe the Corinthian *aedile* but calls him *oikonomos*.[98]

Theissen argues that many cities other than Corinth also conducted such games but special officers were not appointed to supervise them. Although the Isthmian games were not being held under their supervision, the *aedile*'s role was important for the city. They were not just confined to tackling local economic issues but also oversee and maintain public buildings, and by carrying out this responsibility they made their impression on the public's awareness.[99] He proposes another solution by saying that, because an *aedile* was chosen for one year, it is scarcely imaginable that the city's leadership would be entrusted to men who had already proven themselves in more modest positions. Thus, the director of public works (*oikonomos tēs poleōs*) was a position lower than that of an *aedile*, which Erastus occupied when the letter to the Romans was being written, and only later was elected to that position which signified the pinnacle of his public career. Bruce too offers the same solution when he says, "The possibility, some would say the probability, must be recognized that the Erastus of the inscription is identical with Paul's Corinthian friend; if so, his service of city treasurer (the post which he was occupying at the beginning of AD 57) proved so satisfactory that some twenty years later he was promoted to the dignity of *aedile* (curator of public works)...."[100] Further, Theissen makes one more observation that "it is quite possible that he was a freedman as the inscription does not mention his father. Add to this the fact that he has a Greek name, and we may perhaps imagine him to be a successful man who has risen in the ranks of the local notables, most of whom were of Latin origin."[101]

As in the first century, occupation is a major criterion to determine one's status in our country today. We need to recognize that this was not the case always. Where occupations at one time were related to one's caste, the British opened up varied occupations based on educational qualifications. This like the first century is one of the major criteria for determining one's class. It is the high government officials, professionals and non-professional educated people who have a steady income who form a major part of the middle-class today also.

Indirect Evidence from the Epistles

We will now look at some of the indirect evidence from the epistles that may point to the social status of the first century Christians.

In Phil. 4:22, Paul in ending the letter with greetings from 'all the saints,' especially those who belong to Caesar's household. We do not know who these people are—whether they are of the royal household or freedmen or slaves. Nevertheless, Meeks says that "the imperial slaves and freedmen as a group had a greater real opportunities for upward social mobility than did any other non-elite segment of the Roman society, and it is precious bit of information that some of the members of this group had found reason to be initiated into Christianity at so early a date."[102] It is no different today where proximity to the power centre gives a better chance of social mobility.

In the ethical sections of most letters of Paul (on Christian behavior), there is a section on slaves and masters. In Col 3:22ff, the section on slaves is rather longer than that of masters. In Eph. 6:5-9, we again have admonitions to the slaves and masters, and here too the section for slaves is longer. Does this mean, as some commentators have concluded, that a majority of the members of these congregations were slaves? Although the letter may not give us a firm indication of the situation, what is obvious is that there were both slaves and masters in these congregations. Moreover, since Ephesians was supposed to be an encyclical letter, we may safely assume that all the congregations had both slaves and masters.

Paul's Corinthian correspondence, especially the first letter, has another indirect evidence for us to consider. The first are the statements about the community as a whole and these have been given in 1Cor.1:26-29 wherein Paul says:

> Brothers, think of what you were when you were called. Not many of you were wise by worldly standards; not many were influential; not many were of noble birth. But God chose the foolish things of the world to shame the strong. He chose the lowly things of the world and the despised things-and the things that are not-to nullify the things that are. So that no one may boast before him.

It is often concluded from these statements that the church in Corinth had a proletarian Christian Community. Tidball, for instance, says that "Paul's statement in 1 Cor 1:26 is partly made for rhetorical effect, but even so, it must have some basis in reality and there must have been many members in the Corinthian church who were slaves or belonged to the common man. Yet we also know that the church contained some wealthier people."[103] Theissen comments that "Paul does not wish to contest the significance of those congregational members from the upper classes but simply objects to their all too well developed consciousness of their own status."[104] Quoting Wilhelm Wuellner, Abraham Malherbe comments thus: "But to use 1Cor 1:26-28 as the most important text in the whole New Testament for allegations of Christianity's proletarian origins is indefensible and no longer tenable simply and chiefly on grammatical grounds."[105] It is thus quite clear that though there were people from different social levels in the Corinthian church, this text cannot be used to determine what levels they belonged to.

Next, we need to consider whether the statements about the division in the church of Corinth indicate anything about people's social status.

The first is the groups which emerge at the Lord's Supper (1Cor. 11:17-22). It is clear from v22 that there was a split between the haves and the have-nots. Theissen, having done an in-depth study of the probable reason of this split, points out that the conflict was in all probability sociological rather than theological in nature. He shows that the Corinthian society was also stratified like any other society and this would show up at different social occasions. One of these occasions was a banquet where there would be quite a heterogeneous group consisting of his freedmen clients and also his own friends. Here, it was not uncommon for the host to serve different quality and quantities of food according to the social status of the people concerned. This practice which had crept into the church seems to have been the cause of the problem. So, Theissen points out that the problem lay in the kind of stratification that existed in the Corinthian society.[106] This shows that the Corinthian church also consisted of people of various strata of the Corinthian society.

It would be difficult for us to appreciate this for we do not experience such blatant inequalities in our church today as those in the early church. But it would be very unrealistic to say that there is no dividing line between the educated and the uneducated, or the highly educated and the lesser educated. Where possible, separate congregations are formed based on wealth, education and along linguistic lines. Where this may not be possible, there is a subtle divide between these groups, with the former taking a leading and dominating role in the congregation.

Another conflict that Paul addresses in 1Cor. 8-10 is that concerning food offered to idols. With his sociological analysis, Theissen shows that the strong were those who had knowledge and hence said that idols really did not mean anything and that they had the right and freedom to eat as they pleased. On the other side were those with a weak conscience who considered eating meat offered to idols as really dangerous. Theissen has reasons to believe that the 'strong,' who were invited to meals where meat offered to idols were served, were also socially powerful.[107] If Theissen is correct in his sociological analysis, then this conflict also shows that the Corinthian church consisted of people of different social strata. It certainly had a small minority who were from the more affluent strata of the society.

The direct statements on the material and financial achievements of the Corinthians also give us some indications of different classes of people being part of the church of Corinth. In 1 Cor16:2 Paul tells the Corinthians to keep aside a sum in keeping with their income every Sabbath as a collection for God's people. Meeks says "this bespeaks the economy of small people, not destitute but not commanding capital either. This he says would fit the picture of fairly well-off artisans and trades-people as the typical Christians."[108] Though Meeks could be correct in his deduction, Theissen thinks that he is writing it for another reason. He says "In my opinion it follows from the controversy of apostolic support that some Corinthian Christians have considerable means at their disposal, for we learn that some Corinthians have evidently provided hospitality for several missionaries..."[109] He further says that in 1 Cor 9:3, Paul defends himself only before some and not before the whole congregation. Hence, it can be assumed that the spokesperson of the Corinthian parties was from the wealthier class of the society.[110] Obviously, both looking at the same text from differing perspectives have come to conclusions which ultimately show us that the Corinthian church was a community of mixed strata. Though not related to the above argument, it needs to be put on record that Paul did expect their help in his routine travel etc. Meeks says that, in 1Cor. 16:6, Paul tells them of his plan to stay with them for a while 'that you may send me on my way (*propempsete*) wherever I go. In such a context, *propempein* generally means "to equip him with all things necessary for the journey"[111] which would involve financial outlay.[112] Such expenses would be taken care of probably by the wealthier class of the Corinthian church.

In 1Cor 6:1-11, Paul addresses the problem of litigations among the Corinthian Christians. The object of these litigations was probably property or income. As Theissen rightly points out, such litigations could be undertaken only by those who had property. Moreover, he says that it was the upper class that had more faith in the courts than the lower class.[113] This again gives us an indication that a small number from the Corinthian church did belong to the upper strata.

In the book of Acts, we have a number of Gentiles known as 'God-fearers' turning to the Lord. We need to investigate who these people were and what was their status in the society. Scholars like Maclennan and A.T. Kraabel have questioned the very existence of any such group called 'God-fearers.'[114] Louis Fieldman in the *Biblical Archeology Review* of Sep-Oct 1986 has shown quite clearly that the evidence tilts more towards the traditional understanding of this term.[115] There is enough epigraphic evidence to show that these gentiles were attracted to Judaism and developed sympathy for it.

There are at least eight instances where the term 'God-fearer' is used apart from the detailed account of Cornelius in Chapter 10. Cornelius is shown to be one who gave generously to the poor and prayed to God regularly and was respected by all Jews. But he is still a Gentile (cf. v28, v45) for the people accompanying Peter were astonished that the Holy Spirit was given to the Gentiles. Irina Levinskaya thus describes Cornelius' position:

> It is of no less importance that Cornelius holds an official position: he is a centurion in the *cohors Italica* which means that he, like the magistrates from Aphrodisias, participated in the official cult. Thus, at the very beginning Luke takes as an example the most complicated case of a God-Fearer who, because of his official duties and despite his belief in one God, has to demonstrate publicly his polytheism. On the one hand, Cornelius is accepted by God since he fears him and works righteousness (10:35); on the other, Cornelius is a Gentile in the true sense of the word: he is an idolater participating in the offerings to the pagan gods.[116]

Cornelius is the first gentile (God-fearer) in the book of Acts to become a believer of Jesus.

While Peter is instrumental in this case, the rest of the instances where God-fearers are mentioned are all related to Paul. In fact, it is these God-fearers who were a majority among Paul's gentile converts. Paul was associated with Titius, Justus and Lydia who were also God-fearers. There are God-fearers among his audience in the synagogue in Pisidian Antioch. In Acts 13:50 we are told that the Jews incited the God-fearing women of high standing and the leading men of the city. From these and other references, two things become clear: One, these Gentile God-fearers were people of high standing in the society. Two, though they were related to Judaism closely, they were not circumcised and hence not full members of the Judaic society.

K.G. Kuhn and H. Stegemann, from their study of excavated inscriptions, conclude: "Among the 'God-fearers' in the Jewish Hellenistic Diaspora the proportion of those of higher social status was greater than among the proselytes who for the most part come from the lowest strata of the people (for example, slaves)."[117] It is seen that they either became the backbone of the Gentile mission of Paul or they became staunch opponents of Christianity. We do not go into the details of the reason of their opposition, but the reason why many of them accepted Christianity is not hard to find. Theissen says:

> God-fearers had already demonstrated an independence with reference to their native traditions and religion. They stood between differing cultural realms and thus were particularly receptive to the Christian faith, which crossed ethnic and cultural boundaries and offered an identity independent of inherited traditions. Judaism could not do this; within it these people would not be fully entitled. Christianity however, especially in its Pauline form, offered them the possibility of acknowledging monotheism and high moral principles and at the same time attaining full religious equality without circumcision, without ritual demands, without restraints which could negatively affect their social status.[118]

Would there be a group today comparable to the God-fearers among the Hindu educated middle-class in our country? Sharma has rightly pointed out that Indians have lost the meaning of religion. He says, "In practice in present-superstitions, fatalism and blind faith are the basic pillars of religion pursued by majority of Indians."[119] Thus what he/she really follows in the name of faith is only blind superstition leading to various practices which are meaningless to him/her. In such a situation, there is a possibility that he/she looks for meaning elsewhere. Herbert Hoefer too thinks so and bases his 'Churchless Christianity'[120] on this very hypothesis. The fact that such seekers do not become full members of any church would place them very close to what the God-fearers were in the New Testament times. If this is true, there is a tremendous opportunity for the church to evangelize the educated middle-class provided it opens its mind to such concept as 'Churchless Christianity'.

Mixed Strata, Ambiguous Status

In conclusion, it would be right to say that the first century Christians were a mixed lot. The top level of the society consisting of the landed aristocrats, Senators, *decurions* etc. are missing. Of course, among the names mentioned in the New Testament, two men belonging clearly to the category of *Decurions* were also Christians—Dionysius, a member of the Aeropagus in Athens (Acts 17:34), and Erastus, the city treasurer of Corinth (Rom. 16:23). And there is not any mentioned from the lowest category either. Theissen arrives at this conclusion from his study: "Hellenistic primitive Christianity was neither a proletarian movement among the lower classes, nor an affair of the upper classes."[121] So, as already discussed, there were a fair sprinkling of those on the fringes of the upper class and a good number from the working classes.

As Meeks points out, "the levels in between are well represented."[122] Agreeing with Meeks, Jeffers says that 'the social statuses of Christians place them for the most part in the middle or lower range of class and status."[123] Because of this, the congregations were never a homogeneous lot, but represented a great variety in culture, customs and thinking. E. A. Judge rightly emphasizes this saying, "The interest brought together in this way probably marked Christians off from other unofficial associations which were generally socially and economically as homogenous as possible. Certainly, this phenomenon led to constant differences among the Christians themselves...."[124] Roland Allen on the other hand says that though Paul did not aim at evangelizing any particular class, his converts were from the middle and lower strata. He quotes Lightfoot as saying, "From the middle and lower classes of the society, it seems probable that the Church drew her largest reinforcements." Similarly, Ramsay declares that "the classes where education and work go hand in hand were the first to come under the influence of the new religion."[125]

Despite the fact that many scholars have argued in favor of a situation where the gospel penetrated the 'middle-class' of the Roman society, it is strange that Garsey and Saller reject their existence, for they say: "There was no genuine middle-class in the sense of an intermediate group with independent economic resources or social standing."[126] Their position is untenable in view of the evidences presented here for the existence of a middle level in the Roman society to which many Christians belonged.

Further, as discussed, this middle level was also layered with various statuses according to the wealth, work and background of the people concerned. Thus, there were those who were wealthy and those of a higher status, as indicated by their names and capacity to use their resources for the church. These were people who had slaves and servants at their disposal. They were able to house the church, support the missionaries, etc. There were also a fair number of business people in this group who had considerable wealth to travel on business tours. The reasonably wealthy God-fearers too were also part of this group. There was another layer probably below this group who were the artisans and small traders. Some in this category, according to Meeks, had houses, slaves and the ability to travel, and other signs of wealth.[127] It is anyway fair to say that most of these people would be people of decent means to make just enough money to take care of their daily life. There were also people from the *familia Caesaris* who were part of the Christian congregation who could be considered to be the few upwardly mobile people of that society. There were prominent women in most of the congregations who stood out for their leadership in the church and society. Along with these groups were the slaves also who can be considered to be much above the menial laborers and the destitute. Tidball says that they were a mixed group as he concludes his discussion on the social status of early Christians: "Acts, Romans and 1Corinthians all demonstrate the existence of the middle level people. Many of them are mentioned by name and without their support Paul would have been unable to carry out his itinerant ministry."[128]

According to Jeffers,

'With each social level, we see several levels of status. A number of Christians mentioned in the New Testament had high status in one area (such as wealth) but low status in another area (such as Roman citizenship). Often, such people had 'status inconsistency' because they were upwardly mobile seeing a change in their status in their life time...."[129]

In line with Jeffers, Meeks too says that a consensus is emerging here since Malherbe's report seems to be valid: a Pauline congregation generally reflected a fair cross section of urban society. He goes on to generalize that the most active and prominent members of Paul's circle (including Paul) were people of high status inconsistency (low status crystallization). They are upwardly mobile; their achieved status is higher than their attributed status. He questions whether this is accidental, and this is a pertinent question for us today. He further questions whether there were some specific characteristics of early Christianity that would be attractive to status-inconsistent.[130] This is something we cannot probably answer at this point but may be probed further to ascertain what made them come into the Christian fold.

Roland Allen's comment on the kind of people that accepted Christianity is revealing though one cannot agree with it completely. He says: "We are all familiar with the experience that people who are most ready to receive new impressions, to follow new ideas, to embrace new creeds, to practice new rites, are by no means the most stable and admirable, sober and trustworthy, high principled and honest hearted of men."[131] Though some of the converts would have come from the category described, it would be difficult to agree with Roland Allen for many of them were of sound ethical background. However, it is interesting to see is that it is the unstable on whom new ideas do make an impression. Can it be that the upwardly mobile, the status-inconsistents, as Meeks calls them, were impressionable due to this? Swanson and Williams give several reasons as to why the church needs to engage with cities. They say that cities have a transforming effect on people, form a creative centre, create fertile ground for thinking and receptivity and help people to live more efficiently and productively.[132]

So, it seems that though there were a few established people in the first century church, most of the people from the upper social status were the upwardly mobile type. That they were city bred would have helped them to consider the claims of the gospel and, in all probability, would have found the missing anchor in urban situations in the gospel.

So, given the evidences, it would be correct to conclude that the churches in the New Testament times were predominantly urban. Urbanization and Hellenisation did help in its growth. The congregation, though socially a mixed group, did have a fair number of people who may have had an ambiguous status but who were wealthy enough to be included among the *decurions*. And this is a trend that continued for a long time.

Endnotes

[1] David S. Lim, "The City in the Bible," *Evangelical Review of Theology, Vol 12, No 2,* (1988), 138.

[2] Robert Linthicum, *City of God, City of Satan* (Grand Rapids: Zondervan Publishing House, 1991), 21.

[3] Sir Leonard Woolley, *Excavations at Ur, A Record of twelve Years' Work* (New York: Barnes and Noble, 1955) cited in Linthicum, *City of God,* 21.

[4] Werner Keller, *The Bible as History* (London: Hodder and Stoughton, 1965), 42 cited in J. N. Manokaran, *Bible and Cities, Transformation of Urban Centres* (Chennai: Mission Educational Books, 2005), 6.

[5] Lewis Mumford, *The City in History,* (New York: Harcourt Brace, 1961), cited in Linthicum, *The City of God,* 21.

[6] Jacques Ellul, *The meaning of the City* (Michigan: William B. Eerdmans Pub. Co. Ltd, 1970), 16.

[7] Harvie M. Conn & Manuel Ortiz, *Urban Ministry, The Kingdom, the City and the People of God* (Illinois: IVP, 2001), 87.

[8] Linthicum, *City of God,* 28.

[9] Conn & Ortiz, *Urban Ministry,* 121.

[10] Conn & Ortiz, *Urban Ministry,* 122-23.

[11] Harvie Conn, "Genesis as Urban Prologue" in Roger Greenway (ed), *Disciplining the City* (Michigan: Baker Book House, 1992), 30.

[12] Harvie Conn, "Genesis as Urban Prologue," 30.

[13] Roger Greenway & Timothy M. Monsma, *Cities-Mission's New Frontiers* (Michigan: Baker Book House, 1989), 4.

[14] David J. Bosch, *Transforming Mission* (Bangalore: Centre for Contemporary Christianity, 2006), 162.

[15] Bosch, *Mission,* 161-62.

[16] Bosch, *Transforming Mission,* 162.

[17] Roland Allen, *Missionary Methods, St. Paul's and Ours* (London: Robert Scott, 1912), 18.

[18] Randy White, *Encountering God in the City* (Illinois: IVP Books, 2006), 72.

[19] White, *Encountering God,* 73.

[20] Mihail Rostovtzeff, *The Social and Economic History of the Roman Empire*, 2 Vol, 2nd ed, Revised by P. M. Fraser (Oxford: Clarendon Press, 1957), 1:49, cited in Wayne Meeks, *The First Urban Christians, The Social World of Apostle Paul* (New Haven: Yale University Press, 1983), 11.

[21]Wayne A. Meeks, *The First Urban Christians, The Social World of Apostle Paul* (New Haven: Yale University Press, 1983), 29.

[22] E. R. Dodds cited in Rodney Stark, *Cities of God*, 30.

[23] Rodney Stark, *Cities of God*, 31.

[24] Gerd Theissen, *Social Reality of Early Christians*, trans. Magaret Kohl (Edinburgh: T&T Clark, 1993), 280.

[25] Theissen, *Social Reality*, 285.

[26] Gerd Theissen, *The Social Setting of Pauline Christianity*, ed.& trans. John H. Schutz (Edinburgh: T&T Clark, 1982), 107.

[27]Theissen, *Pauline Christianity*, 107-110.

[28] Roger Greenway and M Monsma, *Cities-Missions New Frontiers* (Michigan: Baker Book House, 1989), 21.

[29] Dodd, Cited in Stark, *Cities of God*, 33.

[30] Stark, *Cities of God*, 34.

[31] Meeks, *Urban Christian*, 22.

[32] Meeks, *Urban Christian*, 23.

[33] Ramsay MacMullen, "Women in Public in Roman Empire" *Historia* 29 (1980), 211 cited in Meeks, *Urban Christians*, 24.

[34] Thiessen, *Social Reality*, 272.

[35] Thiessen, *Social Reality*, 273.

[36] Meeks, *Urban Christians*, 16.

[37] Theissen, *Pauline Christianity*, 100.

[38] Theissen, *Pauline Christianity*, 100.

[39] Meeks, *Pauline Christianity*, 45.

[40] Stark, *Cities of God*, 125.

[41] Stark, *Cities of God*, 126.

[42] Meeks, *Pauline Christianity*, 39.

[43] Stark, *Cities of God*, 127.

[44] John E. Stambaugh and David L. Balch, *The New Testament in its Social Environment* (Philadelphia: West Minister Press), 110.

[45] Moses I. Finley, *The Ancient Economy*, Sather Classical Lectures (Berkley: University of California Press, 1973), 35-61 cited in Wayne A. Meeks, *The first Urban Christians* (New Haven: Yale University Press, 1983), 53.

[46] Philip Francis Esler, *Community and Gospel in Luke–Acts* (Cambridge: Cambridge University Press, 1987), 171.

[47] Esler, *Community in Luke,* 172.

[48] J.S. Jeffers, *The Greco-Roman World of the New Testament Era* (Illinois: IVP, 1999), 188.

[49] Esler, *Community in Acts,* 173.

[50] Jeffers, *The Greco-Roman World,* 188.

[51] John E. Stambaugh and David Balch, *The New Testament in its Social Environment* (Philadelphia: The Westminster Press, 1986), 112.

[52] Kautsky, *Foundations of Christianity,* (np: Orabis and Windrush, 1973) 9-323 cited in Derek Tidball, *An Introduction to Sociology in the New Testament* (Exeter: The Paternoster Press, 1983), 91.

[53] Derek Tidball, *An Introduction to the Sociology of the New Testament* (Exeter Devon: The Paternoster Press, 1983), 92.

[54] E. A. Judge, *The Social Pattern of Early Christian Groups in the First Century* (London: np, 1960), 60 cited in Gerd Theissen, *The Social setting of Pauline Christianity* (Edinburg: T&T Clark, 1982), 69.

[55] L. Rorhbaugh Richard, "Methodological Consideration in the debate over social class status of Early Christians," *JAAR* 52 (1984) 519-546, web.a.ebscohost.com/ ehost/pdfviewer/pdfviewer? sid=6c9ec145-ca29-403d-b528-a79a03e32656%40sessi onmgr4002&vid=16&hid=4207&bdata (accessed 30th April 2014), 528.

[56] Rorhbaugh Richard, "Methodological Considerations," 542.

[57] Meeks, *Pauline Christianity,* 53.

[58] Jeffers, *The Greco-Roman World,* 181

[59] Jeffers, *The Greco-Roman World,* 182

[60] Meeks, *Pauline Christians,* 54.

[61] Meeks, *Pauline Christians,* 54.

[62] Justin Meggit, *Paul, Poverty and Survival* (Edinburgh: T &T Clarke, 1998), 100-101 cited in Steven J. Friesen, "Poverty in Pauline Studies: Beyond the so called New Consensus," *JSNT* 26.3 (2004) 323-361, 3d-b52 8a79a03e32656%40sessionmgr4002&hid=4207&bdata=JnNpdGU92Whve3QtbG 12ZSZzY29wZT1zaXR1#DB=rfh&AN=ATLA0001394433 (accessed on 30th April 2014), 334.

[63] Tidball, *Sociology of the New Testament,* 96.

[64] Meeks, *Urban Christians,* 61.

[65] Theissen, "Social structure," 68.

[66] Theissen, "Social Structure," 69.

[67] Theissen, "Social Structure," 67.

[68] Theissen, "Social Structure," 73.

[69] Theissen, "Social Structure," 70.

[70] Tidball, *New Testament*, 93.

[71] Steven, "Poverty," 350.

[72] Tidball, *New Testament*, 93-94.

[73] Esler, *Community in Acts*, 184

[74] Esler, *Community in Acts*, 184.

[75] F.F.Bruce, *Paul, Apostle of the free Spirit* (Exeter: The Paternoster Press, 1977), 255.

[76] Bruce, *Paul*, 256.

[77] Gerd Theissen, *The Social Setting of Pauline Christianity* (Edinburg: T & T Clarke, 1982), 92.

[78] Meeks, *The First Urban Christians* (New Haven: Yale University Press, 1983), 57.

[79] Esler, *Community in Acts*, 184.

[80] Meeks, *Urban Christians*, 57.

[81] Theissen, *Pauline Christianity, 89.*

[82] Theissen, *Pauline Christianity*, 89.

[83] F. F. Bruce, *Paul, Apostle of the Free Spirit* (Exeter: The Paternoster Press, 1977), 251.

[84] E. A. Judge, "The Early Christians as a Scholastic Community" *Journal of Religious History* 1 (1960), 129 cited in Meeks, *Urban Christians*, 59.

[85] Tidball, *Sociology*, 97.

[86] Bruce, *Paul*, 251.

[87] Steven, "Poverty" 354.

[88] Theissen, "Social Structure," 82.

[89] Robert Banks, *Paul's idea of Community* (Massachusetts: Hendrickson Publishers, 1994), 123.

[90] Gerd, "Social Structure," 82.

[91] Meeks, *Urban Christians*, 58.

[92] Theissen, *Pauline Christianity*, 91.

[93] Meeks, *Urban Christians*, 63.

[94] Meeks, *Urban Christians*, 60.

[95] Theissen, *Pauline Christianity*, 74.

[96] E. Haenchen, *The Acts of the Apostles* (Philadelphia: np, 1971), cited in Theissen, *Pauline Christianity*, 75.

[97] H. J. Cadbury, "Erastus of Corinth," *JBL* 50 (1931), 42-58 cited in Theissen, *Pauline Christianity*, 75.

[98] J. H. Kent, *The Inscriptions 1926-1950: Corinth, Results of Excavations Conducted by the American School of Classical studies at Athens VIII*, 3. Princeton 1966, 100 cited in Meeks, *Urban Christians*, 59.

[99] Theissen, *Pauline Christianity*, 81.

[100] Bruce, *Paul*, 252.

[101] Theissen, *Pauline Christianity*, 83.

[102] Meeks, *Urban Christians*, 63.

[103] Tidball, *An Introduction to Sociology*, 99.

[104] Theissen, *Pauline Christianity*, 73.

[105] Abraham J. Malherbe, *Social Aspects of Early Christianity, 2nd ed.* (Philadelphia: Fortress Press, 1983), 30.

[106] Theissen, *Pauline Christianity*, 145-168.

[107] Theissen, *Pauline Christianity*, 121-140.

[108] Meeks, *Urban Christians*, 65.

[109] Theissen, *Pauline Christianity*, 96.

[110] Theiseen, *Pauline Christianity*, 97.

[111] Abraham J. Malherbe, "The Inhospitality of Diotrephes" in Jaccob Jervel and Wayne Meeks (eds), *In God's Christ and his People: Studies in honour of Nils Alstrup Dahl* (Oslo Bergen and Tromso: Universitetsforlaget, 1977), 230 cited in Meeks, *Urban Christians*, 66.

[112] Meeks, *Urban Christians*, 66.

[113] Theissen, *Pauline Christianity*, 97.

[114] Robert S. MacLennan and A. Thomas Kraabel, "The God Fearers: A Literary and Theological Invention", *Biblical Archeological Review* 12:5 (Sep-Oct 1986), 46-47, https://members.bib-arch-org/biblical-archeological-review/12/5/4 (accessed 29 April 2014).

[115] Louis Fieldman, "The Omnipresence of God-Fearers," *Biblical Archeological Review* 12:5 (Sep-Oct 1986), 58-59, https://members.bib-arch-org/biblical-archeological-review/12/5/4 (accessed 29 April 2014).

[116] Irina Levenskaya, *The Book of Acts in its 1st Century Setting, Vol 5, Diaspora Setting* (Grand Rapids: W. B. Eerdsmans Pub. Co., 1996), 121.

[117] K. G. Kuhn and H. Stegemann, "Proselyten," PRE-Suppl. 9, 1266-67 cited in Theissen, *Pauline Christianity*, 103.

[118] Theissen, *Pauline Christianity*, 104.

[119] L. P. Sharma, *The Indian Ruling Class*, (New Delhi, Harman Publications), 116.

[120] Herbert E. Hoefer, *Churchless Christianity* (Pasadena: William Carey Library, 991).

[121] Theissen, *Pauline Christianity*, 106.

[122] Meeks, *The First Urban Christians*, 73.

[123] Jeffers, *The Greco-Roman World*, 194.

[124] E. A. Judge, *The Social Pattern of Early Christian Groups* (London: np, 1960), 60 cited in Theissen, *Pauline Christianity*, 106.

[125] Roland Allen, *Missionary Methods*, 23.

[126] Peter Garsey and Richard Saller, *The Roman Empire* (Berkeley: University of California Press, 1987), 116.

[127] Meeks, *Urban Christians*, 73.

[128] Tidball, *An Introduction to Sociology*, 103.

[129] Jeffers, *The Greco-Roman World*, 194.

[130] Meeks, *Urban Christians*, 73.

[131] Allen, *Missionary Methods*, 23.

[132] Eric Swanson and Swan Williams, *Transform a City*, (Michigan: Zondervan, 2010), 30.

Chapter 2

Ahmedabad:
The Expanding Metropolis
A Case Study for Change

1. THE URBANIZATION OF INDIA WITH REFERENCE TO GUJARAT

The world is getting urbanized at a very fast rate. Today more than fifty percent of the world population reside in urban areas. Kai N. Lee, quoting a 2005 report of the UN, writes:

> Thanks to rapid urban growth not only in China but elsewhere in Asia and Africa, sometime in the coming year the population of the world will become mostly urban. By 2005, the world's urban population of 3.18 billion people constituted 49% of the total population of 6.46 billion. Very soon, and for the first time in the history of our species, more humans will live in urban areas than rural places.[1]

India is not far behind with 31.16% of the total population being urban. We may seem to be lagging compared to the world trends. However, we we have come a long way from where we were a century ago. Looking at the total population of India at 1.2 billion, the fact that 377 million people live in urban areas is in itself huge in terms of absolute numbers. Alex Heltmann writes:

> According to a report on 'India's Urban Awakening' by Mckinsey Global Institute, in the next 20 years, India will have 68 cities with a population over one million-up from 42 today. That is twice as many cities as all of Europe. India's urban population will increase from 340 million to 590 million. To put it in global terms, about 10% of humanity will reside in Indian cities.[2]

Such demographic change in the cities has its effect on various aspects of life. However, before we discuss the changes brought about due to urbanization, it is important to define the process of urbanization and move on to focus on urbanization trends in India, and in Gujarat, and in the city of Ahmedabad, with a view to understanding the expanding metropolis.

How do we define the process of urbanization? The various definitions offered reveal the complexity of the subject. A very simple and acceptable definition, according to Mishra, would be as follows: "Urbanization refers to the total population living in the urban settlements or else to the rise in this proportion."[3] Many do not agree to this definition, however, as it has its own limitations. We need to first make clear what is termed as 'urban' in the Indian context. Cities with population greater than 1,00,000 is certainly more than the smaller towns. And in the contemporary context, the 'million plus' cities are the fastest growing in our country. The customary U/T formula, where U is the urban population and T is the total population, does not take this into account. Thus, in any given period, U/T would never give us the correct picture of urbanization. Bose explains this difficulty with the example of urbanization during the 1961-71 intercensal period, wherein the proportion of the total urban population increased only from 18% to 20%. Nevertheless, in the same period the proportion of the population residing in cities with 1,00,000 or more persons to the total population (C/U) increased from about 48% to nearly 56%. Taking a longer-range view, we find that U/T increased from 11% in 1901 to 20% in 1971; whereas C/U increased from 23 to nearly 56% during the same period. In short, in India from the planning and policy point of view C/U is a more sensitive measure of urbanization than U/T.[4]

This also can be modified to include the daily commuters to the city and the turnover migrants to get the real picture. But the census details of our country, as seen from the tables below, still define urbanization in terms of U/T and thus, for our purpose, we will stick to this definition.

Our confusion over the definition of urbanization does not end there. Mishra shows how the perspective on urbanization would differ from person to person depending on the area of interest. In conclusion, he quotes McGee who called urbanization "a balloon into which each social scientist blows his own meaning."[5] He continues that "urbanization is a process which reveals itself from temporal, spatial, and sectoral changes in demographic, social, economic, technological and environment aspects of life in a given society."[6] A well-known historian, Makrand Mehta of Ahmedabad in an informal conversation with me described it with the acronym 'POET' where P stands for population, O for organisation or economy, E for environment and T for technology. All these have an effect on each other at any given point of time. As Mishra rightly says, "When changes in one dimension is not backed by adequate and necessary changes in the other, urban problems in varied forms occurs."[7] Thus we need to understand that urbanization is not just about population increase, but rather a whole gamut of things which have an effect on the relationships, lifestyle and values of people.

Urbanization of Gujarat in the Indian Context

A published report of the census of 2011 shows an unprecedented growth in the level and trend of the urbanization process in India.

Year	No. of Town	Total population	Urban population	Urban population Percentage of Total Population	Decennial Growth Rate of Urban Population (%)	Tempo of urbanization		
						Annual Exponential Growth Rate	Annual Change in % point of Urban Pop.	Annual Rate of Gain in % of Urban Pop.
1901	1915	238,396,327	25,854,967	10.85				
1911	1864	252,093,390	25,948,431	10.29	0.36	0.04	-0.06	-0.51
1921	2018	251,321,213	28,091,299	11.18	8.26	0.79	0.09	0.86
1931	2188	278,977,238	33,462,539	11.99	19.12	1.75	0.08	0.73
1941	2392	318,660,580	44,162,191	13.86	31.98	2.77	0.19	1.55
1951	3035	361,088,090	62,443,709	17.29	41.40	3.46	0.34	2.48
1961	2657	439,234,771	78,936,603	17.97	26.41	2.34	0.07	0.39
1971	3081	548,159,652	109,113,977	19.91	38.23	3.24	0.19	1.08
1981	3891	683,329,097	159,462,547	23.08	46.14	3.79	0.34	1.72
1991	4615	846,302,688	217,565,526	25.49	36.44	3.11	0.24	1.02
2001	5161	1,028,737,436	286,119,689	27.81	31.51	2.74	0.21	0.82
2011	7935	1,210,193,422	377,105,760	31.16	31.80	2.76	0.33	1.20

Figure 4: Urbanization Level in India
(As Published by the Director of Census Operations 2011)

This report shows that today 31% of the Indian population live in urban areas as compared to only 10.85% as the beginning of the last century. The report points out that "in terms of absolute numbers, the urban population has increased more than fourteen times, with 377 million urban population recorded in the current census year, as compared to 25 million urban population at the beginning of the last century."[8]

Urbanization Levels in Gujarat

As obvious from the report below, the level of urbanization of Gujarat is higher than the National Urbanization index. While urbanization at the national level is 31.16%, it is 42.58% for Gujarat. The reports point out that though the urban population to total population of India has grown threefold from 1901 to 2011, as compared to Gujarat, which has only doubled, the growth in the proportion of urban population has been higher for Gujarat (17%) than the national level (13%) during the last 60 years.[9]

| | No. of Town | Total population | Urban population | Urban population Percentage of Total Population | Decennial Growth Rate of Urban Population (%) | Tempo of urbanization | | |
						Annual Exponential Growth Rate	Annual Change in % point of Urban Pop.	Annual Rate of Gain in % of Urban Pop.
1901	166	9094748	2030738	22.33				
1911	155	9,803,587	1,886,775	19.25	-7.09	-0.74	-0.31	-1.38
1921	166	10,174,989	2,050,339	20.15	8.67	0.83	0.09	0.47
1931	172	11,489,828	2,355,009	20.50	14.86	1.39	0.03	0.17
1941	191	13,701,551	3,259,955	23.79	38.43	3.25	0.33	1.61
1951	243	16,262,657	4,427,896	27.23	35.83	3.06	0.34	1.44
1961	181	20,633,350	5,316,624	25.77	20.07	1.83	-0.15	-0.54
1971	216	26,697,475	7,496,500	28.08	41.00	3.44	0.23	0.90
1981	255	34,085,799	10,601,653	31.10	41.42	3.47	0.30	1.08
1991	264	41,309,582	14,246,061	34.49	34.38	2.95	0.34	1.09
2001	242	50,671,017	18,930,250	37.36	32.88	2.84	0.29	0.83
2011	348	60,383,628	25,712,811	42.58	35.83	3.06	0.52	1.40

Figure 5
(As Published by the Director of Census Operations 2011)

Urban Decadal Growth Rate of Gujarat 2001-2011

The report points out that for the period 2001-2011, Gujarat has recorded higher urban decadal growth rate of 35.83% than the national average of 31.80%. Gujarat ranks 14th in terms of urban decadal growth rate, while it ranks 12th and 17th for the male and female urban decadal growth rate. Gujarat has higher urban decadal growth rate than Karnataka, Tamil Nadu, Maharashtra and Madhya Pradesh.[10] This shows that rapid urbanization is taking place in Gujarat.

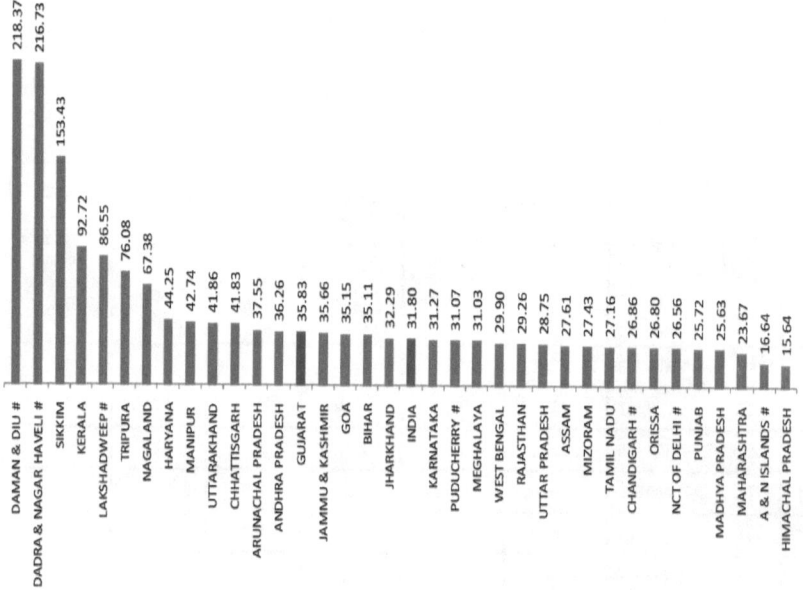

Figure 6: Urban Decadal Growth Rate, India & States (Persons)
(As Published by the Director of Census Operations-2011)

If we compare the district wise levels of urbanization in Gujarat (as shown in the maps below), it is obvious that most of the districts have become more urban. Rajkot, Gandhinagar, Anand, Sabarkanta and Banaskata district have all jumped a notch to go to the next bracket. The state average has also jumped from 37.36% to 42.58%.

The two maps released by the census in its 2011 report show the levels of urbanization districtwise in 2001 and 2011. It can be observed that whereas in 2001 only Ahmedabad and Surat districts had urban populations above 57%, Rajkot district has been added to this in 2011. It is surprising that Vadodara does has not come into this catogery. It could be because Vadorara as a city is not expanding to include its surrounding villages into the municipalty limits. Even the districts with smaller towns (no million plus cities) like Anand, Baruch, Navsari, Valsad etc. have shown an increase in the Urban population. It reveals that Gujarat is a state where development is not concentrated in just one or two areas but is distributed throughout the State.

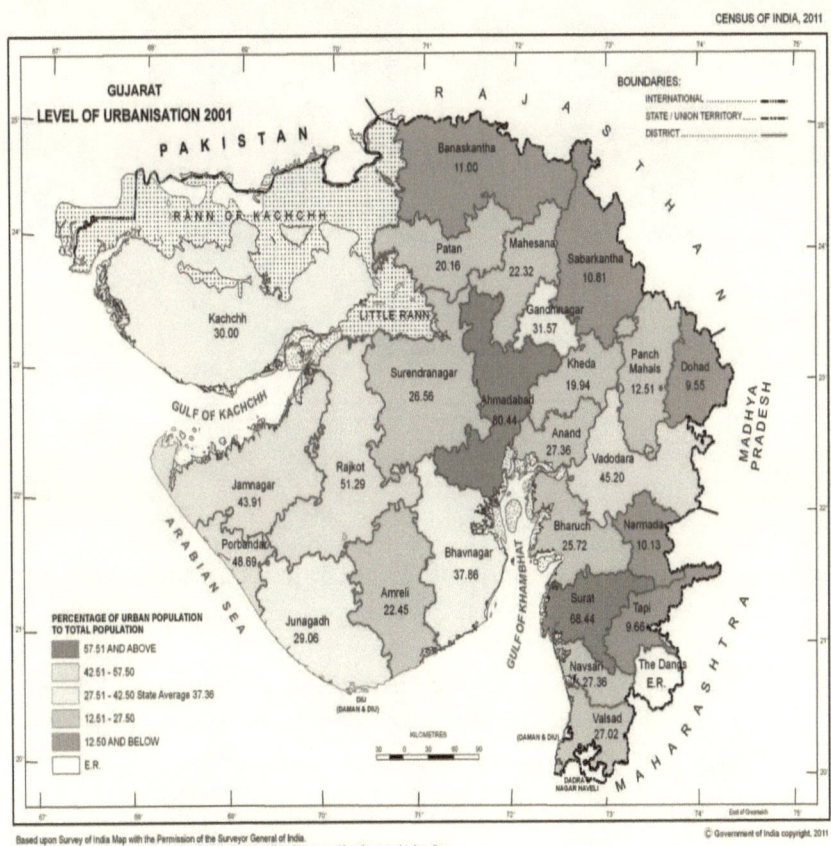

Figure 7

Figure 8

Gujarat has an urban population of 25,712,811, comprising 13,679,307 males and 12,033,504 females. The state has shown an absolute increase of 6,782,561 in urban population, comprising 3,611,501 males and 3,171,060 females. As shown in the chart below (Fig. 9), at the district level, Ahmedabad has the highest urban population followed by Surat, Rajkot, Vadodara and Bhavnagar.

In the context of absolute change of population size during the last decade, Surat (1,917,420) has recorded the largest addition of urban population, followed by Ahmedabad (1,318,586). (Fig 10)

Sr No	District Name	Population
1	Ahmedabad	60,58,764
2	Surat	48,43,722
3	Rajkot	22,08,582
4	Vadodara	20,59,777
5	Bhavnagar	11,80,153

Figure 9

Sr No	District Name	Increase (absolute)
1	Surat	19,17,420
2	Ahmedabad	13,18,586
3	Rajkot	582,720
4	Vadodara	413,555
5	Valsad	252,914

Figure 10

The proportion of urban to total population is highest in Ahmedabad (84.05%), followed by Surat, Rajkot, Vadodara and Porbandar.

Sr No	District Name	Share of Urban Population
1	Ahmedabad	84.05
2	Surat	79.68
3	Rajkot	58.12
4	Vadodara	49.54
5	Porbandar	48.77

Figure 11

In 2001, the total number of UAs cities and towns in Gujarat was 190, with 18,930,250 persons. In 2011, the total number of UAs, cities and towns has increased to 278, holding 25,712,811 persons. Though the maximum additions have been in the size of class-IV and class-V cities, one needs to appreciate that, of the total Gujarat's urban population, 19,850,738 persons are in class-I cities. In terms of population size, Ahmedabad (Ahmedabad and Gandhinagar districts) is the top most UA with more than 6 million persons followed by Surat and Vadodara UAs.[11]

Hence in absolute terms, the 10 million population cities are growing, and it is primarily due to migration of people within the concerned districts, though there is a considerable migration from other districts and also from other states.

2. AHMEDABAD: THE EXPANDING METROPOLIS

Demographic Analysis

Ahmedabad has been a growing city from the time of its founding. Jain traces its growth from 1872 to 1971 and is quite right in saying the rate of increase in population has stabilized at around 40% per decade after 1941.

Table: Ahmedabad City Agglomeration: Growth in Population 1871-1971

Year	Population	Percent increase	Area in Acres
1872	119,672	----	---
1881	127,681	6.64	----
1891	148,412	16.29	---
1901	185,889	25.25	3,808
1911	216,777	16.62	---
1921	247,007	26.40	5,399
1931	313,789	13.14	5,828
1941	595,210	90.73	----
1951	877,329	41.59	12,968
1961	1,206,001	37.36	22,982
1971	1,741,522	38.13	38,026

Figure 12 (Sources-Census Reports-Jain 221)

The succeeding years also show a similar trend.

1981	25,48,000	46.30
1991	3,312,216	29.99
2001	4,448,368	34.30

Figure 13 (Source-Census Reports)

This increase is from intra-state and interstate migration evidenced from the figures below as taken from the census report of 2001.

Migration by place of birth	Ahmedabad-persons	Percentage of Total Migrants
Total Migrants	2,148,464	---
A) Migrants born in Gujarat	1,667,078	77.59
i) Migrants born elsewhere in district of enumeration	7,28,808	33.9
ii) Migrants born in other districts of the state	9,38,270	43.7
B) Migrants born in other states of India	461,126	21.5
Migrants born in other countries	20,260	0.9

Figure 14: Percentage Distribution of Migrants
by Place of Birth - 2001 Census

The above table is self-explanatory. It shows that 48.30% of the population were born outside Ahmedabad and thus can be called migrants. Though 77.59% of these are from Gujarat, 43.7% are from a district other than Ahmedabad. Moreover, 21.5% are from outside this state. Obviously, the intrastate migration is high, and yet the interstate migration is also not very low. The majority of these migrants are from Maharashtra, Rajasthan and Uttar Pradesh. It would be interesting to see the distribution of migrants by place of last residence for that would give us an idea as to whether migration to this city is a continuous process or not.

Distribution of Migrants by Place of Last Residence in Gujarat 2001 Census in Ahmedabad

Migration by place of last residence	Persons	Percentage of total migration
Total Migrants	2,180,885	100
Last residence in other districts of enumeration	952,317	43.7
Last residence in other districts of the State	812,143	37.2%
Last residence in other States of India	401,200	18.4%
Last residence in other countries	15,225	0.7%

Figure 15

If we compare the above two tables, it shows that intrastate and interstate migration to Ahmedabad is a continuous process. This becomes obvious from the decadal increase in population which has stabilized to around 40%. Jain studying the 1971 census report says that migration has played a major role in the growth of Ahmedabad. In studying the occupational structure enumerated in that census, he concludes that the majority of migrants come to the city for jobs (46% employed in manufacturing and processing industry).[12] The trends observed in 1991and 2001 census report reveal that, within Gujarat and to some extent the neighbouring states— Ahmedabad remains the hotbed of migration due to job opportunities available in this city. Has this always been the case for this city founded in medieval times? The next section will explore this question in detail.

A Historical Sketch: The Transformation of Ahmedabad

Ahmedabad was founded in 1411 AD by Sultan Ahmed Shah of Gujarat on a site close to a much older trading centre of Asaval. Historians are divided on the reasons for the founding of this city. It may have been founded for strategic reasons or even for commercial purposes. "Its location," says Jain, "was on the cross roads connecting the caravan routes to Rajasthan and Delhi to the North, Malwa to the east, Sind with its port of Tatta (Lahori Bunder) to the west and the ports of Cambay, Surat and Baroda in the south." [13] Following this line of thought, Jain and a few others seem to be correct that it was for geopolitical and commercial reasons that Ahmed Shah chose Ahmedabad as his capital.

Although the political history of Ahmedabad can be divided into four distinct periods,[14] for our study we will divide it into three periods: (i) the Pre-British period (ii) the British period and (iii) the Post-British period.

The Pre-British Period

The first five decades of the Sultanate was a period of consolidation. All the four kings who ruled during this period were more involved in defending and expanding their kingdom and it is obvious that the city of Ahmedabad would not have received its due attention required for its growth. It was nearly a century after its founding, in Mahamud Begada's rule, that the city enjoyed peace and prosperity. John Burton Page confirms this fact when he writes: "The Gujarat Sultanate in his (Begada's) reign achieved its greatest internal security in the towns and ports and its greatest prosperity."[15] It is likely that craftsmen and artisans came and settled here to practice their trade because of the peace that the city enjoyed during Begada's reign. The author of Haft Iqlim, a well-known geographical and biographical treatise in Persian completed in 1593, gives the following description of the city (as quoted by Commissariat):

> Ahmedabad is unique in the whole of India in the matter of neatness and flourishing condition and it is superior to other cities in the excellence of its monuments. It would be no exaggeration that in the whole world there exist no town so grand and beautiful. Its streets are spacious and well-arranged unlike that in other towns; its shops with two or three storeys each are finely built; and its inhabitants, both men and women are graceful and delicate.[16]

Ahmedabad flourished and became one of the finest cities in its time mainly because it was a business centre. Salim Lakha, who is of the same opinion, says: "Even though it was the capital city, Ahmedabad was distinguished for its commerce and industry rather than its administrative or religious functions."[17] The *Times of India* report that the first permission to trade in India was given to the British through Sir Thomas Roe in Ahmedabad on Feb. 20, 1618.[18]

Lakha quoting Gokhale says, "Textile production in Ahmedabad and Gujarat achieved legendary fame and the existence of skilled artisans helped to make the city a chief supplier of textiles locally and internationally."[19] This depended on the easy availability of raw material like indigo, saltpetre, etc. and the best quality of these were available in or near Ahmedabad. The prominent commercial status of Ahmedabad led to an inflow of foreign wealth through the English, Dutch and French companies which boosted the city's economic growth.[20] Even at this time, one cannot leave out the business acumen of the people of Ahmedabad for which they are famous even today. On the whole, Ahmedabad achieved its prosperity because of the availability of raw materials, good craftsmen, shrewd businessmen and an excellent business structure. Gujarat had a long-established tradition of merchants' guild known as *Mahajan* and artisans' association known as *Panch* which regulated trade and manufacture and were also the face of the business community. These associations obviously set the rules to not only protect themselves from external threats but also maintain internal harmony.

The *Nagarsheth* was another important link between the people and the rulers. Makrand Metha says that he was accepted by the *Mahajans* as their leader and acted as an arbitrator in case of disputes[21]—a process that was carried on through the succeeding generations also. Many interesting incidents reveal their influence upon the rulers. After one such incident where they negotiated with the Marathas and saved the city from being plundered, the *mahajans* in gratitude conferred on his family in perpetuity the right to collect a percentage on the trade of the city.

The merchants of western India consisted of three categories: the *banian*, the *shroff* and the *sahukar*. The banian's dominant role was that of a trader operating at regional, national and international levels involving short-term investments. The *shroff* or *sarafs* played a pivotal role in the system of credit. They performed multiple roles as money changers, buyers and sellers of gold and silver, and as bankers lending and borrowing money and issuing hundis. The last group of commercial men consisted of the *sahukar* or *mahajan* who satisfied the credit and banking requirements of traders, artisans and peasants. They received and advanced money on differing interest rates and profited through transactional fees. Through its local and international trading links, Gujarat was one of the most economically advanced states of India when the Europeans arrived on India's western shores.[22]

Population statistics of Ahmedabad for the seventeenth century is lacking, but the general estimates indicate that the city was comparable to London or Paris in its numbers, that is, about one million, including suburbs. Gillion makes an important observation regarding the social structure of the society of the time. He says, "The social division of Ahmedabad was reflected in the spatial structure of the city."[23] Most of the population lived in *pols* which were house-groups normally associated with caste. Gillion remarks that these *pols,* of which there were 356 in 1872, are still among the curiosities of India. In his description, these pols "comprise a labyrinth of high wooden houses, streets too narrow for wheeled traffic and cul-de-sacs."[24] Forrest in his travelogue commenting on the *pols* wrote: "Nowhere does one feel oneself more thoroughly in an eastern city of past times than in the narrow streets of Ahmedabad, thick with ancient houses, none so poor as not to have a doorway or a window or a wooden pillar carved finely."[25] There is not much information on when and why these *pols* came into existence. If they came into formation for security reasons, then how does one explain the caste-based *pols?* Harish Doshi researching *pols* of Ahmedabad says that each pol had a council called *Pol-nu-panch* which regulated the behaviour of its members and managed local affairs.[26] So, though this was a flourishing heterogeneous population, people lived more like homogeneous groups, each in their own little world. This is not to imply that there was no interaction between these caste-based groups, but rather that their social world was controlled by their own *Panch*.

From the second quarter of the seventeenth century, Ahmedabad experienced a decline. The city was devastated by famines, floods and epidemics from 1681-97 which virtually depopulated the city. There were other geographical, political and historical reasons for the decline. Many thinkers claim that the inefficiency of the Marathas and their inability to rule this marvellous city led to its decline, but it is quite clear that the decline had begun much earlier. Many of the skilled workers also left the city for better pastures. Forbes thus described Ahmedabad as he saw it in 1781:

> Solitude, poverty and desolation. You behold the most heterogeneous mixture of Moghul splendour and Maratha Barbarism; a noble cupola, overshadowing hovels of mud; small windows, ill fashioned doors, dirty cells introduced under a superb portico; a marble corridor filled up with *choolas,* or cooking places, composed of mud, cow-dung and unburnt bricks.[27]

Makrand Metha writes that Forbes noticed the exodus of the artisans from Ahmedabad in search of livelihood wherein he wrote, "Long wars, unstable & oppressive governments and fluctuations of human establishments have brought it to such a state of decay."[28] In fact, Forbes thought that this city was doomed and would never recover from its fall. However, Gillion remarks that though Ahmedabad's economy was eclipsed, her prestige as the first city of Gujarat was still retained, as was the social structure of her resilient and tough people.[29] Gillion was perhaps correct. When the British gave these people the right environment to restart life afresh, they who were in such a dire state grabbed it with both hands and made the best use of it to bring the city back to its former glory.

Under British Rule

Ahmedabad came under British rule in 1817 by treaty with the Peshwa at Poona and the Gaikwad of Baroda after the last Maratha war. They handed over this city rather reluctantly under political and financial compulsions. When John Andrew Dunlop, the first collector, took possession of Ahmedabad on 30ᵗʰ November 1817, the city was a bad sight. Security from the wild animals was the biggest problem. Bhils and Kolis were roaming the streets creating terror. The conditions prevalent at that time were also not conducive for business. Apart from security issues, people faced other issues such as the unreasonable duties on goods imposed by the Marathas for revenue purposes, and other customary duties imposed by tradition such as that paid to the *Nagarsheth*. These had its effects on the population of the city. One can understand the severe limitations under which the British took over this city and yet the British were optimistic. They took several steps to ensure security of the people and gave an impetus to business. The city slowly regained a part of its lost glory as businesses started flourishing and it even survived the foreign competition. Thus, it is clear that the British were able to bring out the entrepreneur in these trading communities of Ahmedabad through their various interventions, and helped the city regain its former glory at least in part.

Another important need was the repairing of the town wall. It is important to note that the British, after much discussion, managed to take the locals into confidence and decided to raise the needed funds for repair through taxes levied on certain items. After completion of the repairs on the wall, which took about a decade, the issue of continuation of taxes came up. Here also, it is the leading citizens of the city who agreed that the taxes should continue, and the money used to for the welfare of the city.

The population rose from about 80,000 in 1817 to 87,000 in 1824 to 90,000 in 1832, to 94,390 in 1846, to 97,048 in 1851, and to 1,16,173 in 1872.[30] There is always an element of doubt in these figures for people had their own fears of giving the correct information in the census. Nevertheless, the improved conditions would have brought in people from the nearby non-British areas under the Gaikwad's dominion. This consisted of not only Hindus, but Jains, Muslims and a few Christians also. Such a cosmopolitan population, in itself, shows how this city was acquiring a secular look. However, as different from the previous reigns, it was the Hindus and Jains who controlled the economy of the city.

A major change took place after the Railways reached Ahmedabad in 1864. There was greater interaction with the outside world which weakened the monopoly of the traditional business houses of Ahmedabad. The railway brought the threat of competition from the mills of Bombay and nearly obliterated Ahmedabad's old reliance on handicraft textile production. As always, the business acumen of the people of the city not only recognised this challenge but also responded to it with gumption to ultimately make this city the Manchester of the East.

The next important phase in the history of this city was the setting up of mills. The mills attracted immigrants to this city from the surrounding districts and from across the nation, thus changing not only the demography of the city but also its landscape. This marked a new phase in Ahmedabad's economy. Leaving behind their older business avenues, the traditional merchant families diverted their resources to modern textile industry though it took a decade before they went into actual manufacturing by establishing their own mills. The following table by Yagnik and Sheth would give us an idea of how mills affected the economy and demography of the city:

Expansion of the Textile Industry in Ahmedabad 1861-1946

Year	Number of Mills	Average Number of Workers Employed Daily
1861	1	63
1879	4	2013
1891	9	7451
1900	27	15,943
1914	49	32,789
1922	56	52,571
1939	77	77,859
1946	74	76,357

Figure 16 (Source: Yagnik & Sheth)

The *Mahajan* and *Panch* system was replaced by owners' associations and workers unions. The mills gave rise to a new working class. The *mukadams* who were responsible for recruiting these mill workers were very powerful people and not only brought in people from their own caste but also exploited them to the core. The caste system was practiced even at the work places. The lower caste untouchables were given work in the spinning section, where the working conditions were tough, and the pay was low, while those from the upper caste would take up work in the weaving section. Their living conditions were deplorable. As many as 7 or 8 people would stay in a single room with common lavatory facilities. The families would be left behind in the villages with rare chances of getting to join these hardworking men.

It is very obvious that the demography of the city also changed drastically due to the establishment of the mills. Quoting figures from the census, Gillion says that the population within the municipal limits rose from 1,16,873 in 1872 to 124,767in 1881, to 1,44451 in 1891 to 1,81744in 1901, to 2,13727 in 1911, and to 2,72007 in 1921 and the city was expanding faster than the municipal limits.[31] A big change in the city's landscape was bound to happen, and such modernization of the city led unfortunately to a divide between the rich and the poor.

Thirdly, Gandhi's presence in Ahmedabad transformed this city. It was from here that Gandhi started his activities for *swaraj*. He founded the *Satyagrah* Ashram at Kochrab and later moved on to the Sabarmati Ashram on the banks of the river Sabarmati. Commenting on the presence of Gandhi at Ahmedabad, Yagnik writes:

> Gandhi's presence effected three powerful changes in the life and status of the city. Ahmedabad became the hub of political activity and thus attracted idealist young people from all over the country and beyond. Second, for a brief moment, Ahmedabad became the important centre for historical research when *Puratatva Mandir* was established at Gujarat Vidyapeeth. Also, with the different *Satyagrahs* that Gandhi launched and especially with the Salt *Satyagrah* Ahmedabad came into international limelight. The fact that Gandhi was in the cover page of Time Magazine in March 1930 and again in January 1931 only added to its importance.[32]

Besides being the textile capital of the country, Ahmedabad also became a centre of national politics. This would have a telling effect on the city in the days to come.

From the initial stages, the British involved the locals in the administration of the city. The municipal presidents and councillors were drawn from the locals. They played a vital role in the development of the city. Vital aspects like water and drainage were given prime importance. As the population jumped in leaps and bounds, the municipality tried its best to look into the aspect of congestion. It was in the 1930s that the western side of the city started developing and it emerged as the centre of premier educational institutions.

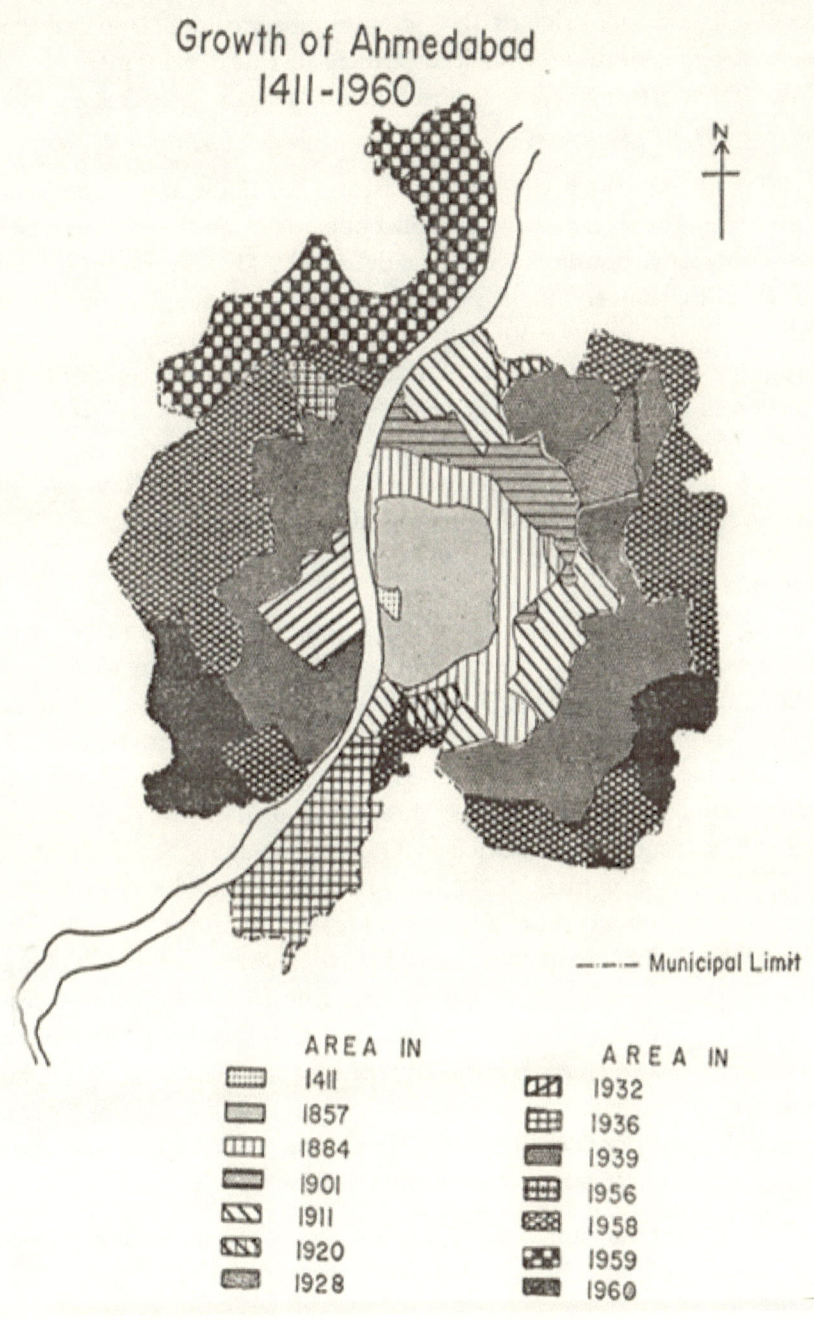

Figure 17 (Source:K.C.Jain in Mishra (ed) Million cities)

This can be seen from the developmental map of the city, shown in Fig. 14. The western side of the city was still agricultural land and there were strong objections from the farmers to this development. It was Vallabhbhai's strong action against agitating farmers of this area which helped this area to develop.

Yagnik and Sheth note that a historic beginning was made in the western side of the river when Vallabhbhai laid the foundation of the first cooperative housing society as early as 1927. The cooperative housing society became a very popular model with the expanding middle-class of the city. By 1935, about 30 such housing societies were established and over the next 15 years another 60 housing societies sprang up in the city. Almost all early housing societies were founded on the basis of caste or community.[33] This was also the time that due attention was given to improve the *chaalis*. The municipality also built housing colonies so that the workers would get better housing facilities at a lower rent.

Post-British

During Partition, Gujarat experienced a two-way migration. Gujarati Muslims belonging to the mercantile communities left the city for Karachi, while a number of Sindhis, Gujarati Hindus and Dalits came to Gujarat. Yagnik says: "We do not have the exact number of Muslims who left the city. But we do know from the 1951 census that in all 41,675 refugees, mainly Sindhis, were settled in Ahmedabad district out of a total of 1,56,677 'refugees' who settled in Gujarat, including Saurashtra State and Kutch State of that time."[34] In 1947, Vikram Sarabhai came back to Ahmedabad with a doctorate in Physics from Cambridge. He along with Kasturbhai Lalbhai worked to make the city and industry more vibrant. They were responsible for institutions like Ahmedabad Textile Industries Research Association (ATIRA), Physical Research Laboratory (PR), Indian Institute of Management (IIM), National Institute of Design (NID), and so on. Even today these are premier institutions in the country. Gujarat was under the Bombay Presidency. It was only after a long and bitter struggle that Gujarat State was born in 1960.

As pointed out earlier, migration has played a vital role in expanding the limits of the city. The inner city, however, remains highly dense. John Brush, from his study of the spatial structure of various Indian cities, says that it follows a typical pattern of concentration. He writes that one of the most typical features of an old city is the high concentration of people in the central wards. He goes on to say that Ahmedabad also follows a similar pattern. He reports that though the city walls have been removed, the density is as high as 300 to 500 persons per acre in the compact core. As we move away from the centre towards the east and the west to new residential areas, the densities vary from 100 to 300 persons. As we go further to the boundary of the municipal area, the density is as low as one person per acre[35] This was the condition in 1961. Of course, though the concentration at the centre is still very high, the city limits are expanding, and the density is increasing considerably at the periphery also.

The crisis in the cotton textile industry did take its toll on the city. The Gazetteer of Ahmedabad district reports:

> In 1967, the cotton textile industry caught between deepening economic and worsening inflationary situation went through a period of unprecedented crisis. The number of mills were reduced from 74 in 1950 to 69 in 1967 but the spinning capacity of the industry kept up its rising trend, no doubt due to the expansion of plants initiated in the earlier years. The year 1973 was a very hard one for the economy and textile industry as a whole. It was a year of shortages of coal, electric power, wagons etc. and as a result half a dozen mills were closed as sick units.[36]

Obviously, thousands of people lost their jobs. Besides unemployment, a severe drought during 1972-75 affected many lives. In 1973, the city was struck by a devastating flood in river Sabarmati, which damaged or destroyed more than a thousand hutments and rendered about 12000 hutment dwellers homeless. These people were settled on the outskirts of the city, which is a Muslim ghetto today. This is now one of the most sensitive areas of the city during communal riots. Communal riots, bad governance and natural calamities and the closure of textile units saw the city hit a rock bottom from 1967 to 1985. The economy was in a bad shape, and more than 40,000 workers in Ahmedabad—most of whom were either Muslims or Dalits—had lost their jobs. Since the 1980s, Ahmedabad has steadily transformed into a city of ghettoes. Today, Muslims have their areas of residence. The Dalits, who were once allies with Muslims, have their own without having any hope of ever getting assimilated in an upper caste area.[37]

The city has once again regained its vibrancy in terms of economy in the last two decades. Dushyant Joshi writes: "The economy of Ahmedabad is exhilarating due to its huge growth in the industrial sector, real estate and service sector."[38] Huge corporate giants in the pharmaceutical, chemical, textile, engineering and automobile industries are housed here. If Tata's Nano has converted this city into an automobile hub, Arvind, Aravee, Ashima and others have made this the denim capital of the country. The *Times of India*, writing on the 50th anniversary of Gujarat, reports that Ahmedabad could well be the single largest denim producing location in the world.[39] Kamath and Randeri report that, in 2002, Gujarat ranked number two in industrial investments in the country. Its share in the country's industrial investments was 16% while in the industrial production was 13%.[40] The Ahmedabad Municipal Corporation has won 14 national and international awards for its various initiatives in the last five years, the latest being 'The Nagar Ratna' from the government of India for the best city in 2011.[41] They further comment that mighty forces of globalization are trying to transform Ahmedabad into a world-class city or 'recreate Shanghai and Singapore' in a medieval city. The Jawaharlal Nehru National Urban Renewal Mission (JNNURM) was launched by the Central Government in 2005. Since 2006, the Gujarat State Government as well as the city governing agencies like Ahmedabad Municipal Corporation (AMC) and Ahmedabad Urban Development Authority (AUDA) have been moving forward with the current mantra of 'creating global cities.' This is not a statement of pride as it may seem but rather of concern. They point out that citizens, academicians and planners have been raising their voice against the exclusion of the labouring poor who constitute a precious half of the population, their concerns find little reflection in the on-going planning of the city.[42]

Yagnik reports that a study done in 1997-98 indicates that the informal sector is growing faster than the formal sector: 76.7% of the people were employed in the informal sector which generated 46.8% of the city's income. This meant that, out of 1.5 million workers in Ahmedabad city, 1.15 million worked in informal sectors.[43] It is obvious that today the informal sector is thriving and offering more jobs to the city's labouring poor. The question we need to ask is whether a city in which half of the population thrives on the informal sector without any social security can really grow to be a world class city. The latest census report of 2011, however, tells another story. The report says that 83% Amdavadi households have toilets while 61.8% have cellphones. This scenario, adds Dilip Patel, is in sharp contrast to the national average of 46.9% households with toilets and 53.2% with cellphones.[44] Though these are important parameters, are they the appropriate measures to understand the prosperity of a city?

The city limits are expanding. The 76 kilometers long Ring Road that passes through 23 villages crosses Sabarmati river twice and encircles the newly extended area of AMC. The new chairman of AUDA announced in mid-2010 that a second Ring Road encircling the extended Megacity would be constructed next. The Figure 15 at the end of the chapter shows the Ahmedabad UA limits and this shows how the city has grown in all directions.

The Role of the Middle-class in Shaping Modern Ahmedabad

The middle-class has played a vital role in fashioning Ahmedabad into a modern city, although it is also blamed for the polarization between the castes, on the one hand, and between the Hindus and Muslims, on the other.

The introduction of modern education in the city by the British was responsible for the formation of the middle-class. Till the British introduced modern education, education was the prerogative of some Brahmin teachers who gave informal education to a select few of the high caste. On the standard of this education, Edalji Dosabhai writes "...the standard of education may be judged from the fact that boys who had learnt to merely read and write and to keep a few simple accounts were regarded as having 'finished their education'."[45] However, since Ahmedabad was integrated into the Bombay Presidency, education in the vernacular and in English flourished. It had a slow beginning, but it provided opportunity not only for boys but also for girls to be educated. The introduction of the press and the formation of the Gujarat Vernacular Society (GVS) gave the needed impetus. Text books and newspapers started getting printed here. College education was also started and in 1879; Gujarat College giving the BA degree was accredited by the University of Bombay. So, education had finally taken roots in the city. Gillion states that "In 1885, there were only six graduates in Ahmedabad, eighteen pleaders and three licentiates of medicine, surgery and civil Engineering"[46] This was only the beginning, for by the mid-19th century a new breed of western educated section emerged in the city. They went on to occupy important positions in the government such as those in judiciary and revenue departments. These developments started a new class of people—those known as the 'middle-class'—who went on to shape the city not only by their knowledge but also by the positions they occupied at various levels.

Ranchodlal Chotalal was one of the pioneers of this class to change not only the economy of this city but also its landscape. He came from the Sathodara Nagar Brahmin community and was trained to take up work in the bureaucracy which he did but later came out to take up business. He was the first to envision the prospect of a textile industry and after great perseverance went on to establish the first Textile mill. Many more followed which gave the nickname 'the Manchester of the East' to this great city. The medieval city was on its way to becoming a modern city, the initiation and growth of which can be attributed to the middle-class of the city. Each bench of judges had at least one native and again it was one of the new breed of educated Ahmedabadis who occupied those positions. Bholanath Sarabhai was one of the earliest to retire as a subordinate judge. The British allowed the locals to be elected to the municipal council and it was the educated middle-class that took advantage of this opportunity. Ranchodlal chotalal, referred earlier as the pioneer of the Textile industry, entered this field. He was followed by Ramanbhai Nilkanth and then by Vallabhbhai Patel. Vallabhbhai Patel came from the small village of Karamsad near Anand from a simple middle-class family but rose up to this position. Such men became role models for those who migrated from little known families and small towns to Ahmedabad not only to rise to greater heights but also contributed towards the growth of the city.

The middle-class played an important role in the field of literature as well. The GVS published the first weekly newspapers called *Vartaman*, besides text books for the schools. Dalpatram Dayabhai, an accomplished poet wrote on contemporary social issues. Later in 1854, GVS started to publish the journal *Buddhiprakash* which had short articles and stories on contemporary social themes. Maganlal Vakhatchand wrote '*Ahmedabad no Ittihas*' and Edalji Dosabhai wrote 'The History of Gujarat' as part of an essay competition organized by GVS. This was the first time that authors had consciously strayed away from religious and mythological stories and ventured into topics related to state and city development. A.H. Somjee writing about the intellectuals of Gujarat says further that

> From the second half of the nineteenth century onwards, Gujarati writers displayed an extraordinary interest in the writings of romantic poets such as Keats, Shelly, Byron; plays of Shakespeare, Ibsen, Shaw.... Such an exposure together with the growth of the Indian National movement and the influence of Gandhi, resulted in their growing interest and involvement in social and political movements of their times. It also resulted in a variety of experiments with literary forms and techniques and the search for universal values which transcend cultural barriers.[47]

Writers who themselves were of the middle-class continued to influence the minds of people post-independence also. People like Yashwant Shukla and Umashankar Joshi were strongly committed to social development and wrote on various social themes. One can go on to name quite a few columnist and social writers who followed in these footsteps and thus influenced the thinking of people.

The Freedom movement also can be traced to this class of people. Gopalrao Hari Deshmukh who was in the judicial service way back in 1870 in Ahmedabad was one of the first to talk of *Swadeshi*. This was followed in a few decades with a call to *Swaraj*. There were the moderates and the extremist on either side of the camp, but I would like to draw attention to a group of people who were experimenting with grassroot mobilization. Sheth and Yagnik point us to Kripashankar Pandit and Professor Barve who created a powerful metaphor of India as a mother goddess[48] which caught the attention of people. We are all aware that Gandhi started his political career from this city and was a great influence on the intellectuals of the city. His Dandi March, experiments at Sabarmati and Kochrab Ashram left an indelible impression on the minds of the intellectuals of the city.

Post-Independence, this class played a major role in the economic development of Gujarat, acting as an agent of change. With the growth of industries in the city, the middle-class also grew. If the textile industries in the city began to decline, there were other giants like the Arvind and Ashima who scaled new heights. Arvind is a world leader in denim manufacturing today. The Pharmaceutical industry in the city is one of the largest in the country. The Tatas brought in Nano and gave a boost not only to the industry but also to the growth of the middle-class in the city. It is difficult to estimate the size of this class but the growth of the real estate market on the western side of the city shows that it is an ever-expanding group.

Further, the middle-class has had considerable involvement in the politics of the State. They led the Maha Gujarat Movement in 1956-57 demanding a separate linguistic state for the Gujaratis. They also led the movement against price rise and corruption which later developed into the *Navnirman Movement headed* by the students which ultimately led to the ouster of the Chief Minister. It is important to note, however, that this middle-class that united together for this cause irrespective of caste, did not hesitate to divide on the basis of caste on the issue of reservation. The anti-reservation agitations in 1980-81 and 1985 are cases in point. Ghanshyam Shah says that "in both these agitations the middle-class of upper and middle caste had an edge over the middle-class of the lower caste, and SCs/STs."[49] He further comments that "Notwithstanding the intra-class differences, the Hindu middle-classes of different caste unite against the Muslims in times of communal riots."[50] The latest was the riots due to the Godhra massacre in which the middle-classes came out openly against this incident and did not hesitate to indulge in arson and looting.

So, in conclusion, one can only say that the middle-class has played a crucial role in shaping not only the economy and culture of the city but is also responsible for the polarization of the city based on caste and religion.

Ahmedabad as a city has had a remarkable history. It has seen its lows which were so bad that many had written it off as dead. In such times the resilience of the city was truly tested. Given the right environment, this city has seen its heights also. On the one hand, this city has been known for its trade and commerce, but on the other hand, Gandhiji made it a hotbed of the freedom struggle.

The middle-class have played a major role in shaping the city, be it economics, or politics, or even the polarization that exists between the Hindus and Muslims. Does this mean that urbanization has not broken the caste barriers or made religion more rational for the educated middle-class? These questions would be discussed in the succeeding chapters.

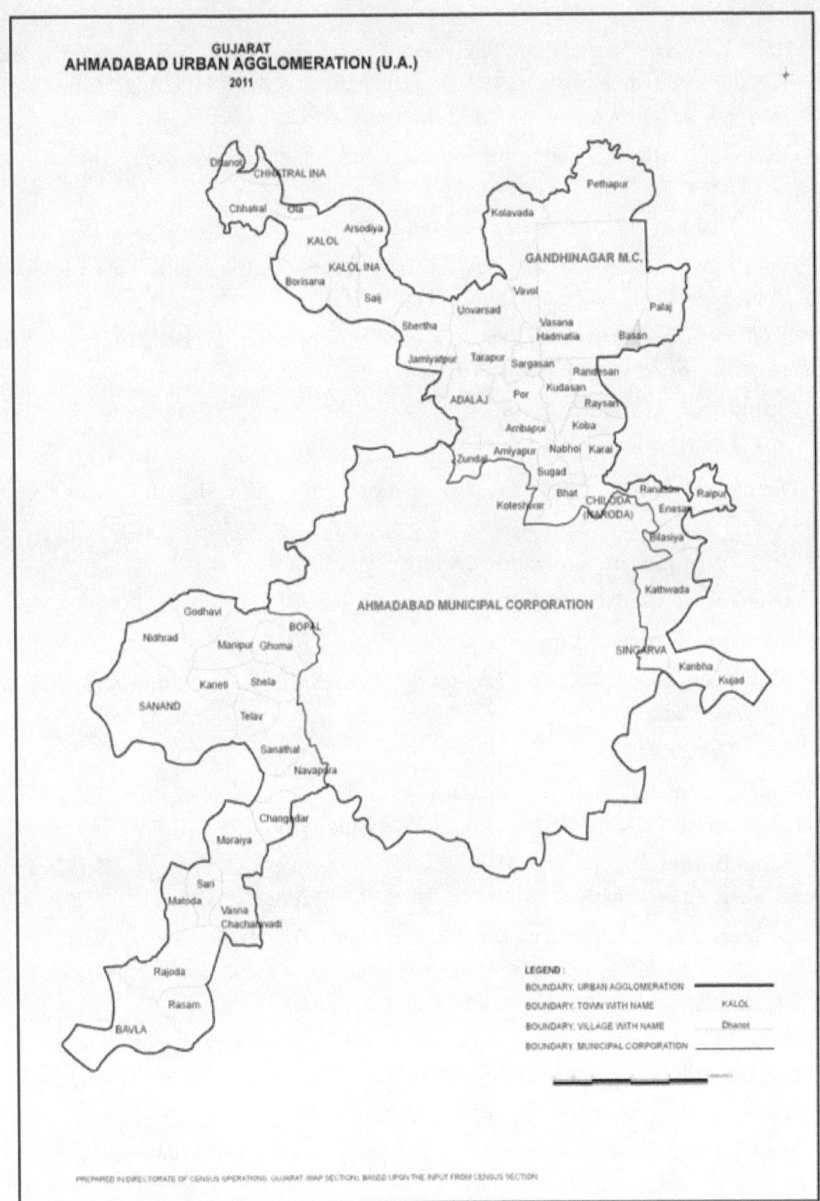

Figure 18 (Source: Census Operations 2011)

Endnotes

[1] United Nations Population Division, *World Urbanization Prospects 2005* (New York: 2006) cited in Kai N. Lee, "An Urbanizing World" in Linda Starke (ed), *State of the World, Our Urban Future* (London: Earthscan, 2007), 4.

[2] Alex C. Heltmann, "Cities are India's future," *The Times of India,* Ahmedabad edn. 31 March 2011, 13.

[3] R. P. Mishra (ed), *Million Cities of India* (Delhi: Vikas Publications, 1978), 15.

[4] Ashish Bose, *India's Urbanization 1901-2001,* 2ⁿᵈ edn (N. Delhi: Tata McGraw Hill Publishing Company Limited, 1978), 49.

[5] T. G. McGee, *Urbanization Process in the World* (London: G. Bell, 1971) cited in Mishra (ed), *Million Cities in India,* 16.

[6] Mishra (ed), *Million Cities,* 16.

[7] Mishra (ed), *Million Cities,* 16.

[8] Director of Census Operation, *Census Report 2011* (Ahmedabad: Census Dept, 2011), 40.

[9] Director of Census Operations, *Census Operations,* 41.

[10] Director of Census Operations, *Census Report 2011.*

[11] Director of Census Operations, *Census Report 2011.*

[12] K. C. Jain, *Ahmedabad: An Expanding Metropolis,* in R. P. Mishra (ed), *Million Cities of India,* 222.

[13] Jain, *Metropolis,* 213.

[14] Independent Sultanate of Gujarat (1411-1573 AD), Mughal Rule (1573-1753 AD), Maratha Rule (1753-1817 AD), British Rule (1817-1947 AD).

[15] John Burton Page, "The History of Ahmedabad" in George Michell and Snehal Shah ed., *Ahmedabad* (Mumbai: Marg Publication, 1988), 11.

[16] Maulavi Abdul Muqtader ed., *The Haif Iqlim (The Seven Climes)* (Bibliotheca Indica), 86-87 in M. S. Commissariat, *A History of Gujarat, Vol I from 1297-8 to 1573* (Bombay: Longmans Green and Company Ltd., 1938), 101.

[17] Salim Lakha, *Capitalism and Class in Colonial India: The Case of Ahmedabad* (Delhi: Sterling Publishers Private Limited, 1988), 13.

[18] Times News Network. *The Times of India,* 8ᵗʰ Feb. 2011.

[19] B. G. Gokhale, *"Ahmedabad in the XVII Century"* Journal of Economic and Social History of the Orient, Vol. XII, Part II, (1969), 189 cited in Lakha, *Capitalism,* 14.

[20] Lakha, *Capitalism,* 16.

[21] Makrand Metha, *The Ahmedabad Cotton Textile Industry: Genesis and Growth* (Ahmedabad: New Order Book Co. 1982), 4.

[22] Lakha, *Capitalism,* 17.

[23]Kenneth L. Gillion, *Ahmedabad, A Study in Indian Urban History* (Berkeley: University of California Press, 1968), 24.

[24] Gillion, *Ahmedabad*, 25.

[25] G. W. Forrest, *Cities of India* (Delhi: Thomson Press, 1991), 72.

[26] Harish Doshi, *Traditional Neighborhood in Modern Ahmedabad: The Pol* in M.S.A.Roa, Chandrashekar Bhatt & Laxmi Narayan Kadekar (eds), *A Reader in Urban Sociology* (Delhi: Orient Longman, 1991), 180.

[27] J. Forbes, *Oriental Memoirs, Vol. III*, (London: n.p., 1913), 120 cited in Gillion, *Ahmedabad*, 32.

[28] J. Forbes, *Oriental, Vol II*, 257-58 cited in Metha, *Ahmedabad Cotton*, 5.

[29] Gillion, *Ahmedabad*, 35.

[30] *Ahmedabad Gazetteer*, 293 cited in Gillion, *Ahmedabad*, 53.

[31] *Census of India, 1921, Vol IX, (II)*, cited in Gillion, *Ahmedabad, 104*.

[32] Achyut Yagnik & Suchitra Sheth, *Ahmedabad, From Royal City to Mega City* (Delhi: Penquin Books, 2011), 220.

[33] Yagnik & Sheth, *Ahmedabad*, 228.

[34] Yagnik & Sheth, *Ahmedabad*, 243.

[35] John E. Brush, "Growth and Spatial Structure of Indian Cities" in Allen G. Noble & Ashok K. Dutt ed, *Indian Urbanization and Planning, Vehicles of Modernization* (Delhi: Tata McGraw-Hill Publishing Co. Ltd, 1977), 67-68.

[36] S. B. Rajgor, S.Triprathy & U.M.Choksi, *Gazetter of India, 1984*.

[37] Yagnik & Sheth, *Ahmedabad*, 285.

[38] Dushyant Joshi, "Enchanting Growth," *Ahmedabad Times*, 14th Aug. 2010, 3.

[39] Times News Network, "Denim Capital of India," *The Times of India*, Ahmedabad edn. 11Feb. 2011.

[40] M. V. Kamath & Kalindi Randeri, *Narendra Modi—The Architect of Modern Gujarat* (Delhi: Rupa & Co, 2009), 113.

[41] Times News Network, "AMC gets Nagar Ratna..." *The Times of India*, 9th July 2011, 14.

[42] Yagnik & Sheth, *Ahmedabad*, 292.

[43] Yagnik & Sheth, *Ahmedabad*, 303.

[44] Dilip Patel, "Ahmedabad is the Best," *Ahmedabad Mirror*, 28th March 2012, 8.

[45] Edalji Dosabhai, *A History of Gujarat* (np:n.pub, 1894), Reprinted (N. Delhi: Asian Educational Services, 1986), 307.

[46] Gillion, *Ahmedabad*, 63.

[47] A. H. Somjee, Gujarati, Social Concerns and Political Involvements of Intellectuals, in Yogendra K. Malik (ed), *South Asian Intellectuals and Social Change* (Delhi: Heritage Publishers, 1982), 192.

[48] Yagnik and Sheth, *Ahmedabad*, 189.

[49] Ghanshyam Shah, Caste Sentiments, Class Formation and Dominance in Gujarat, in K. L. Sharma (ed), *Caste and Class in India* (Jaipur: Rawat Publication, 1994), 254.

[50] Shah, Caste Sentiments, in Sharma (ed), *Caste*, 254.

Chapter 3
The Educated Indian Middle-class

The Indian middle-class has played a crucial role in the formation of modern India. It was always in the limelight, but after the liberalization of the 1990s, the focus became even sharper because the global market saw this class as its principal consumer. It was believed that this class had the buying power and hence manufacturers went all out to woo them. However, in the formative years of the middle-class, they were known not simply for its consumerist behavior, but for the role they played in the formation of the Indian National Congress (INC), their capacity to lead the freedom struggle and control the bureaucracy in independent India. However, this class also has been accused of manipulation of religion, caste and politics to the disadvantage of the downtrodden and marginalized. It thus becomes imperative that we not only define this class, but go on to study its beginnings, evolution and growth in terms of its key characteristics, values and attitudes.

The Concept of 'Class'

Prior to defining the middle-class, it would be appropriate to first understand what is meant by 'class'. According to Schmidt, the class society is "one in which the hierarchy of prestige and status is divisible into groups, each with its own economic, attitudinal and cultural characteristics, and each having differential degrees of power in community decisions."[1] Max Weber defined class as having three elements: (1) Wealth—the economic dimension, (2) Status—the prestige dimension, that is, how others perceive you in respect and deference and (3) Power dimension—the probability that one actor within a social relationship will be in a position to carry out his or her own will despite resistance.[2] Misra says that "the concept of a single social class implies social division which proceeds from the inequalities and differences of man in society, which may be natural or economic. It is chiefly the economic inequality of man that influences, if it does not wholly determine social differentiation. It arises basically from the difference of relationship which a person or a group bears to property or the means of production and distribution.[3] He further clarifies that society is thus divided into classes or groups of people joined together from motives of common economic interest, common ways of behavior and common traits of character. Each such class forms a hierarchy of status according to the varying quality of social prestige and power expressed through the standard of living, nature of occupation, and wealth.[4]

We can understand from these above definitions that each talks of a hierarchy of prestige, status and power depending on one's economic status expressed in one's standard and lifestyle. It is the economic status of the members of a particular group which differentiates and then determines the characteristics of that group. But it needs to be recognized that there may be horizontal differentiation within a class depending on certain other characteristics. Eg. A middle-class may be highly heterogeneous consisting of the educated or professionals, the merchants who may not be so educated or the small entrepreneurs who again may or may not be educated. Thus, within the middle-class, there may be two more classes—that of the educated and the uneducated, and there may not be much in common between them, at times.

The Middle-class

The origin of the middle-class as a social category has a long history. At the least, one has to go back to the emergence of the 'burgher' in the towns of Central and Western Europe in the course of the Middle ages. They formed a separate social, legal and functional category somewhere between the aristocracy on one hand and the lower, working classes on the other.[5] The origin of the concept can be traced back to the era of Aristotle (384-322 BC), for he used the term 'middle-class' and considered them to be crucial for the very existence of the society. The definition of this term has undergone subtle changes over the last two hundred years. Thus when Thomas Gisborne first employed the term in 1785 in a sociological sense (in his work, *Class*), he used it to refer to the propertied and largely entrepreneurial located between the land owners on one hand and industrial and agricultural workers on the other.[6] C. Wright Mills (1972) explained the heterogeneity of the middle-class and included three occupational sub-categories: (i) owners of small businesses (ii) most professional men and (iii) various levels of salaried individuals. These sub categories differ in income, education, family background, ideology and group participation and yet the binding factor was its economic status. As an economic category, middle-class occupies an intermediate position between the propertied and the working class.[7]

George Bernard Shaw in his own characteristic style defines a middle-class as one with a moderately useful education, a moderately decent job, a moderately beautiful wife and leading a moderately honest life with a moderate ambition.[8] While this definition may be appropriate for literary purposes, but it does not relate well to our discussion here.

We need to have a sharper, specific and penetrative definition. Accordingly, Richard Dobbs and others, in their report for Mckinsey Global Institute, call this the consuming class and define it as "individuals with disposable incomes of more than $10 per day or over $36000 per annum at 2005 PPP (Purchasing Power Parity). Our purpose is to focus on that segment of the population with enough income for discretion spending on a range of consumer products. The threshold of $10 per day corresponds to the income level of which the consumption of many goods begins to grow rapidly."[9] A reasonably good restaurant would cost anywhere between Rs.500 to 700/- per person. And such meals could only be afforded by people whose income fall into the range of above figures.

The Indian Middle-class

Pre-British Period

The Indian Middle-class was in an embryonic stage in pre-British times (especially under the Mughal rule in the 17th century) and it came into prominence only during the British rule. The merchants who were third in the class hierarchy were not allowed to grow, despite having a potential for growth. Misra says:

> Indeed, the traditional segregation of occupational groups, the supremacy of the literary and bureaucratic classes, and the hegemony of the commercial monopolist were some of the factors which prejudiced the growth of the

middle-classes. Their general tendency was to keep society rigid and divided principally into two categories: rich and poor.[10]

We could see glimpses of the middle-class in areas where the Mughal presence was not very strong, as in Gujarat and the Western coast. Misra goes on to explain that these people had the acumen for business and were accumulating wealth. Yet, a different problem they faced was that they had no hope of going up the ladder due to caste discrimination. Misra rightly comments: Caste stood in the way: It did not allow wealth to supersede status by birth. Indian society was in-fact not a money dominated society with freedom for individuals to move up or down the social scale according to the economic circumstances.[11]

Writing about the artisans, Misra says that their skills in various trades were comparable to any in the world and at times even better. "But the excellence of manufacturers in India did not generally signify any social advancement of the manufacturers.[12] He says that Bernier goes on to suggest that the situation under which the artisans worked was such that they could never hope to attain any distinction or to effect any savings with which to purchase either office or land.[13] Gurcharan Singh argues that the middle-class did not grow in this period because of the well-established organizational structure which did not necessitate the formation of a new class. He says that all those who would be part of this class, viz officials, traders and merchants and craftsmen and artisans were all directly or indirectly supported from the surplus from land and ultimately were integrated into the agricultural economy.[14] He also argues that "new researches have proved beyond doubt, that Indian caste system was as flexible as any other society. Many alien people came from outside India, caste system adopted them and adapted with the requirements of those times."[15] It would be difficult to come to any conclusion as to why this group did not develop. Misra seems to be correct to a greater extent for given the opportunity in British times, this group developed very fast. Thus, it seems that these were the people who had the potential and yet were waiting in the wings for the right opportunity and environment.

British Period

The British East India Company made situations favorable for the Indian middle-class to grow. According to Misra,

These new conditions were, for example, the mild and constitutional character of Government and the rule of the law, the security of private property and the defined rights of agricultural classes, a national system of education and a period of continued peace, an economy of *laissez-faire* and a liberal policy of employment and social reform.[16]

They introduced new relationships which tended to transform society from a basis of status to contract.

As in other parts of the world, this class was highly heterogeneous in nature and hence could rightly be labeled as 'Middle-classes'—the plural being used to denote the heterogeneity.

- One of the groups to emerge was the "commercial middle-class," which consisted of groups of people to carry out business as agents to mercantile and banking houses. The British generally referred to them as 'banyans' or 'brokers'.

- The second group in this class was the "industrial middle-class." The growth of industry in India was rather slow, but the industry gave employment to the artisans and the like which gave rise to the industrial middle-class.

- The third was the "landed middle-class." There existed a class of people in the Mughal times between the Zamindars and the working class which was responsible for the growth of this class.

- The fourth group of persons to comprise this class and which is of special interest to us was the "educated middle-class." By this we mean those who received higher education through the medium of English and were engaged in the various recognized professions that grew in modern times as a result of Western Education and Capitalist economy. This education was based on the principle of liberalism and directed against exercise of any monopoly.

Prior to the British system of education, the Brahmins had completely monopolized education. As there was no fixed curriculum, everything was left to the fancies of the Brahmin teacher. Thus, the Brahmins asserted their superiority over other castes and kept them in slavish submission. The British threw open the doors of education to all and this introduced the concept of equality. Their basic aim was to train the Indian to become their intermediaries in the government so that they could rule the country effectively. As Misra says:

English education was thus considered useful and expedient as well as consistent with the political requirements of British rule in India. But although the basic policy of Government was to widen its scope, practical considerations demanded that it should be limited to the upper and middle-classes of urban society.[17]

Macaulay had this class in view when, in his minute of 2 February 1835, he declared: "We must at present do our best to form a class who may be interpreters between us and the millions whom we govern—a class of persons Indian in blood and color, but English in taste, in opinions, in morals and in intellect".[18]

The expansion of the middle-class depended very much on the opportunities available under the British rule. The end of the Company's rule in 1858 marked the real beginning of an era of *laissez-faire,* of free enterprise of commerce and industry. As the industry grew, so did the need of new functional groups to manage these businesses. Here is where the Indian middle-class came into picture and filled in the gaps. Thus, the number of the middle-classes grew. Though the Indians were given subordinate posts, this contributed to occupational mobility, eventually weakening the bonds of caste to a great degree. Thus, the Professional classes were the first ones to break through caste or regional barriers and to develop a sense of unity and solidarity which made possible the development of nationhood in India.

What was the character and role of the middle-class during this period? Prior to 1892, the upper class always dominated. With the introduction of English education, an educated middle-class emerged, and they made their presence felt in every field—politics, nationalism or religious revival. In his letters to Northbrook, Dufferin bore testimony to their potential and rising influence in politics. He wrote:

> In conclusion, however, I think I can safely say that however annoying may be the violence, childishness and perversity of the Bengalee Press and the young Babu Politicians, their influence is neither extensive nor dangerous. The mass meetings and all the paraphernalia of the Indian Caucus, though they may make a noise and may appear effective and formidable in the telegrams not follow that some years hence what is now in the germ may not grow into a very formidable product.[19]

So, it become clear that the "Babu Politicians" (as the British referred to the educated middle-class involved in politics) were making their presence felt and they dominated the Congress in this period. Besides being partly responsible for curbing the British rule, the middle-class was also responsible for not allowing the downtrodden and marginalized to be lifted up. They opposed the Tenants' Rights Bill, and any bill on Factory Reforms for the betterment of the workers basically because these Bills did not suit the advancement of the middle-class. So, while various authors described the middle-class as a 'selfish group' in independent India, it cannot be forgotten that this class had its roots in the time it was formed.

It would not be appropriate to paint just a negative picture of this group. The middle-class played a key and sacrificial role in India's fight for independence. The period after 1905 saw the rise of nationalism demanding political freedom. It started as a revolutionary movement with its roots in the middle-class.

It was the middle-class who responded to the call of the national leaders to stand against the British. A number of historians including Misra have noted that those who were actively involved in the struggle against the British included teachers, students, landowners and people in Government services. This shows us that given a mission and an ideological anchor, this class has the potential of overcoming many hurdle.

Independent India

The middle-class played an important role in the post independent India. They formed the ruling class that eventually shaped the country's social, economic, political, cultural and technological spheres. It is important to note that the heterogeneity of the educated Indian middle-class continued on even during this period. Initially, it was only the upper caste (the Brahmins, Khastriyas and Vaisyas called the "twice born." They claimed to have spiritual birth/second birth at their Thread ceremony/initiation ceremony) which represented the middle-class. Varma points out that the upper caste dominated the Indian middle-class during its formative years and later. Prominent among its members were Punjabi Khatris, Kashmiri Pandits and South Indian Brahmins. Then there were the 'traditional urban-oriented professional castes such as the Nagars of Gujarat, the Chitpawans and the CKPs (Chandrasenya Kayashtha Prabhus) of Maharashtra and the Kayasthas of North India.[20] Sheth further says, "Also included were the 'old elite groups which emerged during the colonial rule: the Probasi and Bhadralok Benagalis, the Parsis, and the upper crust of the Muslim and Christian communities."[21] Post-independence, there has been a fair addition of the "non-twice born"—the Dalit community—to this group.

Though the British offered educational opportunities to the Dalits, they were rather employed for manual labor than white collar jobs. It is only after independence that the Indian state opened the door for the Dalits to be employed in the public sector through various reservation policies. Yet, the growth of the middle-class among the Dalits was not uniform throughout the country. It was concentrated in the Metros and more so in the western and southern India than in the North. Being identified as part of the middle-class was liberating to the Dalits. It was based on merit, excellence and efficiency. It was the individual alone who was responsible for his status rather than the caste he/she belonged to and hence mobility within this group was possible. This liberated the individual from the stigma associated with a particular caste. The middle-class all over the globe carries a modernist identity, which is secular. To this extent a middle-class identity holds out opportunity to transcend their ascribed identity which is demeaning within the Indian caste system.[22]

Yet, Gopal Guru says that the Indian middle-class does not seem to have adopted and imbibed the liberal character sufficiently as it has adopted different value premises from which it seems to be operating. Thus, it does not access Dalit mobility on the principle enshrined in the spirit of individualism. The Dalits were and are always judged by their caste by the "twice-born" rather than their achievements and efficiency. Such caste discrimination is perpetuated because the upper castes feel threatened as the Dalit community keeps challenging them in every sphere of life. Hence, according to Guru, in the private sphere, social interaction between the Dalit middle-class and the "twice born" middle-class has been full of social tension which finds articulation at the psychological level. The Dalit middle-class members are psychologically excluded from the larger middle-class imagination.[23] This finds expression in excluding the Dalits from the middle caste localities which are dominated by the "twice born".

So, what is the social status of the educated Dalits? Guru says that the Dalit middle-class faces radical exclusion from the general middle-class but at the same time does not want to draw its resources from the community where it has its roots. It is true of almost every part of the country that the Dalit middle-class members have sought total emotional, social and cultural departure from other Dalits. In such a scenario, the Dalit community has tried to create its own social and cultural world. Guru says that the Dalit middle-class value structures have undergone such a huge change that their past is disgusting and humiliating to them, and they always seek a departure from it. The educated Dalit would like to become an ideal bureaucrat, and this ambition demands bureaucratically correct behavior—impartiality, efficiency, sincerity and honesty—to be able to live up to the standard of the larger middle-class.[24] But that does not make him part of the middle-class in general. Thus, the Dalit middle-class person feels emancipated from both sides and thus his identity truly hangs in the air.

Post 1990 Period

In 1991, P.V. Narsimha Rao, the then Prime Minister, under the able guidance of Dr. Manmohan Singh, initiated several economic reforms wherein he opened up the country for foreign investments. This gave a tremendous boost to the sagging economy and in no time jobs in the service sector, particularly IT and hospitality sectors, multiplied greatly. Cities like Mumbai, Bangalore, Pune and Hyderabad and to some extent even Ahmedabad became the new destination of the IT professionals. As IT parks were developed in many of these cities with new infrastructure, the cities themselves began to gain a new look. People who got into these jobs not only redefined urbanization but also added in great number to the Indian middle-class. Gurcharan Das says that this class started expanding after 1980 while there was the entrepreneurial surge after 1991. He reasons that the former was due to economic growth while the latter was due to economic reforms. The economic growth from 1950 to 1980 was at an average of 3.5% yearly, but in the eighties the growth rate increased to 5.6% while in the nineties it rose to 6.3%. In these two decades, he says, the middle-class more than tripled.[25] This may be true statistically, but it cannot be denied that the middle-class gained prominence after the economic reforms. It is true that these economic reforms gave rise to many new entrepreneurs who through their ingenuity and hard work have made a fortune.

Vinita Pandey explains the size of the middle-class by quoting from two surveys—one by the National Council of Applied Economic Research (NCAER) and the other by the Confederation of Indian Industry (CII). NCAER divided the middle-class into three segments. The consuming class accounted for 30 million households or 180 million people; the climbers consisted of 50 million household or 275 million people; the aspirants were another 275 million people. The average annual income range taken for this survey was Rs. 45,000—2,15,000. The CII according to its survey concluded that that there were 180 million people in India with an annual income exceeding Rs.1,20,000. Another estimate put this size at 400 million which was expected to rise to 450 million by 2010. This comprises of nearly 39% of the total Indian population.[26] This certainly is no small number by any means. Homi Kharas says that "India could witness a dramatic expansion of its middle-class from 5-10% of its population today to 90% on 30 years. With a population of 1.6 billion forecast for 2039, India could well add over 1 billion people to its middle-class ranks by 2039."[27]

Key Characteristics of the Middle-class

The middle-class could be described in a variety of ways. Sometimes, they are described as the educated class with an intense desire for upward mobility. At other times, they are also called the consuming class for they are the ones who virtually decide the size and quality of the markets and goods. With all the modern amenities at their disposal, they tend to adopt a modern lifestyle—perhaps more westernized—as depicted by the kind of clothes they wear, the social circles they interact with, their eating habits, and even the way their leisure is spent. *The Economist* says,

> As people emerge into the middle-class, they do not merely create a new market. They think and behave differently. They are more open-minded, more concerned about their children's future, more influenced by abstract values than traditional mores. In the words of David Riesman, an American sociologist, their minds work like radar, taking in signals from near and far, not like a gyroscope, pivoting on a point. Ideologically they lean towards free markets and democracy, which tend to be better than other systems at balancing out varied and conflicting interests.[28]

While it is granted that the middle-class is highly materialistic, their outlook or worldview still tends to be traditional. Gurcharan Das makes a distinction between the old and new middle-class, the latter being the ones who benefited from the opening up of the economy in 1991. He says that the most striking feature of contemporary India is the rise of a confident new middle-class. It is full of energy and drive and it is making things happen. In comparison, he says that the chief virtue of the old middle-class was that it was based on education and merit with relatively free entry, but it was also a class alienated from the masses and unsure of its identity. The new middle-class, on the other hand, is based on money, drive and the ability to get things done. The old middle-class was liberal, idealistic and inhibited but the new order is refreshingly free from colonial hang-ups.[29]

Consumerism

One of the main characteristics of the middle-class is consumerism. The buying power of this class has increased since most homes have a dual income. A great majority of people have changed their buying patterns. Sanjiv Gupta had said as early as 2001 that "a lot of typical middle-class virtues are getting rewritten or even getting lost in the sweeping changes that it is caught in. From a 'save and buy attitude' it is moving into a 'borrow and repay' mode."[30] This is so evident from the fact that finances today are easily available for any and every consumer item sold in the market. Juliet Schor emphasizing the consumption of the middle-class wrote, "I describe these developments as the 'new consumerism' by which I mean a constant upscaling of life style norms; the pervasiveness of conspicuous status goods and of competition for acquiring them and the growing disconnect between consumer desires and incomes."[31] In a more academic vein, Murphy, Shleifer and Vishny have pointed out in their scholarly study that though it is the rich who are able to sustain an industrial economy it is the middle-class who add to the profits. They persuasively point prove that the consumption pattern of any economy increases only when there is a substantial middle-class.[32] Eric Benhocker and others have stated that "Mckinsey Global Institute (MGI) suggests that if India continues its recent growth, average household income will triple over the next two decades and it will become the world's fifth largest consumer economy by 2025 up from twelfth now"[33] is not surprising looking at the spending habits of the middle-class today. Vinita Pandey quoting various studies says that "by 2025, a continuing rise in personal incomes will spur a tenfold increase enlarging the middle-class to about 583 million people, or 41% of the population."[34] Homi Kharas quoting World Bank figures says "today very few Indian households would have income exceeding USD 5 per day. ...But between 2015 and 2025, half the population will surpass the USD 10 per day, our definition of the middle-class."[35]

With continuous increase in the income and population, it is not difficult to understand as to why the world considers India as a major market. The immense success of McDonald's, Pizza Hut and Dominos is just one example of the buying power of this class. In fact, Ahmedabad is traditionally a vegetarian city. When Pizza Hut first opened a restaurant in Ahmedabad in 2000, it was vegetarian. Over time, all the Pizza Hut restaurants have turned Non-Vegetarian and the business is thriving. KFC has also been doing well in business. It simply shows the changing taste of the middle-class.

The consumerist class would inevitably become materialistic. This characteristic becomes more pronounced with the craze for going abroad. Most of the middle-class families would have at least one family member living outside India. Most of the parents take pride in such situations, and Gujarat is no exception. The *Times of India* of Jan 4, 2015 carried an article titled Gujaratis 6% of Indians but 20% of Indian US citizens. It goes on to elaborate that the US today is home to nearly 15 lakh people of Gujarati origin and more than 3.5 lakh who speak Gujarati as their first language. He further says that the US census data shows that Gujaratis who account for 6% of the population back home form more than 20% of the Indian American community.[36]

Education Oriented

Giving importance to English education is another characteristic feature of this group. This stratum has realized that English education is a must for their children to make it big in life. Considering the vast potential in this area, English medium schools have sprung up in vast numbers, which in turn has given rise to many tuition centers, coaching institutes and so on. The steep rise in fees in schools and coaching institutes has not deterred the middle-class from providing their children the kind of education they desire. Families in middle-classes are ready to pay any price to get their admitted into professional colleges that would guarantee them a career in future. Quoting World Values Survey, Homi Kharas highlights that

> From 1990 to 2001, there has been a striking increase in those answering that the following quality was important for their children. Independence: 30% to 56%; hard work: 67% to 85%; thrift and saving: 24% to 62%; determination and perseverance: 28% to 46%. In other words, the changing values associated with the middle-income families are already visible in India and these changing values are conducive to economic development.[37]

Please note that most of the parents may not be in the educated middle-class cadre. Hence, for them to give importance to education shows the deep desire for them along with their children to move into this class.

Careerist

Another key characteristic of this class is that they are careerist. They want to move up the corporate ladder and they want to do it fast. There is nothing problematic in being ambitious, but being a careerist certainly lands people into problems. Beteille says, "Being a careerist means making compromises, cutting corners and putting self before others."[38] This would mean that a middle-class person is unprincipled to the extent that he would not mind breaking rules which he would expect others to keep. Not everyone would agree to this or possibly one would say that there has been a major shift in thinking with time. Quoting survey findings, Homi Kharas says:

> In 1995, only 47% of the respondents felt it important that their job be interesting. They valued pay and security as the only important elements of the job. By 2001, while pay and security remained important, 74% called job interest important. The percentage of respondents who felt that opportunity to use initiative in a job was important rose from 46% to 64% between 1995 to 2001. The data suggest a changing work ethic. Where interest and initiative are important, it is likely that labor productivity and job satisfaction will also be high.[39]

Such findings show that there is a major shift in the way people of the middle-class perceive their jobs. Such attitudinal changes are showing up already because India today is a major market for all the major IT companies, call centers, etc. Nevertheless, if we take Beteille's words seriously, that is a major opportunity to initiate change.

The Working Women/Nuclear Family

A woman working for the corporate world was a rare scenario until the 90s. If women did work, it was either in schools or hospitals or banks. The Engineering colleges and the Engineering industry were a male prerogative. But not so anymore! Girls from middle-class families have moved on in large numbers to get employed at call centers, the IT industry and other corporate companies. It is not an uncommon sight to see girls taking up careers in project management supervising at some project sites. This is a major shift that has taken place because of the educated middle-class which would again redefine many social values. There are issues that a girl would have to face at the workplace, but things are changing for the better even here.

The impact of such fast-changing scenario on the nuclear family system needs to be understood. It is contended that urbanization causes joint families to become nuclear. We will discuss this hypothesis in the next section. It would suffice to say for now that the working women not only change the equations in the family but also bring in various pressures on each family member. This may be one of the negatives of urbanization on the educated middle-class.

Secularization

Another characteristic related to consumerism is secularization. It is generally believed that the educated middle-class is becoming more secular. Vinita Pandey defines this process by saying,

> Secularization is a process which implies that what was previously regarded as religious is now ceasing to be and it also implies the process of differentiation which results in various aspects of society, i.e. economic, political, legal and moral becoming increasingly discrete in relation to each other.[40]

This does not mean that the middle-class person *per se* has become irreligious. Rather, the middle-class person thinks that Hinduism as a way of life is probably no longer valid and would undergo varied changes. It would now be reserved to rituals and customs that have nothing to do with the public life but rather is confined to one's private life. Nirad Chaudhuri confirms this:

> All Hindus of today, if they have any Hindu left in them and have not, through an inefficient Westernization, acquired an unpleasantly shallow anti-religious bias like the anti-clericalism of the French politicians think of themselves as human community almost wholly in a cultural sense, and the religious association felt by the denatured Hindu is hardly present in their mind.[41]

Although Chaudhari had said this of the old ruling class, this may very well apply to the new middle-class also.

The Social Character of the Middle-class

Understanding the social character of this group requires an understanding of its composition. While this class is largely based on income, education and occupation, there is a constant interplay of the multiplicity of languages, religion and caste as well. This interplay causes endless conflicts within this class leading to compromise of one principle or the other. As Beteille rightly points out, "individuals many a times act in ways that they may condemn in others and yet justify their own conduct by the press of circumstances."[42] For instance, let's consider a ritual like matching the horoscopes of the boy and the girl for marriage. On a very popular Reality Show recently, this ritual was criticized as superstitious. Educated young people would agree to such criticism on the show, and yet would not object to it at the time of their own marriage proposal and would readily state parental pressure as a reason for it. Instances of such compromises abound.

The first social characteristic of this class is the reduction of gap between them and the lower classes. Such disparities have been reduced somewhat though it has not disappeared completely. The middle-classes remain very conscious of their schooling and of the fact that their livelihood does not depend on any kind of manual labor.[43] It should be pointed out here that the rules of commensality (that is, restriction to eat and drink within one's own caste), which the upper caste so zealously guarded, are not adhered by most within the middle-class. Not all authors agree to this. In fact, authors like L.P. Sharma and Pavan Varma go on to show that the middle-class is completely removed from the lower classes and live in a world of their own. We see this disparity in the way the middle-class of the upper caste treated the Dalits who entered this class, as already discussed in previous sections. However, it needs to be emphasized that such disparity is on the decline, though slowly. In fact, we need to recognize that this is the class which is in between the upper class and the poorer sections of the society. As such, they are to showcase the needs of the poor to the upper segment so that they may be of help to them. They sacrifice their time and effort to take care of the needs of the poor. This is happening in many spheres. The innumerable NGOs are an evidence of the concern that the middle-class have for the lower classes of people.

Secondly, the social identity of the middle-class person or family is defined not only by occupation, education and income; it is defined also by language, religion and caste. It is the coexistence of these sets of divisions, new and old, that gives the Indian middle-class its distinctive character. The Indian middle-class is unique not so much because of any peculiarity of the Indian occupation and educational system as because of the peculiar way in which class is intertwined with caste and community in contemporary Indian society. This is in keeping with the Indian social tradition which allows the continuance of the old elements despite the adoption of new ones even when they are mutually inconsistent.[44] So, it cannot be denied that caste, religion or language are not the only criteria to determine the identity of the middle-class. Occupation, education and income also play an equally important role. Due credit, therefore, should be given to the middle-class for minimizing the caste and gender bias.

Lastly, it is believed that the traditional Indian society was marked by the hierarchical aspects of caste and gender which created an inequality in the society. It is sad to note that a decline in this aspect has not brought an end to inequality. In fact, new ones have been generated based on income and occupation. So now, there is a class differentiation rather than caste differentiation. The only difference being that in the first case it was recognized and accepted and hence people at least knew that it existed, but this new order is based on equality which in practice does not exist. Thus, as Beteille rightly says, "What we are witnessing in India today may be described as the passage from a harmonic to a disharmonic regime."[45]

I would conclude by saying that the middle-class is on a growth curve and is the future of our country. India's growth of economy is only second to that of China and the middle-class play a very important role in it. The government needs to recognize this phenomenon and provide the necessary infrastructure to facilitate such growth and development. On the other hand, the middle-class need to understand its responsibility towards the poor and the needy of our country. It is then that our country will become a force to reckon with. It will depend to a great extent on how they perceive the strongholds of Hinduism—the core of which is caste discrimination. Only a proper perception of these aspects can make the middle-class a catalyst for change in the Indian society.

Endnotes

[1] Schmidt, 1950 cited in Vinita Pandey, *Crisis of Urban Middle-class* (Jaipur: Rawat Publication, 2009), 2.

[2] Max Weber, *The Economy and Society*, 1922, 24 cited in Pandey, *Urban Middle-class*, 2.

[3] B. B. Misra, *The Indian Middle-classes, Their growth in Modern times*, (Delhi: Oxford University Press, 1961), 2.

[4] Misra, *Indian Middle-class,* 3.

[5] Imitiaz Ahmad and Helmut Reifeld, (eds), *Middle-class values in India and Western Europe* (New Delhi: Social Science Press, 2001), 1.

[6] Pandey, *Indian Middle-class,* 3-4.

[7] Pandey, *Indian Middle-class,* 5.

[8] *The Week,* 30th Dec. 2001, 14.

[9] Richard Dobbs and Others, Cities and the Rise of the Consuming Class, *Insights and Publications,* Mckinsey Global Institute, June 2012, *www.mckinsey.com/ insights/urbanization/urban_world_cities_and_the_rise_of_the_consuming_class* (assessed 22 July 2014), 24.

[10] Misra, *Middle-class,* 27.

[11] Misra, *Middle-class,* 31.

[12] Misra, *Middle-class,* 36

[13] Misra, *Middle-class,* 37.

[14] Gurcharan Singh, *The New Middle-class in India, A Sociological Analysis* (Jaipur: Rawat Publication, 1985), 46.

[15] Singh, *The New Middle-class,* 50.

[16] Misra, *Middle-class,* 69.

[17] Misra, *Middle-class,* 151.

[18] Misra, *Middle-class,* 154.

[19] MSS. Eur.C. 144, no.16, f. 3, 23 June 1886, cited in Misra, *Middle-class,* 348.

[20] D. L. Sheth, 'The Great Language Debate', *Crisis and Change in Contemporary India* in Upendra Baxi and Bhikhu Parekh (eds), (N. Delhi: [np], 1995), 199 in Varma, *Middle-class,* 27.

[21] D. L. Sheth, Contemporary India, 199 in Varma, *Middle-class,* 27.

[22] Gopal Guru, Dalit Middle-class Hangs in the Air" in Imtiaz Ahmad and Helmut Reifeld (eds), *Middle-class Values in India and Western Europe* (N. Delhi: Social Science Press, Konrad Adenauer Foundation, 2007), 144.

[23] Guru, Middle-class Values, 145.

[24] Guru, Middle-class Values, 147-48.

[25] Gurcharan Das, 'Middle-class Values and the Changing Indian Entrepreneur' in Ahmad and Riefeld (eds), *Middle-class Values,* 196.

[26] Pandey, *Indian Middle-class,* 12.

[27] Homi Kharas, "The emerging middle-class in developing countries, *Working Paper No. 285* of OECD Development Centre, in *www.oecd.org/development/pgd/4445738. pdf* (assessed 22 July 2014), 35.

[28] Surjit Bhalla, "The middle-class in emerging markets, two billion more Bourgeois," *The Economist* 12th Feb 2009, *www.economist.com/ node/ 13109687,* (assessed 22 July 2014).

[29] Gurcharan Das, *India Unbound* (N. Delhi: Viking, 2000), 319.

[30] Sanjiv Gupta, "Great Indian Buyers" in *The Week* 30th Dec 2001, 38.

[31] Juliet Schor, "The New Politics of Consumption" in *Boston Review,* 1999, *http:// boston* review.net/archives/BR24.3/schor.html (accessed 31 July 2017).

[32] Murphy, Shliefer and Vishny, "Income Distribution, Market size and Industrialization" in *Quaterly Journal of Economics,* 104(3), 537-564, 1989, *http:// scholar.harvard.edu/ files/ shleifer/ files/ inc_dist.pdf* (accessed on 31 July 2017).

[33] Eric D. Benhocker, Diana Farrell, Adil S. Zainulbhai, "Tracking the growth of the Indian Middle-class" in *The Mckinsey Quarterly* 2007, No.3, 51, *https://ecell. in/ eureka*13/resources/tracking the growth of Indian Middle-class, pdf. (accessed on 1Aug 2017).

[34] Vinita Pandey, *Urban Middle-class,* 15.

[35] Homi Kharas, The emerging Middle-class, 7.

[36] Parth Shastri, "Gujarati 6% of Indians but 20% of US citizens" The Times of India, NRI edn. 4th Jan 2015 in times of india.indiatimes.com/nri/us-canada-news/ Gujarati-6-of-indians-but 20-of-US-indians/articleshow/45746350.cm (accessed on 1 Aug 2017).

[37] Homi Kharas, The emerging Middle-class, 36.

[38] Andrea Beteille, "The Social Character of the Indian Middle-class" in Imitiaz Ahmed & Helmut Reifeld (ed), *Middle-class Values in India and Western Europe* (Delhi: Social Science Press, 2001), 84.

[39] Homi Kharas, The emerging middle-class, 36.

[40] Vinita Pandey, *Middle-class,* 11.

[41] Nirad Chaudari, *The continent of circe,* (Bombay: Jaico Publication House, 1970), 29.

[42] Beteille, Indian Middle-class, 74.

[43] Beteille, Indian Middle-class, 80.

[44] Beteille, Indian Middle-class, 81.

[45] Beteille, Indian Middle-class, 82.

Chapter 4
Social Change in the Urban Context

1. URBANIZATION AND SOCIAL CHANAGE

Sociologists generally hold that urbanization brings with it social change. Eshleman and Cashion are of the opinion that "The size, complexity and density of urban communities have given rise to new forms of social organizations, new behaviours and new attitudes."[1] He says that German Sociologist Ferdinand Tonnies (1887) recognized this and made a distinction between a *gemeinschaft* (rural) and *gesellschaft* (Urban) communities. Weber labelled this as a change from a traditional to a rational society.[2] Not all sociologists agree with this view. Pocock, writing on the Indian scenario, says that there is no dichotomy between the rural and urban societies. He says:

> This taking for granted of urbanization as a process affecting manners and institutions has led to a number of facile assumptions about some important all-Indian features. Urbanization brings about the breakdown of the joint family, slackens the ties of caste and decreases the hold of morality (when urbanization is considered a bad thing) and religion (when urbanization is held to be a good thing). And underlying these assumptions seems to be one only which whether desired or deplored, are finally inevitable.[3]

Rao, on the other hand, responds by saying,

> Whereas Pocock was right in pointing out that urbanization in India is not co-terminus with westernisation, he however oversimplified the similarity

between the village and the traditional city. Although religion, caste, kinship
are the bases for social organisation in both villages and towns, there are
significant differences in the working of these in the two contexts.[4]

Pocock would be right to some extent if he was writing in the mid
twentieth century. Upto that time and even a few decades later, people
lived in tight knit communities and life for them was no different from
that of the village. But what Roa says is very appropriate that even then
there was considerable difference in the way many of the social institutions
functioned even then. But there can be no doubt that urbanization has
brought in major changes in all aspects of life for the city dweller. Now,
if we postulate that urbanization does bring change, we need to also try
to study to what degree the changes take place. The building blocks of
the Indian society are caste, family and religion. We need to see how
urbanization and the related changes have affected the structure of these
institutions and also the cultural traits associated with them.

Understanding Change

How do we explain the changes taking place due to urbanization among
the urban educated middle-class? No one theory can explain these changes,
but probably a combination of a few may help us in this regard.

Among the Western classical theories, the conflict theory can be
used to explain some of the cultural changes. There were the likes of
Karl Marx, Lewis Coser and Ralf Darendorf who espoused this theory.
According to this theory, social behaviour can be best understood in
terms of conflict and tension between groups as this becomes a means
of social change.

Each of these stalwarts used this theory in their own context, and
it can be a useful tool in our context too in understanding changes due
to urbanization. Urbanization will always cause a conflict between the
traditional and the modern, between caste and class, etc. This conflict
is bound to cause change and give rise to something new. This would
also be close to the Dialectical approach which D.P. Mukerjee used quite
effectively. He focused on the encounter of the Indian traditions with that
of the West which, on the one hand, unleashed many forces of cultural
contradictions and, on the other, gave rise to a new middle-class. The rise
of these, according to him, generates a dialectical process of conflict and

synthesis which must be given push by bringing into play the conserved energies of the class structures of the Indian society.[5]

The conflict theory is attractive in its proposition. However, one will have to concede that not all changes in the urban context are due to conflict. There are some which just get refined by their interaction with the urban elite. Probably the Little and Great Tradition approach which also explains the cultural changes in the urban context is helpful in this regard. According to this theory, as popularized by Milton Singer and Mckim Marriot, the structure of traditions grows through indigenous evolution as well as its contact with other cultures. The social structures operate at the peasant level as well as at the elite level. The former is known as the Little Tradition while the latter is known as the Great Tradition. There is a constant interaction between the two levels of tradition giving rise to change. This theory will probably be able to explain most of the changes taking place in the understanding and practice of caste and religion. The traditions within caste and religion would have crystallized after a long evolution in the rural context. But in the urban context, these very age-old institutions came in contact with other religions and traditions, and this brings about changes in these institutions. More so, the urban elite process these traditions through their own education and experiences giving them new forms of interpretation. When these interact with their original or Little traditions, they give rise to a new form of tradition which may be very different from its original form.

A.L. Kroeber, who postulated Diffusion theory, holds that when different cultures come into contact with each other, there is going to be a diffusion of those cultures across each other. Urbanization is a fertile ground to test this theory for herein various cultures and traditions compete for space.

The structural functional theories give us some clue to understand the structural changes in the institutions of caste, family and religion. To understand this theory, one will have to understand what the authors who advocated this theory meant by structure and function. Steven Vago has given a precise definition of these words. He says, "The word 'structure' generally refers to a set of relatively stable and patterned relationships of social units and 'function' refers to those consequences of any social activity that makes for the adaption or adjustment for a given structure or its component parts."[6] Talcott Parson is among the best known of sociologists embracing this approach. He spoke of stability or equilibrium as the defining characteristics of a structure. He showed that there would always be some endogenous and exogenous elements impinging on the structure. If the structure is not able to keep its equilibrium under the influences of these forces, it will change and attain a new state of equilibrium.[7] On theories of structural changes, Singh says: "A structural analysis of change consists of demonstrating the qualitative new nature of adaption in the patterned relationships as when a joint family become nuclear, a caste group is transformed into a class group etc."[8] In fact, the theory of structural changes would apply to a great degree to all the three institutions being considered. All these institutions are constantly being impinged upon by various forces from without and within which would cause the structure to change.

Hence, as seen, it is a combination of these approaches that would help us to understand the changes that are taking place in the urban middle-class with reference to caste, family and religion.

2. CASTE IN THE URBAN CONTEXT

India is known for its caste system which forms a basis of the social stratification in the country. This has been a major area of interest for sociologists and social anthropologists, and much research has also been carried out on the subject. Our concern here is to understand the caste dynamics in the urban contexts and trace the changes that have come about because of various factors.

Features of the Caste System

The caste system has at least six basic characteristics which form the core of this very important institution of Hinduism. Ghurye gives them as:[9]

1. Segmental division of society
2. Hierarchy
3. Restrictions on feeding and social intercourse
4. Civil and religious disabilities and privileges of the different sections
5. Lack of unrestricted choice of occupation
6. Restrictions on marriage

The Hindu society was divided into different segments. One was born into a caste group. The *Panchayat*, which was free to make its own rules for the community, regulated every aspect of life of its members. Obviously, a 'community feeling' that transcends caste distinctions would be missing. Even the moral standards of one caste would be different from that of another. As Prof. Ghurye comments, "...Castes were small and complete social worlds in themselves marked off definitely from one another, though subsisting within the larger society."[10]

What was it that separated these caste groups from each other is a subject of intense debate. Some scholars believe that there is a definite hierarchy that separates them; others believe that it is the distinctiveness of each caste that makes it unique. Writing at the start of the 19th century, C. Bougle said: "The spirit of caste united these three tendencies, repulsion, hierarchy and hereditary specialization, and all three must be borne in mind if one wishes to give a complete definition of the caste system."[11] Bougle's definition of caste in complete for it embodies all aspects of it. Each person was born into a particular caste and each caste was part of a hierarchy. The occupation of a person depended on his position in the hierarchy. And most importantly, this hierarchy also governed the social interaction between people.

The perpetuation of hierarchy had its own far reaching implications. There is a restriction on feeding and social intercourse between the castes. A Brahmin would never accept water, much less any cooked food, from any other caste except another Brahmin. Prof. Ghurye says that the theory of pollution being communicated by some members of the higher caste is also more developed in Gujarat.[12] Of course, the higher castes have found their justification in their scriptures which seem to have strengthened their resolve to perpetuate it.

Every caste was attached with certain civil and religious privileges and/or restrictions. That the low castes and the untouchables were not allowed to draw water from the village well or enter the village temple was only a sample of the kind of ill-treatments that they received at the hand of the high caste. Another very important restriction was on the choice of occupation for each caste. Each caste was assigned with a particular occupation and it was hereditary. The menial tasks were to be handled by the untouchables, while the Sudras took up those involving manual labor. The last but not the least was the restriction of marriage outside its caste. It was not only the caste which was important but also the sub-caste when it came to marriage. Though endogamy was rather quite strict, hypergamy was permitted in certain cases.

So, it is obvious that the Hindu society at large was divided into various caste groups and sub-castes, held together through strict endogamy and restricted social life. Yet, in spite of distinct cultural traditions of each caste, they were able to function as one society. According to Ghurye, the social economic interdependence of each caste held the society together creating a harmony in civil life. Of course, this harmony was not the harmony of parts that are equally valued, but of units which were rigorously subordinated to one another.[13] Many Indian leaders may have exalted the caste system as a means of maintaining order in the society. Yet, it is strongly believed that caste in India has been perpetuated by the upper caste in order to exploit and oppress the lower caste.

Caste and Change

Two centuries ago, Louis Writh had postulated that the city would have profound effect on the traditional social values which would cause irreversible changes in the way people thought and lived. His thesis was found to be largely true in the European and Western countries and it was thought that the same would be the case in India too. Frank Conlon says that

> the dominant anticipatory theme of scholarship on urbanization and society in India seems to have been based upon a Writhian assumption that traditional social institutions—the typical forms of family and caste—would experience profound erosion both as a result of urban experience and as a by-product of the expansion of urban influences into the countryside.[14]

The institution of religion may also be added to the list. But we need to see whether these institutions changed as expected or they underwent only partial changes giving rise to forms, probably a combination of the traditional and the modern.

Impact of British Interventions on Caste

Cities are not a new phenomenon in India. They always existed and new cities came up under the regimes that ruled India from time to time. However, as Pauline Kolenda rightly points out, the cultural patterns of the indigenous city were not distinctly different from those of the village.[15]

There were a few major interventions that the British brought in which had profound effect on the working of the caste system. It should be noted that Islam also superimposed its cultural traits on Hinduism but that did not change its fundamental social structure.

The British introduced a universalistic legal system which was fundamentally different from that followed in India at that time. The legal system in India when the British came was based on the principle of hierarchy. The legality of a matter was decided on the caste of the victim and the perpetrator which meant that the legal system was non-egalitarian in nature. The British introduced various legal innovations which were against the Hindu law and which were based on principles of universalism, rationalism and individualism.[16] This abolished many of the practices which were against human dignity. Singh rightly says that all these changes posed a serious challenge to the two cardinal attributes of the Indian tradition—those of hierarchy and holism.[17] Everyone became equal in the sight of the law and the special privileges that the high caste enjoyed were thus taken away. The caste solidarity also took a big hit because of this.

The British also brought in other legislatives like abolishing untouchability. This along with Industrialization brought with it many changes in the pattern and process of urbanization. Colonies sprang up near the factories which were heterogeneous in nature. Restaurants and public transport, cinema halls, and other public places were open to all without discretion of caste. Work places like factories, hospitals, schools were places where the caste criteria were not taken into account. This was a great blow to the caste system as was practiced traditionally.

Change in Caste Ideology

The urban middle-class had to accept by default all the changes brought about through British legal interventions. However, what we still need to understand is whether these changes enabled them to overcome the caste system along with its prejudices. Their education under the British system made them somewhat unique as it was different from the one practiced before. Based on a modern scientific worldview, the education system of the British taught equality and rational thinking, and it went against the thought pattern espoused by the principle of hierarchy and holism. Did this create a conflict of ideologies and pose a threat to the old system of education? Or did the age-old traditions get transformed by their interaction with the educated elite? Apart from this, the city brought people of different cultures, religions and regions together. This should have caused either the diffusion of ideas giving rise to a syncretic culture or it should have done away with the irrational giving rise to a new rational system. We are all aware that caste was never obliterated then, and it continues to be practiced even today. But there were a number of changes that did take place which are noteworthy.

One area which did change in the urban context for the educated middle-class was their obligation to adhere to the life style of the caste that they are born in and also pursue the occupation allotted to it. All would agree unanimously that the occupation of the forefathers, be it that of a Brahmin priest or a cultivator holds no legitimate meaning to the thoroughly western bred educated Hindu. Hemlata Acharya did a study to analyze the changing role of religious specialist in the pilgrim city of Nasik and found that they are increasingly taking up new and varied jobs.[18] But this does not mean that they are ready to take up the menial and labour oriented work also? The urban middle-class have taken up new jobs irrespective of their caste but refrained from taking up menial and labour oriented jobs. It is heartrending to note that the untouchables are still doing the menial jobs and in most cases the artisan castes (*shudras*) are still involved in the occupation of their forefathers. This shows that India as a country is far from looking at labour with dignity. This gives us an indication that the educated middle-class are selective in choosing the changes that they want to adapt to.

To what extent has the educated urban middle-class dispensed with caste? What is the understanding and importance of caste to this particular class in question? Andre Beteille in his lecture at the University of California in 1992 contented that the educated middle-class seem to be in a state of confusion with respect to the orientation of caste in the society. They knew that caste existed but did not know how to respond to it as educated people living in the modern world. They could see the evils of caste and knew that it had to be done away with if the country had to progress and also had anticipated that it was on its way out. The British on the other hand were of the view that caste was a pre-eminent institution in India which had permeated every area of life and the idea that it should be dispensed with was wishful thinking. The Nationalist view, which the Indian intellectual also subscribed to, held that this was an exaggerated view of caste and that its importance would vane once India gained independence.[19] It was thought so because this group saw caste as a matter of religion and ritual as did many other prominent sociologists. And what did rituals mean to this class who had been brought up with a scientific world view and rational thinking? For this class, "It may be best summed up in the words of Herbert Risley as 'magic tempered with metaphysics'."[20] Thus, if we take this argument into consideration, caste and its rituals should have been dispensed away with long ago. But we are aware that caste and its rituals have gained in strength among the urban middle-class and caste is today being utilized to garner support in other areas too. The conflict within them has led to a compromise because of which they tend to be rational in their public life and yet otherwise in their private life. Prominent men like Bakimchandra Chatterjee and M.K. Gandhi did not shy away from justifying the morality of caste. This was surprising because though caste was based on the law of *Manusmriti*, the Constitution of India completely negated the *Manusmriti*. It looks as if the majority of Middle-class Indians took their cue from these great personalities. Though Gandhi may have justified caste as a means of keeping order in the society, the educated urban middle-class seems to have taken it to justify a graded hierarchy.

Is caste system practiced in the urban India today? Caste system signified rank and status and it is not uncommon for us to encounter this in the offices, schools, colleges, hospitals, etc. V.S. Naipaul wrote of his experiences as he encountered status and rank in different settings in India. His *Area of Darkness* was not taken well by the intellectuals of India as Beteille says that they saw some part of themselves there.[21] Srinivas says that the vast majority of Hindus (including the educated) do not consider caste as evil and do not want it to disappear for they cannot envisage a Hindu society without caste.[22] But there is more heterogeneity among the educated than those who are not. In fact, this heterogeneity is more among the higher strata of the educated groups like judges, lawyers, engineers, doctors, etc. than among the teachers, clerks or the electricians. This becomes evident from the cosmopolitan nature of residential societies of the higher middle-class.

Again, such arguments do not lead to a conclusion that this class of people believe in egalitarianism. Srinivas makes a scathing remark on the middle-class when he says that this class pays lip service to egalitarian ideals, but that should not blind us to the fact that its attitudes are fundamentally hierarchical.[23] Srinivas, writing in early 60's may have been correct, but things have changed at least marginally since then. Empirical researches conducted in this regard in the 70s and 80s show that urbanization is turning people from being outright casteists to taking a middle path or at times leaning more towards secularism.

Empirical Studies on Change in Practice of Caste

B.V. Shah conducted a study with college students of Baroda on their perception of caste. He found that caste considerations played an important role in one's selection of occupation or even friends. With reference to inter-dining which is a core characteristic of caste, he found that "about 51% do accept as inter-diners those individuals of the caste lower than theirs who are culturally advanced and are similar to them in ideas, ways of living and behaviour."[24] He concludes his study with an interesting observation. On this deviations in behaviour with reference to caste, he says that

> it is natural therefore that we find a proportionally greater deviation as regard to caste commensality and caste endogamy among students who come from urban areas and belong to the higher educational level families than among those who belong to rural areas and to families who have a low educational level.[25]

This indicates that urbanization does have its effect on one's thinking on and attitude to age-old rituals as part of the caste systems. But H.D. Laxminarayana's research among students of Bangalore in 1973 did not find encouraging results. He took six groups of students—Brahmins, high caste non-Brahmins, low caste Hindus, Harijan, Muslims and Christians— and tried to find what governed the social distance between them. He concluded that the traditional values were still present in the students. Their social distance was governed very much by their influence of caste and that education had not brought much change in their thinking and their relationship.

Trivedi's research on the attitudes towards caste of the *Patidars* settled in Anand and Naidad reveal some interesting facts.[26] The *Patidars* or the Patels are mainly the landed aristocracy or the *Zamindars* who settled in the towns of Nadiad and Anand. Though these were small towns, they were towns of importance. Anand was known for *Amul*, the milk factory, and other well-known industries such as Elecon, Vallabh Glass and Gujarat Machinary. Vallabhbhai Patel established the Sardar Patel University at Vallabh Vidyanagar, a twin town of Anand. Vallabh Vidyanagar was created specially as an educational centre. Nadiad, on the other hand, could boast of industries like New Shorock, an initiative of the Lalbhai group. These were well developed towns when the researcher undertook his study. He says that an examination of the *Patidars* in regard to caste showed that they valued caste for it gave them a social identity, provided a social milieu and also acted as a platform for marriage alliances. Most of them spoke of their "*Gnati-Samaj*" (Caste Society) by which they meant only the *Leuva Patidar of Charotar* (region). This shows that caste exists and functions at a local level. It was also observed that most of the migrants were well aware of their position in the hierarchy of caste in that region. It was also found that in both the cities the caste organization and solidarity of *Patidar* migrants have not only been maintained but increased. They preferred candidates of their own caste to contest the elections. However, choosing a person for a job was done on the basis of merit because it involved their own finances. It was also found that the majority of the migrants preferred to live in a locality with a high density of their own community. At the same time, the study also revealed that people preferred to have people of their own class in their neighbourhood. Such preferences clearly indicate that, along with caste, class also has become an equally (or even more) important determinant of migrant's residential locality, particularly in close neighbourhoods in the cities under study.

C.T. Kannan, one of the few sociologists who have researched extensively on this subject, considered a sample of 200 inter-caste marriages and found that inter-caste marriages are on the rise and that the difficulties that these couples faced were comparatively mild to what prevailed previously. Ross in her study of the educated middle-class in Bangalore also found that men were more in favour of inter-caste marriages than women. This is not to say that women did not at all favour these kinds of marriages for more than 50% of her female interviewees did favour it.[27] It is to be noted that education, occupation and income, i.e. class, are also important considerations for marriage. From his research on graduate teachers on this subject, Kapadia found that only about 32% of the graduate teachers were strongly in favour of maintaining caste endogamy.[28] However, as he probed further, he found that these teachers were not very keen on co-education for boys and girls at the school or college level. He thus went on to conclude that "the ideological change in favour of marriage outside caste is superficial and more airy than real."[29] So Beteille is right in saying that, in regard to marriage, "it is only rarely that caste considerations are ignored altogether."[30]

Further, Abha Sharma who researched on married couples in Baroda says that "the trend is seen in increasing personal selection in contrast to dependency in parental selection as well as increasing interaction between prospective partners in the middle and upper classes in the urban area."[31] On the other hand, she also found that "similar caste and religion for both the boy and the girl was considered important (72%). The couples had justified their opinions by stating that such similarity will promote family life adjustment because customs will be similar."[32] B.V. Shah had earlier come to similar conclusions from his research on college students in Baroda. But he had also found that those living in urban areas were more liberal and accommodative in their selection of brides than those in rural areas. He went on to point out that "all these factors tend the students to think and assert more in terms of bride's individual qualities and their own individual aspirations about her rather than in terms of group factors and needs."[33] I see this as a major change in the area of selection of brides. In earlier times, the selection was done only by the elders who were more concerned about the group dynamics; but now, the boy and girl were more involved, and they were the ones who ultimately decided. This does not mean that caste has lost its grip on marriage proposals, as evident from the matrimonials in newspapers and websites.

Beteille points out that, apart from the frequency of inter-caste marriages which needs to be studied, we need to also see which rules are followed, and which are not, with reference to marriage. He says that "Where intercaste marriages do take place among the intelligentsia, ignoring for the moment the question of frequency such marriages are in general as likely to be of the *anuloma* (sanctioned) type as of the *Patriloma* (Unsanctioned) type."[34] Thus caste and society continue to play an important role in choosing one's partner though the choice has now become more flexible than before. There seems to be more deviation among the urban educated from the traditional than those in the rural areas. Thus, in choosing one's partner or social circle, there seems to be a strong diffusion of cultures among the educated which has made people more open to others different from them.

Caste Associations: A Symbol of Caste Solidarity

Caste associations were another form of caste manifestation in cities. Caste-based associations do not seem to be affected by secular values. Conlon says that most of the caste associations came up in cities and the majority of its members were those with English education.[35] These caste associations got involved in the betterment of their caste members. They established hostels, scholarships, schools etc. so that their caste members would be able to advance. Srinivas says that because of the work of the associations, the horizontal solidarity of a caste gained at the expense of vertical solidarity of that region. He points out that the last hundred years has seen a great increase in the caste solidarity, and the concomitant decrease of a sense of interdependence between different caste living in that region.[36] This obviously means that each caste because of the caste associations has become an island in itself. Lloyd Rudolf says that this actually hinders the members from fully utilizing their potential because in a way it is limited by the boundaries defined by the association. He goes on to say that the only way to bring about change is through a complete transformation of the associations, which of course can never be fully realized. He further says that modernity like a 'shadow society' can change the existing regime's direction without ever replacing it. He says that modernity has entered Indian character and society, but it has done through assimilation and not replacement. Changes, he says, will occur only when other integrative institutions are allowed to bring about the changes and also when there is a federation or consolidation of caste associations into larger groupings.[37] History has shown that many a times these caste associations disintegrate into smaller splinter groups rather than integrate other caste into it as Lloyd envisaged. But I believe that it is only a matter of time that this group opens itself to the needs of others outside their own caste.

Reinventing Caste in the Urban Context

If Caste Associations in the city are a symbol of the continuation and solidarity of caste, there are other ways that the educated Hindus in the city are putting their effort to see the perpetuation of caste in the urban context. There is a great interest being shown by this group of people in the study of Sanskrit and ancient Indian culture. Ahmedabad can boast of having a *Swaminarayan gurukul* where the traditional form of education is followed. There is a *Bhagwat Vidyapeeth* which teaches its Brahmin students all the rituals associated with caste. It is in the forefront of popularizing yoga. Thus, the desire of a number of educated Hindus to go back to traditional India seems to be quite strong. We can trace the reason for this in another innovation of the British and that is nationalism and the political culture of democracy. These innovations had worked wonders in the Western world. As the feudal structure was replaced by democracy during the Reformation and Enlightenment, communal values were replaced by values of freedom, equality and humanism. But we did not get the same results in India. Singh gives three valid reasons for the same:

> First, these values had been derived from an alien tradition and had grown on the soil of India under a colonial patronage, which was a psychological irksome factor. Secondly, the economic and social structural factors of the contemporary India were not comparable to that of the 17th and 18th century West. Thirdly, for historical reasons, these historical innovations had been injected into the Indian body-politic in a compressed form which in the West had evolved gradually, and this phenomenon created new and far greater cultural stresses than it did in the West.[38]

The growth of nationalism in India is oriented towards the Indian tradition. Singh says that the national leaders were for modernity, but not at the cost of traditional cultural identity. Tilak and Gandhi represent extreme forms of this movement, being the advocates of a kind of nationalism which was deeply embedded in the past Hindu tradition.[39] E.g., Gandhi's idea of secularism did not mean a-religiosity but the spirit of religious tolerance which he postulated on the basis of universalistic ethic of Hinduism itself.[40] So, it seems that there was a constant struggle or conflict between tradition and modernity. What resulted was probably a synthesis of the old and new or a modern public posture while retaining the traditional in private. Nevertheless, Singh says that much legislation against the practices in Hinduism was taken quite positively during the British times and also after independence. The main reason for this trend was the emergence of enlightened elite in the Hindu society with rational commitment to nationalism.[41] This is probably what urbanization coupled with modernisation has contributed towards modernising the Indian tradition.

Hence, I would conclude that urbanization has affected the perception and practice of caste for the urban middle-class in some areas and to some degree. In the upper sections of this class, people have become more open minded socially. There is generally a greater tolerance towards and acceptance of people of other caste and religions. However, the middle-class seems to think that giving up caste distinctions would lead to an identity crisis and hence they do not want to let go of their caste identity, and at times, they strive to even revive and showcase their caste along with its rituals. It is hoped that the recent globalisation will have a greater impact on this age-old institution to loosen its grip on the urban Indian middle-class.

3. FAMILY IN THE URBAN CONTEXT

The joint family pattern was predominantly practiced in rural India. It is assumed that the rapid urbanization of India affected the institution of the family much more than it affected any other. We would like to study in this section what were these effects. Were they such that they changed the family values completely or are the family values of that of the joint families still predominant? Herein, we would use the theories of structural change to help us analyze the changes in the family. We need to first come to a conclusion whether the structure of the family changed from joint to nuclear. And if this has taken place, then, we need to analyse the effect on the relationships and how it affected the functioning of the new family as against that of the conventional joint family.

Defining a Nuclear Family

Karve, who has done an extensive study on kinship in different parts of India, defines joint family as a group of people who generally live under one roof, who eat food cooked at one hearth, who hold property in common and who participate in common family worship and are related to each other as some particular type of kindred.[42] Though this is a concise definition, it has been questioned by many. In J.P. Singh's analysis, "scholars such as Madan (1962:7-16) and Shah (1998) have questioned whether 'common residence' is an essential element to constitute a joint family, they have instead focussed attention on the element of coparcenary."[43] But he rightly points out that there are several autonomous families who have common ancestral property. But can this be taken as a criterion of a family being joint? He rightly says that "the fact that the joint family is a commensal unit cannot be set aside.[44] He further emphasises that "a common kinship bond spread over more than one household alone, despite having separate kitchens and autonomous means of livelihood with individual assets cannot form a joint family in the true sociological sense."[45] Singh is right in his argument because when the residences become different, the functioning of the family also become different from that of the joint family. But as Ross points out, this definition tells nothing of the sentiments, the systems of power and the rights and duties that constitute the effective binding elements of the family unit. Nor does this definition give an adequate framework for analyzing shifts in family relationships in a rapidly changing society.[46] A.A. Khatri says, "Dr. Earnest Burgress was perhaps the first sociologist to have focused attention on interaction patterns within the family which he described as a unity of interacting personalities."[47] This is the most neglected aspect in the study of family in India. Dr. Kapadia points out the importance of this when he says, "the attitude of each person towards his sons or grandsons, daughters or daughter-in-law, will probably be dearer to him than his brothers or collaterals. It is this emotional reaction, the intensity of a person's feeling towards the members of the own family that distinguishes the new family from the conventional family."[48] Ross thus uses the following working definition in her analysis of the urban families that she studied in the city of Bangalore. She says that a family is a group of people usually related as some particular type of kindred, who may live in one household and whose unity resides in a pattern of rights and duties, sentiments and authority.[49] I think, a combination of Karve's and Ross' definitions would be one which would encompass all the factors that govern a joint family.

Structural Changes in Family

It is very difficult to imagine, at times, a situation where people of three generations stayed together under one roof. But it was possible in the simple, agriculture-based societies. In fact, Ross points out that such families were family-centred, characterized by intimacy, mutuality of interest, strong primary group controls and mutual assistance in the time of need.[50] There can be no doubt here that Ross encompasses all aspects of the functioning of the joint family.

The joint family acted as one unit and the interest of the family superseded that of the individual. The role of each in the family was well defined. The women of the house were supposed to take care of the kitchen and raising-up of children while the men would work and take care of the finances and property. The eldest male in the family was accepted as the head of the family and his word was taken as final in all matters. As everyone worked towards one goal, it created a sense of binding and intimacy within the family. Thus, the burdens within the family were shared to the proportion of one's strength. Thus, life was comparatively easy as each knew that the whole family would stand with them in the time of need.

Urbanization greatly influenced the joint family system and effected many changes. On the one hand, as the joint families grew larger, the land that they tilled could not support them and hence they moved to the cities in search of better career opportunities. Did such changes affect the way families functioned? Did the joint family system disintegrate as many had predicted?

Many studies on the subject of joint families indicate that urbanization has not affected the joint family. Agarwal, in his study of the Marwadi joint families living in large cities all over India, found that urbanization has not really affected them. Agarwal claims that it is "an outstanding example of the obdurate continuance of the joint-family and caste-system in spite of industrialization, technocracy and Western Education and in some respects, rather because of them."[51] Desai studied the families in the small town of Mahuva in Gujarat. According to his findings, nearly 96% of the families in Mahuva have some kind of 'jointness,'[52] that is, though the families live as nuclear, they have a close-knit relationship with their kith and kin. The Mahuva families shared very many characteristics of a joint family. However, if there are similarities, there would be dissimilarities also. A pertinent question that could be asked at this point is: 'At what point would we stop calling a family joint or nuclear'? Gore concludes from his study that the difference between the rural and urban families is rather small on questions of actual behaviour such as size and composition of family, decision making, and larger on questions of age of marriage, intercaste marriage, divorce and family preference.[53] But, Sudha Kaldate rightly points out that "while arguing thus, Kapadia and others fail to give proper recognition to the 'cultural lag.'"[54] She means that these authors do not recognise that what they saw then may have been only the intermediate state and the final state would be something very different.

Accordingly, to Oomen, if we accept the above-mentioned findings, then we are compelled to conclude that the nature of household has not changed due to urbanization. Thus, there seems to be no case for pursuing an analysis of the urban family, since it is not a distinct empirical entity. He goes on to point out that a substantial number of families that had settled in cities prior to industrialization were joint families in nature. Thus, pre-industrial urbanization and joint family organization do not seem to be antithetical.[55] But this would not apply to the post industrialization period where there was a huge migration from the villages. This migration was not just of the artisan or labour class, but also to a great extent of the educated middle-class. Students who came into the cities for their studies got jobs and settled there. These families were essentially nuclear because of space constraint and also because the brothers and their families would have settled elsewhere as per the demands of the job. Empirical studies done at various locations at various time intervals also confirm this.   Edwin Driver conducted his research on this subject in Nagpur district and concluded that "the joint family occurs rather infrequently, especially in the city and towns. Furthermore, it is less prominent among younger couples than older ones and the highly educated than those without education."[56] Sudha Kaldate also came to the same conclusion in her study. She wrote "the data presented leads to the conclusion that the joint and quasi joint family patterns are "traditional middle-class village phenomenon; the nuclear family pattern appears more among the nontraditional groupings influenced by the urban-industrial values and attitudes."[57] It would thus only be right to conclude that the nuclear family is the norm of the cities, and the middle-class families are no exception.

We herein look at four variables within the family (as enumerated by Ross)[58] that may be affected by urbanization, namely, (i) the ecological substructure, (ii) the substructure of rights and duties, (iii) the substructure of power and authority and (iv) the substructure of sentiments.

The Ecological Substructure

As already explained earlier, the small joint family (son with his family and parents) is the typical form of family life amongst the middle and upper middle urban classes in India. Lal, who comes to the same conclusion from his study on families in Patna, the capital city of Bihar, calls these units as supplemented nuclear families. His study does not support the proposition that joint families are found more among the upper caste. He further found that there is a correlation between education and nuclearization of families.[59] It is only natural that the distant relatives are less important to the present generation than they were to the previous ones. Singh says that

> changes are noticed in the familial network also. The kinship networks are becoming smaller and with the rise of individualistic sentiment, kinship obligations are steadily decreasing. Personal interests of individuals are steadily becoming important in life that their attachment to their relatives outside the family is gradually decreasing.[60]

K.M. Kapadia researched this subject taking a substantial sample of teachers. He concluded thus from his in-depth research: "Our analysis shows the emergence of the concept of individuality of both the male and the female and its growing impact on the institution of marriage and the family."[61] This shows that urbanization has affected the institution of the family. There is a distinct shift from jointness to nuclear, from holism to individuality. This, I believe, would have become more enhanced with greater urbanization, more education and severe competition that it brings.

The Substructure of Rights and Duties

As stated in an earlier discussion, the role of each member in a traditional joint family is usually well defined, including their responsibility towards the relatives. But in the urban situation, this undergoes a drastic change. We are aware that in the urban situation, it is the role of the women that undergoes a major change, and this brings about a change in the role of the husband also. Sudha Kaldate says that

> ...one aspect of the impact of urbanization on the family can be observed in the change in the role of the woman. In the urban setting largely as a result of various factors affecting traditional family organisation, the woman tends to achieve an egalitarian status and her more scheduled traditional role as wife and mother gives way to a broader participation in the economic, social and political activity of the nation.[62]

Thus, with the new division of labour, the mother now becomes the pivot around which the family revolves. She in fact plays the same role that the eldest male within the family played in the joint families. Agreeing with this change, Rajendra Sharma quotes Mower who opines that the husband is no longer the head of the household in many families; the wife finds herself equal to her husband in the family and she rules the destiny of the family.[63]

What about the duties towards one near and distant relatives? Is it the same as that of the joint family? Oomen goes a little deeper where he talks of a host of things that affect the kin relationship. He says that the kin relationship will depend on ecological factors like physical accessibility, cost of travel, sociological factors such as degree of relatedness, coupled with intensity of interaction and the resultant intimacy, economic factors such as disparity of income between households, and a host of psychological factors such as likes and dislikes, perceived similarities and differences in social status, conscious and unconscious needs and interests.[64] So in the urban situation, class also plays a vital role in determining the kind of relationships that exists between relations. Though it may not be universally true, it is generally seen that many a family tend to isolate themselves from their relations if they do not belong to a comparable class in terms of economy and education. We will have to see whether this is true in Gujarat for the caste solidarity is pretty strong here. It has been observed that families tend to bring in their kin to the city and educate them to further their career prospects.

The Substructure of Power and Authority

In the traditional joint family, the power allotted to each member is very well defined. For instance, the eldest male of the family, usually the grandfather, is the head of the family. The other male members were subordinate to the grandfather. The children along with the wife are subject to the father and husband. Lal says that these postulations highlight two important characteristics of the power structure in the traditional Hindu family, namely, (i) prevalence of centralized pattern of authority instead of diffused and (ii) the norm of making the eldest man as the centre of corporate authority.[65] When the family structure changes, the problem of adjustment to new patterns of authority is always tough. All relationships become more equalitarian which many a times become difficult for the elders in the family to accept as they would like to assert their authority and dominate. Hence, conflicts within the nuclear families in the cities are increasing. The consequences of such conflicts are also obvious and need not be elaborated. Levy, writing about the change in family in Modern China, believes that the two most crucial areas in family change will be found in the attempt of the son to emancipate himself from the dominance of his parents and in women to change from their subordinate positions.[66] This is observed in our country also for it is the relationship between husband and wife which undergoes a major change. As far as the urban middle-class families are concerned, the wife usually comes from a nuclear family where she has been independent. Moreover, her education makes her equal with her husband in every way. If she is working, there is no question of considering her subordinate to anyone. In addition to this, the children also become economically independent. Oomen thus concludes: "All these facilitate the decentralization of authority in these families, and even its relocation to father to sons after the father's retirement, particularly if he becomes dependent on the sons." [67] He also states the overall ethos in such families is one of individualism, at least as compared to other families.[68] We need to recognize that in the urban context, there are various authorities that one comes under and thus the authority of the family is only a small part which ultimately may not play a very crucial role.

In conclusion, it may be said that though the control of elders has not completely disappeared, their domination is not to the same degree as earlier. As Ross puts it, "There is a growing tendency for the younger family members to be treated as individuals rather than as family members."[69]

The Substructure of Sentiments

For a family to be stable, one needs to respect the sentiments within the family. In a joint family, there is usually a bond of affection between the grandparents and grandchildren, between mother and son but more formal relationships between the father and sons. The husband wife relationship is also one of warmth but never very strong. Lal finds that husband and wife usually do not go out together in joint families showing that the bond between them is not so strong. He attributes this to tradition. He further shows that surprisingly this trend does not change in nuclear families thereby showing the stronghold of tradition.[70] There is also preferential treatment among the children depending upon whether you are a son or daughter or even whether you are the eldest, the middle or the youngest. Much of this thinking is based on some mythological stories and also some religious beliefs. However, there is much change when the structure of the family changes to become nuclear. The strongest bond of affection is now found between the husband and wife. There will also be a strong affectionate relationship between the parents and children, but not so much with the grandparents or the uncles or aunts or even with cousins. One of the reasons for this strong bond between the husband and wife is the mutuality of interest and the privacy they can enjoy. As for the relations who are far off, the distance and infrequent meeting causes any warmth that is there to grow cold. The relationship between the members of the nuclear family is more on the lines of friendship where there is freedom of expression and mutual respect for each other.

We need to keep in mind that the strong affection that nuclearization of family brings is many a time offset by the strong sense of individuality which it fosters. Further, these bonds which can grow stronger over time often become weakened due to pressures of time.

The Impact of Social Change on Mental Health
The changes that take place within a family enumerated above have often had an adverse effect as well. Studies show that it creates conflict within one's self, which when left unchecked for long, has its effect on the mental health and also on the family life. This is more so among the caste Hindus who form a major portion of the middle-class in India. The traditional values of caste Hindu families are often incompatible with the urban environment.

A case in point is the lack of importance given to the girl child in a Hindu family. The girl child grows up with a feeling of inferiority with respect to the male in the family. When she enters an urban environment where the male and female are treated by and large as equals, she finds it difficult to adjust. Such difficulty arises from the kind of upbringing she had in a different value system.

Another example is the kind of freedom that the urban male and female have to mingle with each other. Boys and girls freely and closely relate to each other in schools, and more so in colleges and in their workplaces. The traditional Hindu values do not permit such closeness between the sexes.

This strong pull in both directions causes irreparable damage at times, affecting not only the mental health but also the whole relationships in the long run. Khatri says:

> Attitudes may be in some cases also be reactions against consciously first impulses towards socially disapproved behaviour. Verbal expressions of strong adherence to socially sanctioned belief give the impression as if the person is fighting his own impulses in the opposite direction by this process. Finally, we may mention in passing the psycho-analytic view that beliefs and customs of a given culture are defences against unconscious impulses which would drive them otherwise to do the opposite.[71]

The consequences of this inner conflict are so obvious in the behaviour of the young people. If media reports are to be believed, pre-marital sex is on the rise among the youth in a traditional society like Gujarat. Even divorce cases are on the rise in this society which, at least partially, is the result of the maladjustment of families to the urban environment.

It seems that this is one institution that has been affected the most by urbanization. The families that have migrated post industrialization have become more nuclear in their structure. The rights and duties have also changed. The major change is that of the wife who, through her education and sharing the financial burden, has become the pivot of the family structure. There is a more equalitarian relationship within the family and due respect is given to the children in their decision-making, even on major concerns like marriage or career.

4. RELIGION IN THE URBAN CONTEXT

What changes has urbanization brought in the concept and practice of religion among the middle-class? We will limit our discussion to middle-class Hindus and Hinduism.

Urban Middle-class Identity Crisis

It has been contented by various authors that the urban middle-class Hindus have used religion first and foremost as a means of identity. Sanjay Joshi has elaborated on this issue with respect to the emergence of the middle-class during the colonial rule. He says that it felt a strong need to represent the Hindu community which had not existed as a social entity before.[72] This is how they probably would have felt empowered in the face of colonial rule. Various reformers rose from this class and brought in many changes which would make Hinduism more rational in keeping with the ethos of their own class (Instances: Prathna Samaj, Arya Samaj, etc). Recent scholars have also reiterated that such religious resurgence is found among the new middle-class formed as a result of globalization. Writing on the new middle-class, Minna Saalva says that "by actively engaging in religiosities (Plural intended, to point out the multifaceted nature of Hindu religion), new middle-class Hindus mark their difference from a secularized, immoral and Westernized elite. Religion is among the major moral discursive fields in which the superiority of the Middle-class is enacted."[73] Religion was used not only to distinguish them as a morally superior class from their westernized counterparts but also from the elite of their own country. Minna Savaala rightly says, "Thus, for a century and more middle-class Hindu religiosity has evolved in direct interplay with first the colonial power and later in the post-colonial situation with globalizing economic forces."[74] Thus the identity of a middle-class Hindu is a complex mix of his religiosity and his class. This group went on to become the backbone of a religious fundamentalist party especially in the western belt of Gujarat and Maharashtra and to some extent in the northern Hindi speaking belt also.

At this stage, we need to see whether the middle-class used religion only to overcome an identity crisis or they adhered to its precepts. Did urbanization change the way they perceived and practiced their religion? We start off looking at the meaning of the basic tenet of Hinduism, i.e. *moksha/mukti* or salvation and see what it means to this group.

Urbanization and the ideal of *Mukti*

Understanding Mukti

In its traditional sense *mukti* was/is understood in terms of being released from the sufferings of this world and becoming one with Brahman or the Absolute. This is supposed to be the goal of every Hindu. But with Urbanization and Modernization, this concept has encountered several problems.

One of the basic conditions for attaining *mukti* is non-attachment to the material world. The world is taken to be *maya* or illusionary and thus not real, and attachment to this would be detrimental for one's *moksha*. Klive questions the validity of such ideas in a society which requires commitment to the material world to function. "An ideal like *mukti*, thus becomes so far removed from daily experiences of life that it loses its regulative significance as far as human activities are concerned. It ceases to function as a supreme value."[75]

Secondly, the *mukti* ideal encourages a peculiar escapist attitude to the problems of the world. As the world is unreal, there is nothing like good or bad in it. Thus, one can conveniently overlook the issues and evils of the world as if they don't exist—though they are real and need to be tackled.

Thirdly, one is faced with the difficulty of the paradoxical relation of *mukti* to the worth of an individual. On one hand, because *mukti* is concerned about one's own self (one's transformation, reawakening of one's centre, etc.), one tends to move away from the world of others. On the other hand, human beings living in this world of *maya* are themselves an illusion and hence all worthless. *Mukti* is a higher state of existence one tries to achieve where all human individuality is completely extinguished. In either case, it takes you away from the social world of humans.

Implications of Mukti

How is the concept of *mukti* understood and practiced in the contemporary world? Some have rejected this concept altogether saying that it has no relevance to the modern world. Others, however, have tried to redefine the same to include many of the social elements to make it relevant.

Lakshamana Rao was probably one of those who believed that *mukti* as an ideal had lived its life and did not add any value to modern life. He wrote, "As a philosophical theory it is meaningless to propound that man's true home is eternity or that his *Moksha* consists in his merging with the Absolute. 'Absolute', 'Eternity', 'Infinite' are abstractions not entities…"[76]

Others like Aurobindo see Indian philosophy as a sound basis for spiritual reconstruction in the contemporary context. Radhakrishnan thus stated: "By withdrawing from the scene of mankind's social agony, by proclaiming that justice can be found only beyond the grave, religion is robbed of its possibility of social regeneration."[77] There have been many who have followed this thought. Thus, Raghavachar could say: "If the ultimate good within itself does not include within itself genuine social values, it ceases to be all inclusive. The transcendent perfection of the individual must include within its attainment the individual's utmost contribution to the enrichment of social good."[78] There are others like

Gopalan who feel that *mukti* is all about shedding one's egoistic and selfish tendencies and, when a person walks on this path, social work and social action become second nature to him.[79] E. Ramaswari puts it in the form of a question in the magazine *Kalyana Kalpataru*. " 'Is *Karmayoga* suitable to the modern Indian condition?' and which suggest that the highest type of human being is "the thinker engaged in humanistic service."[80]

The question that still remains to be answered is this: What does this ideal mean for the middle-class and the new middle-class which has emerged post liberalization? There is a particular school which believes that this ideal is basically all about attitude. It has been generally observed that the middle-class is a religious lot. They are the ones who sustain the *guru* movement of today. Shri-Shri Ravishankar and the late Sai Baba have a huge following of which a majority belongs to the middle-class. The Swami Narayan sect in Gujarat is supposedly one of the richest religious sects in India and is funded by NRIs who would also fall into the category of the middle-class and also the Indian middle-class. The ashram movement is also sustained by the patronage of the middle-class. Not to forget the huge temples in our country, it is again the middle-class who patronize them.

Does the religious zeal of the middle-class induce them to get involved in social work or social action as suggested by Aurobindo or Radhakrishnan? Are they involved in solving the problems of the poor which is at their footstep? Edwin Masih, a well-known sociologist of Gujarat, has done a study on professionals in Gujarat taking them from large cities like Ahmedabad, medium cities like Bhavanagar and Godhra and small towns like Naswadi on their social engagement in voluntary organization/association and their perception on social issues. In his study that included teachers, doctors, engineers, journalists, lawyers and social workers as samples, he found that the majority of them were not involved in any kind of social work or action. Though a majority of his respondents saw illiteracy and injustice as major social problems, they were themselves not involved in any way to obliterate them. A majority of them did not feel any obligation to the society which had given them their education, made their career and helped them to improve their status in life.[81] It is very clear that their lives are more inward looking, being concerned about their self and family rather than the society at large.

Pavan Varma makes a scathing attack on the middle-class by saying that the reason for their selfishness is their understanding of the concept of *mukti*. He further says that neither urbanization nor modernization has brought any change in the ideal of *mukti*. Since they continue with their traditional mindset they do not seem to acknowledge the problems of the society, and they thus become more selfish. He explains that the predominant emphasis in Hinduism is on personal salvation. It is all about one's *karma* that affects one's future. He says that, in terms of individual's relation to society, this very emphasis on the self as the centrepiece of the spiritual endeavour tends to stunt the growth of a sense of involvement in and concern for the community as a whole.[82] As already mentioned, the middle-class is religious by their interest in godmen and gurus, but this does not translate into any form of social action. Pavan remarks: "The question of using one's wherewithal for the benefit of the deprived may fall into the diffused category of meritorious work, but is just not as efficacious, in terms of spiritual or material benefit, as the private world of personal religious endeavour."[83] The concept of personal salvation is present in certain other great religions of the world, namely Christianity and Islam, but asceticism is never encouraged. Personal salvation is balanced by the need of the person as an individual to get involved in the society and care of the needy.

As already mentioned, the idea of *mukti* is connected to the idea of *maya* or illusion. The world is considered to be an illusion and thus non-real. This consequently meant that there was no concept of sin as sin is a reality in the world of reality. The concept of right and wrong is more relativistic and circumstantial. Thus, how does a person behave at the existential level? Pavan Varma says, "If the foundation itself was considered to be both there and not there, part of the mysterious illusion of *maya*, how could it sustain a moral edifice which could lay claim to immutability."[84] He goes on to show from the Epics and the Gita that this ambiguity is very much part of it where wrong is many times condoned. Thus, the middle-class Hindu does not bat an eyelid before getting involved in wrong as long he is following one of the given *margas* for his personal salvation.

Of course, Minna Savaala does not agree with this. She says, "It appears that Hindu religious practice is here burdened by an unbearably heavy load. Hindu religion *per se* hardly leads to such damaging social consequences, because Hindu practice can accommodate quite opposing strands of thought."[85] Thus, Hinduism comes to terms with the urban situation quite easily. It is not a dogmatic religion with unchangeable doctrines but rather one which is known for its plurality. Thus, Hinduism is able to take in new forms that arise in the urban context. The various philanthropic activities of godmen like Satya Sai Baba and Maharishi Mahesh Yogi are a case in point. They have started various hospitals, schools, colleges, etc. and many of the volunteers in these organizations are highly placed middle-class professionals.

Achieving Mukti

At this stage, we need to also consider how the urban environment has changed the way the middle-class strives to achieve *mukti*. Milton Singer tried to study the changes in the religious orientation adopted by the Madrasi Brahmins under the influence of the urban environment. He thus found that among the city Brahmins, there was a perceptible change in the path they chose for achieving salvation.

The three *margas* that the Hindus adopt for their salvation are *karma-marga* which is the path of ritual observance, *jnana-marga*, which is the path knowledge and the third is the *bhakti Marga* which is the path of devotion.

Milton observes that "the orthodox Brahmins traditionally committed to the path of ritual observance and knowledge are turning to the path of devotion, that they seem to be doing this as a result of moving to the city, and finally, that the paths themselves are acquiring some new content and form in an urban setting"[86] He further justifies this by stating thus: "This turning to devotional religion is, in part, a response to the anti-religious movements and trends, and, in part, represents a distinctive development of religious and popular culture in an urban environment."[87] In the cities, the educated tend to follow their own judgments rather than be dictated by the ethos of the Hindu *shastras*. This was another reason for the popularization of the *bhakti-marga*. The *karma-marga* and the *jnana-marga* were supposedly for those who wanted a better understanding of the subject. These were usually followed by the upper caste. It is an irony that urbanization which has led to knowledge explosion has lessened the number of devotees following this *marga*. Singer says:

> Traditionally the doctrine of *bhakti* taught that religious merit and even
> salvation could be acquired by those deficient in *sastric* learning, ritual

observance, and ascetic penances if they would but love the Lord and sing His name and praises in the presence of other devotees (called *bhagvatas*). This doctrine gave the movement a mildly anti-caste and anti-intellectual tone."[88]

Hence, it is surprising how the Brahmins also have taken to this *marga*. The *bhakti* or devotion takes the form of group singing which is held at one of the devotees' residence, from evening till late night. However, this kind of *bhakti* is observed either among the lower middle-class (the teachers, clerks etc.) or among the upwardly mobile new middle-class. We do not see this happening among the engineers, doctors, lawyers, judges, etc. Most of them do not seem to consciously follow any *Marga* and if they do, it is more of a private affair, more in terms of personal piety.

The Practice of Religion

Creating Auspiciousness

Minna Saavala speaks of the New Middle-class which has come into existence post liberalization of the 1990s. We have already discussed that many of the low caste, viz. shudras and the untouchables, could get themselves educated and improve their economic status. In addition, they wanted to move up the hierarchical order—a process called Sanskritization by Srinivas—and thus they begin to emulate the practices of the higher caste. Herein, they may have a *katha* or *pooja* at their homes to which many are invited. Many of them undergo pilgrimages to places like Sabrimala in Kerala. The aim of such religiosity is to create an auspicious ambience for the future. With their new economic status, they also want to move up socially. It seems that by invoking the deities of a higher caste, they try to fix their positions in the newly acquired class. These are the very people who believe in auspicious and inauspicious moments controlled by the planetary constellations and the divine order. Thus, they are very careful to do things at the auspicious moments so that things may go well with them. Such religious attitude is not to be found in the upper middle-class and the elite. The reason is obvious. The new middle-class want an acceptance into the social fold of the middle-class which their forefathers did not have. But this is not so for the elite. Minna Savaala says:

> The elite do not anchor their Hindu identification in a whole heartedly cosmological construction of Hindu practice but use a more eclectic and anthropocentric-and arguably more politicized-version of Hindu-ness for their purposes. In a way it could be correct to say that they share a more

postmodern view of Hindu religion than the new middle-classes which
are less blasé about the importance of religion.[89]

Asserting Individuality

The elite, on the other hand, may not go on pilgrimages or have *katha's*
in their homes but, as said above, their religion or religious attitude is
more geared towards asserting one's individuality rather than one's piety.
This can be observed from the way they keep their idols of their gods.
There are times when the *pooja* room was kept out of sight of anyone
entering that house. Only if the person was of a high or comparable caste
would the lady of the house take the guest to the *pooja* room. Under no
circumstances would a person of low status be allowed to even look at
the idols which would be considered inauspicious. But such strict vigils
are not observed anymore. A majority of the middle-class elite do not
mind keeping the idol of their gods in a very conspicuous place for
everyone to see. They may even keep it in their front porch or near the
front door, evident to all who enter. As a researcher, I have personally
observed both these situations firsthand in the society where I live. Thus,
religion takes on a form among the urban middle-class according to who
you are and what you want to make of it.

Religious Traditions: Continuity and Change

One last area that we need to consider is the form the religious traditions
take when they move from the rural to the urban. Again, this is related
to the urban middle-class for they are the ones who either reinterpret the
meanings of these traditions or give them new forms.

The traditions of Hinduism are expressed in folk, ritual, popular
devotional, classical forms and interestingly, all of them now have their
modern counterpart. Whereas the place and occasion of the folk plays
and songs were the Temples on festival days, the players and audience
were mostly non-Brahmins. For the ritualistic performances found in
villages too, the Brahmins were the sole perpetrators of the same. These
Vedic texts were used for these rituals and the themes were either Vedic
or Puranic.

The urban environment, however, brought in a number of changes
in such a situation. Whereas the duration of these performances was
much shorter in the cities, the performers and audience were from the

Brahmin and Non-Brahmin communities. Also, many of these traditions shifted from the village temples to theatres and halls in the cities. The caste restrictions also seem to have disappeared. Moreover, as Singer rightly points out, "The greatest transcendence of local folk and ritual forms is reached in the strictly modern urban forms-the social play, the social film, the short story and the novel."[90] These urban forms have, in fact, exploited the *puranic* themes extensively in these social media. The television has also played an important role in popularizing the *puranas* and epics but with an urban flavour which would appeal to the urban mind.

How does this change take place? Singer is very insightful when he says:

...each sphere in culture seems to be subject to opposing directions of change, one type of change tending to push a given cultural sphere in the direction of greater refinement and codification, the other in the direction of maximum popularity and practicality. At any given time, the outcome within a given cultural sphere is something of a compromise between the two extremes, a range of intergrading cultural forms.[91]

Thus, we can observe a shift from ritual observances and sacred learning to the field of popular culture and arts. The urban settings do have the ritualists and the sages who follow the paths of *karma* and *jnana*. But Singer says that they do not feel at home in the urban environment. The literati of old changed their professions as they underwent education and got involved in the role of intelligentsia in the urban situation.

It was expected that urban middle-class would have a more secular outlook to life and be more involved in the civic life of the society. Contrary to it, the middle-class still live a life of individualism fostered by their ideas of *mukti* taught by the Hindu *shastras*. Thus, the religious zeal of the middle-class seems to have increased, and yet the concern is more about one's own wellbeing. One's tendency to follow *bhakti marga* in the city is garnered by his/her desire for personal salvation. The society at large gains nothing from this religious attitude.

On the other hand, there is an increased interest in the traditional religious forms. We tend to see the educated families sending their children to learn the traditional Indian dance and musical forms. These forms are connected to Hindu rituals, but it seems that, in the urban setting, the emphasis is more on the form and less on the ritualistic aspect. This is not to say that the rituals have been eliminated, but rather the meaning has been lost to the urbanite. The media of cinema and plays have not only popularized these Hindu traditions, but also the stories from the Hindu scriptures.

Religion received a new lease of life through the guru movement. A good number of middle-class tend to attend religious discourses on a regular basis. It only remains to be seen how this has affected their attitude to ethics in moral and business dealings.

In general, we can thus conclude that urbanization has caused change in the three variables that we have considered, viz. caste, family and religion. Though the pace of change is slow as compared to the western countries, there can be no doubt that changes *are* taking place. Moreover, the middle-class has grown considerably in the post 1990 period, and the pace of change among the middle-class with respect to the variables has also accelerated. There is a clear prospect of major changes taking place in this class in near future.

Endnotes

[1] J. Ross Eshleman & Barbara G Cashion, *Sociology, An Introduction* (Boston: Little Brown and Company, 1983), 512.

[2] Eshleman & Barbara, *Sociology,* 512-513.

[3] David F. Pocock, "Sociologies: Urban and Rural," in M. S. A. Roa (ed), *Urban Sociology in India, Reader and Source Book,* (Delhi: Orient Longman Ltd, 1974), 20.

[4] M. S. A. Rao, "General Introduction," in Rao (ed), *Urban Sociology,* 2.

[5] Yogendra Singh, *Modernization of Indian Tradition* (Delhi: Thomson Press India Limited, 1972), 19.

[6] Steven Vago, *Social Change* 2nd edn (New Jersey: Prentice Hall, 1989), 41.

[7] Talcott Parson, A Functional theory of Change, in Amitai Etzioni and Eva Etzioni ed., *Social Change, Sources, Patterns and Consequences* (New York: Basic Books Inc. Publishers, 1964), 83-87.

[8] Singh, *Modernization,* 17.

[9] G. S. Ghurye, "Features of the Caste System" in Dipankar Gupta (ed), *Social Stratification* (Bombay: Oxford University Press, 1992), 37-48.

[10] G. S. Ghurye, Features of the Caste System in Dipankar Gupta (ed), *Social Stratification* (Delhi: Oxford University Press, 1992), 38.

[11] C. Bougle, The essence and reality of the caste system in Gupta ed. *Stratification,* 65.

[12] Ghurye, *Stratification,* 40.

[13] Ghurye, *Stratification*, 48.

[14] Frank F. Conlon, Urbanism and Indian Society: The aspect of Caste in Allen G. Noble, Ashok Dutt (eds), *Indian Urbanization and Planning, Vehicles of Modernization* (N. Delhi: Tata McGraw Hill Publishing Co. Ltd, 1977), 127.

[15] Pauline Kolenda, *Caste in Contemporary India* (Illinois: Waveland Press Inc., 1978), 141.

[16] Singh, *Modernization*, 96.

[17] Singh, *Modernization*, 86.

[18] Hemlata Acharya, "Changing Role of Religious Specialist', in M. S. A. Rao, (ed.), *Urban Sociology in India* (Delhi: Orient Longman, 1974), 391-402.

[19] Andre Beteille, "Caste in Contemporary India" in Andre Beteille (ed), *Caste Today* (New Delhi: Oxford University Press, 1996), 152-155.

[20] Herbert Risley, *The People of India* (New Delhi: Oriental Books, 1969), 233.

[21] V. S. Naipaul, *An area of Darkness* (London: Andre Deutsch, 1964) cited in Beteille, *Caste*, 172.

[22] Srinivas, *Caste*, 70.

[23] Srinivas, *Caste*, 88-96.

[24] B. V. Shah, "Gujarati College Students and Caste," [CD-ROM] *SB* 10 (1961), 48.

[25] Shah, "Gujarati," 57.

[26] Jayprakash M. Trivedi, *The Social Structure of Patidar Caste in India* (Delhi: Kanishka Publishing House, 1992), 175-189.

[27] Ross, *Hindu Family*, 270-71.

[28] K. M. Kapadia, "Changing Patterns of Hindu Marriage and Family," [CD-ROM] *SB* 3 (1954), 79.

[29] K. M. Kapadia, "Changing Patterns of Hindu Marriage and Family, II," [CD-ROM] *SB* 3 (1954), 136.

[30] Beteille, "Caste in Contemporary India," 165.

[31] Abha Sharma, "Opinion of Married Couples Regarding the Selection of Marriage Partner," [CD-ROM] *SB* (1979), 72.

[32] Sharma, "Opinion of Married Couples," 76.

[33] B. V. Shah, "Gujarati College Students and the Selection of Bride," [CD-ROM] *SB* 11 (1962), 137.

[34] Beteille, "Caste in Contemporary India," 166.

[35] Frank Conlon, Urbanism and Indian Society: The aspect of Caste, in Allen Noble, Ashok K. Dutt (eds), (N. Delhi: Tata McGraw-Hill Pub. Co. Ltd, 1977), 132.

[36] Srinivas, *Caste*, 74-75.

[37] Lloyd Rudolph, *The Modernity of Tradition*, cited in Singh, *Modernization*, 168.

[38] Singh, *Modernization*, 114.

[39] Singh, *Modernization,* 114.

[40] Singh, *Modernization,* 115.

[41] Singh, *Modernization,* 116.

[42] Aileen D. Ross, *The Hindu family in its Urban Setting* (Delhi: Oxford University Press, 1961), 9.

[43] J. P. Singh, "Nuclearisation of household and family in Urban India," [CD-ROM] *SB* 52 (2003), 56.

[44] Singh, "Nuclearisation," 57.

[45] Singh, "Nuclearisation," 57.

[46] Ross, *The Hindu family,* 30.

[47] A. A. Khatri, "Some neglected approaches and Problems in the study of family in India," [CD-ROM] *SB* 10 (1961), 75.

[48] K.M.Kapadia, *Marriage and Family in India* (Bombay: Oxford University Press, 1949), 264.

[49] Ross, *The Hindu family,* 31.

[50] Ross, *The Hindu family,* 14.

[51] B.R. Agarwala, "Symposium on Caste and Joint family: In a Mobile Commercial Community," [CD-ROM] *SB* 4 (1955) 143.

[52] A. K. Lal, *The Urban Family, A Study of Urban Social System* (New Delhi: Concept Pub. Co., 1990), 17.

[53] M. S. Gore, *Urbanisation and Family Change* (Bombay: Popular Prakashan, 1968), 228.

[54] Kaldate, "Urbanization and Disintegration of Rural Joint Family" [CD-ROM] *SB*11(1&2) 1962, 106.

[55] Oomen, Urban Family, 59-61.

[56] Edwin D. Driver, "Family Structure and the socio-economic status in Central India," [CD-ROM] *SB* (1961), 119.

[57] Kaldate, "Urbanization and Disintegration," 110.

[58] Ross, *The Hindu Family,* 33-177.

[59] Lal, *The Urban Family,* 37.

[60] Singh, "Nuclearisation," 69.

[61] K. M. Kapadia, "Changing patterns of Hindu Marriage and family," [CD-ROM] *SB* 4 (1955), 192.

[62] Kaldate, "Urbanization and Disintegration," 105.

[63] Earnest P. Mower, *The Family* (1932), 274-275 cited in Rajendra K. Sharma, *Urban Sociology* (N. Delhi: Atlantic Publishers and Distributors, 1997), 92-93.

[64] Oomen, Urban family, 69.

[65] Lal, *The Urban Family,* 61.

[66] Marion J. Levy Jr, *The Family Revolution in Modern China* (London: Oxford University Press, 1949), 175 cited in Ross, *Hindu Family*, 99.

[67] Oomen, Urban Family, 78.

[68] Oomen, Urban Family, 79.

[69] Ross, *Hindu Family*, 135.

[70] Lal, *The Urban Family*, 50-51.

[71] A. A. Khatri, "Social Change in the Caste Hindu family and its possible impact on Personality and Mental Health," [CD-ROM] *SB* 11 (1962), 151.

[72] Sanjay Joshi, "Fractured Modernity: Making of a Middle-class in Colonial North India," (New Delhi: Oxford University Press, 2001), cited by Minna Savaala, *Middle-class Moralities* (Delhi: Orient Blackswan Pvt. Ltd, 2010), 150.

[73] Minna Savaala, *Middle-class Moralities* (Delhi: Orient Blackswan Pvt. Ltd., 2010), 152.

[74] Savaala, *Middle-Class*, 154.

[75] Visvaldas Clive, "The ideal of Mukti: Philosophical change in the Contemporary Indian setting" in Allen G. Noble and Ashok K Dutt (eds), *Indian Urbanization and Planning, Vehicles of Modernization* (New Delhi: Tata McGraw-Hill Publishing Co. Ltd., 1977), 115.

[76] A Lakshamana Rao, "Does Indian Philosophy rest on a mistake?" Indian Philosophical Annual V (1969), 1970, 44 cited by Klive, Mukti, 118, in Noble and Dutt (eds), *Modernisation*.

[77] S. Radhakrishnan, *Recovery of faith* (Delhi: Hind Pocket books, 1967), 42 cited by Klive, Mukti, 118, in Noble and Dutt (eds), *Modernisation*.

[78] S. S. Raghavachar, "The concept of liberation," *Indian Philosophical Annual* V 1969, 30, cited by Klive, Mukti, 119, in Noble and Dutt (eds), *Modernisation*.

[79] S. Gopalan, "Concept of Moksha: its Significance for Hindu ethics" *Indian Philosophical Annual* V 1970-71, 161 cited by Klive, Mukti, 119, in Noble and Dutt (eds), *Modernisation*.

[80] *Kalyana Kalpataru*, September 1972, 280 cited by Klive, Mukti, 120, in Noble and Dutt (eds), *Modernisation*.

[81] Edwin Masihi, *Social engagements of Intellectuals in Civil Society with special reference to professionals in Gujarat* (Ahmedabad: AWAG, 2006), 57-86.

[82] Pavan K. Varma, *The Great Indian Middle-class* (N. Delhi: Viking, 1998), 124.

[83] Varma, *Middle-class*, 125.

[84] Varma, *Middle-class*, 127.

[85] Savaala, *Middle-Class*, 155.

[86] Milton Singer, "The Great Tradition in a Metropolitan Centre, Madras" in M. S. A. Rao (ed), *Urban Sociology in India* (New Delhi: Orient Longman, 1974), 369.

[87] Singer, "The Great Tradition…" 370.

[88] Singer, "The Great Tradition..." 371.

[89] Savaala, *Middle-class,* 172.

[90] Singer, "The Great Tradition..." 376.

[91] Singer, "The Great Tradition..." 376.

Chapter 5

Field Survey:
Findings and Analysis

This chapter presents the month-long field survey undertaken in Jan 2014 using snowball sampling methodology and analyses the findings in light of the hypothesis made initially. Although I had personally conducted the study, many of my church members and their acquaintances rendered much help in completing the study.

People who were involved in data collection were from different walks of life—teachers, bankers, managers of private firms, etc. They were given preliminary instructions on the procedures of the study, and the survey forms got circulated among a wide variety of people as they distributed some directly, and others through their friends, colleagues and acquaintances, and so on. So the sample was randomly selected through snowballing (also known as chain-referral methodology).

Pilot survey indicated that doing the survey in English language may pose a barrier for many. Hence, the survey form was translated into Gujarati. Over 150 survey forms were distributed. Out of these, as many as 125 responded, and 111 of them were valid and so were chosen for study and analysis. All the parameters have been noted and analyzed for these 111 respondents. For some crucial parameters I have done cross tabulation in order to gain a better understanding of the results.

The second part of the survey was undertaken to know the response of some of the middle-class Hindu converts. A few respondents were informally interviewed. Efforts were made to find out the reasons for their conversion and compare them with the responses of our Hindu friends who have filled up the survey form.

Basic Information of the Respondents

The first part of the survey was the basic information about the respondents. This consists of the age distribution, male-female ratio, the mother tongue, education levels, caste distribution and the area of residence of the respondents.

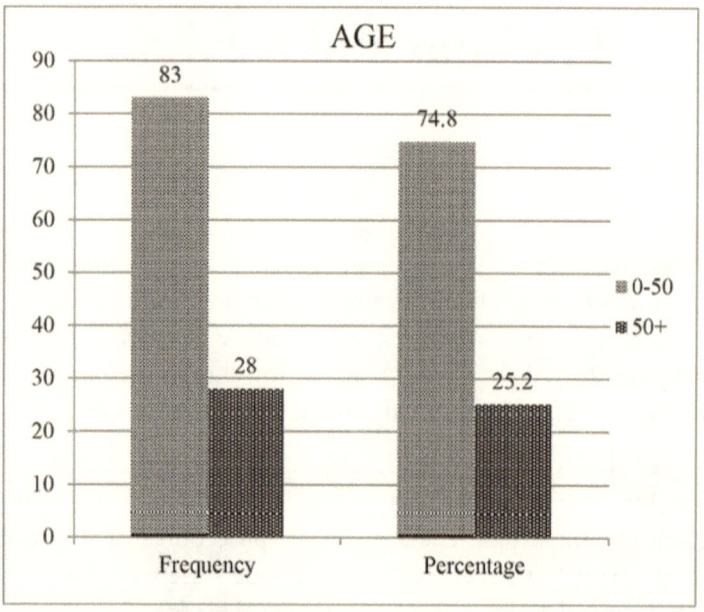

Figure 19

The age of the respondents varied from 22 years to 92 years. More than 70% fell in the age bracket of 30-50, and those at the extreme ends of the age group were just a few. Respondents above the age of 50 were only 25.2% and even here most of them were in the bracket of 50 to 70. Thus, the age bracket can be said to be predominantly below 50 years and a smaller group above 50. Though the survey has been done through the method of snowballing, I feel we have got the right age group which would give a good mix of different perspectives.

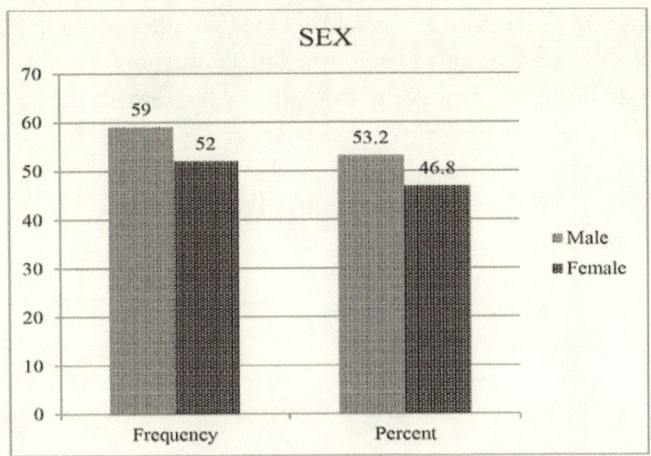

Figure-20

The male-female percentage almost divides in half. This along with age was not deliberately chosen, but when the ratio of male to female is close to 1, we can expect a good balance in the responses as well. I say this because it is usually assumed that the effect of urbanization with reference to the parameters being analyzed, viz caste, family and religion are different on males and females. Though, it is generally agreed that there are other factors like education, or family background etc which come into play, one will have to agree that males and females do have their own peculiar way of interacting and reacting to the environment.

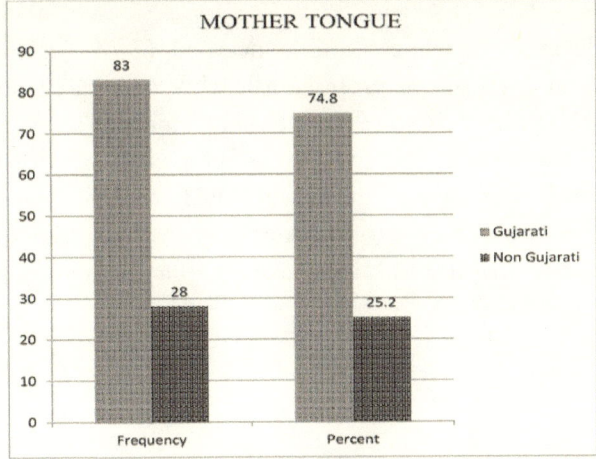

Figure-21

The number of Guajaratis is three times that of the non-Gujaratis. This ratio does, to some extent, indicate the actual situation. Though this has no deliberate designs, I wonder if the ratio would remain the same when we take only the educated into consideration.

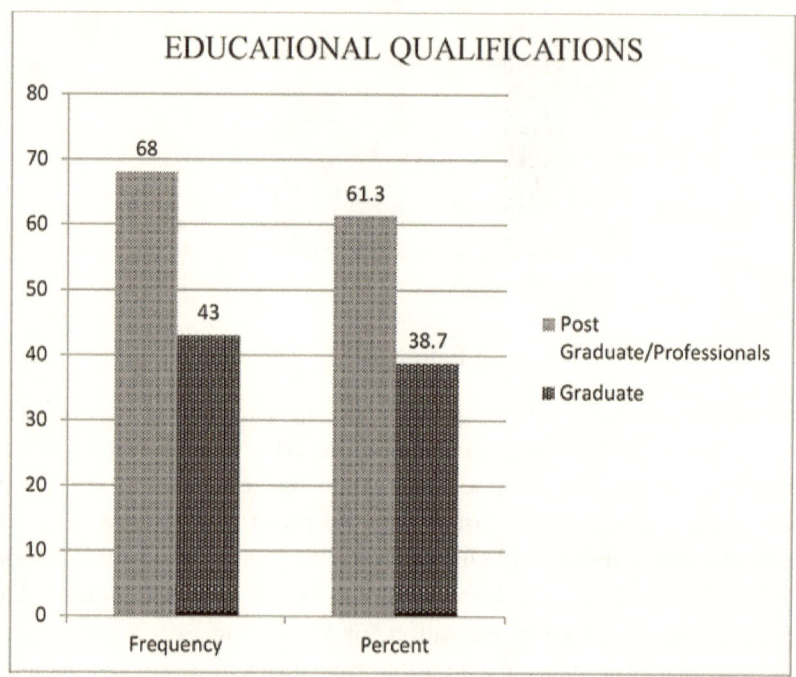

Figure-22

As far as educational qualification is concerned, 68 of the respondents were either post graduates or professionals while 43 were graduates. The professionals in this survey were very few and hence the researcher hasn't taken them as a separate group but has merged them with the post-graduates. The percentages of these were 61.3% and 38.7% respectively. It is generally thought that education does have an effect on one's thought pattern. Hence if urbanization does have an effect on people, the group that has been contacted is the right one.

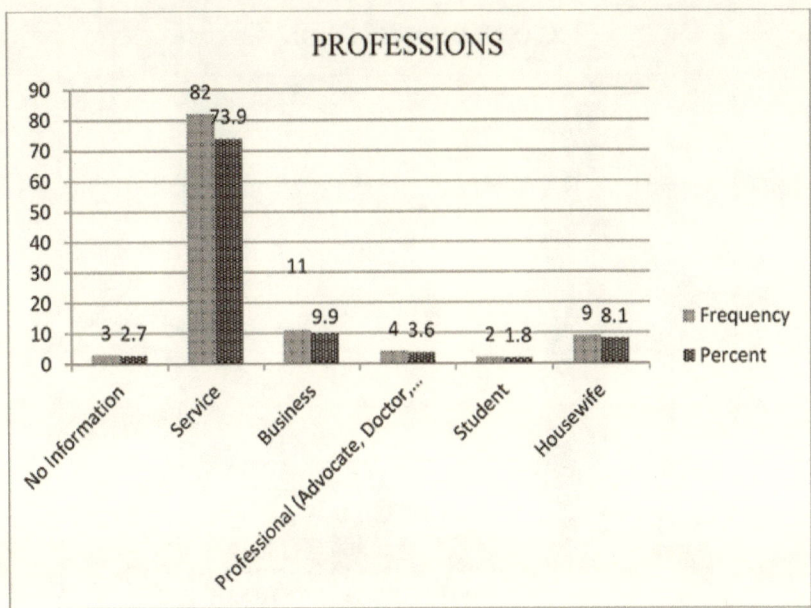

Figure-23

The majority of the respondents were employed either in Government or private sector, besides some who have retired. I've attempted to differentiate between those in service and the professionals. The professionals are those who have got a professional degree and are in that particular profession, for instance, an engineer, a doctor, or a lawyer, a professor etc. They constituted a small percentage, but along with the business people they constituted a good 13.5%. Housewives are in a moderate measure occupying about 8.1% of the total number. Thus, though the response can be taken to be predominantly from the service sector, one needs to keep in mind that the professionals along with the business people are not miniscule, though not substantial. The housewives probably play a balancing role in this analysis because their response may be different from those in service and the business and professional class as their interaction with their surroundings are different.

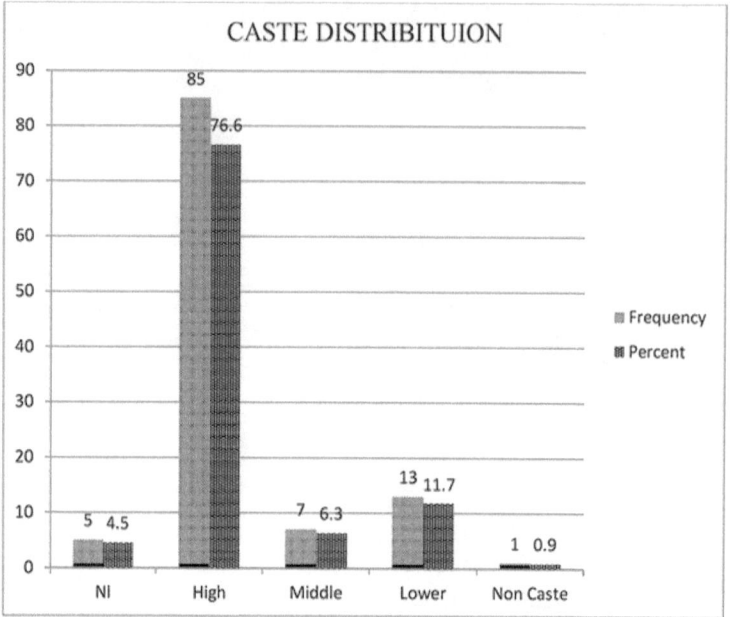

Figure-24

The majority of the respondents are from the higher caste which includes Brahmins, Banias, Patels etc. So, with the high caste being in such a predominant number in this survey, one may tend to conclude that the response is basically from this category. Thus, one may conveniently say the middle-class mainly consists of the people of the higher castes. Though the middle caste is only 6.3%, the lower caste is a good 11.7%. Probably, this latter group would like the housewives in the previous category play a balancing act in this survey because, as various authors have said, the response of the lower caste in the urban situation is quite different from the others. However, the graph below also shows that it is the high caste that is predominantly moving into the middle-class.

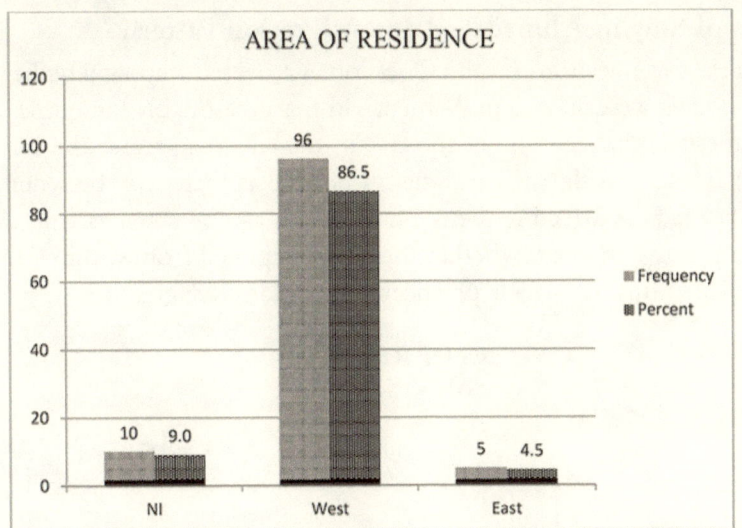

Figure-25

While a few of the respondents have not indicated their area of residence, the majority (86.5%) come from the western part of Ahmedabad. This is deliberate. Central Ahmedabad is the original walled city built by Ahmed Shah as discussed in chapter II. With the British establishing the textile industry in the mid-19th century, the eastern part of the city was used to accommodate the migrant workers of this industry. The development on the western part of the city (across the river Sabarmati) was rather slow. Though it housed the Gujarat University and institutions like Indian Institute of Management and Physical Research Laboratory, this area developed as a major residential and commercial centre only in the last 30 years or so. Today, people have shifted from the central Ahmedabad to the western side. The educated migrants also reside in this part of the city. One should note that most of the western side of Ahmedabad is a suburb. But looking at the kind of people there, one can safely assume that the effect of urbanization may be the highest in this part of the city.

The forgone discussion has been enabled by the basic personal information provided by the respondents.

Years of Stay in Ahmedabad and Migration Pattern

The first two questions of the Questionnaire were to know whether the respondents were staying in Ahmedabad for a reasonably long time. The hypothesis is that the longer the stay in the city, the greater the impact. I understand that this may not always be true as there may be a number of other factors affecting them, but largely it can be taken as true. Also, it is imperative to know whether they have migrated from within Gujarat or outside Gujarat as their perspectives would differ greatly.

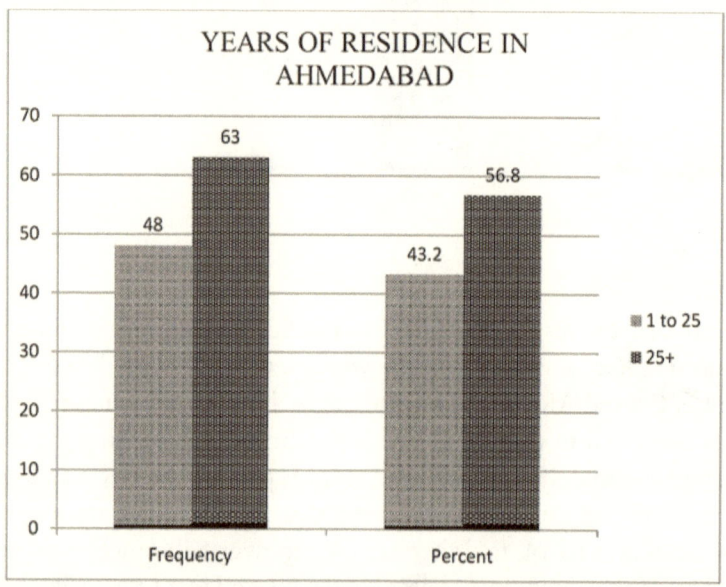

Figure-26

The duration of the respondents' life in the city varied from a few years to 30 to 50 years. As seen from the graph, 56.8% have been in the city for more than 25 years. Even from the 43.2%, who have been in Ahmedabad for less than 25 years, a good number have crossed 15 years. Considering the long stay people have had in the city, it can be assumed that the longer one stays in the city, the better chances one has to enter the middle-class. Thus, we can safely say that the majority of the respondents had a good interaction with the city and the city would have had its effect on them.

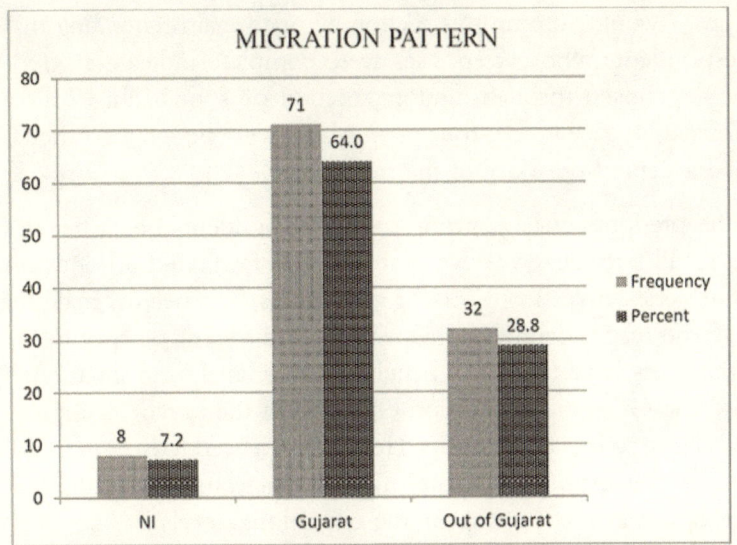

Figure-27

This migration chart does not say anything about the people who were in Ahmedabad from their birth for there were a few that would fall in this category. This number has been merged with those who have migrated from within Gujarat. The majority have migrated either from within Gujarat or from outside. The migration from within the State is nearly double that of those coming from outside the State and this may present the actual situation also. This pattern of migration is very different from that in cities like Bangalore and Bombay. Bangalore has only 38% of Kannadigas while Bombay has approximately the same number of Maharashtrians. This shows that though the cities of Gujarat do attract migration from inside the state, those coming from outside is not as high as other similar cities. It could be because the IT industry has not entered Gujarat in a big way though the industrial giants have come here. In fact, TATAs were probably the first giants to come to Ahmedabad with their Nano plant after being rejected by the Government of Bengal. This itself has brought in a good number of automotive professionals in the city. It was also noticed that those who migrated from within Gujarat came either from the rural areas or from small towns. But those coming from outside usually have migrated from cities. The migration from rural or the semi-urban to this city would certainly result in a major shift in the environment and change in the values, living style etc.

Thus, I would sum up this section by once again reiterating that the 111 respondents whose responses were complete indicate a good mix of people, chosen through random method of snowballing. I also had an informal interview with four people who were people of other faiths and had accepted the Lord in the recent past.

The predominant age group of the respondents being below fifty, with a small percentage above that age, has facilitated a good mix of different perspectives from varying age groups. The healthy male-female ratio of the respondents also helped us get different perspectives since both the sexes have their own peculiar way of analyzing situations. The ratio of the Gujaratis to the non-Gujaratis in the survey is approx. 3:1 which is close to the actual reality. However, we need to bear in mind that the census which puts the figure of migrants from outside the State at 22% does not give a breakup of the educational levels of the migrants. Hence it would be difficult to say precisely how close the ratio depicted for this category comes to the reality among the educated. Nevertheless, I feel we did get a good perspective from both these angles. All the respondents were graduates or post-graduates. I have divided this group into these two categories only to give us an idea of the educational levels of the respondents.

Further, it may be affirmed that, as we are looking at the effect of urbanization of the educated Hindus, the group that has emerged is certainly the right one. The caste distribution shows that the group is predominantly from the high caste which may be an indication that it is this group that is moving into the middle-class. The majority of the respondents were from the western part of the city which is a recently developed area and which resides mainly the educated crowd. It can safely be assumed that these are the people who have been affected the most by urbanization. Most of the respondents were residing in the city for over 15 years, with many crossing even 25 years. This would mean that they were very part of the culture of this great city. Finally, it is observed that the migration to this city is pretty high with the majority being intra-state migrants, though the inter-state migration is not a very small number either. Of course, most of the intra-state migrants came from rural or small towns. Urbanization would have a great impact on such migrants.

Measuring Caste Perceptions in the Urban Contexts

The next 12 questions deal with the changes in caste perception in the urban context.

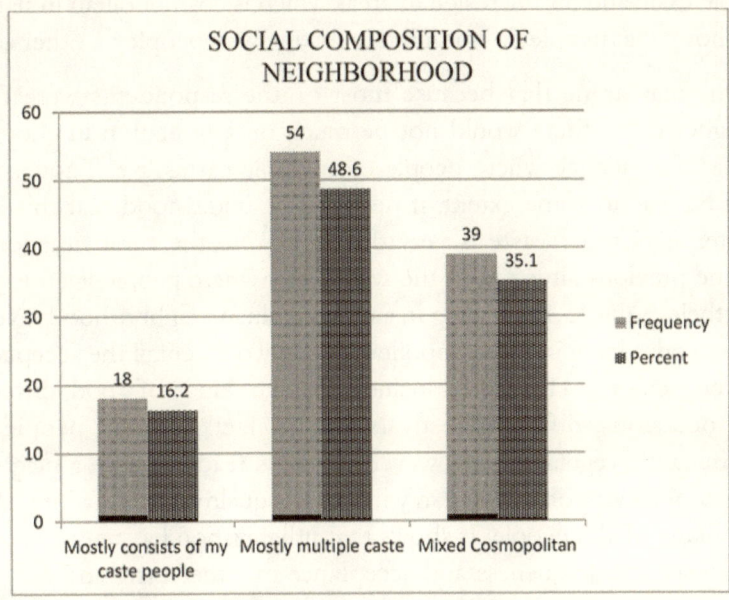

Figure-28

The first of these questions aims at identifying the kind of areas where the respondents reside. The composition of the neighborhood will usually give a fairly good idea of how one perceives people of other castes. This will not always be true if one is not free to choose one's area of residence. I do not think it was the case here because these are all developing areas and the respondents would have deliberately chosen their residence. The researcher would like to clarify that the options 'my caste people' or 'mostly multiple caste' meant Gujarati people only while 'cosmopolitan' would include people from outside Gujarat also.

We are aware that, in rural areas, people preferred to reside among those of equal caste status. This, in fact, was translated to the urban situation in old Ahmedabad (the walled city). The old city consisted of closed communities in vast numbers, and their places of residence are called *Pols*. Each *Pol* was a self-sufficient unit of people of the same caste. Thus, there were 'Desai ni *Pol*', or 'Jain ni *Pol*', etc. Even when societies came up in the western side of the city in the initial stages, they were of a particular caste or developed as caste-based societies. In comparison, the above graph shows that 48.6% reside in neighborhoods consisting of multiple caste and 35.1% reside in areas which is cosmopolitan in nature. This shows that people do not mind in mixing with people of other caste.

One may argue that because most of the respondents were from the higher caste, there would not be much of a hesitation in choosing an area of residence where people of multiple castes live. Though this would be true to some extent, it needs to be understood that this kind of heterogeneity of caste is very different from the rural situation or even the previous situation in the walled city where people lived in *pols*. Nevertheless, the 35.1% staying in a cosmopolitan neighborhood reveal a recent trend. Living in a cosmopolitan set up would entail the acceptance of diverse culture. This would include different kinds of food, different social occasions, different festivals, etc. In fact, Gujarati people are predominantly vegetarians. However, if one is ready to have a neighbor who is probably a non-vegetarian without any qualms, it is a major shift in the thinking of the people. It shows that urbanization has opened up the mind to see the uniqueness and acceptance of other caste and cultures.

q-4 interactions you have with your neighbors of other castes				
Rank	1	2	3	Total
Frequent exchange of food	43	1	2	46
Visiting on social occasions	78	8	1	87
Taking part in religious functions	46	6	2	54
Exchange Pleasantries	28	1	2	31
No interaction	2	-	-	2

Figure-29

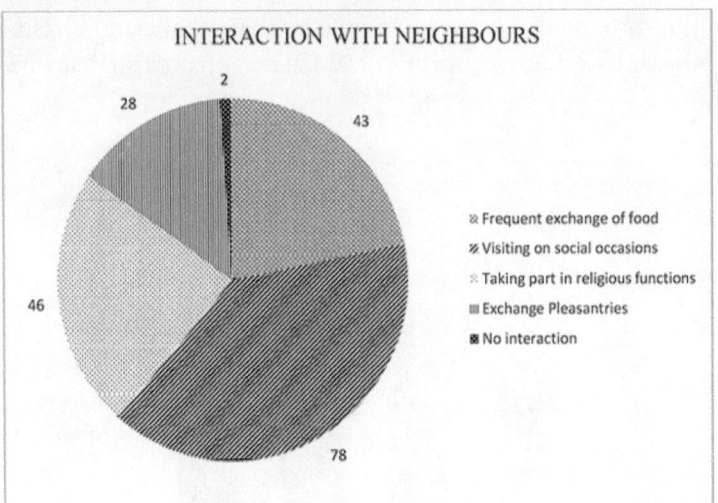

INTERACTION WITH NEIGHBOURS

- Frequent exchange of food
- Visiting on social occasions
- Taking part in religious functions
- Exchange Pleasantries
- No interaction

Figure-30

The respondents were asked to rank their interaction with their neighbors. As many as 78 ranked the category of "visiting on social occasions" as No.1. This shows that visiting on social occasions is the norm of an urban society. This, I think would include visiting on festivals, participating in social functions like marriages, birthday parties, and so on.

In comparison, only 43 ranked "exchange of food" as No. 1. How would we interpret this ranking? If people are ready to visit others on social occasions and yet not have that relationship of exchange of food, it probably shows a relationship which is not very personal. This is one of the negatives of urbanization. It makes people too individualistic. People tend to want to live in their own cocoon, not wanting to share their lives to others.

Further, it is interesting that 46 have ranked visiting on religious occasions as No. 1. Do these people visit their own caste people on religious occasions, or are they involved in visiting people of other caste also? This is difficult to say though is a good possibility that they do visit people of other caste also. This possibility cannot be ruled out because as seen in another response, the social circle is mainly of persons of other caste. And there is a fairly good engagement between them at various levels. But the overall assessment would be that urbanization has broken down at least to some extent the social barriers that existed at one time.

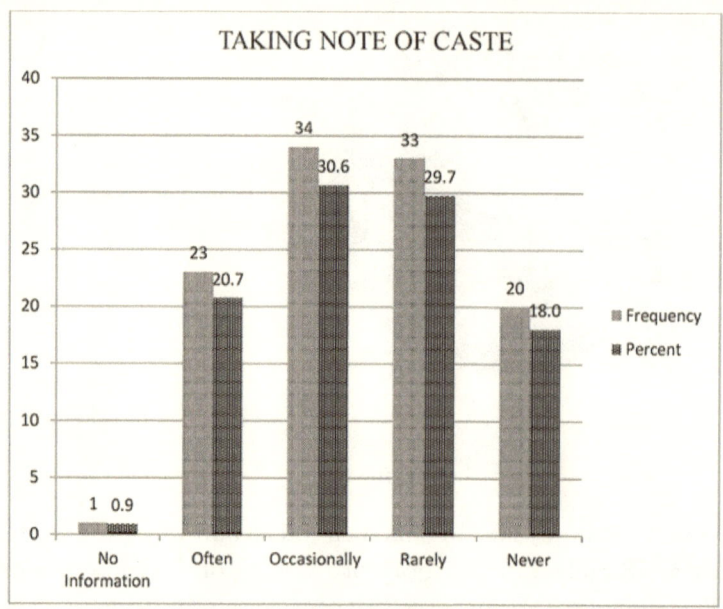

Figure-31

One of the important questions was whether they took note of the caste of the people they came across in their daily walk of life. It is interesting to note that 53 respondents representing about 48% of the total respondents said that they rarely or never took note of the caste of people. This would mean that at least in their daily life in the office or neighborhood or among their friends, there are a good number of people who are not concerned about the caste of the people they are dealing with. This would mean that in business dealings, employment of white and blue-collar workers etc, people do not consider caste as a criterion for relationships. In fact, this group of people has broken most of the caste barriers except for probably marriage alliances. This would also mean that these people have no inhibitions of sharing their lives with other people. These are the people who are usually open to new ideas. This certainly is one of the effects of urbanization. But it should also be noted that about 51% together either take note of caste often or occasionally. Those who 'often' take note of caste are 20.7% of the 51%. These probably are the ones who still are very conscious of their caste. Their caste consciousness being so high, probably all their interaction at any level would be controlled by caste. The 30.6% who say that they 'occasionally' take note of caste are probably indicating that they take note of caste in some special situations or occasions, but not much concerned about it in their everyday life. This shows that they have opened themselves to others to a limited extent but are still caste conscious when it comes to personal occasions.

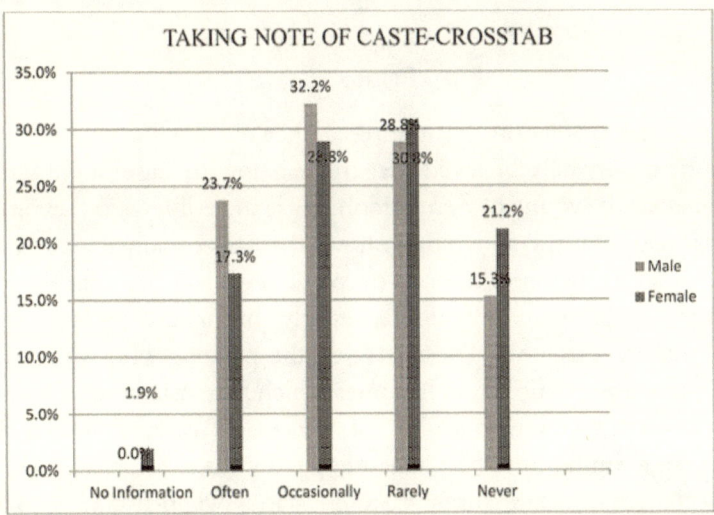

Figure-32

The researcher also did a cross tabulation on this data to see whether it is the male or the female who take note of the caste more often. It is usually thought that the females are more caste conscious. But it came as a surprise that it is the male who seems to be more caste conscious, taking note of caste more often than the female. The females lead in the "rarely" or "never" category of taking note of caste. Does this mean that the middle-class educated females have been able to imbibe secular values to a greater extent than the males in the urban context? It does seem so.

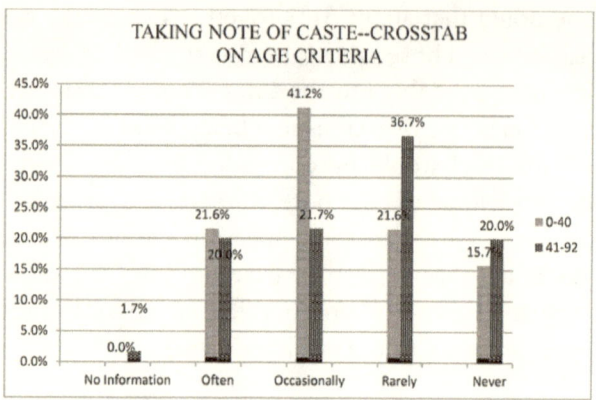

Figure-33

Another cross tabulation that the researcher did was keeping age as the criteria. It is generally believed that those below the age of 40 who are considered as the young by demographers are more liberal in their attitude towards caste. But the above data shows that it is equally divided among those who very often take note of caste. This -shows that there is a certain group of people distributed evenly throughout the society who are very caste conscious. These may be the persons who have a rather strong orthodox culture at their homes which is translated in their public stance. It is the young who lead in the 'occasional' category which shows that even a good number of young people do not consider caste in their normal dealings but are surely caste conscious when it comes to some special occasions, religious functions at home etc.

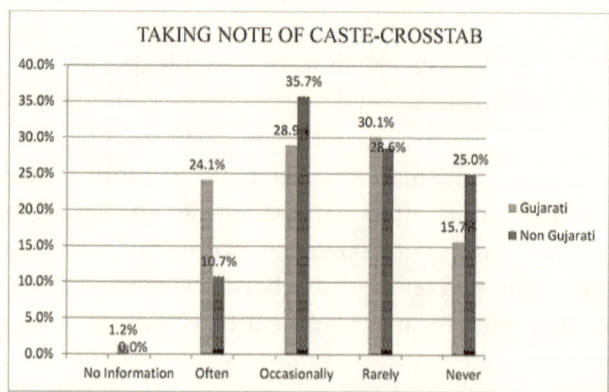

Figure-34

One more cross tabulation that the researcher did was taking the mother tongue into consideration. Those speaking Gujarati may have been residents of Ahmedabad or migrated from within Gujarat, but those whose mother tongue is not Gujarati are certainly those who migrated from outside Gujarat. Here it follows a predictable pattern. The Gujarati residents are certainly more caste conscious than the non-Gujarati when it comes to those who take note of caste very often. This may be because the non-Gujarati in trying to adjust with the new environment have no choice but to except people of all castes. One of the respondents clearly stated during my informal interviews that their neighbors were a mix of different castes and religions. The mother of the respondent was very orthodox but in the given situation, she let go of all caste restrictions to be socially accepted by their neighbors. It was not only their house which was open to people of all religions and castes but even the kitchen was open to all. Usually the high castes are very conscious of who enters their kitchen, but not so in this case. This shows how urbanization breaks down caste and religious barriers, especially among the educated. Though in the other categories, it seems to be equally divided showing that irrespective of your mother tongue, there a good number of people who do not give importance to caste at all. This is probably a good effect of urbanization.

This, however, does not mean that the Gujaratis cannot be reached. Three of the respondents to my informal interviews came from high caste orthodox families, and yet none of them was caste conscious.

The next question was to gauge how the social position/status of a person is determined in the present day urban India. This was an opinion given by the respondents.

Basis of the social position/ status of a person determined in the present day urban India						
Rank	1	2	3	4	5	Total
On the basis of Caste	10	-	2	1	-	13
On the basis of economic status	37	8	4	-	-	49
On the basis of education	85	4	1	-	-	90
On the basis of religion	11	1	2	-	2	16
On the basis of the job of the person	39	10	4	1		54
Having human values	3	-	-	-	-	

Figure-35

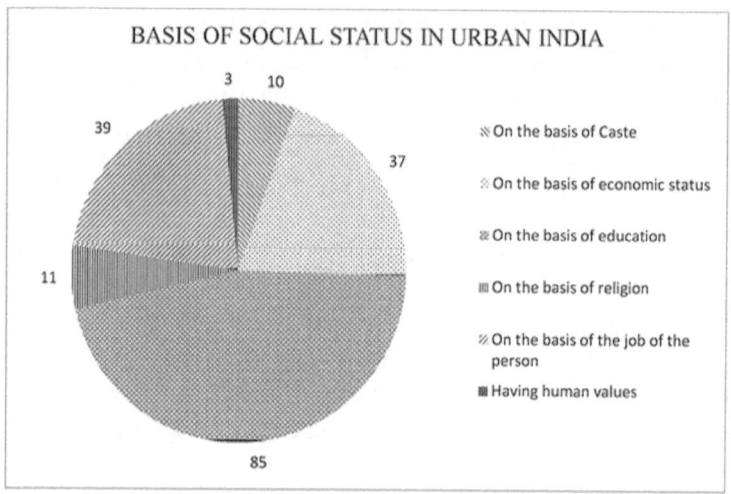

Figure 36

The respondents were asked to rank the options if they had more than one answer, and the results are given in the chart. The pie chart gives only the No.1 ranking. Here, 85 persons said that education is the basis of the status of a person in urban India. This is probably the reason why the upper castes who are caste and class-conscious give so much importance to education. Along with formal education, the middle-class are now also getting involved in arts like music and painting which was formerly the domain of the upper class. There is also marked interest in personality development, sports etc. which the Gujarati business class have exploited to such a great extent that it is a multimillion market today. Job and economic status come next in the order of importance to gauge the status of the person. The job of a person and his/her economic status is usually connected, though not always. Hence, education along with the kind of job you hold and the money power that you command are all intricately linked and that determines the status of the person. These three cannot be strictly taken together at all times, because at times only two may play a role as in the case of academicians or social workers etc. But usually all these three go together. It is interesting to note that caste or religion does not play much of a part as far as the status of a person is concerned. This probably shows that in our public life, we seem to be going towards secularism and materialism which is what the Western society is today. This needs to be taken with a pinch of salt. One of the respondents to my informal interview, a medical doctor by profession, stated that many of the doctors and medical professors from the low caste category are still looked down upon by their peers. They are not considered by many as their equals. This may not be true in all cases but it only brings to light that education does not always help override caste feelings.

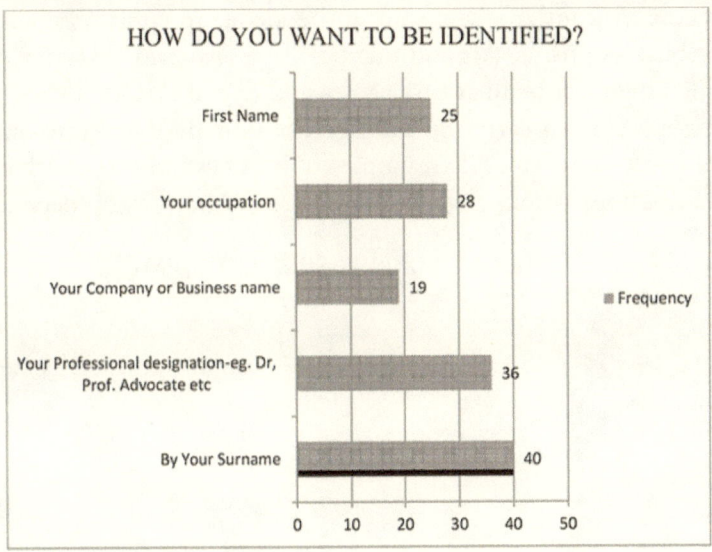

Figure-37

How a person wants to be identified shows what he/she gives importance to. Here the respondents were asked to identify only one, but many of them ticked two or at times three options. I have taken for my analysis all the options that they ticked and hence they will not add to the number of the respondents. When a respondent ticks more than one option in this category, it shows that he/she feels the need to be identified in more than one way. Eg. A person may tick the following options: a) By Surname b) Occupation c) Professional Designation. This would probably indicate that by his surname, he wants the people to know his caste. Eg. Patel or Dixit or Purohit or Shah would indicate a high caste. But he is not satisfied with that and also wants to be identified by the work that he does and his professional designation which probably shows the class that he belongs to. Thus, many a times the identity of a person is linked to the complex interaction of caste and class.

It is to be noted that 40 people have shown their desire to be identified by their surname. This amounts to about 36% of the respondents. This shows that there is a sizable number among the educated urban middle-class who still are caste conscious if the surname does indicate caste. We need to keep in mind that the desire to be known by the surname is not always an indication of caste consciousness but I believe it usually is. However, a majority of them want to be identified either through their jobs or business firms. A good number have also said that they prefer to be identified just by their first names and that also is a good sign that some people do not carry the baggage not only of their caste but also of their professions etc. The response to this question very much agrees with that of the last one that the status is education or job dependent.

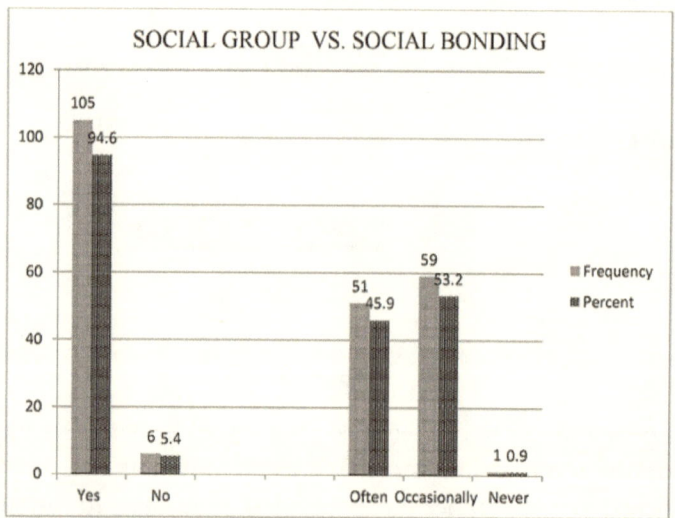

Figure-38

The researcher tried to find out whether people had a social circle outside their caste and if so, whether their bonding was superficial or much deeper. *Fig. 38* is a comparison of these two aspects. The first of these questions was *whether their social group consisted of people other than their own caste members* to which 94.6% have answered in the positive (as shown in the above graph under the heading 'social group'). This indicates that people tend to bond together irrespective of caste. Though it was not clarified who these people were, it can be safely assumed that they would be from their place of work or from their neighborhood or at times be even childhood friends. To that extent, the hold of caste is not so strong in the cities.

However, social bonding (as inquired by the question of *how often they include their social group in their social functions*, shown by the same graph) is strong among 45.9% who call their acquaintances for their social functions often. More than 53.2% only call them occasionally. This may mean that this latter group probably do not include their acquaintances in family functions like birthdays, anniversaries etc, but would call them for a marriage in the family etc. Nevertheless, the overall picture we get from the analysis of these two questions is that there seems to be a homogeneity that is forming at a social level in the cities.

The researcher did some crosstab on this question of social bonding. The question was: how often did they invite people of other caste to their social function? Herein are some of the results of the crosstab. The first crosstab was to gauge how male and female responded to this question and it is as seen in the graph below.

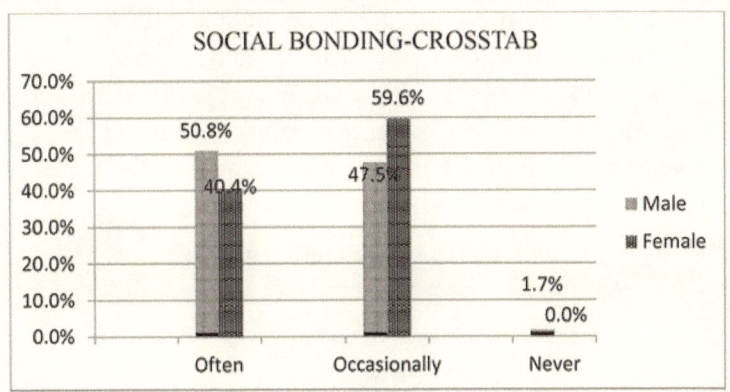

Figure-39

In terms of social bonding which includes inviting people of other caste to your homes and including them in your social functions, it can be seen from the cross tabulation keeping the male and female as the criteria that men seem to be marginally more open than woman in this regard. But as the difference is not very high, it can also be assumed that as educated men and women of the middle-class mingle with people of other caste and religion in their work places, the importance of caste usually wanes.

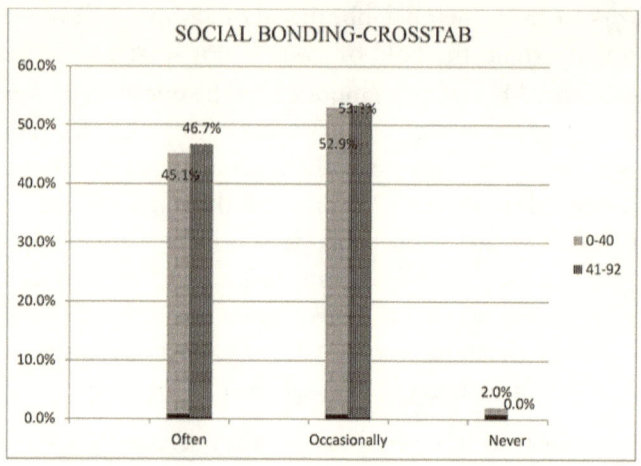

Figure-40

What was found with reference to males and females was also confirmed when considering the age criteria. The above graph shows that the social bonding occurs in all categories of people irrespective of age. This probably is an indication that social bonding among the educated middle-class is subject more to the environment that you are subject to rather than your age. It may happen that people in the higher age group may be resistant to change, but the circumstances in the urban set up forces a person to change.

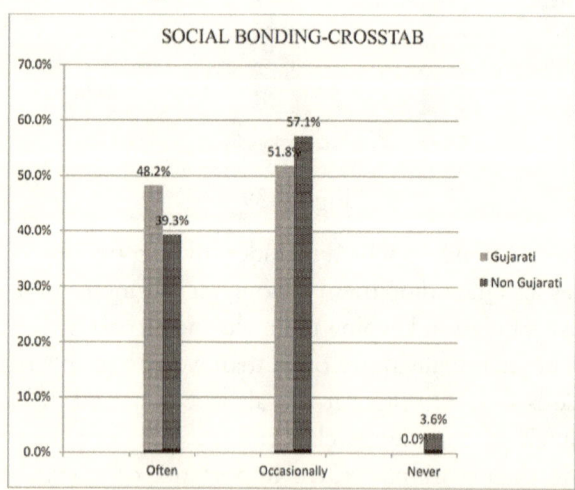

Figure 41

When we do a cross tabulation keeping the mother tongue as the criterion we see that the Guajarati's bond more often with people of other castes than non-Gujaratis. But occasionally, it is the non-Gujaratis who have a higher bonding percentage. Does this show that the Gujaratis have become more open to other castes? Probably, it may have to do with the soft and peace-loving nature of the Gujaratis. On the other hand, the non-Gujarati is open occasionally, which may be more of compulsion rather than as a voluntary act.

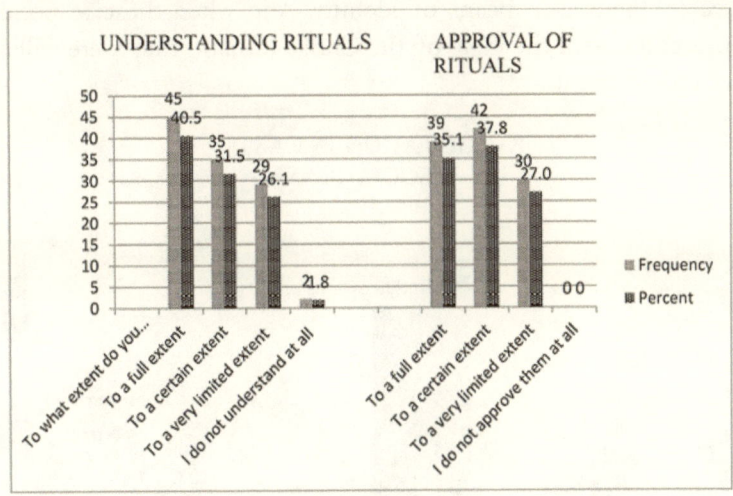

Figure-42

The Researcher tried to gauge how much the respondents understood what caste was all about. The most important aspect of caste is the rituals which are performed at various occasions like birth, marriage, pregnancy, death etc. The Researcher asked the Respondents whether they understood what these rituals stood for and whether they approved of them. There is a general notion that people in the cities because of their rational thinking and approach do not see much meaning in the rituals and thereby do not approve of them. But this survey shows that to be partially true. Where 40.5% said that they understood rituals to the fullest extent, 31.5% said that they understood them to certain extent. This means that 72% understood what rituals in their own caste meant at least to a certain extent. It is therefore not surprising that nearly 72.9% approve of the rituals fully or to a certain extent. The Researcher feels that this needs to be investigated further. Though approving the rituals is a very subjective matter, the understanding of it is objective and it needs to be investigated further how much they understand the rituals. One needs to investigate whether the understanding of rituals has changed over a period of time. Nevertheless, for the purpose of this research, we need to take the response that urbanization which leads to rationalization among the educated has not loosened the hold of caste and its rituals on the middle-class. However, by contrast, the respondents of my informal interviews categorically stated that they never understood rituals though they did approve of them as a means of identity. And when these respondents were presented with the logic of the Christian faith, they were willing to let go of their rituals.

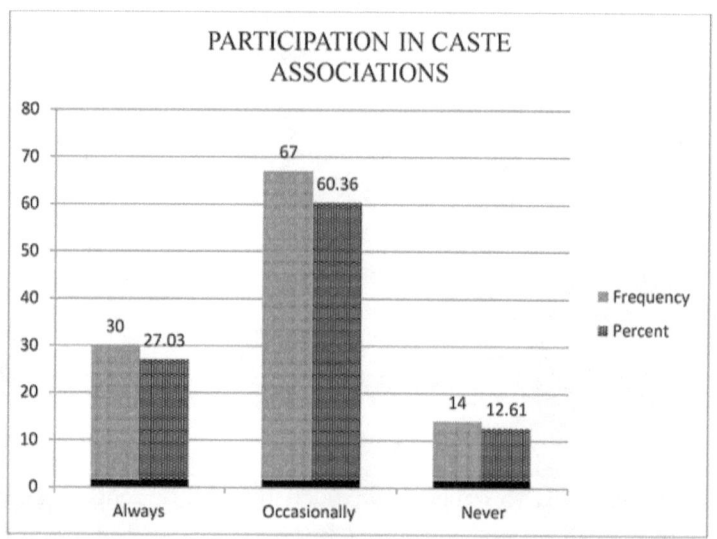

Figure-43

Though only 27.03% said that they always attended their caste associations, an overwhelming 60.36% said that they attended occasionally. Though the majority attended only occasionally, they did have a link with their caste associations which shows that they approved of them. A small minority of 12.61% did say that they never go to their caste meetings and thus can be deduced that they do not really approve of caste.

The caste associations are involved in a number of things. Apart from keeping the caste distinctions alive through various programs, they are involved in upliftment of the caste members through various social measures and most important is their political involvement. The caste associations become a means of gaining political mileage. Looking at the class of people involved, their association may be first and foremost for political reasons, but looking at the response on rituals, one cannot rule out the second reason that they want to keep their caste distinction alive.

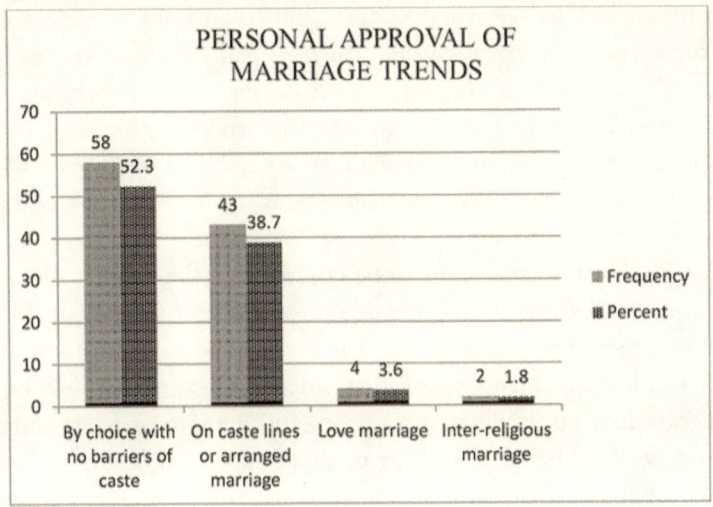

Figure-44

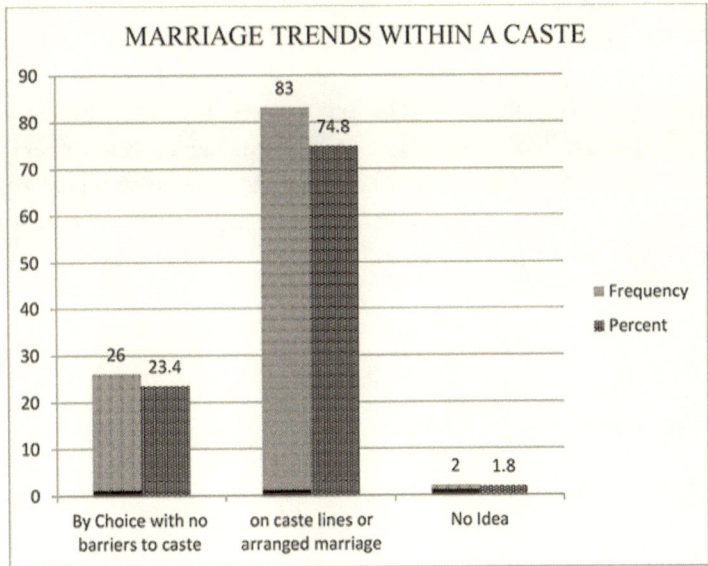

Figure-45

The last two questions in this section on caste were on marriage because caste plays a major role in marriages. Evidently, marriages in India were caste-based. We have already discussed in Chapter IV on the kinds of marriages that were approved and the rules and regulations thereof. Here, my attempt was to see whether caste still has a hold on marriages. The first question, here, was regarding the personal choice of marriage. Here about 52.3% said that they approved of marriages by choice without barriers to caste. When it came to marriage trends within their own caste group, this came down by nearly half. It was reduced to 23.4% while those on caste lines or arranged marriages went up to 74.8%. A comparison of both these trends is quite revealing. What does this show? Personally, the respondents do not want to be confined to their caste; they want to move out and explore things outside the confines of the caste. However, the pressure of the society keeps them confined to their caste.

It is a known phenomenon that when these very people who are so caste conscious go to Western countries, they tend to open up and explore the new world. They are not only ready to explore different relationships outside their caste, but also are open to new ideas of religion and faith. This shows that caste does play a major role in marriage. Yet, I would say that the hold is not so very strong since, if need be, people may marry outside their caste without much inhibitions. How much this would hold for marriage alliance with a low caste person is a matter of debate, and I do not intend to take it up here.

The study also involved some crosstab to see how different categories of people approved of marriage at a personal level. Such crosstab is essential because it is generally agreed that the one place where caste is so strong is in the area of marriage. The first was to see how males and females responded to this question.

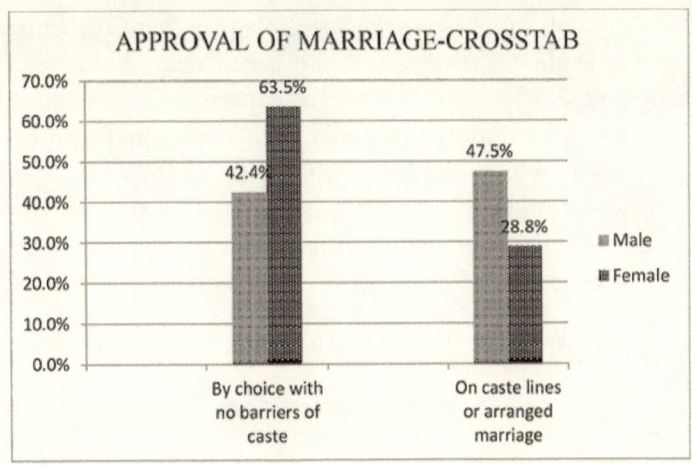

Figure-46

This cross tabulation comes as a surprise. The long-held idea that women are conservative with respect to marriage does not seem to be true. Very clearly, women want freedom when it comes to marriage. She probably looks for important needs such as education, economic status and/or financial security, job and so on; once she has access to these things, she is probably ready to forego caste. As compared to that a higher percentage of males seem to want their marriages to be planned along the caste lines. It may be difficult to really find out the reason here, although family honor or even dowry could play a role.

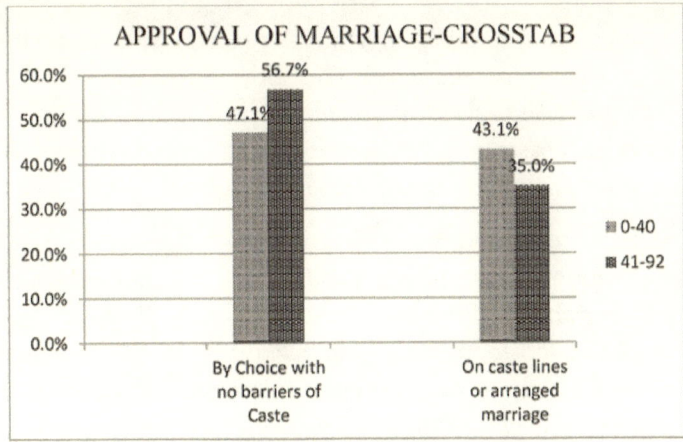

Figure-47

When we crosstab with reference to age, it is seen that a higher percentage of those in the above 40 age group opt for marriage by choice. This is a surprising scenario. Does this mean that experience has taught this group that there are more important criteria to be considered than caste when it comes to marriage? In the below 40 age group, the choice seems to be equally divided. The 43.1% of those below 40 who approve of marriage on caste lines shows again that there is a section of society which is caste conscious irrespective of their age.

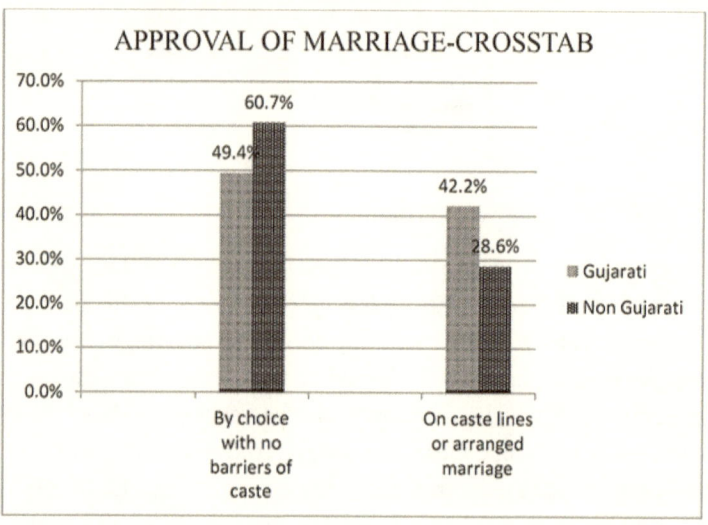

Figure-48

Does migration from another state affect your thinking when it comes to important aspects like marriage? The above tabulation makes it clear. If 60.7% of the non-Gujarati population opts for a marriage based on choice rather than caste, it indicates that urbanization does have an effect on the way one makes his/her choices.

In the forgone section, we analyzed people's perception of caste in the urban situation. The social composition of the neighborhood usually gives us a fairly good idea of how one perceives caste. The fact that about 35% have chosen cosmopolitan neighborhoods shows that people are ready to accept people of diverse cultures. I would also like to state here that cosmopolitan neighborhoods are a more recent phenomenon. This usually translates into more social interaction, as seen in the responses. As many as 78 of the respondents ranked visiting on a social occasion as No.1 in the social interaction category. This shows that, whereas previously this was absent, urbanization has broken down at least some of the barriers. About 50% of the respondents said that they never took note of the caste of the people they were dealing with or the ones they came across in their daily life. Again the 30% who have said that they occasionally look at caste probably are the ones who are caste conscious. On the whole, this indicates that a general openness to people of other castes is steadily growing, and this is a positive effect of urbanization.

A crosstab of males and females in this category reveals that the women are more open to people of other castes. Does this mean that women have become less caste conscious? A crosstab of age groups in this category shows that age did not have much to do with caste consciousness. Of course, it does seem that the young are more open to people of other castes in normal dealings but are still caste conscious on certain occasions. Of course, the interviewees were all below forty and not very caste conscious, which may have been the reason for their conversion. When the same question was analyzed for Gujarati and non-Gujarati categories, it was seen that the non-Gujarati migrant is more open on this subject. This is because he himself is trying to adjust to a new society and culture. Nonetheless, this is not to conclude that the Gujarati cannot be reached, for the views shared by the informal interviewees show otherwise.

Through our efforts to find out how one's social status or position is gauged in the modern society, it revealed that education played a major role in the same. It is obvious that, at some point, class overtook caste in determining one's social position. However, it needs to be asked if this is true for those belonging to the lower castes? Are the educated low caste people accepted into this class because of their education? This is highly debatable and needs further investigation. Closely related with social status is one's identity. In fact, both these questions overlap and need to be understood together. If education determined the status of the person, so should his identity. But it was noted that, apart from education, people also wanted to be known by their caste. This shows that caste and class constantly rub shoulders when it comes to determining one's own identity. Of course, the majority of people base their identity on their jobs and businesses, which is a clear indication that one's identity and status depend on education or job.

The social group (friendship group) of people seems to be more homogenous in terms of caste. Though this may not always result in greater social bonding, it certainly shows that certain homogeneity is being formed at the social level in the cities. This is observed both among men and women. It seems that as people, irrespective of sex, mingle with each other at their work places, the hold of caste usually wanes. When the same responses are analyzed for the categories of locals and the interstate migrants, it is seen that the locals show a higher bonding with other caste people. Whether the bonding is with their same language group or across cultures is not known but it certainly shows that a general openness is being seen in the urbanite in these days. The fact that a staggering 87% participate in caste associations may do so for political reasons, but there may also be a desire to keep alive the caste distinctions and rituals associated with it. A discussion on caste cannot be complete without some reference to marriage. When this was probed, it was observed that people want a choice in marriage with no barriers to caste and religion. This means that they do want to come out of the confines of their own caste but unable to do so due to social pressures. This desire for freedom is seen more among the educated women. Education and modernity has brought the desire for liberation from the age-old traditions that are binding them. This desire seems to go up with age thereby probably showing that experience has taught them that life is more than what they have experienced within the boundaries of their own closed society. The fact that the non-Gujarati person approves marriage based on choice shows that urbanization does have an effect on the way a person thinks and acts.

To sum up, it may be said that there is a general openness to people of other castes and, to some extent, religion as well. The caste and religious barriers seem to have broken down to a great extent. However, it has not taken away the caste consciousness of a person. People want to keep their caste distinctions alive more as a means of identity though, at some points, class takes precedence over caste.

Measuring Changes in the Family in the Urban Context

Urbanization brings drastic changes in the family setup along with changes in values. The decision-making process within the family also undergoes change. I've attempted to study if this is true, using just a few basic parameters here. There is great scope for further research in this particular area.

The first area investigated was whether the families have become more nuclear in their setup. This according to many authors is the first change that will occur when families shift from the rural to the urban.

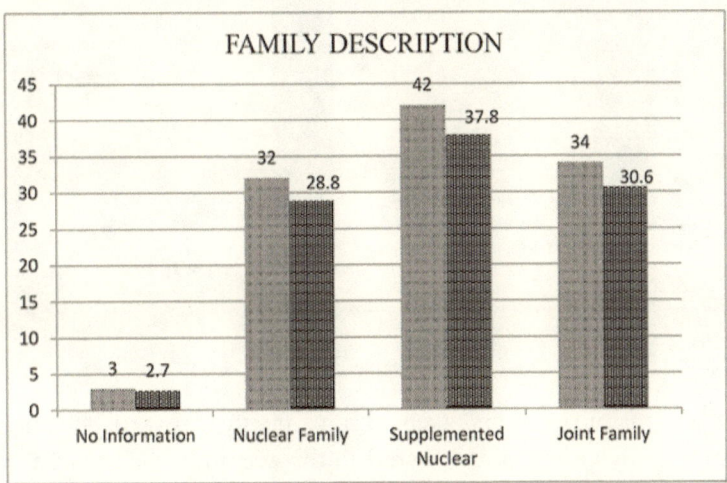

Figure-49

It is seen that nearly 66.6% of the families live in either nuclear or supplemented nuclear families. The supplemented nuclear families are those in which the parents live along with the children. This family is different in its ecological structure and its functioning from the joint family as described in the section on families, hence I would go along with Lal in calling this a supplemented nuclear family. The nuclear and supplemented nuclear families are the expected outcome of urbanization, particularly in view of the constraint of space. Further, the independence that urbanization brings is sometimes difficult to handle in joint families. However, it is surprising that a good 30.6% of people live in joint families according to the survey. Nevertheless, the majority of the families live in either nuclear or supplemented nuclear families.

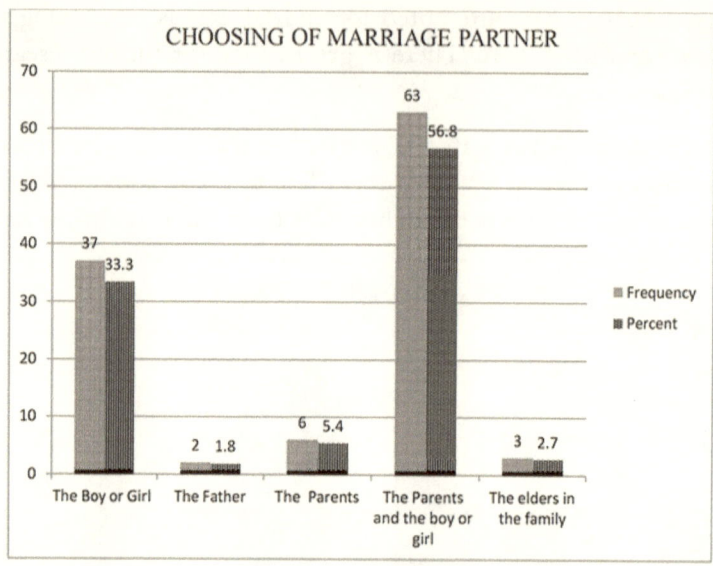

Figure-50

One of the major decisions taken within a family is that of choosing the life partner. We witness a major shift in this regard in the urban context. Whereas previously, it was either the Father or the elders of the family that decided, here the onus is more on the person getting married. Accordingly, 33.3% have said that it is the sole decision of the boy or girl getting married, although 56.8% have said that the parents are also involved in the decision making along with the boy or girl getting married. Education, job and financial security bring with it independence in decision making not only in regard to marriage, but also in other important areas such as purchase of property, investments, and so on. In other words, the control of parents in the urban situation has slackened to a great deal. This independence in decision making comes probably from the importance to individuality which may be the effect of nuclearization of families.

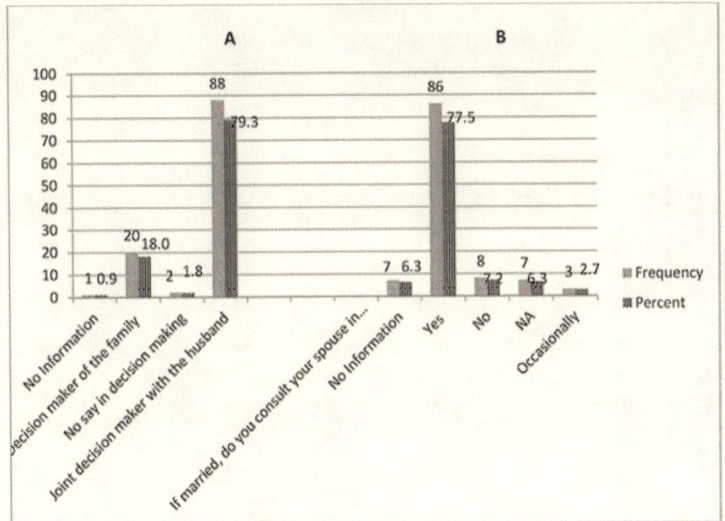

Figure-51

The research also focused on the role and authority of the woman of the house. In the joint family system, the woman was relegated to raising children and to kitchen work. This has changed drastically in the urban situation and is also confirmed by the survey. The first question was to know what the role of the woman was in the urban household. The answer represented in graph under A shows that, in about 80% of the cases, the woman is the joint decision maker in the house. What is surprising is that about 18% have said that she is the decision maker of the family. This I feel is a great role reversal in comparison with their previous condition in the rural joint families. The graph under B above only reinforces that of A. To the question of whether they consulted their spouses in taking major decisions, such as investing in stocks or buying a property, an overwhelming 77.5% of the respondents have answered "yes." This may have been higher as the remaining 12% either did not give an answer or it was not applicable to them. In short, the woman today plays a major role in every aspect of the household. If she is a working woman, she has a higher share in the authority of the spouse.

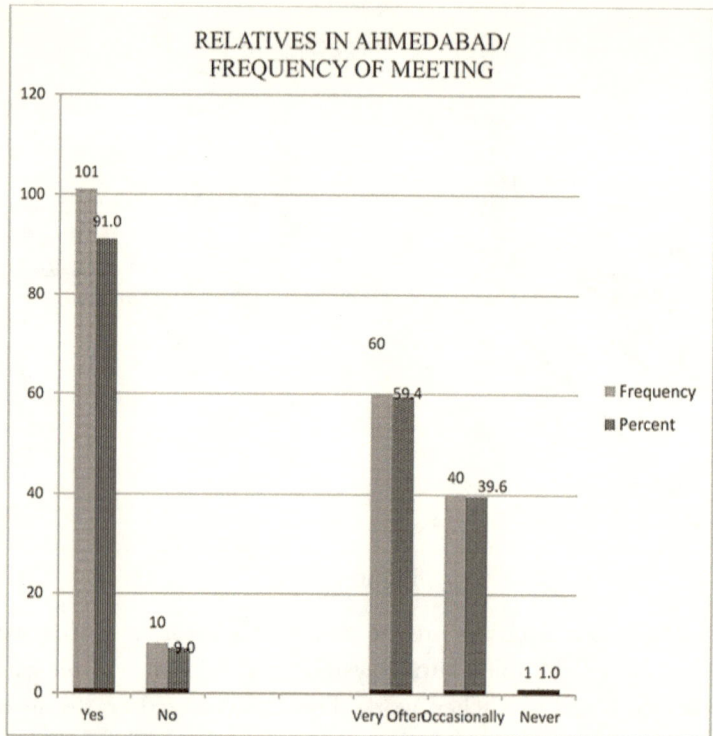

Figure-52

In the joint family, there was a great bonding between the family members. As the family had a common purse, irrespective of what one earned, everyone had a right to it and it was used as the need arose. When the families became nuclear, did this bonding remain? If the relatives are staying in distant places, probably in other cities or States, where it is not possible to meet often, probably this bonding is loosened overa period of time. But what about the families who stay in the same city? In fact, 91% said that they have relations in the city, and 59.4% also said that they meet them very often. About 39.6% said that they meet their relatives occasionally. Are they helpful to each other in economic and social terms? The next graph will show this.

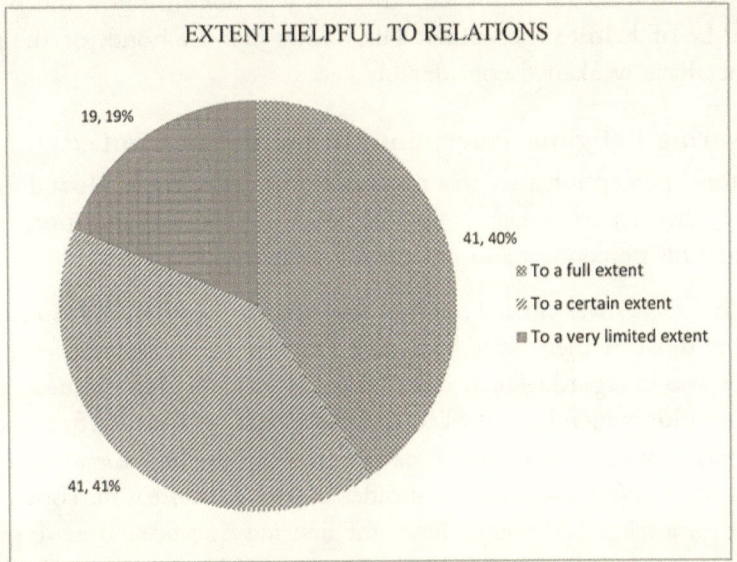

Figure-53

The help we envisage is economic and social. If 40% say that the help is to the fullest extent, it would mean that the rest either help in a limited way or do not help at all. This shows that the unity and oneness exhibited by the joint families, which was its main strength, has weakened now. More so, if the relatives live far apart geographically, the bonds are weakened still further. Even the 40% who claim to help to the fullest extent may probably be nothing more than a socially acceptable answer than the ground reality. It is generally agreed that the pressure of urban life make it difficult to help others above a particular limit. This is open to further research.

Thus, we may conclude that, as the families are turning nuclear in the cities, the authority of parents on the children has loosened, and the children have more independence in taking decisions, even major ones. The role and authority of women is also changing. The woman seems to have taken on more responsibility and also has more authority in the affairs of the household. She is the one around whom the house revolves. Thus, it is not surprising that she either becomes the decision maker in the house or the joint decision maker in the family. This is a major role reversal in comparison with their earlier status in the rural joint families.

Relatives do meet up with each other but it is doubtful how much they would be of help to each other. This shows that the bonds of the joint families have weakened considerably.

Measuring Religious Perceptions in the Urban Contexts

The third perception that was measured was on religion. How does an urban person perceive and practice religion? Has urbanization really changed his perception and practice of religion?

This survey was carried out primarily among the Hindus. It so turned out that most of them were high caste Hindus. The first question in this section was in regard to their belief about after-life. Hinduism believes in reincarnation which is controlled by one's deeds or *karma*. After a series of rebirths, when one's good *karma* cancels out the bad *karma,* one gets salvation or *mukti/moksha*. Thus, the idea of *moksha/mukti* is the controlling factor for a religious Hindu. Hence the first few questions were to gauge whether they believed in this ideal of *mukti* and how they practiced it.

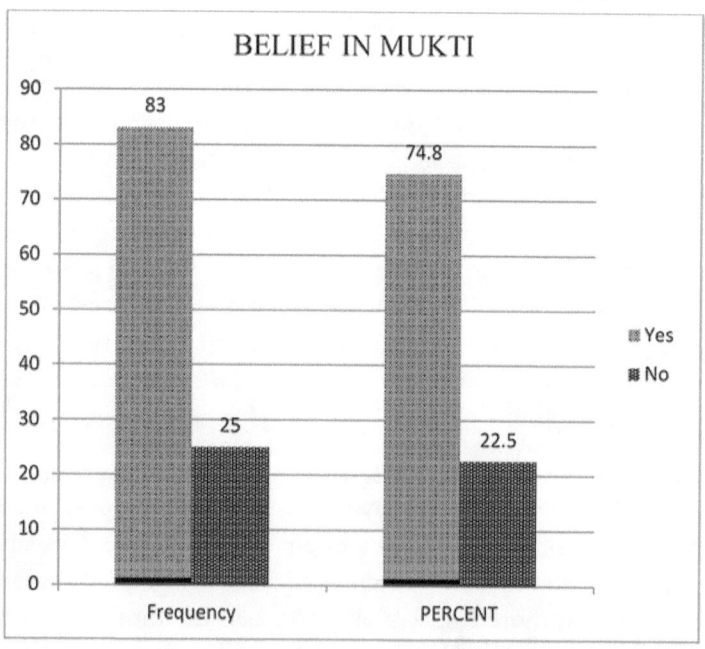

Figure-54

As seen, while 74.8% answered in the positive, about 22.5% said that they did not believe in the concept of *mukti*. A few did not answer this question, and that is not included for our calculation. So, a majority of the middle-class educated Indians find the concept of *mukti* meaningful. The focus was not on what constituted their belief since it was assumed that they knew it. If those who believed in this concept is so high, it should naturally mean that people are overtly religious, practicing diligently one of the ways or *marga to* achieve it. The next few questions focused on what they did to achieve salvation.

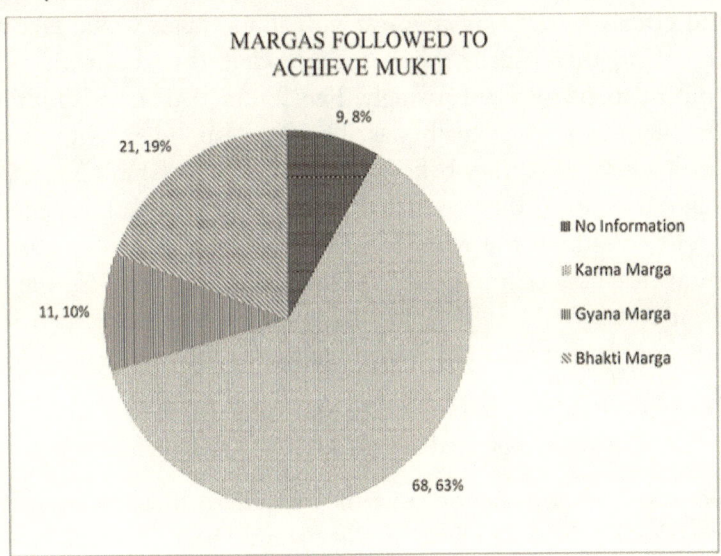

Figure-55

Hinduism prescribes three *margas* mentioned in the pie chart to achieve *moksha*. It is to be noted that even though 22.5% said that they did not believe in this concept, only 8% did not give any information. Ideally speaking, these two percentages should match. Interestingly, data from survey forms show that many of those who did not believe in this concept did follow some *marga*. This is an area which is worth investigating for it looks as though many people are not convinced about the logic of this concept of *moksha* as understood in Hinduism and yet know that there is something beyond this life and hence do want to follow some way or the other to reach there.

What is surprising is that 63% said that they follow the *karma marga* to achieve their *moksha*. It is surprising because urban sociologists have said that the educated middle-class in the cities tend to follow the *bhakti marga* because of lack of time and desire to go deeper into the rituals of the *karma marga*. The chapter on Urbanization and Change discusses the findings of Milton Singer on why the educated city people tend to follow *bhakti marga*. This is well supported by the findings of Minna Saalva, a more recent sociologist. The perception of these authors is quite correct for it seems that time is a controlling factor in people's choice of a particular *marga*. However, does following *karma marga* not require time and effort? In fact, *karma marga* with all its rituals would take more time and effort than usually thought. I intended to find out what *karma marga* meant to people. Surprisingly, I've found that it had nothing to do with what this *marga* actually was. The few respondents with whom I had clarified it said that they believed that 'work is worship'. Accordingly, they believed in doing their secular work with integrity and diligence and that would give them the reward. Such thinking is probably based on the famous teaching of the Gita on 'work without looking for the fruit.' Further, it certainly shows that, to a large extent, a secular urban Hindu does not want to get involved in religion as a ritual.

Those who follow *bhakti* are to the tune of 19% which is also substantial. The *gyana marga* adherents at 10% are a dwindling lot.

The next question was on how they practiced their religion. If the question on *margas* is any indication, there should be a substantial number who do not follow any particular religious practice.

q- 24 What best describes your regular Spiritual Life/activity?					
Rank	1	2	3	4	Total
Performing Rituals	30	4	-	-	34
Studying the Scriptures	23	6	-	-	29
Performing Pooja, Singing Bhajans	46	4	2	-	52
Attending Spiritual discourses	22	-	2	1	25
Nothing in particular	22	-	-	-	22
Work is worship, Introspection, Interaction with Nature etc	11	-	-	-	11

Figure-56

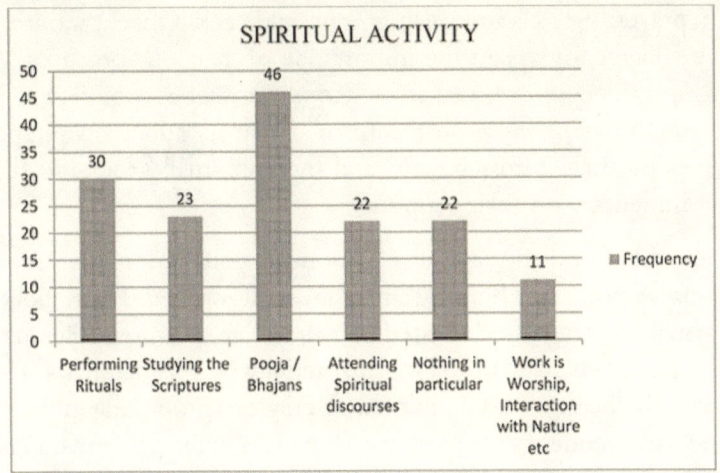

Figure-57

Spiritual activities may vary from person to person, and so it would be difficult to describe it just as one activity. The respondents were asked to rank their spiritual activity in the order of preference, which is presented in the table. For our understanding though, I've taken that which is ranked as No.1 and represented it graphically. As seen from the chart, there are 33 responses which say that they do not have any particular spiritual activity and that for them their work is worship. These are probably the non-religious *karma margis*. I would put the 46 who have said that doing *pooja* and singing *bhajans* is their spiritual activity in this category as well. It may be that many from this group do these things primarily because of family pressure or as a tradition. So, together, this is a good number and it would mean that a majority of the middle-class Hindus fall in the non-religious class. Those involved in performing rituals or studying the scriptures or attending discourses are the more serious ones, and they form a sizable number. Hence, we may conclude that the educated middle-class consists of one section that does not believe in and is not involved in any particular spiritual activity, and another section which is deeply religious.

That a section of the middle-class is deeply religious is evident from the various spiritual activities they attend at regular interval in the cities. The Pandurang Shastri's *Swadyay* has a good number of adherents. An adherent of this group informed that, apart from their Sunday morning time of prayer, they also meet in groups midweek. Once a month, they visit the villages to explain the importance of religious practices. Thus, this group is deeply involved in religion. Another respondent, who is part of the *Swami Narayan* sect, informed that its adherents attend the discourses of their guru regularly, and meet in small groups to discuss some commentary on their scripture.

Thus, the so called religious and non-religious among the educated middle-class among the Hindus seem to be equally divided. The respondents of informal interviews have stated that they were the non-religious type and were hardly involved in any spiritual activity on a regular basis. Thus, it seems that the people who do not have a religious grounding in their own religion have a tendency of accepting new ideas when presented logically.

Spiritual activities are a sure way a religion is manifested. There is another way in which one's spirituality is expressed, that is, through his/her involvement in the society, particularly the works done for the development of the poor and the marginalized. This is also true of Hinduism which believes that doing good works is one way of nullifying your bad *karma*. The reality, however, as various authors have said, is that this group is too self-centered and cares only about its own self and not seriously work towards the development of the needy and poor.

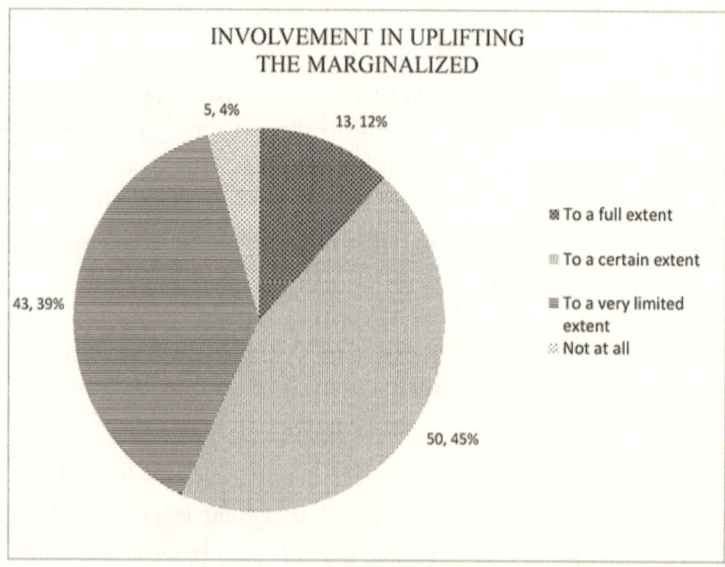

Figure-58

It was found that only 12% of the respondents were involved to a full extent. I would group those involved to certain extent and those involved to a limited extent together because the extent of involvement is again dependent on one's perspective. Those who fall in these two categories usually would be involved in some philanthropic work to some extent. There is no serious involvement with the work or a concern for the people affected. Thus, I would say that the majority of the people are not involved with the poor in any substantial way. Does this not in a way confirm the opinion of various authors that the middle-class people are very self-centered. For those who are involved in social welfare activities, the reasons are far from being religious.

If Yes, then why?				
Rank	1	2	3	Total
Because it leads to gain *punya* for one's *Mukti*	10	1	-	11
Because it is my religious duty	20	3	1	24
It is a way of showing gratitude towards society	33	4	1	38
It gives me satisfaction	74	3	-	77
Serving with foundation having philanthropy activity	1	-	-	1
Being a "HUMAN" it is our duty	1	-	-	1

Figure-59

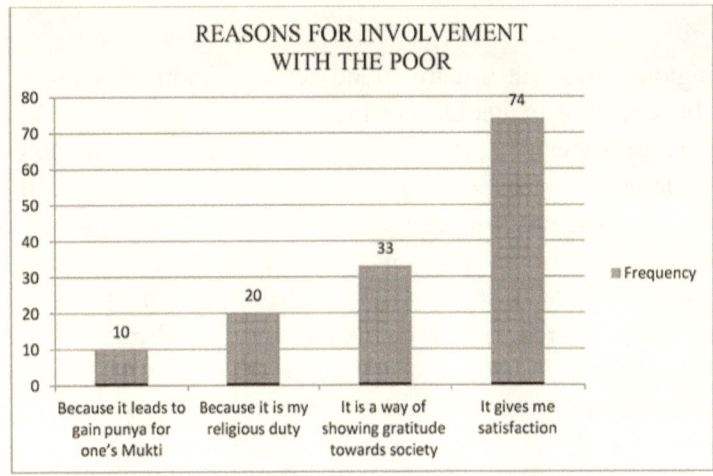

Figure-60

Taking only the values of Rank 1 from the above chart, we understand that the few who do get involved in helping the poor in some concrete way do it primarily for their satisfaction or as a way of showing their gratitude to the society. There are very few who do it because their religion tells them to do so. This in a way again shows that religion does not have much of a hold on the lives of people.

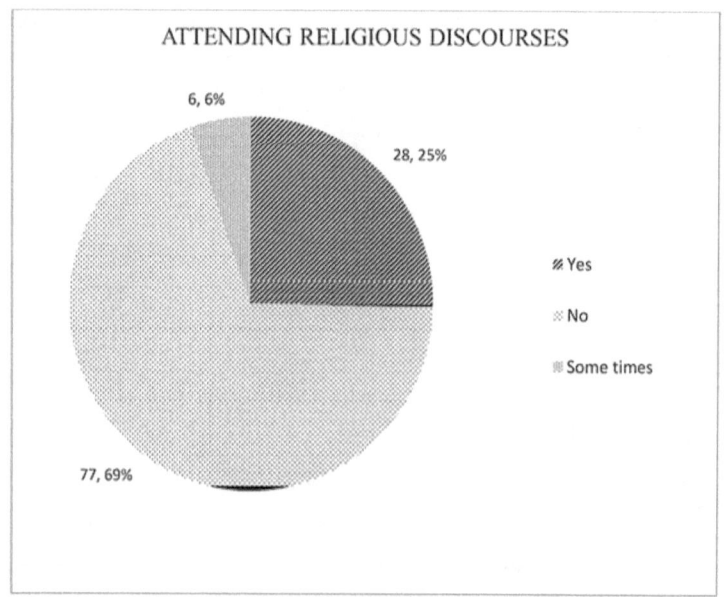

ATTENDING RELIGIOUS DISCOURSES

6, 6%

28, 25%

Yes

No

Some times

77, 69%

Figure-61

The religious ones will usually attend some religious discourse. They would be attending religious meetings on a regular basis to listen to some guru or leader. E.g., Art of Living, *Swadyay Parivar* and so on. As per the survey, an overwhelming 69% of the respondents said they do not attend any religious discourse as such. This itself is an indication that religion does not have so much of a hold of the educated middle-class. In fact, the respondents of informal interviews also confirmed that they did not attend any religious discourses. For the small minority who do attend these discourses give two basic reasons for the same. It gives them an understanding of scripture and also connects them to their religious heritage. So, for a few, religious heritage holds importance as they may feel that they have found their roots in them. The vast majority, however, do not either have the time or the inclination to attend any such discourses.

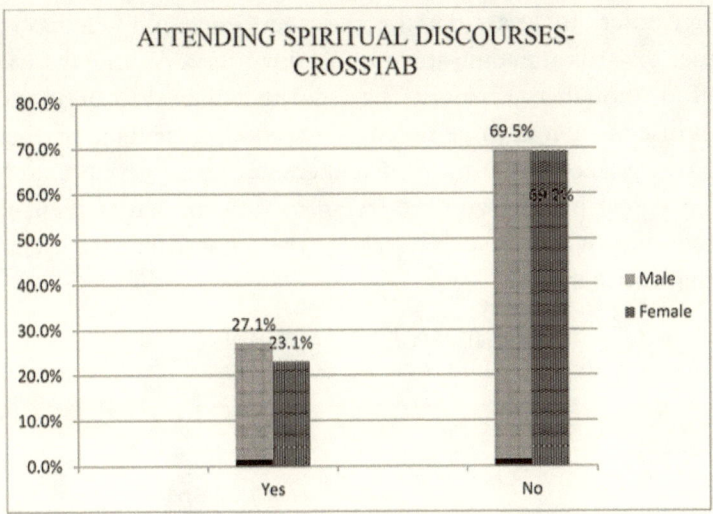

Figure-62

In regard to spiritual activities too, there is no difference among the male and female. If one of the indications of spirituality is attending spiritual discourses, there is an equal percentage of male and female who do not get involved in this activity. This again shows that, among the educated working middle-class, the thinking is similar irrespective of whether you are a male or female.

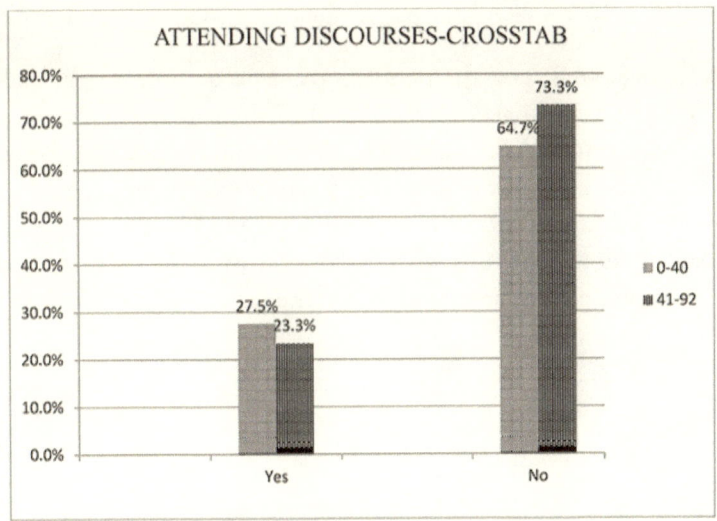

Figure-63

In the age criterion, we see that it is the older generation who has shown reluctance towards attending any spiritual discourses. Among the younger generation, though the majority has said that they do not attend any spiritual discourse, it is to be noted that a good percentage of them do attend. If we take this to mean that there is a small group among the educated young people who are trying to find the truth, then, this is consistent with what Meeks says about the inconsistent—the climbers accepting Christianity.

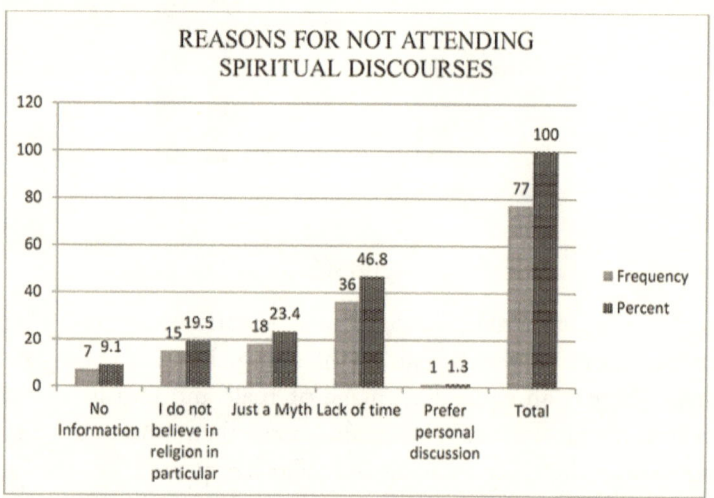

Figure-64

As seen above, 46.8% of the people gave 'lack of time' as their reason for not attending spiritual discourses. And 23.4% said that such discourses were not related to real life, while 19.5% said that they did not believe in religion in particular. Lack of inclination seems to be the real reason here. Perhaps the educated middle-class is only inclined to what is profitable and what works for them. It is probable that most of them do not see any value in these discourses and hence the lack of interest.

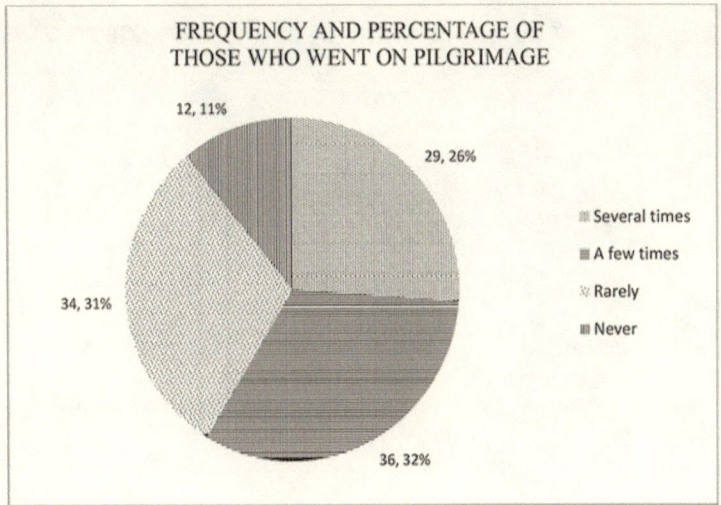

FREQUENCY AND PERCENTAGE OF
THOSE WHO WENT ON PILGRIMAGE

12, 11%

29, 26%

Several times

A few times

Rarely

Never

34, 31%

36, 32%

Figure-65

The above figure shows the number of people who undertook pilgrimages. It was only 26% who went on pilgrimage 'several times.' These are the people who undertake pilgrimage with a purpose. The 36% who go on pilgrimages 'a few times' are those who accompany parents or friends. They are not usually the religious type, as I have observed through some informal conversations with those who have gone on pilgrimages. The rest, which will add up to 42% of the respondents, do not go on pilgrimages. Thus, it is very clear that pilgrimages as a means of gaining *punya* or washing away one's sins etc has lost its glitter.

Now, it would be even more surprising to look at the figures on the reasons for people going on pilgrimages.

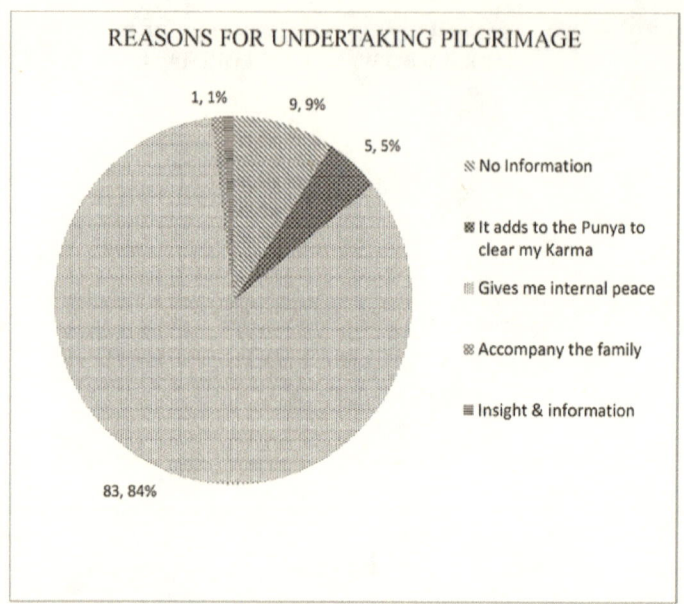

Figure-66

It is very clear that an overwhelming majority of people undertake pilgrimages more for getting internal peace than for any other reason. Again, there does not seem to be a religious reason for the pilgrimage.

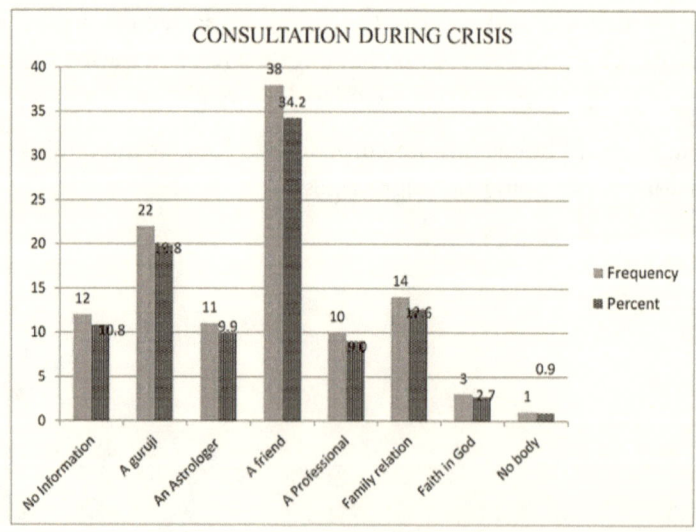

Figure-67

Crisis is a time when a person usually takes the help of religion if he/she is religious. The above chart is quite revealing in this that only about 30% of the respondents sought the help of religion in some form or the other. They either said that they go to a *guru* for help or consult an astrologer. This means that an overwhelming 60% sought help from other sources. A whopping 34% said that they would consult a friend, while another 13% said that they would consult their relative. So, crisis management for the educated middle-class is limited to one's own close circles of friendships, and does not even include the professionals, leave aside religion. It seems correct to say that the educated middle-class do not seem to have much faith in religion.

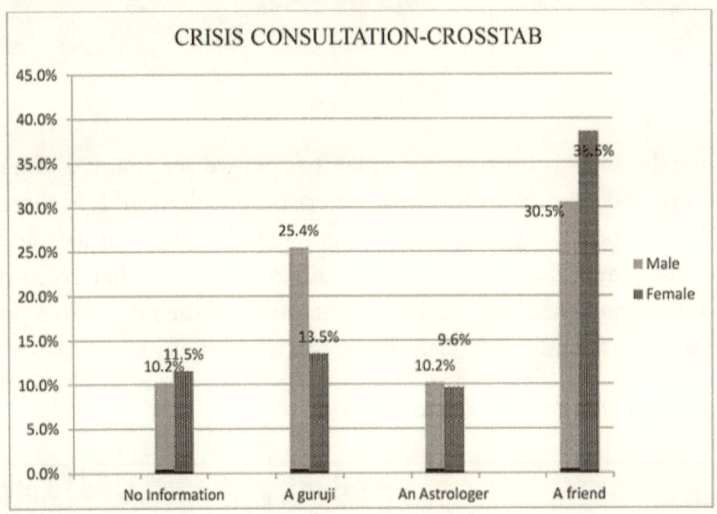

Figure-68

Bifurcating the data for male-female categories, we get surprising results in that the percentage of woman consulting *gurus* is glaringly lower than that of men. Does this mean that the woman prefers to endure rather than go to a source which may or may not be reliable? The male and female prefer to confide in friends and relatives, though here also the percentage is higher for the female than the male. It looks like the woman is affected more by urbanization than men and they are ready to leave their traditional thinking and adopt new ideas more easily.

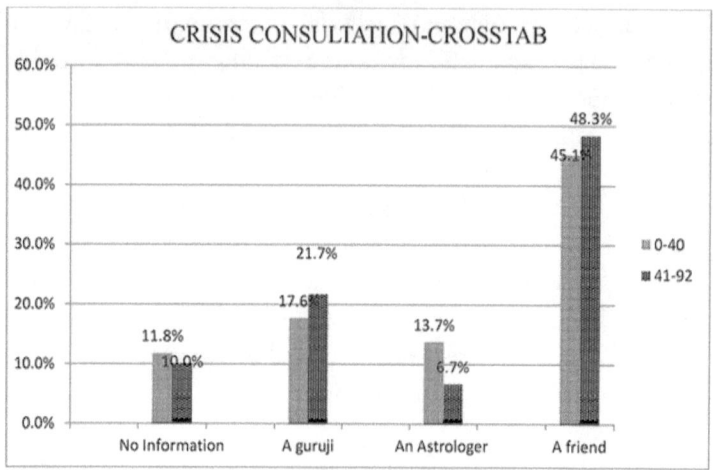

Figure-69

When we do a bifurcation with respect to age, we see that it is the older generation who want to go to a *guru* for crisis consultation. It is surprising that a higher percentage of the younger people go to an astrologer. I fail to understand the reason for this and recommend that an in-depth research be done in this regard. But the majority of the people irrespective of age rely on friends and relations in the time of crisis.

q-34 What kind of literature do you read?					
Rank	1	2	3	4	Total
Related to my Profession	50	5	3	-	58
Related to Religion	49	6	1	2	58
Related to life issues	40	5	2	-	47
Related to Politics	14	1	3	1	19
Related to Entertainment	56	-	1	2	59

Figure-70

q -35 What do you usually discuss with your relatives/friends?						
Rank	1	2	3	4	5	Total
Regarding current affairs	80	4	1	-	-	85
Regarding religious issues	25	5	2	-	1	33
Regarding social issues	56	4	7	2	-	69
Regarding Entertainment	35	2	-	-	-	37
Regarding Professional issues	56	5	1	1	-	63

Figure-71

The kind of literature one reads and topics one discusses with friends is an indicator of his/her inclination. This has been put in the above chart with rankings. If we just take the ranking No. 1, the pie chart would give us a fair idea of the reading habits of people.

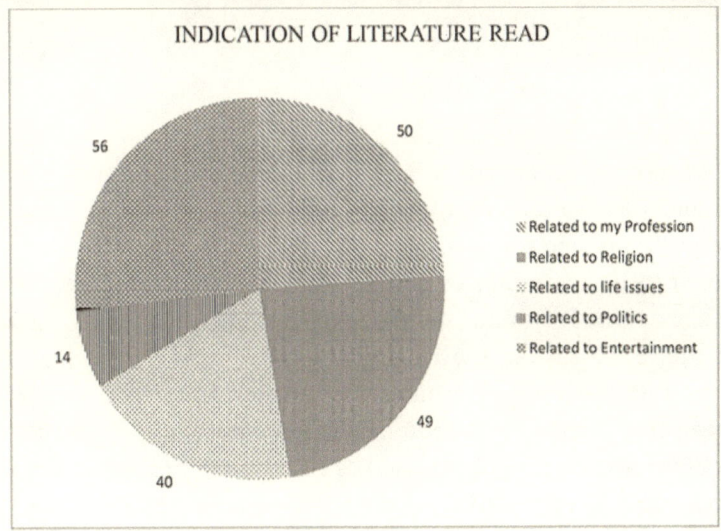

Figure-72

It is very clear that literature related to profession, religion, life issues and entertainment, all hold equal interest for the educated middle-class. Politics is one area which people do not seem to be interested in reading.

In regard to discussions with their social group, considering the data that has been ranked as No. 1 results in the following:

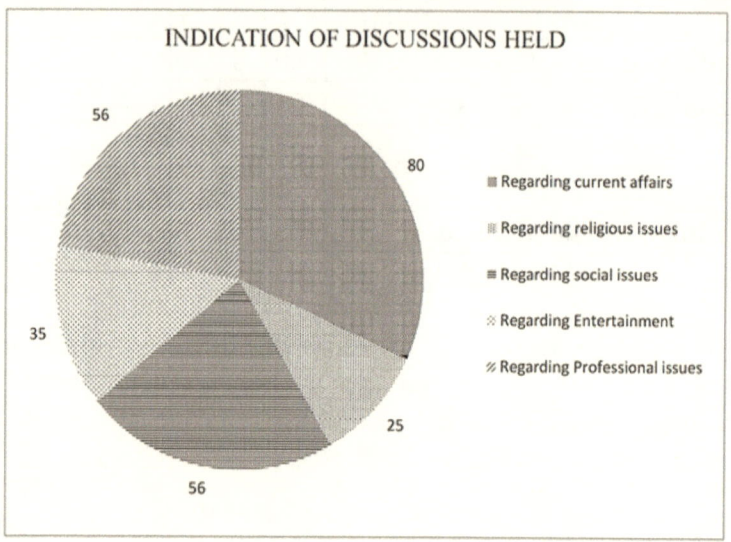

Figure-73

As far as discussions are concerned, people would prefer current affairs. This is surprising for this held the last position as far as reading is concerned. The other topics like social issues, entertainment and professional issues also seem to be the topics of interest in their discussions. But the one which has got the least value in this category is religion. This is surprising for, in the reading habit, the religious literature held quite a high place. Does this mean that people want to keep religion as a private affair? Does this mean that there is an interest in religion and yet people do not want to discuss it for the fear of branded as narrow-minded or communal or even religious? It seems that people have questions relating to religion but prefer not to discuss them very much.

Therefore, in regard to the religious perception of the urban middle-class, we may conclude by saying that, generally, there is confusion about how one can attain *mukti*. As the basic condition of non-attachment is not fulfilled in the urban context, it tends to leave the middle-class in a state of flux. Though the majority in this class believe in the ideal of *mukti*, they are not able follow any religious precepts to achieve it. The modern man believes that 'work is worship' and that it would give him the *moksha* he seeks. His religious activity is also limited to either daily pooja which may consist of some *mantras*. Apart from that he/she is not involved in religion in any serious way. One cannot, however, forget that a good number of the middle-class are involved in a serious way with religious precepts and work.

There is hardly any involvement in the uplifting of the poor and marginalized and those involved do it more for satisfaction than for one's *mukti* or any other religious reason. Looking at this, one gets feeling that either this response is not the complete truth or that they do not really believe firmly in the concept of *mukti*. The study also indicates that religion does not have much hold on the lives of people. The majority do not attend any spiritual discourses which would keep them in their spiritual path, with lack of time and interest cited as reasons. However, there are other things to occupy their mind and thereby pushing religion to the backseat.

The educated is more interested in what is profitable and what brings immediate results. This finding is similar for males and females. For the middle-class Hindu, pilgrimage also does not carry much weight. The reasons may be the same as cited for not attending spiritual discourses. It certainly seems that pilgrimage as a means of gaining *punya* has lost its glitter. People who do undertake pilgrimages do it to gain some measure of internal peace. Even during crisis, they prefer to consult a friend or relatives rather than go to a spiritual *guru*. It may not be wrong to conclude that the average middle-class Hindu does not have much faith in religion. Of course, the surprise was in the reading habit. There was a good number who indicated to reading religious literature, but when it came to discussions, religion again took the back seat.

So, it is evident that the educated middle-class people appear to be more materialistic, non-religious externally and yet wants to strengthen their grips on their worldview which, they believe, would give meaning to life.

Chapter 6

Recommendations and Conclusion

The study that I undertook aimed to measure the changes that urbanization has brought about in three important aspects of Hindu life—caste, family and religion. In this chapter, I would like to highlight the implications of the study and make recommendations that would help develop a framework for Christian witness among the educated Hindu middle-class.

1. IMPLICATIONS OF THE STUDY

The Urban Dynamic of Caste

Urbanization coupled with education has brought about several changes among the educated middle-class with reference to caste. This does not in any way imply that caste has lost its hold completely. There are two sides to this change and both need to be acknowledged and kept in view in formulating any strategy to reach this class with the gospel. On the one hand, there is a general openness among this class towards other castes or even people of other religions. Importance is given to education, high profile jobs and economic status when it comes to social status. The social grouping has also changed drastically. Usually there are people of various castes in a person's social circle which again would depend probably on the class rather than the caste. Thus, there is certainly greater interaction between people of different caste and religions though this also has its reservations.

It has been assumed that women in this class would be more conservative in their thought patterns, but the study indicates that on many fronts they were found to be more progressive. Fewer women took note of caste while interacting on a day-to-day basis. Women favored inter-caste marriages more than males. This may probably mean that they are frustrated within the boundaries of their own caste and want to explore the world outside. Of course, a good number of males also favored inter-caste marriages. Thus, it may be said that a sizable section of the middle-class wants to explore life outside their caste.

Going by the age criterion, there is openness across all age groups. This implies that though the young people may generally be found to be open to new ideas, the older ones are also not far behind. Probably they may not accept them in public due to social pressure and prestige.

One particular group among the middle-class that has shown more openness than others is the educated migrants. They are the ones who are most open to people of other castes and would have a social circle which is varied rather than of one's own caste.

Here again, as already said, it does not mean that caste has lost its hold completely. People who want to be identified by their education and jobs also want to be recognized by their caste. So, the identity of an educated middle-class person is a complex of class and caste. People's approval of rituals also shows that they want to keep their caste identities alive. For those who belong to the high caste, it must be giving them a sense of pride and a sense of being different from others. Further, if an overwhelming majority is comfortable with 'Caste Associations' it shows that they want to identify themselves with that group.

In this situation, a Christian will have to keep in mind that he does not do anything to antagonize the caste conscious Hindu or to alienate him and yet, at the same time, take advantage of their social openness and their desire to explore new avenues. This, indeed, is like walking on a tight rope.

Change in Family Dynamics

As in other parts of the world, urbanization brings with it change in the family structure. Families in India are also becoming more nuclear in the cities, and this change leads to various other changes within the family. The first pertains to decisions making. In important matters like marriage, the girl or boy are very much part of the decision making. The same applies to other aspects of life such as choosing a career or a place of work. The children in the urban context have become more individualistic. They are independent in taking decisions, even major ones like conversion. It is also true that such decisions of the children have any major adverse effect on the families in the urban context. This independent decision making happens due to education of the children and the lack of oneness in the family due to pressures of time. Another major change is the role of woman. Many a times, she is the pivot on which the family revolves. She is either the major decision maker of the family or at least a joint decision maker with the husband on various aspects of life, including financial matters. The bonds with the relatives living in the same city have certainly weakened as compared to that of the joint families.

Change in Religion: Theory and Practice

This is one area which is full of contradictions. While a majority of the educated middle-class believes in the ideal of *mukti*, this ideal is not connected with the original concept of non-attachment. Similarly, most of the people of this class do not follow any particular *marga* but take their work to be worship. Most of them do not attend any spiritual discourse for spiritual upliftment; their religious activity is limited to some *pooja* or *mantras*. Most of them cite lack of time or inclination as reasons for not engaging in any kind of religious activity. As *karma yogis*, they are to engage in good works such as the development of the poor, but most of them do not. A majority of them do not go on pilgrimages. Their visit to temples is meant for leisure and pleasure than for serious worship as such. The visible religious symbols at their residences are probably to show their religious identity rather than their faith. They do read religious literature, but they are not ready to discuss religious ideas or teachings with their friends or colleagues. This shows that religion for the middle-class Hindus has become a private affair. It is usually thought that females engage themselves in religious activity, but this survey shows that, among the educated middle-class, both the male or female are disinterested in religion as a whole.

All these parameters put together would imply that this particular class is highly materialistic and non-religious externally. However, they have a desire to know the truth and firm up their world-view which would give them meaning to life.

The greatest influence that religious themes have on the urban middle-class is through plays, cinema and fictional literature. They consider forms of religious expressions like dance and music merely as art forms rather than depicting religion. This, I feel needs to be exploited for reaching this class with the gospel.

Crisis management is very important in life. For some communities like Christians, the priest is the focal point for crisis management. He in turn becomes a counselor trying to bring the counselee to see most of the solutions in their faith in Jesus Christ. This kind of structure seems to be absent among the Hindus and hence crisis management for them revolves around friends, relatives, parents etc. It should be mentioned here that the females are less prone to go to *gurus* or consult astrologers than their male counterparts. The female surprisingly shows more inclination to consult friends and relatives in their times of need. Though this is good, it has its limitations in many cases. Thus, it may be said that crisis management is an area of concern for the educated Hindu Middle-class and is a potential area of development.

2. TOWARDS A FRAMEWORK FOR CHRISTIAN WITNESS

Building Bridges

Looking at the fact that the high caste middle-class educated Hindus are socially more open today, we need to look for avenues to interact with them.

i.   Christians need to be encouraged to interact with their colleagues, neighbors without compromising the uniqueness of the gospel. They need to be taught to differentiate religious from social concerns among the Hindus. Social visits, participating in social events and inviting people of different caste for our social functions will help people open up and share their needs. If Christian lay people are taught how to handle these needs sensitively, it will help the Hindus to be open to listen to the gospel.

ii. It has been observed that Christians usually limit their socializing to their church members. They need to be encouraged to form friendships with the people of other communities and caste. They need to have strong friendship ties with their professional colleagues, fellow students, etc.

iii. Christians need to be encouraged to be part of NGOs or other professional or social organizations where they can act as a catalyst and also enlarge their social networking and bonding.

iv. Christians need to be encouraged to form home fellowships where they may socialize with their friends, colleagues, etc. which may become means of sharing one's faith when an occasion arises.

v. The church needs to create platforms for interaction on themes of common social interest. These may be termed as Christian clubs which the middle-class can perceive as a place of relaxation and yet a place where truth prevails.

vi. The one group that is more open than the others is the educated migrant. Interaction with this group is much easier and needs to be exploited.

Making Christian Presence Felt

It is important that the Christian presence be felt and acknowledged by the middle-class in this city.

i. English education is a big attraction for the middle-class in any city. Whereas Christian institutions were sought after at one time, there are several well-known institutions which have taken over this area of work. But we still can make an impact if we are able to have a good mix of the middle-class with the lower middle-class and the poor. This is how we may be able to differentiate ourselves from the elite schools of the city.

ii. Christians need to be encouraged to open Spoken English classes for there is a great demand for it among those wishing to go abroad.

iii. Hobby classes, summer training programs etc. needs to be explored by the churches. These would be hugely successful for the middle-class who want to upgrade the skills of their children and themselves.

Addressing Relevant Personal and Social Issues

The churches need to create platforms to address the relevant personal and social issues relevant to the middle-class.

i.   These could be issues of women like gender bias, domestic violence, environmental issues, those pertaining to the poor etc.

ii. Marriage enrichment and child development programs need to be developed for the people of other faiths as these issues remain largely unaddressed among them.

iii. The church also need to address issues of the Corporate Sector like corporate ethics, moral ethics, avoiding burn-out, stress management, work-leisure cycle etc. These are issues on which the Bible has much to say.

Create Counseling Centres

As seen, crisis management is certainly an area of concern for this class of people. Whereas the problems they face at the domestic and professional level are many, they usually do not have any place to go to for counseling.

i.   It is required that counseling centers be opened where people are able to share their issues and problems and get professional and proper advice.

ii. The church needs to train their lay people for counseling in general and also for special ministries relating to, for instances, domestic violence, single mothers, abortion, etc.

Create Awareness through Creative Exploration

i.   The medium of arts—painting, music, dance, literature, theatre, cinema etc.—need to be explored to present Christian thought to help the educated middle-class explore the world outside their caste confines. They need to be aware of the liberation of the spirit and abundance of life available in the Christian faith.

ii. These need to be held in neutral places where the educated middle-class do not feel threatened to come.

Christian Ministry and Witness

i.   Evangelism needs to be focused on the individual rather than the family. This is because urbanization has made people more individualistic and family ties are not that strong.

ii.   The church and mission agencies need to explore apologetic approaches for dealing with the issues of *moksha/karma,* etc. and also for the presentation of the Christian gospel.

iii. Christians need to be trained for one to one evangelism which will include pre-evangelism also. Care need to be taken not to antagonize this class as they are caste conscious to some extent.

iv.   Religious discourses need to be made relevant to daily life issues and they need to be time bound.

v.   Converts need to be trained to share their experiences as a Christian to their friends and colleagues.

vi.   The educated Hindus need to be encouraged to view Christian sites which would enable them to study Christian thought while remaining anonymous.

vii. TV programs need to be developed to showcase holistic Christian thought, rather than showing Christ as a healer alone.

3. IMPLICATIONS FROM THE STUDY OF BIBLICAL PERSPECTIVE

In this section, I confine the discussion to Paul and his strategy for mission among the middle-class. He travelled throughout the then known world and planted churches in cities with a mixture of different classes of people.

Paul strategized mission, especially his activities in the cities. He found strategic centers (nerve centers) within the district from where the gospel could branch out to smaller towns and the countryside. Paul planted churches in the provincial capitals of the empire. This is probably compared to the capital of the State, this in the present case being Ahmedabad. (It may be called the commercial capital for Gandinagar is the capital of the State). We also need to look at other cities like Baroda that are the cultural capitals of the State and Surat which can be called the industrial capital of the State. The peculiar characteristics of these cities need to be studied, analyzed and strategies drawn for the gospel to be propagated.

The middle level of the Roman society was reached fairly well. This compares well to the middle-class of the Indian society today. If this is so, it implies that this class, which the Church has not focused on for evangelism, can be reached with a proper strategy. The God-fearer's attraction to Judaism implies that there is always an attraction to monotheism and high ethical standards. It would imply that in the polytheistic Indian society, there exist a good number of seekers who would be attracted to Christianity because of the same reason. (Of course, we do recognize the fact that there are other monotheistic religions in India apart from Christianity).

Paul's method of holding discussions at the Tyrannus hall at Ephesus and its success implies that the method of dialogue is a useful method to propagate the gospel provided the essence of the gospel is not compromised with. In addition, Paul's method of evangelism was based on partnership. He sought the help of people like Acquilla and Priscilla, Lydia, Phoebe, Jason, and others who would have been instrumental in not only extending their hospitality but also using their influence to bring in contacts into the Christian faith.

A few from high public positions got converted and this implies that witness among that class also cannot be neglected. We do not know whether Paul deliberately targeted the household of Caesar. This implies that we should not leave out the people in the high places but strategize how to reach them through the people working in their household.

Christianity was attractive to the "status inconsistents," as Meeks calls them, who were economically well off but were of a low status. These are the upwardly mobile. Though much research needs to be done in this regard, we can use this unverified finding to our advantage. Equality in status, oneness, inclusiveness and similar other virtues attracted a good number of people into the Christian fold. This implies that sociological implications of the gospel are as important as the spiritual reasons though both need to be kept in proper perspective.

4. RECOMMENDATIONS BASED ON IMPLICATIONS FROM BIBLICAL PERSPECTIVE

i.   Cities need to be the focus of Christian mission. A research agency needs to be set up to study the cities, the kind of people living there, the migration pattern, the characteristics of that city etc.

ii. The Tyrannus hall model needs to be experimented out here. A neutral avenue like the Tyrannus hall coupled with a dialogical approach would go a long way in propagating the gospel. Christian homes would be an ideal place for such an activity in our country.

iii. Except where language is a barrier, the church should not think ethnically as the city cuts across ethnic lines. Hence one should look to develop multilingual or multicultural churches.

iv. The Church/Mission Agencies need to recognize those who like the God-fearers are attracted to Christianity and yet cannot take baptism for various social reasons and give them all the nurture required for discipleship.

v. Partnership and networking among churches and para-church organizations in the city is a must to utilize talents effectively and adopt best practices.

vi. Special efforts need to be taken to reach those in placed in high positions of work. Strategically evangelize those connected with people on high places through whom the gospel can reach them.

vii. Identify the 'status inconsistent' of the society. Here it would be the 'educated dalits' who are economically on an equal footing with the other middle-class and yet are not readily accepted as the elite of the society. Make special effort to present the gospel with special emphasis on the sociology of Christianity.

Conclusion

'Can the educated be reached with the gospel?' is a question that is often asked. This study, though a preliminary one in this area, certainly shows that the educated in India can be reached with the gospel.

Paul's strategy of mission was not only urban in nature, but he also made efforts to reach the educated and wealthy, those who were the middle-class of his times. The study of Acts of the Apostles and Paul's letters show clearly that the churches he formed had a mix of various classes of people, many of whom were wealthy businessmen and a few of whom were in the administration of the city council. If this is so, then, two very important conclusions emerge. Mission in India need to have a paradigm shift:

1. Whereas missions in India are geared to reach the tribal and the village population, Paul's strategy shows us that we need to shift our mission emphasis to the city.

2. We need to make evangelistic efforts to reach the educated middle-class of our cities.

This study has revealed that urbanization has made the educated middle-class in India, who are mainly from the upper caste, more open in their social interaction with people of the other castes. The social groups are more class-oriented than caste-oriented. There is a greater acceptance of inter-caste and inter-religious marriages now, although caste does remain a major criterion in many cases. It should be noted that urbanization has affected the educated middle-class women as much as their male counterparts. The educated middle-class migrant is probably the most open to new ideas, and thus, is probably the one who would accept the gospel more readily.

This, however, does not mean that caste has completely lost its grip on people in urban contexts. The identity of a person is a complex intermingling of caste and class. It appears that the upper castes do not want to let go of their caste identity for it defines their status within the Hindu fold, as it is seen in the evidence by their treatment of the dalit counterparts. It is observed that the middle-class dalits are in a state of flux as the upper castes do not accept them and hence they usually cut off their roots with their own caste.

Urbanization has affected the family as well. Nuclearization of families has altered the equations within the family. Families have become more egalitarian and individualistic. The role of the women has changed drastically, and she has become the pivot on which the family revolves.

The educated middle-class does not show much interest in ritualistic religion. He neither has a clear understanding of *moksha* nor does he make a focused effort to gain it. While, on the one hand, the careerist and consumerist trait is domineering in this class, they are marked on the other hand by a desire to know the truth and firm up their worldview.

The church needs to become more sensitive to these changes and challenges that urbanization coupled with education has brought about in the middle-class. Christians need to identify themselves with this class in their needs and help them find solutions to their problems in the light of the gospel and their relationship with Jesus Christ. The church needs to create the right environment for interacting with this class at the social and intellectual level. The church also needs to train her laity to present the gospel apologetically yet with sensitivity.

Bibliography

BOOKS AND ARTICLES

Acharya, Hemlata. "Changing Role of Religious Specialist', in M.S. A. Rao, (ed.), *Urban Sociology in India*. Delhi: Orient Longman, 1974.

Ahuja, Ram. *Indian Social System*. Jaipur: Rawat Publication, 1993.

Allen, Roland. *Missionary Methods, St. Paul's and Ours*. London: Robert Scott, 1912.

Bakke, Ray. *A Theology as Big as the City*. Illinois: IVP, 1997.

Bala, Raj. *Trends of Urbanization in India, 1901-1981*. Jaipur: Rawat Publication, 1986.

Banks, Robert. *Paul's Idea of Community*. Massachusetts: Hendrickson Publishers, 1994.

Barot, Jyoti. "Modern Trends in Marital Relations", in John S. Augustine (ed). *The Indian Family in Transition*. New Delhi: Sterling Publications Pvt. Ltd, 1972.

Beteille, Andre *Caste: Old and New, Essays in Social stratification*. Delhi: Asia Publishing House, 1969.

Beteille, Andre. The Social Character of the Indian Middle-class in Ahmad, Imitiaz. & Reifeld, Helmut (ed). *Middle-class Values in India and Western Europe*. New Delhi: Social Science Press, 2000.

Beteille, Andre. "Caste in Contemporary India" in Andre Beteille, (ed), *Caste Today* (New Delhi: Oxford University Press, 1996)

Bhatia, B.M. *India's Middle-class, Role in Nation Building*. New Delhi: Konark Publishers Pvt. Ltd., 1993.

Bhatt, S.C.(ed). *The Enclyopaedic District Gazetters of India-Western Zone, Vol 7*. New Delhi: Gyan Publishing House, 1997.

Bhoite, U.B. *Sociology of Indian Intellectuals*. Jaipur: Rawat Publications, 1987.

Bosch, David J. *Transforming Mission*. Bangalore: Centre for Contemporary Christianity, 2006.

Bose, Ashish. *India's Urbanization: 1901-2001, 2nd* edn. Delhi: Tata Mcgraw Hill Publishing Co. Ltd, 1978.

Bougle, C. The essence and reality of the caste system in Gupta ed, *Social Stratification.* Delhi:Oxford University Press, 1992.

Boyd, R.H.S. *A Church History of Gujarat.* Madras: The Christian Literature Society, 1981.

Bruce, F.F. *Paul, Apostle of the free Spirit.* Exeter: The Paternoster Press, 1977.

Brush, John E. "Growth and Spatial Structure of Indian Cities" in Allen G. Noble & Ashok K. Dutt ed. *Indian Urbanisation and Planning, Vehicles of Modernisation.* Delhi: Tata McGraw-Hill Publishing Co. Ltd, 1977.

Burnett, David G. *The Spirit of Hinduism.* Turnbridge Wells: Monarch Publications, 1992.

Clive, Visvaldas. "The ideal of Mukti: Philosophical change in the Contemporary Indian setting" in Allen G. Noble and Ashok K Dutt (eds), *Indian Urbanization and Planning, Vehicles of Modernization.* New Delhi: Tata McGraw-Hill Publishing Co. Ltd., 1977.

Commissariat, M.S. *A History of Gujarat, Vol I from 1297-8 to 1573.* Bombay: Longmans Green and Company Ltd., 1938.

Conlon, Frank F. Urbanism and Indian Society: The aspect of Caste in Allen G. Noble, Ashok Dutt (eds), *Indian Urbanization and Planning, Vehicles of Modernization.* N. Delhi: Tata McGraw Hill Publishing Co. Ltd, 1977.

Conn, Harvie M. & Ortiz, Manuel. *Urban Ministry.* Illinois: IVP, 2001.

Daniel, P.S. David Scott, David C. & Singh, G.R. *Religious Traditions in India.* Delhi: ISPCK, 2002.

Das, Gurcharan. *India Unbound.* New Delhi: Viking Penguin Book India, 2000.

Desai, I.P. *Some Aspects of Family in Mahuva.* Bombay: Asia Publishing House, 1964.

Desai, S.D. *Images-Finer Contours of Ahmedabad.* Gandhinagar: Gujarat Sahitya Academy, 2005.

Devi, Shakuntala. *Caste System in India.* Jaipur: Pointer Publications, 1999.

Diddee, Jaymala, & Rangaswamy, Vimala (eds). *Urbanization, Trends, Perspectives and Challenges.* Jaipur: Rawat Publication, 1992.

Director of Census Operation, *Census Report 2011.* Ahmedabad: Census Dept, 2011.

Directorate of Census Operations, *District Census Handbook-200, Part XII-A&B* Ahmedabad: Directorate of Census Operations, 2001.

Dosabhai, Edalji. *A history of Gujarat-From the earliest Period to the Present time.* New Delhi: Asian Educational Services, 1981.

Doshi, Harish. "Traditional Neighbourhood in Modern Ahmedabad: The Pol," in M.S.A. Rao, Chandrashekar Bhat, and Laxmi Narayan Kadekar, (eds). *A Reader in Urban Sociology.* Delhi: Orient Longman, 1991.

Driver, Edwin D. "Family Structure and the socio-economic status in Central India," [CD-ROM] *SB* (1961) 119.

Dumont, Louis. *Homo Hierarchicus,* trans. Mark Sainsbury, Louis Dumont & Basia Gulati. Delhi: Oxford University Press, 1988.

Dushyant Joshi, "Enchanting Growth," *Ahmedabad Times,* 14th Aug. 2010. 3.

Ellul, Jacques. *The Meaning of the City*. Michigan: William B. Eerdmans Pub. Co., 1970.

Eric Swanson, Eric and Swan Williams, Swan. *Transform a City*. Michigan: Zondervan, 2010.

Eshleman, Ross J. & Cashion, Barbara G. *Sociology, An Introduction*. Boston: Little Brown and Company, 1983.

Esler, Francis Philip. *Community and gospel in Luke –Acts*. Cambridge: Cambridge University Press, 1987.

Etzioni, Amitai & Etzioni, Eva. *Social Change-Sources, Patterns and Consequences*. New York: Basic Books INC Publishers, 1964.

Forrest, G.W. *Cities of India*. Delhi: Thomson Press, 1991.

Fox, Richard G. "Tezibazaar: Colonial Town in Prismatic Society" in M.S.A.Rao, Chandrashekar Bhat, & Laxmi Narayan Kadekar (eds), *A Reader in Urban Sociology*, New Delhi: Orient Longman, 1991.

Garsey, Peter and Saller, Richard. *The Roman Empire*. Berkeley: University of California Press, 1987.

Ghanshyam Shah, Caste Sentiments, Class Formation and Dominance in Gujarat, in K.L. Sharma (ed). *Caste and Class in India*. Jaipur: Rawat Publication, 1994.

Ghanshyam Shah, Communalization and Participation of Dalits in Gujarat 2002 Riots in Lancy Lobo, and Biswaroop Das (ed), *Communal Violence and Minorities*. Jaipur: Rawat Publication, 2006. 77-86

Ghurye, G.S. *Caste, Class and Occupation*. Bombay: Popular Book Depot, 1961.

Ghurye, G.S. Features of the Caste System in Dipankar Gupta (ed), *Social Stratification*. Delhi: Oxford University Press, 1992.

Gillion, Kenneth. *A study in Urban Indian History-Ahmedabad*. Ahmedabad: New Order Books, 1968.

Goldstein, Sydney & Sly, David F. (eds). *Patterns of Urbanisation: Comparative Country Studies*. Belgium: Ordina editions, 1976.

Gore, M.S., *Urbanisation and Family Change*. Bombay: Popular Prakashan, 1968.

Gould, Harold. *The Hindu Caste System*. Delhi: Chanakya Publication, 1987.

Green, Michael. *Evangelism through the Local church*. London: Hodder and Stoughton, 1990.

Greenway, Roger and Monsma, M. *Cities-Missions New Frontiers*. Michigan: Baker Book House, 1989.

Gupta, Sanjiv. "Great Indian Buyers" in *The Week* 30th Dec 2001, 38.

Guru, Gopal. Dalit Middle-class hangs in the air, in Imtiaz Ahmad and Helmut Reifeld (eds), *Middle-class Values in India and Western Europe*. N. Delhi: Social Science Press, Konrad Adenauer Foundation, 2007.

Heltmann, Alex. C. "Cities are India's future." *The Times of India*. Ahmedabad edn. 31 March 2011. 13.

Hemer, Colin J.& Gempf, Conrad H. (ed). *The Book of Acts in the Setting of the Hellenistic History*. Indiana: Eisenbrauns.

Hunter III, George G. *How to Reach Secular People*. Nashville: Abingdon Press, 1992.

Hutton, J.H. *Caste in India: Its Nature, Function and Origin*. Bombay: Oxford University Press, 1961.

Irina Levenskaya, Irina. *The Book of Acts in its 1ˢᵗ Century Setting, Vol 5, Diaspora Setting*. Grand Rapids: W.B. Eerdmans Pub. Co., 1996.

Jain, K. C. "Ahmadabad: An Expanding Metropolis," in R.P. Mishra (ed.). *Million Cities of India*. Delhi: Vikas Publications, 1978.

Jeffers, J.S. *The Greco-Roman World of the New Testament Era*. Illinios : IVP, 1999.

Jha, Nirmala. *Law of Karma as prescribed by Mahatma Gandhi, Aurobindo, Vikekananda & Radhakhrisnan*. New Delhi: Capital Publishing House, 1985.

Joshi, P.C. *Culture, Communication & Social Change*. New Delhi: Vikas Publication House Pvt. Ltd.,1989.

Kamath M.V. & Randeri, Kalindi. *Narendra Modi, The Architect of a Modern State* Delhi: Rupa and Co., 2009.

Kannan, C.T. *Intercaste and Intercommunity marriages in India*, Bombay: Allied Pub. Pvt. Ltd, 1963.

Kapadia, K.M. *Marriage and Family in India*. Bombay: Oxford University Press, 1949.

Kapoor, Saroj. "Family and kinship Groups among the Khatris in Delhi, " *Sociological Bulletin*, Vol XIV (2), 1965.

Kapur, Promilla. "The Changing role of Status of Women", in John S. Augustine, *The Indian Family in Transition*. New Delhi: Sterling Publications (P) Ltd, 1972.

Karve, Iravati. *Kinship Organization in India*, Bombay: Asia Publishing House, 1965.

Khan, Ali Mohammed. *Mirat Ahmadi*, trans. James Bird. New Delhi: Asian Educational Services, 2005.

Klive, Visvaldis. "The ideal of Mukti: Philosophical Change in the Contemporary Indian Setting", in Allen G. Noble & Ashok K. Bhatt (eds), *Indian Urbanization and Planning, Vehicles of Modernization*. New Delhi: Tata McGraw-Hill Publishing Co. Ltd.

Kolenda, Pauline. *Caste in Contemporary India*. Illinois: Waveland Press Inc., 1978.

Kosambi, Meera. *Urbanization and Urban Development in India*. Delhi: Cambridge Press, 1994.

Kraft, Charles. *Anthropology of Christian Witness*. New York: Orbis Books, 1996.

Lakha, Salim. *Capitalism and Class in Colonial India: The Case of Ahmedabad*. Delhi: Sterling Publishers Private Limited, 1988.

Lal, A.K. *The Urban Family, A Study of the Hindu Social System*. New Delhi: Concept Publishing company, 1990.

Lewis Mumford, *The City in History*. Middlesex: Penguin Books, 1961.

Lightfoot, J.B. 2ⁿᵈ Print *Commentary on St. Paul's Epistle to the Romans*. Massachusetts: Hendrickson Publishers, 1993.

Linthicum, Robert. *City of God, City of Satan*. Michigan: Zondervan Pub. House, 1991.

Madan, T.N. (ed), *Religion in India*. Delhi: Oxford University Press, 1992.

Malherbe, Abraham J. *Social Aspects of Early Christianity.* 2" ed. Philadelphia: Fortress Press, 1983.

Mandelbaum, David. "The Family in India" in Ruth Anshen (ed), *The Family: Its function and destiny.* New York: Harper and Brothers, 1949.

Masih, Edwin *Social Engagements of Intellectuals in Civil Society with special reference to Gujarat.* Ahmedabad: AWAG, 2006.

Meeks, Wayne A. *The First Urban Christians, The Social World of Apostle Paul.* New Haven: Yale University Press, 1983.

Metha, Makrand. *The Ahmedabad Cotton Textile Industry, Genesis and Growth.* Ahmedabad: New Order Books Co., 1982.

Michell, George and Shah, Snehal ed. *Ahmedabad.* Mumbai: Marg Publication, 1988.

Milton Singer, Milton. "The Indian Joint family in Modern Industry" in M. Singer and B.S.Cohn (eds), *Structure and Change in Indian Society.* Chicago: Aldine Pub. Co., 1968.

Mishra, R.P. (ed). *Million Cities of India.* Delhi: Vikas Publication, 1978.

Mishra, B.B. *The Indian Middle-class, Their Growth in Modern Times.* Delhi: Oxford University Press, 1961.

Moore, Wilbert. *Social Change.* New Jersey: Prentice Hall, 1963.

Mukerjee, Ramkhrisna. *Sociologist and Social Change in India today,* New Delhi: Prentice Hall, 1965.

Nagpaul, Hans. *Modernisation and Urbanization in India, Problems and Issues.* Jaipur: Rawat Publication, 1996.

National Commission on Urbanisation. *Report, Vol I & II.* Delhi: National Commission on Urbanisation, 1988.

National Institute of Urban Affairs. *State of India's Urbanization.* Delhi: National Institutes of Urban Affairs, 1988.

Oommen, T.K. "The Urban Family in Transition" in John S. Augustine (ed), *The Indian Family in Transition, New* Delhi: Vikas Publishing House Pvt. Ltd., 1982.

Pandey, Vinita. *Crisis of the Urban Middle-class.* Jaipur: Rawat Publications, 2009.

Parson, Talcott. A Functional theory of Change, in Amitai Etzioni and Eva Etzioni (eds), *Social Change, Sources, Patterns and Consequences.* New York: Basic Books Inc. Publishers, 1964.

Patel, Dilip. "Ahmedabad is the Best," *Ahmedabad Mirror,* 28th March 2012. 8.

Paul, John & Dave, Kapil. "Urbanization erodes the role of castes," *The Times of India,* Ahmedabad edn, 14th March 2014, 2.

Pocock, David F. "Sociologies: Urban and Rural," in M.S. A. Roa (ed), *Urban Sociology in India, Reader and Source Book.* Delhi: Orient Longman Ltd, 1974.

Rajgor, S.B. Tripathy, S. & Choksi, V.M. (eds). *Gazeeter of India, Gujarat State, Ahmedabad District.* Ahmedabad: Gujarat Govt. Publication, 1984.

Ram, Nandu. *The Mobile Schedule Caste: The Rise of the New Middle-class.* Delhi: Hindustan Publishing Corporation, 1988.

Ramchandra, R. *Urbanization and Urban Systems in India.* Delhi: Oxford University Press, 1989.

Ramsay, W.M. *St. Paul the Traveller and the Roman Citizen.* Michigan: Baker Book House, 1949.

Rao, M.S.A. (ed). *Urban Sociology in India.* Delhi: Orient Longman, 1974.

Rao, M.S.A. Bhatt, C & Khandekar L.N. (ed), *A Reader in Urban Sociology.* New Delhi: Orient Longman, 1991.

Rao, Nandini V. & Rao, V.V. "Desired Qualities in a future mate in India", in Mansingh Dal and Vijaykumar Gupta (eds), *Social values among young adults, A changing scenario.* New Delhi: M.D. Pub. Pvt. Ltd, 1995.

Rao, M.S.A. "General Introduction," in M.S.A Rao (ed), *Urban Sociology in India, Reader and Source Book.* Delhi: Orient Longman Ltd, 1974.

Ray, Pranabranjan. "Urbanization in Colonial Situation: Serampore " in M.S.A. Rao. (ed). *Urban Sociology in India,* New Delhi: Orient Longman, 1974.

Risley, Herbert. *The People of India.* New Delhi: Oriental Books, 1969.

Roland Allen, *Missionary Methods: St. Paul's and Ours* (Michigan: Wm. B. Eerdman's Publishing Co., 1962), 24.

Ross, Aileen. *The Hindu Family in its Urban Setting.* Bombay: Oxford University Press, 1961

Sanghvi, Nagindas. *Gujarat at Cross-Roads.* Mumbai: Bharatiya Vidya Bhavan, 2010.

Savaala, Minna. *Middle-class Moralities.* New Delhi: Orient Blackswan Pvt. Ltd., 2010.

Shah, A.M. & Desai, I.P. *Division and Hierarchy, An Overview of Caste in Gujarat* Delhi: Hindustan Publishing Corporation, 1988.

Shah, A.M. Baviskar, B.S. & Ramaswamy, E.A. *Social Structure and Change, Complex Organizations and Urban Communities.* New Delhi: Sage Publications, 1996.

Shah, Vimal, "Mate Selection: Theories and Educated Youth, Attitudes Towards Mate Selection" in Narain Dhirendra (ed), *Explorations in the family and other Essays.* Bombay: Thacker and Co., 1975.

Sharma, L.P. *The Indian Ruling Class.* New Delhi: Harnam Publication, 1982.

Sharma, Rajendra K. *Urban Sociology.* N. Delhi: Atlantic Publishers and Distributors, 1997.

Shivramakhrisnan, K.C. Kundu, Amitabh. & Singh, B.N. *Oxford Handbook of Urbanization in India.* Delhi: Oxford University Press, 2005.

Shukla, S.S. "Understanding Modern Indian Youth" in John S. Augustine (ed), *The Indian Family in Transition.* New Delhi: Sterling Publishers (P) Ltd, 1972.

Singer, Milton. "The Great Tradition in a Metropolitan Centre, Madras" in M.S.A. Rao (ed), *Urban Sociology in India.* New Delhi: Orient Longman, 1974.

Singh, Gurcharan. *The New Middle-class of India.* Jaipur: Rawat Publication, 1985.

Singh, Yogendra. *Modernization of Indian Tradition.* New Delhi: Thomson Press, 1973.

Somjee, A.H. Gujarati, Social Concerns and Political Involvements of Intellectuals, in Yogendra K.Malik (ed). *South Asian Intellectuals and Social Change*. Delhi: Heritage Publishers, 1982.

Srinivas, M.N. *Caste in Modern India and other essays*. Bombay: Media Publishers, 1962.

Stambaugh, John E. and Balch, David. *The New Testament in its Social Environment*. Philadelphia: The Westminster Press, 1986.

Starke, Linda. (ed). *State of the World, Our Urban Future*. London: Earthscan, 2007.

Stott, John (ed). *Making Christ Known: Historic Mission Documents from the Lausanne Movement 1974-1989*. Cumbria: Paternoster Press, 1996.

Stott, John. *Christian Mission in the Modern World*. Illinois: Intervarsity Press, 1975.

Thiessen, Gerd. *Social Reality of Early Christians*. trans. Magaret Kohl. Edingburh: T&T Clark, 1993.

Thissen, Gerd ed. and trans. John H. Schutz, *The social setting of Pauline Christianity* Edingburgh: T&T Clark, 1982.

Tidball, Derek. *An Introduction to the Sociology of the New Testament*. Exeter Devon: The Paternoster Press, 1983.

Times News Network, "Denim Capital of India," *The Times of India*, Ahmedabad edn. 11Feb. 2011.

Times News Network, "AMC gets Nagar Ratna..." *The Times of India*, 9th July 2011. 14.

Times News Network. *The Times of India*, 8th Feb. 2011.

Toynbee, Arnold. *Cities on the Move*. London: Oxford University Press, 1970.

Trivedi, Jayprakash M. *The Social Structure of Patidar Caste in India*. Delhi: Kanishka Publishing House, 1992.

Vago, Steven. *Social Change*. New Jersey: Prentice Hall, 1989.

Vajpai, Virendra. *Modernization and Social Change*. New Delhi: Manohar Press, 1979.

Varma, Pavan K. *The Great Indian Middle-class*. New Delhi: Penguin Books (I) Pvt. Ltd., 1998.

Vastu Shilp Foundation. *The Ahmedabad Chronicle-Imprints of a Millenium*. Ahmedabad: Vastu Shilp Foundation for studies and Research in Environmental design, 2002.

Walli, Koshelya. *Theory of Karma in Indian Thought*. Varanasi: Bharata Manisha, 1977.

Weber, Max. *The City*, trans & ed. Don Martindale, & Getrude Newrith. New York: The Free Press, 1958.

White, Randy. *Encountering God in the City*. Illinios : IVP Books, 2006.

Yagnik Achyut & Sheth, Suchitra. *The Shaping of Modern Gujarat*. Delhi: Penguin Books, 2005.

Yagnik, Achyut. & Sheth, Suchitra. *Ahmedabad-From Royal City to Mega City*. Delhi: Penguin Books, 2011.

ELECTRONIC/ONLINE SOURCES

Agarwala, B.R. "Symposium on Caste and Joint family: In a Mobile Commercial Community," [CD-ROM] *SB* 4 (1955) 143.

Benhocker Eric D, Farrell Diana, Zainulbhai Adil S., "Tracking the growth of the Indian Middle-class" in *The Mckinsey Quarterly* 2007, No.3, 51, *https://ecell.in/eureka*13/resources/tracking the growth of Indian Middle-class.pdf. (accessed on 1Aug 2017).

Bhalla, Surjit. "The middle-class in emerging markets, two billion more Bourgeois," *The Economist* 12th Feb 2009, *www.economist.com/node/13109687* (assessed 22 July 2014).

Dobbs, Richard and others, "Cities in the rise of the consuming class." *Insights and Publications,*MckinseyGlobalInstitute.June2014, *www.mckinsey.com/insights/urbanization/urban_world_cities_and_the_rise_of_the_consuming_class* (assessed on 22 July 31, 2014).

Fieldman Louis, "The Omnipresence of God-Fearers," *Biblical Archeological Review* 12:5 (Sep-Oct 1986) 58-59, *https://members.bib-arch-org/biblical-archeological-review/12/5/4* (accessed 29 April 2014).

Kapadia, K.M. "Changing Patterns of Hindu Marriage and Family, II," [CD-ROM] *SB* 3 (1954) 136.

Kaldate, Sudha. "Urbanization and Disintegration of Rural Joint Family" [CD-ROM] *SB*11(1&2) 1962, 103-111.

Kapadia, K.M. "Changing Patterns of Hindu Marriage and Family," [CD-ROM] *SB* 3 (1954) 79.

Kapadia, K.M. "Changing patterns of Hindu Marriage and family," [CD-ROM] *SB* 4 (1955) 192.

Kharas, Homi. "The emerging middle-class in developing countries, *Working Paper No. 285* of OECD Development Centre, in *www.oecd.org/development/pgd/4445738.pdf* (assessed 22 July 2014).

Khatri, A.A "Social Change in the Caste Hindu family and its possible impact on Personality and Mental Health," [CD-ROM] *SB* 11 (1962) 151.

Khatri, A.A. "Some neglected approaches and Problems in the study of family in India," [CD-ROM] *SB* 10 (1961) 75.

Laxminarayana, H.D. "Caste, Class, Sex and Social distance among College Students in South India," [CD-ROM] *SB* 24 (1975) 190.

MacLennan Robert S, and Kraabel Thomas A, "The God Fearers: A Literary and Theological Invention", *Biblical Archaeological Review* 12:5 (Sep-Oct 1986) 46-47, *https://members.bib-arch-org/biblical-archeological-review/12/5/4* (accessed 29 April 2014).

Murphy, Shliefer and Vishny, "Income Distribution, Market size and Industrialization" in *Quarterly Journal of Economics*, 104(3), 537-564, 1989, *http://scholar.harvard.edu/files/shleifer/files/inc_dist.pdf* (accessed on 31July 2017).

Richard, Rohrbaugh L. "Methodological Consideration in the debate over social class status of Early Christians," *JAAR* 52 (1984) 519-546, web.a.ebscohost. com/ehost/pdfviewer/pdfviewer? sid=6c9ec145-ca29-403d-b528-a79a03e326 56%40sessionmgr4002&vid=16&hid=4207&bdata (accessed 30th April 2014).

Schor Juliet, "The New Politics of Consumption" in *Boston Review,*1999, *http://boston* review.net/archives/BR24.3/schor.html (accessed 31 July 2017).

Shah, B.V. "Gujarati College Students and Caste," [CD-ROM] *SB* 10 (1961) 48.

Shah, B.V. "Gujarati College Students and the Selection of Bride," [CD-ROM] *SB* 11 (1962) 137.

Sharma, Abha. "Opinion of Married Couples Regarding the Selection of Marriage Partner," [CD-ROM] *SB* (1979) 72.

Shastri Parth, "Gujarati 6% of Indians but 20% of US citizens" The Times of India, NRI edn. 4th Jan 2015 in times of india.indiatimes.com/nri/us-canada-news/Gujarati-6-of-indians-but 20-of-US-indians/articleshow/45746350.cm. (accessed on 1 Aug 2017).

Singh, J.P. "Nuclearisation of household and family in Urban India," [CD-ROM] *SB* 52 (2003) 56.

Steven J. Friesen, "Poverty in Pauline studies: Beyond the so called New Consensus," *JSNT* 26.3 (2004) 323-361, 3d-b528-a79a03e32656%40sessionmgr4002&hid =4207&bdata=JnNpdGU92Whve3QtbG12ZSZzY29wZT1zaXR1#DB=rfh &AN=ATLA0001394433 (accessed on 30th April 2014).

Theissen, Gerd. "The Social structure of Pauline Communities" *JSNT* 84(2001)65-84, web.a.ebscohost.com/ehost/detail/detail? vid=23&sid=6c9ec145-caZ9-403d-b528-079a033265640%sessionmgr4002&hid=4207&bdata (accessed on 30th April 2014).